Beyond the Black Stump

Nevil Shute

Pan Books
in association with
Heinemann

First published 1956 by William Heinemann Ltd
This edition published 1972 by Pan Books Ltd,
Cavaye Place, London SW10 9PG
in association with William Heinemann Ltd
9 8 7 6
All rights reserved
ISBN 0 330 02965 7
Printed and bound in Great Britain by
Hazell Watson & Viney Limited,
Member of the BPCC Group,
Aylesbury, Bucks

My mother used to say to me,
'When you grow up, my son,
I hope you're a bum like your father was
'Cos a good man ain't no fun!'

Stonecutters cut it on stone,
Woodpeckers peck it on wood,
There's nothing so bad for a woman as
A man who thinks he's good.

Carousel
Oscar Hammerstein II

ACKNOWLEDGEMENTS

The lines from *Carousel* by Oscar Hammerstein II are printed by permission of Williamson Music Ltd. The eight lines from *A Shropshire Lad* by A. E. Housman are printed by permission of The Society of Authors as the Literary Representative of the Trustees of the estate of the late A. E. Housman, and Messrs Jonathan Cape Ltd, publishers of *The Collected Poems* of A. E. Housman.

ONE

A NUMBER of substances that are trapped in the earth's crust will influence a Geiger counter sufficiently to set it clicking, and one of the feeblest of these influences is oil imprisoned in a salt dome or an anticline. Stanton Laird sat in an office of the Topeka Exploration Company Inc, on the eighteenth floor of the Topex Building in Cedar Street in downtown New York City, and explained his work again to Mr Sam Johnson. He believed that the work that he had done upon his own initiative in analysing the radioactive indications at the bottom of the pilot drillings at Abu Quaiyah had shortened the seismic observation programme by some weeks and had brought the No 3 well to production so much sooner, and this was the first bore on that site to produce oil in commercial quantities. He had explained this previously to Mr Johnson in a fairly lengthy report that he had typed with sweating, gritty hands in the hut beside the oil rig where he had lived with the drilling crew, and he had known as he typed that Mr Johnson would either be too busy to read it at all or, at best, he would skim it through and merely study the conclusions at the end. In fact, he had done the latter, and he had forgotten all the detail. Only a vague impression on his mind remained, that Stanton Laird was a good youngster who didn't sit around complaining of the heat but got on with his job.

Mr Johnson didn't say much while the young man talked, for the simple reason that he couldn't trust himself. Like all oil executives he had a general knowledge of petrology, but he had never himself been a geologist. He had come into the oil industry forty years before as an organic chemist, but he had been on the executive of Topex now for many years and his organic chemistry was thirty years out of date, and half forgotten. In dealing with the young technicians who worked under his control he had developed a technique of making them do the talking while he sat back and listened, encouraging them on with phrases such as 'Surely', or 'That sounds reasonable to me', or 'Dr Streeter was working on this last fall. I'd like you to have a talk with him.' In this way he maintained the fiction that he understood what Stanton Laird was talking about, while his acute subconscious mind summed the young man up and filed the essential data that would determine his advancement in the Topex organization. Long years of practice had made him clever with these phrases, so that Stanton Laird believed that his painstaking techniques had made a good impression on his boss. In that he was correct, but not quite in the way he thought. His techniques meant little to Mr Johnson because he didn't fully understand them, but his approach to the job and his industry meant quite a lot.

Presently the older man glanced at the clock, which showed ten minutes past noon, and steered the conversation to a close. 'I guess we'll go and get some lunch,' he said. 'Which hotel are you staying at?'

'I checked my bags,' the young man said. 'I've got a friend has an apartment in Peter Cooper Village. I'll call him later on, see if he's got a bed.'

'Didn't you get in yesterday?'

Stanton shook his head. 'We got a twenty hours' delay at Lisbon. They had to change a motor on the plane.'

Mr Johnson glanced again at his technician. He had always been a pale young man, with very short mousy hair and little colour in his face. Three years in Arabia had bronzed him to a deep yellow rather than a brown; he seemed more adult and self-reliant than when he had last sat in that office, but he did not look very well. Perhaps that was fatigue.

'What time did you get in?'

'I'd say we landed around eight o'clock,' the young man replied. 'I took a shower at the airport, 'n came on in to town.'

'Get any sleep on the way over?'

'Not very much.'

Mr Johnson pressed a bell on the side of his desk, and when the girl came in, sleek and young and well groomed, he said, 'Sharon, call the club and tell them I'll be bringing a guest in for lunch. Table for two. I'll be right over.' The young man's eyes flickered quickly over the stenographer, a motion which did not escape the notice of his boss. Three years in Arabia was tough on a young man.

When the girl had gone out, Mr Johnson said, 'Have any trouble with your health?'

'Not a thing. You don't have to, if you stick by the rules. I'm glad to be out of it before the real hot weather, though.'

His boss nodded. 'Three summers is enough in Arabia, out in the field.' The sun of mid-July streamed in through the slats of the Venetian blind. 'I suppose you wouldn't call this a hot day.'

The young man smiled. 'Kind of humid, after the dry heat. I wouldn't want to work here through the summer.'

'We all come to it as we get on in life,' said Mr Johnson. 'That's unless we fail to make it, and go run a gas station. There's worse things to do than that, too. That's what I think sometimes, commuting from Norwalk through August, with the temperature way up in the nineties.' He heaved his massive body up from the desk. 'Let's go and get some lunch. How much leave have you got coming? Ten weeks?'

'Nine,' said Stanton. 'I took a week in Cairo last year.'

'That time you flew up to meet P.K. about the core analysis?'

'That's right.'

'Maybe we'll give you that. Where are you going for it? Out West?'

Stanton nodded. 'I'll go home and stay with my folks, for a while, anyway. I guess I'll be around there most of the time.'

They left the office and walked to the elevator. 'Oregon, isn't it?' said the older man. 'Way in from Portland somewhere?'

'That's right,' said the geologist. 'Place called Hazel, in the back of the state. That's where I come from.'

As they descended in the elevator the older man said vaguely, 'I knew a man one time went fishing in the Hazel River, runs into the Snake. Would that be the same?'

'That's right,' said Stanton. 'Hazel's on the Hazel River, in the north-east corner of the state. There's good fishing in the river – trout.'

'Is Hazel a big place?'

The young man shook his head. 'About ten thousand at the last count, I think.'

At the entrance to the Topex Building and in the street the crowds thronged around them, making conversation impossible; they walked in silence for a couple of blocks and went into another building and up in another elevator. They walked out into the air-conditioned coolness of the club and checked their hats. They went to the washroom and then Mr Johnson led his guest into the bar. 'What's it to be?'

'Orange juice,' said the young man.

Mr Johnson ordered it, with rye on the rocks for himself. 'Still sticking to your principles?'

'I guess so,' said the geologist. 'It's mighty easy to stick to some principles.' He laughed. 'I just don't like it.'

In fact he had an aversion to alcoholic beverages that was almost pathological. He felt about alcohol as other people might feel about cocaine, that it was most dangerous stuff to take even in the smallest quantities. It was habit-forming. If you took one drink you would want another, and another, and another; with each essay the craving would increase till it became overpowering. The end, inevitably, was that you would become an alcoholic, unable to hold down a job, unable to walk down the street without falling flat on your face, fit only for Skid Row. If you were very fortunate you might be rehabilitated by Alcoholics Anonymous, but throughout your life thereafter you would be wrestling with the ever-present temptation. In many ways cocaine was less dangerous, because it was less readily obtainable.

These feelings were connected, rather strangely, with his

first driving licence; he had sowed his wild oats younger than most men. His father, Stanton Laird, was a Presbyterian of remote Scots descent; he had married early and had had four children, two daughters, Stanton Junior, and Dwight. Both daughters were now married, and Dwight was serving with the US Army on the Rhine. In his youth the father had founded the Hazel Cold Storage Corporation, and he had worked it up into a sizeable concern by 1938. With the coming of war to the world he had guessed shrewdly that cattle might prove more profitable than cold storage, and this change in his views corresponded with a restless wish to change his way of life. He had sold the cold storage business and had bought three ranches in the district, and he had profited over the war years from the demand for beef for the armies. As peace approached he looked ahead to the peacetime demand for automobiles, and in 1944 he bought a gas station in Hazel with a vacant lot beside it and two more behind. In 1945 he sold his ranches and in 1946 he built a showroom and extensive modern workshops behind his gas station, with the result that in 1949 he succeeded in wresting the Ford franchise from the ageing local dealer. Since then he had prospered more than ever.

The change from cold storage to ranching had come when Junior was fourteen years old, and leaving grade school for Hazel High. The change meant that the family removed from the house on Franklin Avenue, which was now too small for them anyway, and went to live about fifteen miles from Hazel on a ranch. In a district where boarding schools were virtually unknown this would have made difficulties in the education of the children but for a thoughtful provision of the State of Oregon, which decreed that in such circumstances a child could get a driving licence, theoretically limited to the route between his home and school. Accordingly Stanton Junior got his first motor car driving licence at the age of fourteen when he entered Hazel High School, driving Dwight to grade school every day in an old Chevrolet and going on himself to High

School. With the driving licence and the car he became free from all parental or any other control.

Like most reputable citizens of Hazel, Stanton Laird never drank in his home town. At cold storage Conventions in Portland or Seattle he would drink whisky for business conviviality in a naïve ignorance of when to stop, so that he got sick and had a hangover next morning, ailments which he regarded as a necessary part of business life like a sagging abdomen due to sitting at a desk all day, and which had influenced his restless change to ranching. His home was happy and well ordered but no tobacco and no alcohol ever entered it, so that it was only natural for Junior, on attaining to the freedom of his own car at the age of four-teen, to start experimenting with both. Since Hazel High School was, of course, coeducational, his experimenting wasn't limited to whisky and cigarettes.

It is a deep conviction of all right-thinking Americans that a boy shows independence, manliness, and self-respect by working his way through college, and a good preparation for this way of life is to encourage him to earn his pocket money while he is in High School. While the Lairds had lived in Hazel they had encouraged Junior to earn by de-livering newspapers around the district where they lived. With the coming of war to the world the demand for such services increased, and soon after they moved to the ranch he took on the delivery of Donald Duck bread in the Chev as well as the newspapers, wearing a peaked cap embellished with the emblem of the order, rampant. This new assign-ment took a good deal longer and made his hours away from home irregular; at the same time it provided him with a considerable income, the extent of which was unknown to his parents, which he could spend on cigarettes, rye whisky, and girls.

By the time he was sixteen he was leading a thoroughly dissipated life and was giving his parents a good deal of anxiety, though they had no idea of the full scope of his misdoings. There was little left for him to experiment with in the spheres of tobacco, alcohol, or girls, but marijuana cigarettes had just been placed before the youth of Hazel by a Mexican-Negro halfbreed who worked in a liquor store. Few of the boys or girls at the High School really enjoyed them, being healthy young people raised in the clean conditions of a small town in the country, but the cigarettes were obviously vicious and so fit subjects for experiment by broad-minded adolescents learning about Life.

The end of it all came when Stanton Junior was in the last term of his junior year. He had a friend called Chuck Sheraton who came to school in an old Plymouth tourer, a merry and inconsequent young man whose one ambition was to fly aeroplanes. Being friends, they made common property of many of their belongings, including their girls. One evening in the early summer they were playing a complicated game based on 'touch last' in their two cars around the streets of suburban Hazel, Diana Fawsitt driving with Chuck and Ruth Eberhart, a notable cheer-leader at the football game for Hazel High, with Stanton. It was a good game, though rough upon the fenders, but that evening they carried it a bit too far. Stanton, coming down 4th Street and crossing Roosevelt Avenue at seventy miles an hour, hit the Plymouth broadside on and hurled it on its side on to the sidewalk. Diana was thrown out and killed almost instantaneously. Chuck got concussion and a fractured shoulder, but made a good recovery. Ruth got scars upon her face and arms that would last her lifetime as she went through the windscreen, and Stanton got three fractured ribs upon the steering wheel. An empty bottle of whisky was found in the Chev, the doctor pronounced both boys and Ruth to be under the influence of liquor, the post mortem revealed Diana to have been pregnant, and a further research revealed that Ruth was pregnant, too. All the participants were sixteen years of age.

This happened a few months after Pearl Harbor when the citizens of the United States, including even Hazel, had more important things to think about than the misdeeds of their teenagers. Moreover, it was less than eighty years since Hazel had been established as a town, and only about

13

fifty since the trails leading to the east had been made safe from the marauding bands of Indians. In such a place the legislature acts more directly and with fewer inhibitions than in districts with a longer record as communities. Diana Fawsitt was dead and nothing would bring her back to life, and though these boys had killed her it was difficult to argue that she was entirely blameless in the matter; all four of them were culpable in some degree. It seemed profitless to Judge Hadley to start anyone upon a road that might end at the penitentiary; he dealt with the case summarily in ten minutes when the boys came out of hospital and sentenced Chuck and Stanton to a year in the reform school, suspending the sentence indefinitely subject to satisfactory reports from the police. It only remained for the parents to clean up the mess.

When the Eberharts pressed Ruth to declare the father of her child she took two days to think about it in the hospital, and finally decided that Chuck Sheraton was more fun that Stanton. Accordingly when they came out of hospital Ruth and Chuck were married, rather quietly in the circumstances, the bridegroom being still in High School though Ruth's education was considered to be finished. Stanton was left to re-model his life alone, guided by the practical good sense of a father who was ruefully conscious of incidents in his own youth that would not bear a close examination, and who was inclined to blame himself for not looking after his son better.

The weeks that followed were not happy ones for Stanton. Because he was in hospital with broken ribs and possible internal injuries nobody cared to rub it in that he had killed Diana Fawsitt, but he suffered a good deal from frustration in his first love. Ruth had been his girl, not Chuck's, and if she was pregnant he had a good idea which of them was probably responsible. That she had thrown him over for Chuck was a bitter blow to him, a blow which struck far deeper than the general disgrace. It was intensified when he was able to meet Chuck in the Piggy-Wiggy café and found, as they discussed their position over a milk shake, that although Chuck liked Ruth well enough he didn't particularly want to marry her or anybody else at the age of sixteen. They were in the grip of forces more powerful than they were themselves, however. Neither of them was old enough to stand up and flout the opinion of the whole community in their hour of disgrace. Chuck was not prepared to stand up to the citizens of Hazel and declare he wasn't going to marry Ruth when she claimed him as the father of her child, which he might well have been, and Stanton was not prepared to stand up in the face of all his other sins and claim paternity from Chuck. A succession of milk shakes did nothing to resolve their problems but left them better friends than ever, united in the disapproval of all Hazel. From their meeting at the Piggy-Wiggy café Chuck went on to matrimony with Ruth and Stanton turned to work for an anodyne, his grief for Ruth tempered by a secret relief that it had proved impossible for him to get married at sixteen.

He worked very hard in his last year at High School, abandoning his former ways of life. He had a good brain and a good background, with sensible and sympathetic parents to encourage him. It was his intention to go on to the University of Oregon at Eugene but he put in as a long shot for admission to Leland Stanford and, somewhat to his own surprise, he got in. He stayed there for four years, a sober-minded, hardworking, rather pale young man doing physics and geology, and he graduated with some distinction but no girl. From the university he had got a research job with the Carnegie Institution in Washington DC working on geophysics, and two years later he had joined the Topex team.

At the time when he returned from Arabia he would drink no alcohol at all nor had he done so since his High School accident; his renunciation of it had been absolute. He smoked very little, perhaps one pack of cigarettes a month, fearing perhaps that the tobacco habit, too, could get hold of a man and lead him into gross excesses of the flesh. In compensation he still ate a good many candies at the age of twenty-eight; a can of wrapped peppermints was generally to be found in one of the drawers of his desk, and he had a weakness for milk shakes and ice cream in its various forms. He was an active and a healthy man, the more so for his abstinence, physically well developed though sallow in appearance.

In the club bar he raised the question of his next employment with his boss. 'Will you want me to go back to Arabia after this vacation?' he inquired. 'I'd like to know ahead if it's to be back there.'

Mr Johnson shook his head. 'Not Arabia. Have you got any preference?'

'I could do with a domestic assignment for a time,' Stanton suggested. 'I've been out of the United States now for three years.'

'Are you getting married?'

The geologist shook his head reluctantly; he had expected that. Domestic assignments for geological work within the United States or Canada were usually reserved for men with families. 'Not that I know of,' he said.

'We usually try to work married men into the domestic assignments,' Mr Johnson said. 'It's fairer on the kids.'

'I know it.'

'Have you got any other preference?'

'I'd just as soon it was a white country,' said Stanton. 'I've seen enough of sand and Arabs to last me for a while.'

Mr Johnson finished his drink, offered Stanton another orange juice, and when that was refused led the way into the dining-room. He ordered Crab Louis with a large cup of white coffee for them both, and when that was on the table he said, 'What would you think of Paraguay?'

'That's the new concession?'

'Surely. We'll need geologists in the field there.'

Stanton ate in silence for a minute. 'I'll have to admit I don't know much about Paraguay,' he said at last. 'Not desert, is it?'

His boss shook his head. 'I was never there myself, but

16

I was in East Bolivia one time, and that's just about the same. It's forest country, jungle you might say. Communications aren't so hot, apart from airstrips. Most of the heavy material goes up and down the rivers.'

'What's the capital of Paraguay?'

'Asuncion.'

'Is the concession near there?'

'Well,' said Mr Johnson, 'it's quite an area of country, of course. I'd say the nearest point would be about two hundred miles from Asuncion. It's in the Chaco Boreal, around Fort Diaz.'

'The people would be Spanish – like in Argentina?'

'I guess so. The executives and the technicians would be Spanish Americans. Do you know any Spanish?'

'Only a few words.'

'I'd say you'd have to learn some. It's an easy language to get along in – not so easy to speak well. I don't know that you'd find a lot of Spanish society out in the field. The labour would be mostly Indian.'

'Be a change from Arabia, anyway,' said Stanton.

They said no more about the future work, but sat for a time in the club lounge after the meal talking of other aspects of the Topex organization. In the end Mr Johnson said, 'You're going out West tomorrow, I suppose?'

'Unless you want me here.'

The older man shook his head. 'I'll talk to P.K. about the new assignment for you, but he's in Canada right now, and after that he's going off on his vacation. I'll have to write you, maybe in two weeks from now.' He pulled out his pocket diary. 'Let's see, you've got ten weeks' vacation coming to you – that takes us to September twentieth. I'll see you again then.'

They walked back together to the office, where Stanton spent half an hour in the Treasurer's office putting in expense accounts and drawing money; from the office he telephoned his friend about a bed in his apartment, telephoned an airline office for a reservation to the West next day, and sent a telegram to his parents in Hazel. Then he walked out into the streets of downtown New York and took a bus up Broadway, savouring the city.

He loved his country very dearly, without realizing it. He was a technician, and nothing technical was worth much to him that did not come from the United States. Overseas he had wondered at the little cramped style of the foreign motor cars; now that he was back in his own country the glorious, spacious vehicles of his own land were an acute pleasure to him; the cars that he had seen in his travels overseas could not compare with the new Oldsmobiles or Cadillacs. The origins of the techniques that pleased him so did not affect his thinking; that Otto was a German and Whittle an Englishman did not seem relevant when he considered the superiority of American motor cars and American jet aircraft. Nothing was very real to him that did not happen in the United States.

His personal experience of the world outside America had been limited to Cairo, the Arabian desert, two days in Rome while waiting for air connexions, and twenty-four hours in Lisbon. He had been impressed by the motor scooters in Rome, but they were the only things that he had seen in all his travels that had made him feel his own country behindhand. He was sensible enough to realize that there was more to the world than that, that London and Paris might have things to show him that he would admire, but the United States was his home, the place with the highest standard of living in the world, the place with the most glorious technical achievements, the place where he loved to be.

In the late afternoon he found his way into Abercrombie and Fitch and spent a delightful hour looking over the new styles in fishing rods with reels incorporated with the handle, the new styles in outboard motors and fibreglass boats, in camping gear and sleeping bags. A stainless steel barbecue set with fork, spoon, and skewer three feet long, with steel hand shields gleaming and bright, took his fancy and he bought it as a present for his father though his luggage was already overweight for the airline, and then the shops were closing and he made his way happily through the thronging crowds around Grand Central Station towards his friends in Peter Cooper Village. It was grand to be back in the United States again, but it would be even better to be back in Oregon again tomorrow, his own place.

He was a Westerner, born and raised in Oregon and educated in California. All the United States was good in his eyes, the meanest part better than the best of the outside world, but of the United States some parts were better than others. He did not greatly care for the Eastern states, infiltrated as they were with European influences and already burdened with three centuries of tradition. The racial problems of the South distressed him mildly, to the extent that he would not have chosen to live there, and although the technical advances of the Middle West were stimulating he knew a better country to live in than the plains of Michigan or Ohio. It was not until you crossed the mountains that you came, in his opinion, to the vital and virile heart of the United States, the states where men were men. Less than a hundred years ago the immigrants had poured into his home country over the Oregon trail, travelling hard by covered wagon, fighting the Indians, facing death and injury each day of the six months' journey that would lead them to the glorious new country in the West. The men, the women, and the children who had opened up the Pacific slopes were hard, competent, and virile types, and they influenced their country still. Stanton's grandfather had made that journey as a child in 1861; at the age of eight he had seen men killed in an attack by Indians upon the wagon convoy, had helped his father hew a farm out of the wilderness a little to the east of where the town of Hazel now stood. Stanton knew that old man intimately for he had lived till the boy was fifteen, and he had heard from him the history of Hazel as it had grown in one man's lifetime from the first shack in the virgin prairie on the edge of the forests and the mountains to the place that it was now, a place of paved streets, of drug stores, of quiet, decent homes in shaded avenues, of theatres and railway tracks and aeroplanes, of the Safeway and the Piggy-Wiggy café. In his view the people of Washington, Oregon, and Northern California constituted the best stock in the United States because their descent from the pioneers was the shortest; he was proud to be one of them, and infinitely happy now that he was going home.

He did not think of these things in that detail, but they formed together to create the general happiness that stayed with him all next day as he flew westwards in the Constellation. He changed planes at Chicago about noon, and flew on through the interminable afternoon, stretched out by changes in the local time, over South Dakota and Montana to the high mountains that delighted him, that heralded the Coast. In the evening light Mount Rainier showed up ahead, snow-capped and symmetrical and lovely, and the aircraft started to lose height; they landed at Seattle in the dusk. The fresh, salt-laden breeze from the Pacific was a tonic as he stepped out of the aeroplane.

He could not get home that night, but he could at least sleep in his own state. He telephoned from the airport for a hotel reservation and took a Convair southwards from Seattle to Portland. With each hour that he flew the sense of coming home grew stronger in him, the airports less magnificent and friendlier. He had not been home for three years, but the United dispatcher at the gate of Portland airport came from Portage, a village not far from Hazel, and knew Stanton, and greeted him by name.

'Hi-yah, Stanton,' he said. 'Quite a time since we saw you here.'

The young man paused, delighted, but unable to remember the dispatcher's name. 'That's right,' he said. 'I've been away.'

'I know it,' said the fat, uniformed man. 'Some place in the East, was it?'

'That's right. Arabia.'

'Uh-huh. You going on by Flight 173 in the morning?'

'That's right.'

'Saw your name down on the list. Where are you stopping tonight?'

'I'll be at the Congress Hotel.'

The official scribbled a note upon a pad. 'I'll fix the airport limousine for you. Five minutes past seven at the hotel.'

'Thanks a lot.'

'Your mother, she came through about two weeks back. Your father, of course – he comes through quite a bit. They're looking fine.'

'You don't look bad yourself.'

'Putting on weight,' said the official sadly.

The limousine was waiting to take Stanton to the city. With the homecoming he reverted to the idiom of his boyhood. 'You know somethin'?' he inquired.

'What's that?'

'It's kind of nice to be back.'

The dispatcher laughed. ' 'Bye now.'

He got to the hotel at about ten o'clock, tired, but not too tired to ring his parents from the hotel bedroom. He spoke to his father and mother for some minutes and told them the time when he would land at Hazel airport; then he rang off and undressed slowly, savouring the comforts of the bedroom and the shower. It was a warm night, though much cooler than New York, and he lay for a time before sleep came to him. He had nothing to read till he discovered the Gideon Bible in the drawer of the bedside table; he leafed it through as he grew drowsy, remembering the intonations of the minister in church as the familiar phrases met his eye, one after the other.

The sun shall not smite thee by day, nor the moon by night.

That meant Arabia, of course. Well, it hadn't.

The Lord shall preserve thy going out and thy coming in from this time forth, and even for evermore.

Well, He had. That motor might have failed way out over the Atlantic instead of half an hour before they were due to land at Lisbon.

This is my rest for ever; here will I dwell, for I have desired it.

He was home again, back from his travels, in one piece. Back in his own state of Oregon, in his home town to-morrow. Gee, this Book had messages, skads and skads of them, if only you bothered to look.

Presently he slept.

He flew next morning in an old DC3 eastwards from Portland up the Columbia River valley, landing once at The Dalles. The DC3 put down on the small Hazel airport in the middle of the morning and taxied into the minature airport building, and there at the fence he could see a little crowd of people waiting to meet him. He got out of the machine carrying his plastic overnight bag and the wrapped parcel that contained the barbecue set, and walked quickly to the barrier. There were his mother and his father, clean-shaven and portly, and his sister Shelley with her husband Sam Rapke who ran his father's business, the biggest hard-ware store in Hazel, and their two children, Lance, aged six, and Avril, aged four; they must have left the baby at home. All the family were there to meet him, those who lived in Hazel, and he was glad of it.

'Hi-yah, Mom,' he said, and kissed her. She said, 'Junior, you're so *brown!*'

He turned from her to his father. 'Hi, Dad.' His father said, 'Welcome home, son. You're looking mighty well.'

'I feel pretty good,' Stanton said. 'Glad to be back again.'

His mother asked, 'Did you get sick at all, out in those hot places, Jun? You never said in any of your letters.'

'I wasn't sick a day,' he assured her.

'Well now, isn't that just wonderful! I got so worried you might have been sick and not told us.'

'I wouldn't have done that, Mom.'

He turned to greet his sister and the children and Sam Rapke, and when that was over he turned to his father again. 'Say, Dad, I got this for you when I stopped off in

22

New York.' He handed him the parcel. To his mother he said, 'I got your present in one of the bags, Mom.' The barbecue set was unwrapped there and then as they stood by the airport barrier. His father said, 'Say, that's just what we've been needing! We built an outdoor barbecue this spring.'

'I know it, Dad. You wrote and told me.'

His mother said, 'Oh Junior! They're so *elegant.*'

The few bags were taken from the aeroplane and wheeled into the baggage room, and they went in to claim them. Carrying his grips they went out to the park. His father said, 'I got something for you, son. How long a leave do you get now?'

'Till September twentieth, Dad.'

'Good enough. Well, that's it. There she is.' There were only two cars in the park, a Dodge with a family already getting into it, and a great Lincoln convertible in two-tone blue, with blue upholstery, gleaming and bright. Stanton stared at it.

'Gee, Dad – not the convertible?' They walked towards it.

'Yours for your leave, son.'

'But, Dad, it's just about new!'

'Done nine thousand miles. I sold it to Dirk Hronsky last fall.' Dirk Hronsky was the local lumber magnate. 'He didn't like it, didn't like the power steering. He's a wee bit heavy-handed driving on an icy road, an' got himself a couple of skids, and his wife just didn't care for it. So he traded it in for a new Mercury this spring, only a month or two back, an' I kept it for your leave.'

'Gee, Dad, that's swell of you!' Now that he was home again the schoolboy phrases, half forgotten in his wider life, came tumbling out one after the other.

His father and Sam Rapke put the suitcase into the trunk and closed it down; they had not allowed Stanton to carry anything. At the huge door of the car his mother said, 'Now I'm getting in back while Junior drives us home.'

He said, 'You come up front with Shelley, Mom, and let Dad drive. I'll get in back.' All his life he had longed for a great modern car like that, but now that it was his he was half afraid of it, unwilling to experiment with it before his family.

His mother said, 'No, Junior. You must drive your own car.'

He glanced at the floor, devoid of any clutch pedal. 'I don't suppose I know how, Mom. I've never driven an automatic shift.' He had left the country before they had come into very general use.

His mother said, 'Why, Junior, even I can drive a car like this. You get right in and drive it!'

He slipped into the driver's seat and explored the controls for a minute. His father got in beside him. Very gingerly, bearing in mind the motor of two hundred horsepower, he touched the accelerator. Nothing happened.

'You got to pour it on, son, to get rolling,' his father said. 'Just pour it on.'

He poured it on, and the big car moved off. He drove it with increasing confidence and delight down the familiar highway to the town, past the well remembered stores and gas stations, across the railway tracks and into the quiet, shaded streets where all Hazel lived, between Main Street and the High School. He drew up carefully beside the sidewalk opposite his home and stopped the motor. He sat motionless in the driver's seat for a moment. 'She's certainly a lovely car,' he said quietly, and his parents beamed at his pleasure. He touched one of the stops upon the organ-like console in front of him, and said, 'What does this one do, Dad?'

'Raises the aerial.' He pulled it, and the radio mast grew magically upwards. He pressed it, and the mast sank down again. 'Well, what do you know!' breathed the geologist. 'I bet she can pick up her heels and go, on a clear run.'

'Pass anything on the road, except a gas station,' his father laughed. 'I've opened a charge account for you down at the garage.'

In the house his room was exactly as he had left it three years previously, the same college banners on the wall, his fishing rods, his guns, his steel bow and arrows, his skiing boots, all carefully dusted and tended and exactly as he had left them. He was glad of it, and yet they made him feel that he had grown in stature during his travels; to some extent he had outgrown these things and if he were to live in Hazel now for any length of time his room would not be quite the same. Downstairs the house was as he had known it from the time when they had bought it in his early manhood, and yet there were changes to be seen. The old electric range that had dominated the kitchen had been ripped out and a more modern one installed that dominated it more, a new dishwasher stood where the old one had stood, a larger, grander, and more elaborate refrigerator. In the living-room a television set had appeared. In the basement the old heating plant had been ripped out and a new one installed, fully automatic, with time clocks and thermostats to control the temperature in every room. which his father demonstrated to him with great pride. A new outboard motor of improved design had replaced the old one, a new boat the old boat, and a new boat trailer the old boat trailer. His father's Mercury and his mother's Ford convertible were both the latest models, but that, of course, to some extent concerned the business. A used electric washing machine isn't very easy to trade in, so three of them stood in the basement in a row, each marking a stage further in development. His father was responsible for all these innovations. As each new machine had been introduced, Mrs Laird had smiled quietly and had displayed a distressing tendency to go on using the old one if it had been left for her to use. It took her about two years normally to get accustomed to a new machine and to cease grieving for the old, out-dated one, and by that time the new machine itself was obsolete and due to be replaced. It was a gentle joke within the family that Mom had never ceased to grieve for the Model T Ford that they had driven in the early years of marriage. 'It was a lovely car,' she had once said quietly. 'You couldn't ever grind the gears, it wouldn't go fast, and **you** could see where you were going.'

Stanton Junior settled down to his ten weeks' leave happily enough, in his home town, in summer weather. Hazel lies in a bowl of the foothills of the Rocky Mountain range on the edge of the Hazel National Forest. The National Forest is a tract of mountain country about fifty miles long and thirty miles wide, designated by the Federal Government as a Primitive Area. In a Primitive Area no house or road may be constructed and no internal combustion engine may run; if you go into it you go on horseback or on foot. In the high mountains the lakes are full of trout, and deer roam the mountain slopes. Few of the active citizens of Hazel did not fish the rivers and the lakes, may of them kept horses and packhorses for adventures in the wilderness that lay above the town. After the deserts of Arabia his home town was like a drink of clear, cool water to the geologist.

He could not, of course, resist considerable journeys in the Lincoln. A week after he got home he drove his mother on a visit to his other sister, Cathy, married to a sawmill manager at Bellingham, just short of the Canadian border, and a week or two after that he drove southwards for seven hundred miles down California to Stanford University to see old friends, covering five hundred and fifty miles in one day. He fished a good deal in the Hazel River, mostly with a spinner, and he made a few short trips into the mountains on horseback, staying out each time for a couple of nights and sleeping in a sleeping bag under the stars.

His chief difficulty, of course, was to find anyone to play with him. The men of his generation were dispersed, married, and working in jobs, and none of his generation of High School girls remained unmarried in the district. Chuck Sheraton was a lieutenant in the US Air Force and likely to remain so; he had flown Sabres in Korea with a good combat record, but he was allergic to discipline and every time he rose a little in the estimation of the Air Force he got out of line, and got slammed down again. He was stationed at an Air Force base down in Texas now as an instructor, with Ruth and their four children; they were coming home on leave to Hazel in September, and Stanton looked forward to their coming. In the meantime fishing and riding in the mountains did not occupy him fully, and for the first time in his life he began to take an interest in his father's business.

He was no salesman, though he delighted in the glorious new motor cars. Laird Motors Inc, however, had developed a large tractor business in that agricultural community, and the adaptation of the tractors to various uses in the lumber industry had caused them to set up a considerable workshop for the manufacture of special parts and tools. Behind the automobile showroom and the service station was a busy general engineering shop, and this the geologist began to find absorbing in its interest. He had a good theoretical knowledge of metals and their properties but he had never before seen much of their manipulation. The conception, the design of a special forklift for a certain purpose in the Hronsky sawmill which should button on to an existing tractor interested him greatly; when it failed on test owing to a burnt weld he found that he could offer some constructive help in the selection of a better type of steel, based on his experiences at the drilling rigs. These minor engineering creations became of real interest to him in the weeks he was at home, and whenever he had nothing else to do he would find his way down to the shop and sit about watching the lathes and milling machines paring down the steel, and chatting to the men.

It was the middle of August before the letter from Mr Johnson arrived. The mail reached Hazel at noon, and he found it waiting for him when he returned after a day's fishing. 'There's a letter from New York for you, Junior,' his mother said. 'Maybe it's the one that you've been waiting for.'

'I guess it is,' he said. He went into the kitchen and unloaded five small trout and two rainbows on to the steel drainboard. His father came through. 'That's a good fish,' he said, pointing. 'Want your letter now?'

'I'll wash my hands first, Dad,' he said. He did so, and

27

slit the letter open with the patent opener that stood upon his father's desk. He stood in fishing clothes reading it in silence, while his parents watched. The he folded the letter and put it in his pocket.

His mother asked, 'Do they say where you're going?'

'Kind of difficult, Mom,' he said thoughtfully. 'They've given me a choice – Paraguay or Australia. I'll have to think it over.'

Disappointed, his mother said, 'There wouldn't be a chance of a job here in the United States?'

He had explained this to her before. 'Not unless I get myself married, Mom.'

She said nothing, and he went slowly to his room to park his fishing gear, unreel his line to dry, and change his clothes. Later in the evening, when they switched off after *I Love Lucy*, he said thoughtfully to his father, 'You know what, Dad? I believe I'll go to Australia.'

His mother said, 'Why, Junior? It's much farther away for coming home on leave.'

'I like the sound of it better, Mom.' For half an hour he laid out the alternatives before them. In each case Topex were to function, in a sense, as exploration contractors working for a national company. In each case the assignment would be for approximately two years. In Paraguay the location would be jungle country, hot and wet and humid, and Spanish-speaking. In West Australia the location would be sheep country just above the tropic, near desert, hot, waterless, and English-speaking. 'I guess the country might be somethin' like Arabia,' he said. 'Maybe not quite so bad. You couldn't have run sheep at Abu Quaiyah.'

His mother said, 'I don't like the thought of you going back to a place like that, Junior.'

'It's healthy enough, Mom,' he said. 'I wasn't sick a day. I'd be more scared of getting sick in Paraguay than I would back in Arabia. Marshes and flies and fevers, 'n all that.'

'I know it,' said his father. 'A dry place is better, honey.'

'There's the language, too,' the geologist said. 'Two years is neither one thing nor the other. By the time you'd learned to speak well enough to get on with people, it'ld be time to come back home.' He grinned. 'Not that there'd be anyone to talk to in either place.'

'What would Australians be like?' his mother asked presently. 'Would they be like Canadians?'

'More like English,' his father told her. 'They say tomahto instead of tomato. We had some of them at the airport, training, in the war. Didn't you meet them?'

She shook her head. 'I never did.' And then she asked, 'Do they have coloured people there, like Africa?'

That perplexed them. 'I saw a piece in the *National Geographic* about Australian black boys,' her husband said. 'Pretty near naked, like savages. The ones I saw when they came here were white like you or me.'

'They make good soldiers,' said her son.

He took a couple of days to think it over before answering the letter. Like most young men in Hazel he was accustomed at home to doing his own laundry; ironing a couple of shirts one morning in the kitchen while his mother prepared lunch, he said, 'I just about made up my mind, Mom. I think I'll go to Australia.'

She said, 'Will it always have to be places such a long way away, son?'

'Depends how I get on,' he said. 'Maybe the head office one day, if I'm good enough.'

'That would be in New York?'

'Uh-huh.'

'Do you want a city life, even if it means a lot of money?'

'I don't know, Mom,' he said slowly. 'I wouldn't like living in New York.'

'A small town's the best for small town people,' she said quietly. 'Your father and I, we've been mighty happy here.'

He smiled. 'Go easy, Mom – all small towns aren't like Hazel. This is one of the best towns in the whole of the United States. Why, people come here from the East for their vacations!'

'I was just saying it's a mighty good place to live, son.'

There was a long pause while he ran the iron carefully

around a collar. 'There'd be nothing I could do in a town like this,' he said. 'I don't know that there's any place I'd rather live in, but you got to be practical.' He grinned. 'There's not an oil rig in five hundred miles.'

His mother said nothing, and the conversation lapsed.

He wrote next day to Mr Johnson accepting the Australian assignment and asking if they wanted him to report back to New York on the conclusion of his leave, since in Oregon he was three thousand miles or so towards Australia. He did not get an answer for a week, and then he got a fat letter with many papers enclosed giving him preliminary information of the Topex business in Australia, a general account of the geological situation in the Hammersley Ranges, a detailed geological report of the probable formations under a place called Laragh deduced from surface indications, and a map. The covering letter instructed him to report to the Topex agent in San Francisco on September the twentieth, who would supply him with expense money and any final instructions, and who was securing airline reservations for him. He would make his way directly to Perth in West Australia and report to the local Topex manager, Mr Colin Spriggs, who had an office in Barrack St.

In the next fortnight he began to overhaul his kit; he would want very much the same outfit of tropical clothes that he had worn in Arabia, but many replenishments were needed. In the field he usually wore US Army clothing, battledress trousers and blouse of light fabric, jungle-green in colour, but these suits were threadbare and in need of much replacement. He drove down to Portland in the Lincoln upon this and other matters of his kit, trading in his typewriter for a new one and buying a new electric razor, an essential in his mind for a sojourn in the desert. Water might be brackish and in short supply, and usually had been so at Abu Quaiyah, but practically every aspect of his work demanded electricity; he could not explore the strata far below the ground nor sink a bore for exploration at the point he had selected without the assistance of a considerable power station. He bought a new camp bed with a mosquito

30

net attached and had it shipped to Perth, and stocked up his medicine chest with two years's supply of the American drugs that he knew and was accustomed to.

All these things he distributed around his bedroom on the floor, with many others, as he started to get organized. His mother gave up all attempts to clean his room, but she paused in the open doorway one morning to watch him sewing on a button. 'I'll do that for you,' she offered.

'It's no trouble, Mom,' he said. 'It's easy to do them as I find them.'

She looked around the room. 'You taking any books along?'

'I thought maybe I'd take this one along, this time,' he said. He indicated a small Bible on the dressing table.

'That might be a good thing to do,' she observed. 'You didn't take it with you last time.'

'No,' he replied. 'Guess I'm getting old.'

She did not comment, but said, 'Taking any other books?'

'I don't think so, Mom. I'd like it if you could keep sending the *Saturday Evening Post* and *Life*.'

'Surely,' she said. 'If you read those papers I don't know that you want to read anything else.'

There was a pause, and then he said, 'You know somethin'?'

'What's that?'

'I'd kind of like to see the *Hazel Advertiser* now 'n then. Not every week, just now 'n then.' He looked up and grinned at her. 'See what movie's playing at the theatre.'

She nodded. 'I'll have that mailed to you from the office. Your Dad, he sometimes cuts bits out of our copy. You want a Portland paper, say the *Sunday Oregonian* as well?'

'I dunno that I'd read it. Maybe there'll be an Australian paper that I'll have to read, out there. I guess if I have the *Saturday Evening Post* and *Life* and the *Hazel Advertiser*, that's all I'll want to read.'

'And the Bible,' said his mother.

He looked up, grinning. 'Kind of makes the library complete.'

Three weeks before the end of his leave Chuck Sheraton arrived from Texas, his Chev full to the brim with wife, four children, two dogs, a pushcart, luggage, camp kit, and appurtenances. The Sheraton home was in Lindbergh Avenue two blocks from the Laird home on 2nd St, and Stanton strolled round to visit with them the morning after they arrived. As he approached the house a boy of eleven came out of the basement garage sucking a Coke through a straw, and Stanton got his shock. When he had last seen him four years previously this kid had been getting most uncomfortably like himself, and quite unlike his father or his mother. Now, at eleven, he was the very spit and image of Stanton at that age.

The geologist said, 'Hi-yah, Tony. You remember me?'

The boy said, 'You're Stan Laird.'

'That's right. Have a good ride up?'

'Gloria was sick, and Imogen was sick, and Peter was sick, *I* wasn't sick.'

The geologist wrinkled his brows, a little dazed. 'Is Imogen the baby, or is that Peter?'

The child said scornfully, 'They're dogs.'

'Oh, sure. Your Dad inside?'

'I guess so.'

He found Ruth and Chuck in the house. He had not seen Ruth for four years and probably he had not met her half a dozen times since their disgrace; he thought he had got over that, and he was surprised that she could still give his heart a little twist when she said, 'Why Stan, it's real nice to see you!' Chuck was in a clean drill summer uniform shirt and slacks, sorting out a tangled mass of baggage and kit on the floor of the video alcove off the living-room. He said, 'Hi-yah, fellow. How you doing?'

'Okay,' said Stan. 'You still in one piece?'

Chuck stood up, grinning, a bulging haversack in hand. 'More'n one piece. Either one or two more since I saw you – I kinda lose track of them. You better ask Ruthie. She might know.'

'It's one more, Stan,' she said. 'Gloria was born just before you went away, remember?'

'Uh-huh. This the one born last fall?'

'That's right – Jasmine. She's asleep right now, but she's a lovely baby.'

Chuck said, 'Sure, she's a lovely baby. Ruthie, what about a rum 'n Coke?'

She went to get the bottles of Coca-cola from the refrigerator, and Chuck produced a half-empty bottle of rum from the haversack. Stanton said, 'Not for me, pal. I don't use the stuff.'

'Not even in Arabia?' Chuck grinned.

Stanton shook his head. 'Just Coke.'

'Okay, fellow. Ruthie, bring some ice along.'

They sat down, sucking Cokes and rum and Cokes through straws as they compared experiences. Chuck had achieved the Distinguished Flying Cross in Korea after shooting down three MIGs, and in celebration at a party in Tokio he had crashed an Army jeep, had been arrested by the military police, and had spent a night in the cooler. He was now instructing fighter pilots at an airbase near Houston, and he had developed a technique which was giving him a good deal of pleasure. In that district the railways were mostly single track. When night-flying he would cruise around until he saw a train, the engine decorated with one bright headlight. He would then retire fifteen miles ahead of it and bring his aircraft down to track level, flying towards the train with one landing light on, exactly above the track. So far no engineer had actually died of fright but he understood that several had come very near it, and that half the locomotives in Texas were progressing in a series of leaps with flats on the wheels.

Stanton told them all about Arabia, or what he knew of it; it took him about three minutes. They then turned to gossip about their schoolmates in Hazel, far more interesting and important topics, and the prospects in the forthcoming World Series. They sat together gossiping for half an hour, and got on to the subject of the deer.

33

'I got to get going on September nineteenth,' the geologist said.

'Only gives us three days of the shooting season,' said Chuck. 'Kind of short.'

Stanton said, 'You know somethin'? I'd like to try it with the bow and arrow.'

In the Hazel National Forest the deer were strictly protected. There was a shooting season of one month in the fall, but before the shooting season it was legal to attack the deer with bows and arrows for a fortnight.

'Might do that,' said Chuck. 'You got a bow?'

Stanton nodded. Before leaving for Arabia he had bought himself a fine new modern bow the like of which was never seen at Agincourt, made by the American Steel Tube Co, Inc in Springfield, Illinois, delicately tapered and immensely powerful; he had only used this outfit once and longed to use it again. 'Hank Fisher got himself a bow like mine,' he said. 'He'd lend it you.'

Chuck smiled. 'Go at it the hard way, like boy scouts.'

'I guess it wouldn't do us any harm, take off a bit of weight.'

'I'll say it wouldn't,' said Ruth feelingly.

They started three days later, Chuck and Stanton alone. They went on horseback, Chuck riding Mrs Eberhart's grey mare and Stanton riding a bay gelding called Scamp that belonged to his father; they led a packhorse loaded with their sleeping bags, hobbles, and food, for they intended to stay out for a week or so. They rode in the blue riding jeans that they called levis, with thick woollen shirts and windproof jackets suitable for the high altitudes that they were bound for; they rode in saddles with saddlebags, and they carried their bows slung across their backs. All this was normal to them, as it was to most of the citizens of Hazel; they had made this sort of expedition in most of the summer vacations of their lives. They were skilled and experienced horsemen in the mountains, and their equipment was superbly good.

Hazel lies in a shallow, fertile valley beside the mountains, at an altitude of about three thousand feet. It took them half a day to reach the edge of the Primitive Area; they camped there at about six thousand feet, making a short day of the first one. The next day they were up at dawn and in the saddle by eight o'clock. They descended by rocky trails into the valley of the Duncan River and commenced the long climb up the side of Sugar Mountain, zig-zagging all through the hot afternoon across the grassy slopes and in and out of the fir woods.

They camped that night in a pasture with good feed for the horses by Emerald Lake at about eight thousand feet, and went on next day above the tree line across granite screes still covered in the shaded parts with patches of snow. They descended a little and camped soon after midday by the edge of Duncan's Lake in a little grassy meadow between high screes, with the twin peaks of Saddle Mountain tower-ing up above them, snow-clad, to about eleven thousand feet. This was their permanent camp from which they would proceed on foot after the deer.

They ate well that evening, for they would be travelling hard and eating only cold food for the next day or two. They had brought with them a five-foot spinning rod and had no difficulty in catching half a dozen eager little trout in half an hour. They made a fire and cooked a supper of hot buck-wheat cakes and syrup, with bacon, trout, and a fried egg all piled together on the plate and eaten together, with hot muffins, butter, and jam as a side dish and a huge pot of hot, sweet coffee to wash it down. Replete and comatose in the dusk by the lakeside they discussed their plans.

'I guess we'd better try it up the north side, by Cooper's Gully, as if you were going to Trout Falls,' Chuck said. 'The wind's been in the south the last two days. I reckon they'll be there, if they're anywhere.'

'They'll be feeding in the sun by midday,' Stanton said. 'They always get into the sun when they're up high. You know somethin'? I think they'll be on the far side of the gully, up by Indian Hat.'

They started on foot soon after dawn, after a breakfast

cooked before the sun got up. They left the horses hobbled in the meadow and left their sleeping bags and most of their equipment; they went with packs upon their backs consisting of a little bread and tinned meat wrapped up in a blanket, and their pockets full of wrapped candies.

For three hours they climbed the northern spur of Saddle Mountain, getting up above the tree line again in the granite screes. From the ridge they could look down into the wooded, pasture cleft of Cooper's Gully. On the sunny side facing them they saw deer feeding, in among the trees, perhaps two miles away. They had no glasses with them because of the weight, but the animals were distinct in the clear air.

Chuck said, 'I guess we've got to get down wind from them. Get up behind them, 'n come down from the top.'

The geologist said. 'They'll move down the valley as the shadow comes round – keep in the sun. We'll have to cross way down below them.'

'Uh-huh. We got quite a walk.'

They made their way down into Cooper's Gully, moving down the scree as quietly as they could go, for they were in full view of the deer. Two hours later they were in position three hundred feet above the animals and within half a mile of them, with the wind blowing gently in their faces. They studied the position and made plans for the stalk. The sloping meadow where the deer were feeding was bounded on three sides with trees; the open side led upwards to the heights. They decided that Chuck should stalk them through the trees and try to shoot a buck as they grazed. Stanton would place himself three hundred yards towards the open, to try a second shot when they were startled and made for the heights. There were fourteen animals in the herd, three of them good bucks with antlers.

They left their packs, and separated, creeping forward on their stomachs in the grass, moving cautiously from rock to tree, infinitely low. Stanton had the shorter and the easier stalk, designed to enable him to get into position long before Chuck was in range for a shot. He reached the place that he had planned in about twenty minutes, a comfortable hide behind two fir trees and a rock at a place where the deer must pass within twenty yards of him if they made for the heights. He laid out four birch arrows on a flat rock convenient to his hand, braced his bow, and nocked a fifth arrow to the bowstring, ready to draw. Then he waited, motionless.

It was very quiet in the glade. He could hear some of the animals grazing still, but they were getting restless now, lifting their heads and looking around. He could see nothing of Chuck, but judged that he must be near them. Then as he watched he saw the pilot rising slowly to his feet behind a .ree. Stanton made ready, glanced at the arrows he had laid out on the rock, felt for the arrows in his quiver.

Then Chuck shot. The herd wheeled around, and came galloping up the glade towards Stanton, headed by an antlered buck. He drew his bow, waited till they were within fifty yards, and stepped out from behind the tree. The buck checked at the sight of him and wheeled, stationary for an instant and presenting his flank, and at that moment Stanton shot. As he shot he noted a wound already in the flank, rather low down. His arrow sped true and hit the beast just behind the shoulder, going in about six inches and lodging there. The buck leaped round and tore on past him for the open heights, followed by the herd; Stanton nocked another arrow and shot again at the same beast; the arrow hit it in the rump making a long flesh wound, and fell to the ground. Then the animals were gone over the hill.

Chuck came walking up the pasture to him. 'Do any good, Stan?'

The geologist told him what had happened.

Chuck said, 'I hit one a bit low, one of the bucks. The arrow went right through him. Then I shot at him again and missed.'

'That's the one I shot at,' Stanton said. 'I saw he'd been wounded. I got him just behind the shoulder, 'n a flesh wound in the rump.'

They discussed the matter as they made their way back

up the hill to fetch their packs. 'I guess this is where we start and take the fat off, Stan,' said Chuck.

It was then about three o'clock in the afternoon. They shouldered their packs, collected their arrows, and stood in the tracks of the departed herd. They had no idea which way the herd would run, or how far the wounded buck would go before he paused to rest. The trail up the hill was clear, however, and they set off in the hot sun to follow up the herd. Presently they noticed bloodstains on the grass and knew that the buck was seriously wounded.

The tracks led them up out of Cooper's Gully, over the ridge and along the side of Saddle Mountain towards Indian Hat, leading away from their camp and their horses all the time. They paused on the ridge, looking out over the wide sweep of the mountains, streaked and patched with snow upon the northern slopes. To go back to the camp and fetch the horses would delay them for a day; it might be quickest in the long run, but in that day the trail would grow cold and probably become windswept and obliterated. They decided to go on on foot while the trail was fresh.

They followed the trail on till dark, with no sight of the animals. Once they found a patch of crushed and blood-stained grass where the buck had rested in the shelter of some scrub; the grass did not seem warm, so they judged that he was still some way ahead. When dusk came they were still following the trail on the southern slopes of the peak that they called Indian Hat, fifteen or sixteen miles away from their horses.

They dared not make a fire, for fear of stampeding the deer if they were near at hand. They ate about half the bread and meat they had brought with them and lay down to sleep, huddled together for warmth. They got little sleep, for it was bitterly cold at that high altitude and the two blankets that they had were quite inadequate. As soon as it was light enough to see, they got stiffly to their feet. They had no appetite for food and there was nothing to drink, but the trail of the deer was still clear and they went on. Presently they came upon a little cold stream running down out of the snow, and paused to drink, and ate a little of the cold meat that was left.

About two miles from where they had camped they found another bloodstained patch of ground where the buck had rested, and now the grass and the blood were still warm. A few minutes after that they saw the herd ahead of them, about two miles away, galloping across a grassy hillside and over a shoulder, but the wounded buck was not with them.

'He'll be lying up some place between here and there,' said Chuck. 'I guess we'd better get one of us each side of him. You stay behind him here, and I'll go round, 'n get ahead of him. Gimme an hour from now, and then come on.'

He went off up the hill and Stanton sat down upon a rock to wait. It was warm now in the rising sun. Up on the heights there he could see snow-capped peaks tipped by a golden light, over in Idaho, maybe a hundred miles away, distinct in that clear air. This was his country and he consciously rejoiced in it; it was better for him than anything that he had seen outside America. The fact that it was under snow for nine months of the year and so quite inaccessible did not affect his pleasure; the outside world, he felt, had nothing to show him that was so good as this.

Presently his self-winding wrist watch showed him that the hour was up. He got to his feet, adjusted the aluminium-framed pack upon his back, pulled up the zip of his feather-weight wind jacket, put on his scientifically designed tinted glasses, for the sun was now strong, picked up his tubular steel bow, put one of his few remaining candies in his mouth, and went on, following the trail.

Half a mile farther on there was a struggling and a crashing in the scrub ahead of him and he saw the buck getting to his feet, barely two hundred yards away. It went on weakly but still faster than Stanton could run, stumbling now and then, following the trail left by the herd. Stanton followed in pursuit at a fast walk. If Chuck was in position it was now all his.

Presently, far ahead of him, he heard the twang of

Chuck's bow borne on the still air, and then another, and another, and then a crashing in the scrub, and a shout from Chuck. He quickened his pace to a run, and presently he came on Chuck sitting on the ground by the dead buck. He had shot five more arrows into it so that it looked like something out of a bull fight, and then, when it went down, he had run in rather rashly and had grappled with its antlers, and had cut its throat with his long aluminium-handled hunting knife; that was the end.

They stood resting for a time, exulting in their prowess and retrieving their steel-barbed birch arrows. They were determined to get the head and antlers back to Hazel with them and into cold storage as a preliminary to being mounted as a trophy, but they were all of twenty miles now from the horses, the sun was getting up, and they were very hungry.

'I guess we'd better make a fire and have a steak, first thing of all,' said Stanton. 'It's going to be tough meat.'

He set to work to build a fire, while Chuck commenced the butchering, a gory business, for there was no water on the hillside. He decapitated the buck and slung the head up in the fork of a tree till they could fetch it with the pack-horse; they were at too high an altitude for flies to attack it. They cut steaks from the buck and grilled them in small pieces on a sharpened stick, but they could eat little for the lack of water and the toughness of the meat. Then they set out on the long walk back to the horses and the camp, leaving their hunting gear cached near the carcase of the buck, unloading themselves of everything they could spare.

They got back to their camp by Duncan's Lake beneath Saddle Mountain just before sunset, tired but exultant. They gave the horses a feed of oats and made a huge stew of the deer meat and a tin of beef, topping off with crackers and jam and about a gallon of coffee. Then they blew up the air beds incorporated with their sleeping bags and crept into the warm comfort of the blankets in the light of the dying fire, and lay together under the bright stars for a few minutes before sleep, discussing the events of the day and what they would do in the morning.

Presently Stanton said sleepily, 'You know somethin'?'

'What's that?'

'That boy Tony of yours. He's getting to look the hell of a lot like me.'

The other chuckled. 'Ruth and me, we don't say nothing about that.'

'I guess you're the only people in all Hazel that don't.'

'So what?' said Chuck. 'There's nothing anybody can do about it now. I reckon we were all just a little bit hasty in those days.'

'Maybe we were. Anyway,' Stanton said sleepily, 'it's all come out all right.'

There was a short silence, and then Chuck said, 'You never going to get married, Stan?'

'I guess I will one day. There aren't too many girls around the places where I work.'

'Ruth and I, we get kind of worried sometimes.'

'About me?'

'Uh-huh.'

'What about?'

'I dunno. Seems like you got the smutty end of the stick in that deal of ours.'

'I made out all right,' said the geologist. 'Reckon I got a long ways further than if I'd married in High School.'

Chuck said sleepily, 'Maybe so. You got the book learning and turned into somebody. I got Ruth and turned into a bum. I dunno which of us got the better deal.'

Stanton laughed. 'Go to sleep, you big bum.'

'Okay. G'night, Stan.'

'G'night.'

They set off next day soon after dawn and made their way on horseback to retrieve the head and antlers of the buck. On the ridge above Cooper's Gully they met a forest ranger riding down towards his cabin, and told him about the buck. The ranger had two-way radio at his cabin, and they gave him a telegram to Stanton's father asking to be met with a horse truck at Beaver River dude ranch next morning; this was fifty miles from Hazel but was the shortest way out of the Primitive Area for them, and would save them a couple of days on the homeward trail.

On the next day they were home, displaying their gory trophy to their slightly horrified relations before rushing it down to Portland in the Lincoln, packed in dry ice, to be mounted before the processes of death went too far. They had been away from home a week, and each of them had lost three or four pounds in weight.

That was the last trip into the mountains that Stanton made before leaving for Australia. On his last day he drove the Lincoln down to the garage to turn it in; his father came out of his office to look it over. 'If there's a scratch on it I'll bill you for it,' he threatened, laughing.

'Nary a scratch, Dad. That one was there when I got it.'

'I know it. Dirk Hronsky did that when he went off the road.' He turned to his son, more serious. 'Got a minute to spare?'

'Sure, Dad.' They went into the office.

His father closed the door. 'I wanted to talk without your mother hearing everything,' he said. 'You all right in your job?'

The geologist opened his eyes. 'Sure, Dad. I got a swell job. What makes you think it's not?'

'I just got an idea that living in Arabia and Australia and all those sort of places – maybe you'd be getting tired of it by now.'

'I kind of like the work, Dad. The places aren't much to live in, but I make good money.'

'I know it, son.' He paused. 'You wouldn't rather work here?'

'Here in Hazel?'

'Here in this office.'

There was a pause. 'I never thought about it, Dad. I dunno that there's much here I could do. I'd never make a salesman.'

'No, you wouldn't. But I can hire good salesmen for five

hundred a month 'n commission. What you could do is run the business and the engineering side.'

'What about you, Dad? That's what you're doing.'

'There's a lot of other things I'd like to do, son, before I get too old. I'd like to expand this business in a lot of ways. Moving earth, for one. There's not a real road contractor this side of Portland. We could use one here, with the equipment based on Hazel. I'd like to have a parking lot for the equipment up on 5th Street.'

Stanton realized that his father had got this all figured out. It was in keeping with his restless energy; as soon as he had got one business established and running profitably he itched to start another one. The urge to move earth lies deep in the heart of a number of Americans. To use great bulldozers, graders, and Euclids to drive a road through a hill or cut a grade along the shoulder of a mountain had been a secret ambition of his father for some time; little casual remarks passed in the home had warned the geologist of this enthusiasm since he had returned to Oregon. While his son worked in places like Arabia or Australia, Stanton Laird was tied to the automobiles, but if his son were to come in and help him, he would be free to adventure again before he grew too old.

'I'd like to think about it, Dad. I certainly would like to live in Hazel, but it'd take some thought.'

'Sure,' said his father. 'It'ld be quite a change from being a geologist.'

'I'll have to go to Australia now, Dad, anyway. I couldn't just walk out on Topex at a minutes's notice 'n leave them flat.'

'Sure you can't,' his father said. 'I wouldn't want you in the business if you were liable to behave like that.' He paused. 'How long do you reckon to be in Australia?'

'I wouldn't know, Dad. I've got just the one hole to dig, so far as I know – take about a year, maybe. I could make a break then, if they want me to go on out there. But I guess I'll have to go and dig that one.'

'I could wait a year,' his father said, 'so long as I knew

43

you were coming. I'd appreciate it if you could make your mind up one way or the other before Christmas. The business is big enough to carry both of us, right now.' He went on to discuss the salary and the percentage of the profits. ''Course, in the end it'll all come to you, to you and Dwight between you. If you don't want to leave the oil business and come into it, I'll probably up-grade McKenzie from the shop.'

The geologist nodded slowly, thinking over that proposal. 'He'd be the one. He's a mighty fine boy, that ...' He grinned at his father. 'I guess I'd be sorry to see that happen, all the same.'

'Well, don't jump at a decision,' said his father. 'Take a bit of time, 'n think it over. Hazel's a small town, and you've been travelling around the world, and going places. Maybe you'd find Hazel a bit small. You want to think it over.'

'I wouldn't mind spending my life here,' Stanton said. 'I don't think it's small.'

'It *is* small, 'n you can't get away from it.'

'None of the West's small, Dad,' said his son. 'It's still the Frontier here. Hazel's not the same as a small town back East, say in Connecticut. It's still pioneering here, opening things up 'n getting new things started. Why, lots of the roads around here aren't paved yet, 'n you can go thirty miles and never pass a gas station. It's pioneering here, Dad, still – and will be for a long time.'

His father's heart glowed. 'That's the way I feel about this place myself,' he said. 'I didn't know you did.'

'Sure it's the way I feel about it,' his son said emphatically. 'It's pioneering here, Dad, still. It's not so long since everything came here by ox cart. Grandpa used to drive one. He took me riding in it once.'

'You remember that, son? You were only about three years old.'

'Sure I remember it. This is a Frontier town, and that's all part of it. Maybe it's not so undeveloped now as it was in Grandpa's time and we don't ride round in ox carts, but it's mighty undeveloped still. It's only two years since we

44

got television, 'n we can only get two channels even now. There's plenty of pioneering to be done here yet, Dad – here on the Frontier. Small town or not, that's the kind of place I like to work in, not in the big cities.'

His father said, 'Well, think it over, son, and let me know before Christmas.'

TWO

It is doubtful if much pioneering in the State of West Australia ever was done by ox cart, for oxen need water, a commodity that has always been in short supply over most of the state. The diesel semi-trailer takes its place, and about a week later the semi-trailer driven by Spinifex Joe ground to a standstill in a swirl of red dust before the homestead of Laragh Station.

Spinifex Joe looked like a half-caste and may have been one, for he was vague himself about his father and not much more certain of his mother. He was a small, lean man about fifty years of age, good with diesel engines, a good bush mechanic capable of making quite a tolerable repair by welding when the need arose. He had use for these qualities, because he was the postman. Each week he started on Monday morning from the post office at Onslow on the coast of West Australia just inside the tropic and drove eastwards, loaded with two or three sacks of mail that had reached Onslow by air, an assortment of packing cases destined for the stations that he served, a number of drums of fuel and kerosene, and all the aboriginals who cared to climb on board.

His route took him eastwards through the stations for about two hundred miles to a property called Malvern Downs, the end of the so-called road. From there he took to the bush tracks, lurching and swaying over the bare red earth, hard baked in the sun; when one bit of his road became worn out he deviated and made another track. From Malvern he went to Mannahill, from Mannahill to Laragh, from Laragh on to Poonda, Mulga Downs, and Millstream, and so back to Onslow. The whole journey was about six hundred and fifty miles and it took him a week of blazing sun, red dust, and small mechanical repairs. He never travelled without a forty-gallon drum of water on the back and he frequently had need of it when tyre trouble or breakdowns delayed him. Normally he slept on the bare earth underneath the trailer, his head pillowed on a tarpaulin. That was his whole life; he had no other home.

On the flat tray of his semi-trailer when he stopped at Laragh were three bales of wool trimmings that stank in the hot sun, about thirty drums of various fuels with a few empties, eleven packing cases, two coloured stockmen with their wives, or gins, and their many children on their way to Poonda, and five assorted full-bloods probably just coming for the ride. In addition, he brought three small sacks of mail.

Mrs Regan was waiting for him on the verandah of the homestead, a tall, commanding woman about fifty years of age, born in Edinburgh and brought to West Australia as a child. With her was her twenty-year-old daughter, Mollie, one of her eleven children, and David Cope. David was English, twenty-two years old, born and bred upon a farm near Newbury. His parents' farm had been requisitioned for an aerodrome during the war, and covered with great concrete runways. For the first years of peace they had battled with the Ministry to get their land back, and had failed; they had then emigrated as a family to West Australia and had bought a farm at Armadale, near Perth. At the age of sixteen David had gone as a jackeroo upon a sheep station, to learn the business. He had stayed there for four years and had remained enthusiastic about sheep, with the result that now, only two years later, he was manager and part owner of Lucinda Station, white enthusiasts being something of a rarity in the far north of West Australia.

Lucinda was a property of about three hundred and

twenty thousand acres that lay to the west of Laragh, a sizeable stretch of country somewhat hampered by a water supply that would have been deemed inadequate for a three-hundred-acre farm in England. The mail truck did not come to Lucinda, but David had a radio transreceiver for use with the Flying Doctor service, and so he kept himself informed of the progress of the mail truck as the housewives gossiped together on the natter session after the scheduled calls. That morning he had driven thirty miles in his jeep to collect his letters at Laragh, a cheerful, energetic young man in a torn khaki shirt, shorts, and sandals on his bare feet, all thickly powdered with red dust.

He had been sitting with the women on the verandah drinking tea and waiting for the truck. As it ground to a standstill he got up and went out into the sun to meet the driver. Mrs Regan followed him.

'Morning, Joe,' he said. 'How are you today?'

'Good,' said the driver. 'Country drying up again.' He selected one of the three mail sacks that rode with him in the cab, and pulled it out on to the ground.

Mrs Regan cast an eye over the loaded tray. None of the blacks meant anything to her, but the drums did. 'You brought my kerosene, Joe?' she inquired.

'Two kero,' he said laconically. 'Six diesel and four petrol. That right?'

'Aye,' she replied, 'that's right. Will ye have a cup of tea? Pat'll be down with the boys in a minute to unload.'

He followed her to the verandah, carrying the mail sack, and sat down on the edge of it while he sorted through the letters; she did not ask him to sit in a chair with them. Mollie poured out a large cup of very strong tea with a great spoonful of sugar in it, and took it to him on the edge of the verandah. At the truck the aboriginals got down on to the ground and squatted underneath the trailer in the shade.

Beside the homestead stood the station store, a large, dimly lit building full of every kind of hardware ranged on shelves, where the blacks and half-castes could buy blankets, shirts, trousers, dresses, stockwhips, red and yellow scarves, stockmen's hats, and riding boots, together with a small variety of sweets and chocolate, and soft drinks. Beside that was a smaller building that served as the station office and the school. The door opened now and a flood of children burst out into the sun, children of all colours from the deepest black to pure tanned white, all ages from four to twelve. There were about thirty of them; the two white ones came over to the homestead. These were Mrs Regan's youngest children, Maggie and Shamus. The station book-keeper, who also served as the schoolmaster, followed them.

He was a shambling, grey-haired, scholarly-looking man, well into his sixties. Spinifex Joe handed a bundle of letters and parcels to Mrs Regan, who took them on her lap and began to sort them through. She looked up as the schoolmaster approached. 'Here's one for you, Judge,' she called. 'And here's your newspaper from England.'

He approached, and took them from her. 'Thank you indeed,' he said. 'My sister is a very regular correspondent, is she not.'

'Aye,' said Mrs Regan. 'Never forgets to write.'

A Land Rover appeared from the direction of the station stockyard half a mile away. Mrs Regan said to the postman, 'Here's Pat and the boys, Joe. They'll get the drums off.' To her daughter she said, 'Get the bottle, Mollie, and the cold water and the glasses.'

The girl went off and turned the corner of the verandah towards the kitchen; the eyes of the young Englishman from Lucinda followed her. The little truck drew up beside the semi-trailer and two young half-caste men got out. From the driver's seat a huge, powerful old man emerged. He was over seventy years of age, but he still boasted a shock of bright red hair. He was dressed in soiled trousers of jungle-green and a khaki shirt, with elastic-sided riding boots. He had come from breaking horses with his sons down at the yard, and he carried a stockwhip in his hand. On his shoulder perched a kangaroo mouse.

48

David Cope got to his feet as the old man came to the verandah. 'Morning, Mr Regan,' he said. He eyed the long-legged mouse. 'What's that you've got there – a hopper?'

'What else would it be?' asked Mr Regan. 'The kindest hopper this side of the black stump.' He paid no more attention to the young man but took the bunch of letters from his wife and shuffled them through. Spinifex Joe crossed to his truck and began to lay the skids down from the trailer to the ground to get the drums off, helped by the young men. David Cope sat down again upon the edge of the verandah.

Pat Regan picked out a letter in a long official envelope and peered at it suspiciously. The mouse peered with him from his shoulder. There was an official imprint on the envelope; he would not admit that he now needed glasses, and he had never read well anyway. 'In the Name of God!' he exclaimed, 'what would this one be?'

His wife took it from him and screwed up her eyes. 'It says, Bureau of Mineral Resources,' she told him. 'That will be those people that were here before, fossicking about after the oil.'

'God mend them! They'll not be after coming back again?'

'It may say in the letter.'

'Well, open it and read it, woman,' said the old man testily. 'Open it and read it, and see what it says.'

His wife put on her iron-rimmed glasses and opened the letter. She read it through in silence. 'It's from that man Bruce who was here before,' she said. 'He says he's coming here again about the first of the month and bringing with him six Americans belonging to the Topeka Exploration Company to make a seismic survey. I don't know what that is, or how you say it. He says that they'll be working on our land about fourteen miles west of the homestead. He says they'll be a party of seven, with three trucks.'

'Did ye ever hear the like of that!' exclaimed the old man angrily.

'That's what he says,' his wife remarked equably. 'He

says at the end that the something survey will decide whether they drill a test well here or not.'

The girl came back carrying a tray and set it down on the table. Her father said irritably, 'Will ye write straight back and say that they're not wanted here. I'll have no part of them, no part at all.'

'Go easy now, and have your shot of rum,' his wife said quietly. She laid the letter down and reached out for the bottle and poured out half a tumbler of neat overproof rum into one glass, and half a tumbler of ice-cold water into another. 'Take that, and then come on and sit down in the shade.'

The old man lifted the mouse carefully down from his shoulder and set it down upon the ground at the end of the verandah; he gave it a gentle pat behind and it ran under the house. Then he came up on to the verandah and took the glass of rum his wife held out to him, shot it down in one swallow, and followed it with a chaser of water from the other glass. Then he sat down heavily beside his wife. 'Give yeself a rum, Judge,' he said. 'Give yeself one, David. Americans, is it? Americans on Laragh Station!' He spat scornfully on to the withered grass lawn of the homestead. 'If there's money to be gathered any place in the wide world those boys are after it, deep down in the earth on other men's land, ten thousand weary miles from their own rightful place. They'll be after the smell of it, like a pack of rats will find a bit of stinking fish.'

He flared up suddenly into a fury. 'Go on and write the letter, Judge. I'll not have Americans on Laragh Station, not if the Holy Father was to write from Rome itself.'

The old man that he called the Judge snuffled and rubbed a hand across his nose, a habitual gesture when he was perplexed. 'I doubt if we have any right to refuse them, Mr Regan,' he said gently. 'We hold this land upon a pastoral lease. There is a clause in the agreement that reserves the mineral rights to the State of West Australia, and that binds us to give reasonable access to any part of the land for the exploitation of the mineral resources.'

'And would ye call it reasonable that they should bring Americans to Laragh? Will ye answer me that, now?'

The Judge poured himself a rum and shot it down, following it with a chaser of water. 'Some Americans are very pleasant people,' he observed. 'I met a bishop once, an Episcopalian, who was quite charming. But mundane, I am afraid. Very, very mundane.' He sucked a drop of rum from his thin, straggling moustache.

David Cope poured about half an inch of rum into the bottom of a tumbler and filled it up with water. He did not dare to risk the old man's displeasure by refusing a drink, and he had not yet learned to drink rum neat. He said, 'They'll be working not far from our fence, Pat. They'll probably be nearer my place than they are to you, in fact. I think it might be rather fun, having some Americans around.'

'Fun, is it?' exclaimed Mr Regan. 'Would ye be after calling fun the way they carried on in Alice Springs all through the war? Glory be to God, no young girl living in the town that wasn't raped, and no old woman safe save in the house itself and the door locked and bars on all the windows and Father O'Connor praying with her on their bended knees, with the American soldiers bellowing around the house like raging bulls! Is it fun ye call it?'

'It was not like that at all, Pat,' said Mrs Regan placidly. 'If there's any raping done on Laragh it won't be by the Americans.'

David Cope said in mock alarm, 'I hope you don't mean me, Mrs Regan.'

'No,' she said tranquilly, 'I don't mean you. There's going to be no raping here on Laragh Station. Heaven knows, the Judge's got enough children in the school already.'

The old man rubbed his nose and snuffled. 'That is very true. I shall have six more children in the school next month than we have desks for – the Vogue twins, and Mrs Stockton's Elsie, and little Johnny Six, and Palmolive's little girl, and the Yardley boy. I think we ought to order eight more desks, Mr Regan. I cannot rebuke them for bad

51

writing when they have to balance their slates on their knees.'

The old man grunted. His wife said, 'We will need the desks, Pat. Let the Judge write the order now, and Spinifex can take it with the mail.'

Her daughter said, 'Here's Uncle Tom coming.'

Tom Regan appeared around the corner of the verandah. He was a very thin man, recently aroused from sleep; he had not shaved for several days. He had not the exuberant virility of his brother Pat because he had gastric ulcers, aggravated no doubt by the rum he loved to shoot down neat. He now did little work upon the property, yet his was still the directing mind. He shuffled down the verandah. Mrs Regan poured him a rum and a glass of water. He took them from her without a word.

'A letter from Mr Bruce, Tom,' Mrs Regan said. 'He's coming back with some American engineers to do another survey.'

'How many of them?'

'Seven, with three trucks.' She paused. 'We can't have that many in the house.'

'It's all a part of it,' said Tom dolefully.

His brother Pat said, 'Isn't there the shearers' quarters empty for them to sleep in, with wire beds for their bedding and a stove for them to cook on?'

'Aye,' said Mrs Regan doubtfully, 'they might go there.'

The girl said impulsively, 'You can't put Americans in the shearers' quarters, Ma.'

'In the Name of God,' asked Pat, 'why not?'

'They live differently to that,' his daughter said stubbornly. 'I've seen how they live on the pictures, father, down in Perth. They live in lovely sort of flats called penthouses on the top of skyscrapers, or in big white houses about a hundred feet high with columns in front. It wouldn't do to put them in the shearers' quarters.'

'Did you ever hear the like of that!' exclaimed her father. 'It's a queer thing, I'm thinking, that the shearers' quarters would be good enough for an Australian shearer and not

52

good enough for an American, with all the lechery and evil in the world in his black heart.'

David Cope laughed. 'I see we're going to have some fun and games round here in the next week or two,' he said. 'I can put a couple of them up at my place if they can make do with the gins' cooking.'

'They'd be better doing their own cooking in the shearers' quarters,' said Mrs Regan drily. 'No, leave it, David. Mr Bruce knows the way things are with us and that we can't accommodate that many. They'll have everything they need for camping by their trucks, or they can sleep in the shearers' place. I might make shift to feed them if it comes to that.'

She turned to the other letters on her lap. The Judge went off to his desk in the store office to write an order for school desks and slates, and Mrs Regan opened all the other letters for the two men. Spinifex Joe vanished in the direction of the kitchen; he would wait at Laragh till the letters were written before going on. The two half-caste boys began rolling the drums of kerosene and petrol towards the store. The aboriginals squatted motionless in the dust beneath the truck.

David Cope picked up his own letters and glanced them through. There was nothing that required immediate attention. He slipped the letters he had brought with him in the breast pocket of his shirt into the post bag, said goodbye to Mrs Regan, and walked towards his jeep. Mollie got up and walked out into the sun with him, to see him off.

She was a red-headed girl like her father, and she had something of the same square line to her chin. She was wearing very light, loose khaki linen slacks and a khaki shirt; she wore soiled leather sandals on her bare feet, as he did. 'How are you off for water at Lucinda?' she asked as they walked.

'Not too good,' he said. 'We've got a little left in the big dam – last about a month. The bores are running well, though.' He had two bores that produced water from a depth of about seven hundred feet; a windmill over each

53

pumped up this water to a raised storage pool from which it was piped to troughs. His property was chronically short of water. Though Lucinda Station comprised over three hundred thousand acres, most of this land was useless to him when the heat of summer had dried up the few natural pools. The sheep then congregated about the two bores that supplied the only water left upon the property. They would graze for a radius of about two miles from the water; in a bad summer they would eat out every blade of grass within this area and then die of starvation by the water. For this reason Lucinda Station could only carry about four thousand sheep on its three hundred and twenty thousand acres, and a dry summer would imperil even those.

'Are you going to put down any more bores?' she asked.

'I'm not sure that it's worth it.'

'They cost an awful lot of money,' she agreed. 'What are they quoting now? Thirty bob a foot?'

'Two quid,' he said. 'It's not the money, though. We're making enough from the wool cheque to put down one a year, say. But I don't think there's any water there. We've got the two along the line of Blackman's Creek, and there's no sign of water anywhere else. We might put one down between them to spread the feed, but it'ld probably reduce the flow of the ones we've got.'

She nodded. She had lived all her life on Laragh but for periods at boarding school, and in her short memory four graziers had tried their luck on Lucinda Station and had given it up after a year or two. When David had come, this young English boy so full of energy and hope, the Regans had been sorry for him, the more so because he worked so hard on his depressing property. He lived quite alone, being unmarried, with only his half-caste and aboriginal stockmen for company. By his enthusiastic energy he had achieved more than his predecessors; he ran four thousand sheep without disaster where the best of them had run a bare three thousand, by dint of herding them by night out to the fresh pastures and herding them back again to water after a few hours; he had a lucerne paddock where he grew

54

a hay crop in the rainy season, an unheard-of innovation in the district. He had sheared ninety-eight bales of wool in the previous year, which had given him a wool cheque of nearly nine thousand pounds; after paying expenses this still left him a considerable income on his sixty per cent share of the property, good money for a boy of twenty-two. The Regans, good graziers themselves upon a million acres of very much better watered land, respected him and showed him kindness, while they waited for the years of drought that would dry up his bores and finish him completely, and send him back into some city for a job, a ruined man.

'Any news of Charlie?' he asked.

'He's still in England.'

'Is he coming back here?'

'I don't think so,' she replied. 'Not for a long time, anyway.' Charlie was her half-brother, for he had been born to Mrs Regan in the days when she was married to Uncle Tom. 'He's still working on cancer, at the London Hospital. He's setting up as a consultant now, in a place called Harley Street. That's something good, isn't it?'

'It's where all the big doctors live,' he said. 'He must be doing very well.'

'He's awfully clever.'

He glanced down at her. 'You know, you're a pretty bright family. Is Bridget still in Canberra?'

She shook her head. 'She's still in the Department of External Affairs, but she's doing a course of Chinese, somewhere near Melbourne.'

'I thought she was absolutely brilliant when she was here last year,' he said. 'I was scared stiff of opening my mouth.'

She laughed. 'Not like me.'

'I don't know about that,' he said. 'You took a second, didn't you?' She had been home from Perth University for some months.

'Only in History,' she said. 'That's an easy school.'

'It'ld be damn difficult for me,' he said. 'You're a clever family.'

They paused by his jeep. 'We aren't really,' she said. 'I don't think so. Ma says it's all the Judge's doing. I think he's a wonderful teacher. I got really interested in history before I left here to go to school. And Bridget was the same. She could speak French and German before she was ten.'

David blinked. It seemed incredible on Laragh Station. 'Tell me,' he asked, 'why do you all call him the Judge? What's his real name?'

'I don't know his real name,' she replied. 'I suppose he doesn't want people to know it. He's called the Judge because he is one – or he was. I don't think he was a very important one – County Court or something. He got the sack.'

He grinned. 'I didn't know a judge *could* get the sack.'

'Well,' she said, 'there's one that did.'

'What did he get pushed out for?'

She dimpled. 'I'm not supposed to know. I think it was for taking too much interest in delinquent girls.'

'Too bad. When did that happen?'

'Oh, ages ago, before I was born. Uncle Tom found him stinking drunk in a hotel at Geraldton and took him on as book-keeper. He's been here ever since.'

'Where was he a judge?'

'In England somewhere,' she replied. 'He talks about Dunchester sometimes – it might have been there.' She paused. 'Ma says he was a schoolmaster when he was a young man at a place called Eton. That's a good school, isn't it?'

'That's right,' he said. 'It's supposed to be the best school in England.'

'Were you there?' she asked.

'Me? Never came within a mile of it. I went to the grammar school at Newbury.' He paused. 'You were at school in Perth, weren't you?'

She nodded. 'Ma said all of us must go away to boarding schools. She's Scotch, you see. Father and Uncle Tom wouldn't have bothered if we went to school or not, because they're Irish. Ma's very firm about school. I think that's why she's put up with the Judge all these years – because he's a good schoolmaster. He's not much of a book-keeper, really. Mike checks the books over when he comes up for his summer holiday each year, and he finds an awful lot of mistakes.'

'Is Mike one of your brothers?'

'Well – sort of. He's Uncle Tom's son, when Ma was married to him. Mike and Charlie and Bridget – they're all Uncle Tom's. Mike's a chartered accountant, with Gordon and Bottomley, in Perth.'

He wrinkled his eyebrows. 'Well, who's Stanley?'

'Stanley and Phyllis,' she explained, '—they're Fosters. You see, Ma was a Mrs Foster and she had two children. Then Foster got killed in a car crash and Ma hadn't any money, so she worked in a bar in the Unicorn Hotel in Perth. Uncle Tom went down to Perth for a holiday and met Ma in the bar and married her, and brought her and Stanley and Phyllis back here to the Lunatic. Before that, of course, they only had the gins.'

His head was swimming. 'It all sounds a bit complicated,' he said.

'It isn't really. It's just that there are rather a lot of us. Ma had eleven children, and then of course there were all the others.'

'Quite a lot of kids to send to school.'

She laughed. 'The schools round Perth just live on us. Stanley and Phyllis went to Church of England schools, of course, but all the rest of us are Micks. We girls all went to Loreto and all the boys to Aquinas, and the half-castes to Alvan House and MacDonald House.'

'Are you going to be here for long?' he asked.

'I don't know. I want to be a teacher, but Ma's not getting any younger. I think I'll stay here for a year till Elspeth leaves college and then let her come home and take a turn. Ma wants me to go home to Scotland then, and to France and Italy. I'd like to do that before I settle down and take a job.'

'That'ld be a grand trip. You could come back through America.'

'I never thought of that,' she said. 'I say, won't it be beaut having Americans here?'

'Your father doesn't seem to think so.'

She laughed. 'Do you think they'll be like people on the movies?'

'I shouldn't think so,' he replied. 'If you think they live in penthouses on the top of skyscrapers or in old Southern mansions you've probably got another think coming.'

'They don't live in places like our shearers' quarters, anyway,' she said.

'No, I don't suppose they do that. Talking of the movies, are you going to Mannahill on Saturday?' Mr Clem Rogerson of Mannahill Station fifty-six miles away over the bush tracks had a sixteen-millimetre talkie outfit, and gave a show in his garden each Saturday night, on films flown up from Perth.

'I don't know. Are you going?'

'I usually go over. Makes a change.'

'I don't know if they're going over this time or not. Ma sometimes likes to go.'

'Tell me on the air tomorrow night, in the natter session. I'll call in here and pick you up if no one else wants to go.'

She smiled at him. 'All right.'

He drove off in the jeep, and she turned back to the homestead. James Connolly and Joseph Plunkett had finished unloading the drums from the semi-trailer, and had gone back to the stockyard with their father, to go on with the horses. Their mother, the Countess Markievicz, came out of the laundry with a great basket of damp clothes and began to hang them on the wires strung between the laundry and the store, a shapeless, coal-black woman, very ugly, who had been slim and even good-looking in an aboriginal way thirty years before. By the time she had finished hanging out the last garments in the basket the first ones would be ready to take down to iron, which she would do in the verandah of the laundry. That was her daily work for all the days of the year; it did not seem to her monotonous.

The Judge came out with the letters he had written and

showed them to Uncle Tom and Mrs Regan, who approved them. The letters were sealed up and stamped, and given to Spinifex Joe, now waiting for them at his truck. He dropped them in the mail bag, said goodbye, and got into the cab. The starter groaned, the diesel belched black smoke, the blacks got up on to the tray, and the vehicle moved off upon the next stage of its week-long journey. Life at Laragh Station sank back into its normal, quiet routine. The women cooked and mended, the aboriginal women moved languidly about the housework. Outside, Pat Regan and his half-caste sons broke horses in slow time and rode out quietly to the water-holes to move the sheep around, generally in the cool of the early morning. In the heat of the day they worked in the shade, maintaining the cars and trucks and pumps and lighting system. The Judge taught school in the morning and took a siesta in the afternoon, dreaming perhaps of Waynflete's chapel or of the cloisters of Dunchester Cathedral, or merely of the incredible and ever increasing current account in the Commonwealth Bank in Perth. Mrs Regan wrote letters every afternoon in the verandah, rather illiterate letters to each of her children; her main interests lay with them. Nobody at Laragh Station worked very hard; they bred a great many children, drank a good deal of rum, and made a good deal of money that they seemed to be unable to dispose of and that was rapidly becoming a responsibility to them, and a nuisance.

Mr Bruce and his party arrived in the district a few days later. They came with two closed vans full of electrical recording gear, and a big four-wheel-drive truck containing all their other equipment. These were brand new American vehicles that attracted a good deal of interest at the places they had stopped at on their route. Donald Bruce was the only Australian in the party, and the only one who had taken part in the previous geological survey of the district. He was a public servant from the Bureau of Mineral Resources. The other six members of the party were American employees of the Topeka Exploration Company Inc, headed by a Mr Stanton Laird. When Mr Bruce had introduced his party to the pastoralists upon whose properties they were to work he would retire to his office in Melbourne and leave them to their job.

They had hoped to arrive at Laragh Station on a Saturday afternoon. In fact, they took a wrong track between Malvern Downs and Mannahill which took them fifteen miles out of their way and landed them on the edge of a dry creek that Mr Bruce could not recognize and knew to be wrong. They stopped and rigged their radio and made contact with the Flying Doctor service on the midday schedule, and spoke to Mr Rogerson at Mannahill Station, who told them where they had gone astray. By the time they had got going again and had retraced their steps they had lost three hours, arriving at Mannahill at about five in the afternoon.

It was too late for them to go on to Laragh that night, over strange bush tracks in the dark; the chances of getting lost again were too great. They stayed that night as guests of the Rogersons at Mannahill, and found that they had come in for the big social event of the district, the weekly picture show. There were several Land Rovers and Jeeps from the adjoining stations, one of which had come over a hundred miles. Amongst the visitors Stanton was quick to notice a remarkably pretty girl, red-headed and white-skinned, who had come in a jeep with a young man called David Cope from Lucinda Station.

Mr Bruce knew her well. 'Hullo, Mollie,' he said. 'How are you today?'

'Good,' she replied.

'Are your father and mother here?'

'They didn't come. They were expecting you with the Americans. Ma said they'd better stay at home in case you came. David brought me over.'

'We got held up upon the road,' he said. 'Look, let me introduce you to Mr Laird. He's the one who'll be in charge of the party on your father's land.' He called out down the verandah. 'Hey – Stan! Come over here a minute. I want you to meet Miss Mollie Regan, from Laragh.'

60

Stanton held out his hand. 'Why, hello, Miss Regan, I'm certainly glad to know you,' he said. 'I hoped we'd get on to your property today, but Don will have told you that we're running late.'

'I know,' she said. 'What happened?'

'I guess we just naturally got lost,' he said. 'It's kind of easy to go off on the wrong trail in this country.'

'You got lost between here and Malvern Downs?'

'That's right.'

'But didn't you follow the tracks that the mail truck makes?'

'One wheel rut's just like another wheel rut to me, Miss Regan. I reckon when you've lived in Australia for a time you get so you can tell them apart.'

She laughed. 'Mollie's the name, Mr Laird. We use Christian names in this country unless you're trying to be very formal.'

'Fine,' he said. 'I'm Stanton.'

She turned, for David was behind her. 'David,' she said, 'this is Stanton Laird. They got lost between here and Malvern!'

He laughed. 'I got lost all along the road when I came up here first.'

She wrinkled her brows. 'It doesn't seem possible. I mean, you just turn left at the burnt Mulga tree and go straight on.'

He laughed again. 'You'll get a lot of this, Mr Laird. When an Australian says you can't mistake the road, that's the time to get out your compass and start navigating.'

The girl flushed and laughed. 'I suppose it *is* a bit difficult for strangers.'

'I'd agree with that,' said Stanton. He turned to David. 'You aren't Australian?'

The other shook his head. 'I'm English. They call us Pommies here. I've got Lucinda Station, next to Laragh.'

The geologist nodded slowly, his mind running over the maps that he had studied. 'That's to the west of Laragh,' he said. 'I guess we'll be operating pretty near your boundary.'

61

'That's right,' said David. 'If I can give you any help I hope you'll come and tell me.'

'That's mighty nice of you.'

Mr Rogerson turned the corner of the verandah and came to the little group. 'Drinks just outside the dining-room,' he said cheerfully. 'Mr Laird, what can I get you? Gin, whisky, or rum?'

Stanton had travelled far, but Hazel still held him very close. 'Thank you,' he said a little awkwardly, 'but I don't believe I'll take anything right now.'

'Nothing at all? Everybody's drinking like so many fishes just around the corner.'

It was getting a little more awkward, and Stanton became aware that they were all looking at him curiously. Moreover, he was very thirsty. 'Maybe something soft,' he suggested.

'Why – yes. What would you like?'

'You wouldn't have a Coke?'

'What's that?'

'Coca-cola.' There had always been a Coke at Abu Quaiyah, but there Americans had run the commissariat.

'No – I'm sorry, we haven't got that. Lime juice, or lemon squash?'

'Lime juice – a long one.'

'Sure you won't have a drop of gin in it?' asked Mr Rogerson hospitably. 'Liven it up?'

'Thank you – I'd prefer just the lime.'

It was Mollie who asked what they all wanted to know. 'Don't you drink, Stanton?' she asked kindly.

'Not alcohol,' he said. 'Not many people do back home, where I come from. I never got the habit.'

'I thought all Americans drank terrifically,' she said. 'I suppose I'm going by the movies.'

'Some of the boys drink,' he said, referring to his crew of five. 'Bob and Hank, they'll drink anything they can get hold of. Ted's a light drinker. Dwight and Tex – they're like me, don't drink alcohol at all.' He smiled at her. 'I'd say the movies aren't a very safe guide to America.'

'I suppose not,' she replied.

Clem Rogerson came back with a very large glass of lime juice and soda, with ice tinkling at the brim. The geologist took it from him gratefully. 'Let's all move round the corner to the drinks,' the grazier said. 'Mollie, what can I get you?'

'I'll have a gin and lime, a long one,' she said. 'Just a very little gin, Mr Rogerson – really a little. About half an inch.'

'All right.' As they moved round the corner of the verandah he said to the geologist, 'I'm sorry we couldn't fix you up in the house, Mr Laird. The shearers' quarters aren't too bad, though. We had to rebuild them all two years ago, to bring them up to the award conditions.'

'They're mighty comfortable, Mr Rogerson,' the geologist said. 'I never reckoned that we'd find accommodation so good as that. We brought along a whole truckload of stuff for camping, so as not to be a nuisance to anyone. It's mighty good of you to let us use your shearers' quarters.'

'Oh, that's all right. They're empty for eleven months of the year, you know.'

He went off to the table to get Mollie her drink, and she turned to the American. 'Do you really camp out, when you're working in a place like this?' she asked.

'Sure,' he said. 'We've got everything in the truck, food for about three months, tents, sleeping bags, stretchers – everything. Ted's the camp cook. The other four and myself – we're technical. Ted runs the camp.'

'Can you do your work, living like that?' she asked.

'Why, yes. We've got one tent we rig up as a drafting office. We always live that way when we're on survey work. Later on, if it comes to setting up a drilling rig, then we have to make a better camp, of course, with a power station and portable buildings with air-conditioning, and everything like that. But on a survey we just live in tents.'

She was relieved. 'We didn't realize that you'd be used to that,' she said. 'We've got shearers' quarters at Laragh, of course. You'd be welcome to use those. I was afraid they might not be the sort of thing that you were used to.'

David Cope said mischievously, 'Too many movies again,

63

Stan. She thought that you all lived in penthouses on top of skyscrapers in New York.'

She said indignantly, 'I didn't, Stan! At least, not all Americans.'

He said, 'America's a pretty big place, Miss Regan. Some Americans do live that way or they couldn't make movies about them. At least,' he said, 'I guess they can do anything in Hollywood.' They all laughed. 'But I come from the West, where we don't live that way at all. It's still kind of frontier where I come from – ranching and riding horseback over the trails.'

She asked in wonder, 'Do you still use horses in your part of America?'

'Why, certainly,' he said. 'Where I live there's nearly three hundred square miles right close in to town where you can only go on a horse. No roads at all. It's frontier still, the part of the United States I come from.'

'What part of the United States is that?' she asked. 'Where is your home?'

'Oregon,' he said. 'In back of the state, close to Idaho.'

David Cope asked, 'Do you know how big Laragh Station is, Stan?'

The geologist shook his head. 'I'd only be guessing.'

'It's just under a million acres – fifteen hundred square miles. That's five times the size of your bit, and that's just one property. How many horses does Pat use, Mollie?'

'Oh, I don't know,' she said. 'I think we've got about three hundred, but I'm really not sure.'

Stanton said, 'My face is sure red. I'd better quit talking about our ranches while I'm in Australia. Is Laragh Station really that big?'

'We've got a million acres,' Mollie said. 'It's not big as properties go, up in the north. We feel it's just a comfortable size.'

He turned to her, smiling. 'You know what? I'm going to keep my mouth shut about America till I learn something about this country.'

'Don't do that,' she said. 'We've all been looking forward

to hearing how you live and everything. We very seldom get a visitor at Laragh, and I don't ever remember anybody coming from abroad. Except David,' she added.

The Rogersons were used to an influx of visitors for their movie show and enjoyed having them, but that night they had to have tea in relays; with the surveyors they had over thirty people to feed in the dining-room. After the meal Clem Rogerson set up his projector and amplifiers while the visitors arranged chairs on the lawn in rows. The hostess with her guests sat in the front, four or five white stockmen behind, a miscellaneous assortment of half-castes and aboriginals behind them again, and the show commenced.

The main feature was one that Stanton had seen first in New York four years previously, again in Hazel with his family before leaving for Arabia, and again at Abu Quaiyah. Seen for the fourth time, it failed to hold his attention; he had leisure to study the audience and to reflect on his surroundings. Before leaving Hazel he had considered that this assignment would be just such another one as Abu Quaiyah had been, a hot desert where they had lived in social isolation amongst an Arab population. He was already realizing that here it was not going to be like that at all. Distances were enormous in Australia but in spite of them there seemed to be definite social life. There was no poverty as there had been amongst the Arabs, indeed there was some evidence of a good deal of money; Clem Rogerson's Jaguar was exactly the same motor car as rolled down Wilshire Boulevard in Hollywood with a millionaire film actor at the wheel. The women were well got up and attractive in their summer dresses, particularly Mollie Regan sitting by his side, deeply absorbed in the vicissitudes of Marilyn Monroe. He sat among the moonlit audience before the screen, a little sleepy, feeling that he was entering on to a strange, unknown stage where all eyes were upon him, as indeed they were.

The movies came to an end about ten o'clock, and the Rogersons dispensed more drinks, with tea for the women. Stanton avoided alcohol this time by electing for tea. He

65

seldom drank tea, and when he did he was accustomed to being presented with a cup of hot water and tea in a hygienic little bag; here tea was served barbarously from an enormous enamelled teapot, very black and strong. He didn't really like it as a drink but the alternative seemed to be alcohol which was worse because it was habit-forming. He stood telling Mrs Rogerson how much he had enjoyed the movie and what a good actress Miss Monroe was, and while his attention was engaged on these politenesses somebody refilled his cup, to his dismay.

Mollie Regan came up to him. 'I'm going off now with David,' she said. 'We've got rather a long way to go. You'll be coming along to Laragh in the morning, I suppose?'

'I guess so,' he replied. 'Mr Bruce, he's in charge. Does it make any difference being Sunday?'

She shook her head. 'Father Ryan comes through about once a year, but he doesn't approve of us really, of course.' He didn't understand that, and it didn't seem quite the moment to pursue the matter. 'The Judge holds a Mass in the dining-room after breakfast – lasts about half an hour. After that it's just like any other day, except that nobody does any work.'

'I'd say we'd be along in the morning, then,' he said.

'That's fine. I've just got to go and find Mrs Rogerson to say goodbye, and then I'll be going off. See you tomorrow.'

She smiled, and he smiled back at her. ' 'Bye now,' he said. The girl went off to find her hostess to say goodbye.

David Cope came up to him. The geologist strolled out towards the jeep with the young grazier, glad to abandon his cup of tea. 'Mr and Mrs Rogerson are very kind people,' he said. 'Donald Bruce tells me that they have a movie show like this each week.'

'That's right. It's rather a good thing.'

Stanton looked round him in the quiet, moonlit night. In the stockmen's quarters over on the right a few lights showed; from the foreman's house came the faint wail of a baby roused for a feed. Over to the left was a long shed for vehicles; half a mile out in the bush he could see the iron

66

roofs of the shearing camp, his quarters for the night. Behind them was a cheerful noise of talk and laughter as men and women got into the parked cars and jeeps, and said goodbye to the Rogersons. 'It's quite a place,' the geologist said at last. 'Are all these properties like this?'

The Englishman said, 'This is a particularly good one. They vary, you know. Mine isn't this sort of a place at all.'

'What's Laragh like?'

'That's different again.'

'Smaller than this?'

'No,' said David. 'It's a good bit bigger, and it's got more water. It's a better property all round than this. But – well, the Rogersons are different to the Regans. You'll see when you get there. Rogerson runs this place with white stockmen. I believe he's got five of them here now. Laragh runs on aboriginals and half-castes. That's one difference, for a start.'

'They're Catholics at Laragh, aren't they? Something Miss Regan said just now seemed to mean that.'

David Cope laughed, unreasonably, it seemed to Stanton. 'Well, yes, I suppose they might be. The two Regan brothers, the old boys, they're Irish, of course. The mother's a Scot. Did Don Bruce tell you anything about them?'

'No.'

'Oh ...' The Englishman considered for a moment. 'They're southern Irish,' he said at last. 'They were in the IRA.'

'What's that?'

'The Irish Republican Army. I suppose you wouldn't know about that. They rebelled against the British Government in 1916, and went on fighting them for years. It's no secret – Pat Regan 'll tell you all about it any time he gets a skinful. How he sniped the dastardly British from Jacob's biscuit factory in Dublin and carved notches on the stock of his Mauser for each one he killed. They've got the pistol in the homestead still – they'll probably show it you. Then, later, they were out against the Black and Tans – they were a sort of an armed police force that we had in Ireland, rather a tough army of Commando types. There was a price on both their heads at one time – five hundred pounds on Pat and a thousand on Tom, dead or alive.' He paused. 'Pat's never forgiven Tom for that, being worth more than him.'

The geologist blinked. Nothing in his previous experience had prepared him for this. 'Is that still current?' he asked anxiously.

'The rewards? I shouldn't think so. There was a pardon, or something. They got away from Ireland before the British put them up against a wall, and came out here as stockmen. Then new land was opened up for settlement and they put in for it in the ballot, and got it. After that they never looked back. They're worth a lot of money now.'

Stanton was a little dazed. 'Would one of them be the father of Miss Regan, then?'

'Mollie's Pat's daughter. It's a complicated family, as you'll find out. But clever. They're as clever as a wagonload of monkeys – all the children are.' He dropped his voice. 'Here she comes. The cream of the joke is, my Dad was in the Black and Tans.' He laughed uproariously. 'Pat doesn't know that yet.'

Stanton laughed dutifully with him. Mollie, coming to the jeep, asked. 'What's the joke?'

'Stan was telling me a rude story,' David said. 'Very American, and very rude. I wouldn't like to repeat it to you, Mollie.'

Stanton was staggered. 'Hey, Miss Regan, that's not—' he began, but the noise of the starter drowned his words, and when the engine caught David revved it up. The jeep slid off upon the moonlit track, and Stanton was left wondering whether he had been the victim of an English joke. If so, he thought, it was a joke in very poor taste.

THREE

WHEN Donald Bruce drove up to Laragh Station next morning with his party of Americans Mrs Regan was there to welcome them, with Mollie and the two youngest children, Shamus and Maggie, aged twelve and ten respectively. Tom and the Judge were lying on their beds somewhat unwell; the Judge had got up to celebrate the weekly Mass quite unconstitutionally before a miscellaneous congregation and had gone back to bed again, for Saturday night at Laragh was marked by a different social formula from that of Mannahill. At Laragh on Saturday night the men would get together in the store office after tea and commence the serious business of the week, which was drinking rum. The store office had an old-fashioned, elevated accountant's desk with the high stool that went with it; this was the only furniture apart from the children's desks and forms, too small for the men. They sat around on packing cases or on the floor, debating alcoholically the work of the station and the state of the surrounding district. The debate that Saturday had been a depressing one, being mainly concerned with the advent of the Americans and the chaos that it was expected to create upon the property. Even the news of a substantial rise in the price of wool had done nothing to dispel the gloom, for the economics of the station had long ceased to be critical. That fact did nothing to alleviate the impression that ruin stared them in the face through the advent of the American oil men and, as a minor side issue, that Stanton Laird and his seismic crew intended to seduce every woman on the place, white and black.

'I'm thinking the Lord God has sent them to us as a visitation', Pat said. 'A visitation on account of all our mortal sins that Father Ryan keeps on telling us about, the way He'll have us destroyed entirely.'

'It's all part of it', said Tom Regan gloomily. They stumbled to their beds at half past one in the morning, in black despair.

An excess of alcohol never kept Pat Regan in his bed; his massive frame carried the rum well. Disappointed in the ways of God to man, he turned for solace to the animal kingdom. He loved all animals, and he was very good with them. There was generally a little kangaroo hopping about Laragh homestead, a joey brought in by one of his stockmen. On Laragh Station kangaroos were a pest, eating the feed that should have been reserved for the sheep, multiplying in their hundreds. The Regans were good managers and could not tolerate the kangaroos; from time to time the Judge wrote a letter asking for a permit to shoot the protected animals and once a year would get a permit to shoot a hundred; with that authorization shooting went on merrily all the year round, so that it was not uncommon for them to shoot as many as a thousand of the vermin in a year. Inevitably from time to time a joey would be found by a shot dam, and if there was not at that time a little kangaroo about the place it would be reared at Laragh Station as a pet; in later life it would go off into the bush, probably to be shot a month later in the normal course of keeping the beasts down.

The hopping mouse was the latest triumph of the man who could tame anything. He had found it as a youngster only about two inches long out in the bush at the foot of the windmill that pumped one of his bores, and had brought it back to the homestead in the toolbox of a truck, the tools thrown out and the box lined with gum tree leaves.

Pat Regan read no books or newspapers, nor did the radio appeal to him. His simple interests lay in taming animals and drinking rum. For weeks he had fed the mouse small dead beetles, cheese, and young shoots of the eucalypt, had played with it and made a fuss of it. It had ridden on his shoulder through much of each day, in the truck or jeep or, more aristocratically, in the Humber Super-Snipe bought new the previous year and used on Laragh Station principally as a nest box for the hens, who laid in it whenever a window was left open. That morning he had retired on to the back verandah of the store with the mouse, for he was developing a wonder with which to surprise and amuse his wife. He was training the mouse to come to him and hop up on his shoulder whenever he called 'Hop!', and he was achieving some success.

As the trucks approached Laragh, Donald Bruce, driving with Stan Laird, said, 'All these properties are a bit different, you know. You mustn't expect this one to be like Mannahill.'

Stan smiled. 'I know it, Mr Cope was telling me last night. He said these people are Irish.'

'That's right. You may think them a queer lot, to start with. Take them the right way, and you'll find they can't do enough for you. Get their backs up, and they could be very troublesome.'

'I wouldn't expect that we'd create any trouble for them,' the geologist said. 'We'll be operating quite a ways out from the ranch house.'

'That's true.' They drove on in silence for a minute. 'You won't mind if I explain to them that you don't drink?'

'I'd appreciate it if you would. I see it's kind of awkward here, but I just don't like the stuff.'

'Oh, that's all right,' said Mr Bruce without much confidence. 'I'll fix that up for you. They're very hospitable, you know, and that's about the only hospitality they understand. They're really very nice people when you get to know them. They're immensely kind.'

'Kind?'

The other nodded. 'The kindest people this side of the black stump.'

'The black stump?'

'It's what they say round here. It just means – anywhere.'

They drove up to the homestead about midday. The single-storey building stood drenched in blazing sunshine under a cloudless sky; its white-painted iron roof hurt the eyes. The men got out of the trucks and Mrs Regan came out to meet them, with Mollie and the children. The girl said, 'Ma, this is Stan Laird, from America.'

Stanton said, 'I'm certainly glad to know you, Mrs Regan.'

'You picked a hot time of day to come over,' she said. She was introduced in turn to all the others. 'Well, don't let's stand here in the sun. Come on into the shade.'

The geologist laughed. 'I guess we're all used to the sun, Mrs Regan. We'll see plenty more of it before we're through.'

'No need to stand out in it when you haven't got to,' she replied. She led the way to the verandah. 'Mollie, get the tray and the glasses.' She turned again to Stanton. 'You've been working up in the north here for some time?'

'Most of us are new to this country, Mrs Regan,' he said. 'I only landed in Australia a week ago.'

She wrinkled her forehead. 'Is it as hot as this in America?'

'It gets quite hot down in New Mexico,' he said. 'I wouldn't say it's quite as hot as this. But most of us came right here from Arabia. That was my last assignment before coming here.'

'Well,' she said drily, 'welcome to the Lunatic.'

He blinked. 'The Lunatic?'

Donald Bruce said, 'I should have told you that one, Stan. It's what they call this end of the Hammersley Range, the Lunatic Range.'

He smiled. 'Why do they call it that? Because only lunatics live here?'

'Aye,' said Mrs Regan. 'They're all right when they come.'

The girl came down the verandah with the tray and set it down upon the table. Stanton was relieved to see that there was a bottle of lemon squash there by the rum bottle, and a large glass jug of ice-cold water from the refrigerator. Mrs Regan said, 'Help yourself, now, gentlemen.' There was still a faint flavour of the barmaid in her manner.

Mollie said, 'Stan doesn't drink, Ma.'

'Do ye tell me that! Would ye have a lemon squash, then, Mr Laird?'

'I'd appreciate that, Mrs Regan. About half of us don't drink alcohol. Dwight and Tex here, they're the same as me.'

'That's something new for the Lunatic,' said Mrs Regan. 'Well, help yourselves. Mr Bruce, I know that you're not one of them.'

Pat Regan appeared around the corner of the verandah, the mouse perched upon his shoulder. His wife said, 'Pat, this is Mr Laird with his party.'

'God save you,' said the grazier. He did not seem particularly enthusiastic in his welcome. Stanton studied the old man with some concern, the massive frame, the dour look, the thick red hair only touched with grey, the little creature on his shoulder. Pat Regan's eye fell on the glass that his wife handed to the geologist. 'In the Name of God,' he said, 'what would that be you're after giving him to drink?'

'Lemon squash,' she said equably. 'Mr Laird and two of his party don't drink spirits.'

'There's queer fellows,' said the grazier. He turned to Stanton. 'If it's the stomach ulcers you'd be suffering, there's no harm in the rum. The whisky is a poor thing for an ulcer, and the gin will do it no good at all. But rum is a smooth liquor, Mr Laird; it lies as soft upon an ulcer as the feathers of a goose.'

Stanton smiled. 'I guess I'll stay on lemon squash,' he said. 'I just don't like the taste of alcohol.'

'Well, isn't that a wonder!' He turned to Bruce. 'Ye didn't bring Jock McKenzie with you this time, Don?'

The Australian laughed. 'No, he's still in Canberra.'

'Well, give yeself a rum, and make pretence you're him.' Pat turned to Stanton. 'I should be after telling you, this Jock McKenzie from the Mineral Resources down in Canberra, he's a heavy drinker, Mr Laird. A very, very heavy drinker. We aren't like that at all up here.'

Donald Bruce laughed. 'Three drinks to a bottle.'

'Aye. Isn't it a queer thing now, and he a public servant working in an office, in Canberra itself? Four drinks it should be. There's some, like the Judge, would say five, or six even. But four drinks it should be. Four makes a comfortable, friendly kind of drink. Three is too much, too much altogether.' He poured himself a quarter of a bottle of rum into the tumbler and shot it down before the eyes of the startled Americans, following it with a chaser of water. 'And now, Mr Laird, where is it that you want to sink your bore?'

'I wouldn't say we'd gotten quite so far as that just yet, Mr Regan,' said the geologist. 'We'll have quite a bit of exploratory work to do before we make our minds up if we're going to drill a well right here at all. I haven't been out on the location yet, of course. I've got some air photographs of the district the last party picked as interesting enough for us to investigate more closely. Would you like to see them?'

'I would so. Would it be pictures that the aeroplane was after taking a while back, and him so high up in the Heaven he might have been the Archangel himself?'

'He was up here in June,' said Mr Bruce. 'Most of the photographs were taken at fifteen thousand feet.'

'Well, Glory be to God, isn't that a great height for a man to be flying? How far would that be in miles?'

'About three miles.'

The old man shook his head. 'They'll be no use to you, no use at all. Ye'll see nothing any good to you at that distance. Ye should have told him to fly lower.'

'They tell us all we need to know,' said Stanton. 'I have the prints right here in the truck.'

He walked over to the truck, opened one of his dustproof tin boxes, and brought a sheaf of half a dozen large prints back to the verandah. He handed one to the grazier. 'This is the best general view,' he said. 'The centre of this picture would be about fourteen miles from here, and practically due west. The scale would be about four miles from edge to edge of the print.'

74

Mrs Regan said, 'Mollie, go and get your father his glasses. They're in the right-hand small drawer of the bureau.'

She did so, and the old man adjusted the unfamiliar things on to his nose and ears. He peered at the print, and the mouse peered with him from his shoulder. 'Well, isn't that the queer thing to be a picture of the property. Ye'd say to look at it that there'd be no feed on the ground, no feed at all, and the countryside in June as green with spinifex as all the fields of County Wicklow put together.'

'They always look like that,' said Donald Bruce. The photographs were passed from hand to hand. He took one, and said to the grazier. 'Look, this is where we are. You see this river bed?' He traced upon the print with his finger. 'Well, that's what you call Brown Ewe Creek.'

'Do ye tell me that!'

'And this line, this very faint, straight one. Can you see it? There.' The grazier blinked behind the unaccustomed spectacles. 'Well, that's the fence between your property and Lucinda Station.'

'Well, Glory be to God! Isn't it a great wonder to be taking pictures like that from the air?' He turned to his daughter. 'Go tell your Uncle Tom to come and see these pictures, and then tell the Judge himself.'

Presently Tom and the Judge appeared, somewhat the worse for wear, but a neat rum revived them and they began to take an intelligent interest in the photographs. Stanton took the opportunity to give them a short lecture on the discovery of oil. 'This, right here,' he said, tracing it with his finger, 'this is a limestone outcrop such as might hold oil. Or it might not. This, here, is another one. Along this southern edge of both there's a layer of clay. You can't see it in the picture, but the geological survey says it's there.'

'That's right,' said Mr Bruce. 'There's nothing much to see upon the surface, but the limestone – just about *there* – that limestone shows an oil trace when you crack the rock.'

'I'd say that it's a typical folded structure with oil traces,' said the geologist. 'I'd say *this* might be a small dead fold

75

and *this*. But *this* one, I'd say he might run right under, with a fold beneath the gypsum outcrops *here*, and *here*. I wouldn't know yet, but it looks like that to me.'

'Is that where there'd be oil?' asked Tom.

'I wouldn't know, Mr Regan,' said the geologist. 'If there's a fold in the limestone there it's my job to find it. If we find one or more folds with an impervious layer on top, then that's the sort of a formation that is capable of holding oil. We do know this much that there has been oil here once, maybe centuries ago. The traces in the limestone tell us that. Whether there's any down there now is anybody's guess.'

'But if ye find the folds ye talk about, then you'll sink a bore down to the oil?'

'We might do that,' said the geologist. 'It would depend a lot how promising it looks. We might decide to drill a hole and see what's there. But that's no guarantee that we'll strike oil. We'd be mighty lucky to strike oil with the first hole.' He turned to them. 'You know somethin'? For every hole we drill in the United States that produces oil in commercial quantity, we drill five that don't. That's about the ratio – five dry holes to every one that produces. Over 'n over again I've drilled a hole down maybe to seven or ten thousand feet not expecting to find oil at all with that one, just to examine the rock cores coming up 'n find for certain how the strata run down there. Then with that evidence, maybe we drill a good one in some other place, 'n get the oil.'

They stared at him, this queer stranger who wouldn't drink spirits, with some respect. He spoke as if he knew what he was talking about and they could recognize competence when they met it, even in fields remote from their experience. 'How much does it cost to drill a hole?' asked Tom.

'I wouldn't be able to put a finger on it,' Stanton said. 'It depends how deep you go, what sort of rock you strike. On skads of things.'

'About how much?'

'In this country here? I'd say perhaps three hundred thousand dollars.'

'How much would that be in pounds?'

Donald Bruce said, 'About a hundred and thirty thousand.'

'And ye'd spend that much money on a bore and then maybe to find no oil at all?'

'That's right,' said Stanton. 'I spend most of my life doing that. Then one day we drill a good producer, and that pays for all the rest.'

They had no comment to make on that. Such figures were beyond all their experience, or so they thought. In fact the annual gross income of Laragh Station was considerably more than half the figure that had just been mentioned, but this was not real money to them. It is doubtful if any member of the Regan family even knew what the gross income of their property was; the Judge knew the figures, for he kept the books, and the fact that the current account of Laragh Station was just about enough to pay for the restoration of Dunchester Cathedral was a perpetual worry to him, the more so because he could not get the Regans to display the slightest interest in it. Tom was the only one with any money sense, but that was mostly turned to the economies of good management. Mrs Regan could appreciate the fact that they were wealthy people, but the figures meant little to her in terms of holidays or goods; her instinct always was to save money for a rainy day. Of all the children, Mike, the chartered accountant in Perth, was the only one who really understood the situation of the family, and he knew better than to trouble them about it. Reserves were building up – well, let them build. So long as the Regans had a quiet life upon their property, an occasional new truck and plenty of rum, they lived as happy and contented people. They had no other ambitions.

It was arranged that the survey party should stay to dinner and then go out to their location to make their camp. It was the custom upon Laragh Station that the men should eat alone, somewhat in the Moslem style. This curious habit had originated in the old reprobate days before Tom Regan had gone down to Perth to meet Mrs Foster in the bar. In those days they had lived somewhat indiscriminately with the gins, though the Countess Markievicz had been Pat's favourite and ranked as the chief wife. The Countess was unaccustomed to a lavatory and her table manners had left much to be desired, so the men had fallen into the habit of dining alone while the black women took their meals out in the kitchen, or in any place they wished. When Mrs Foster, now Mrs Tom Regan, had arrived upon the scene with two young children, she had found too much to be reformed to cope with everything at once. Moreover, it was necessary for her to look after the children at their meals, and she did not want to bother the men with them. So she pushed the blacks out of the kitchen to eat in the scullery, and took the kitchen as her own domain, where she ate with the children. The custom, once established, had endured throughout the years.

Stanton, accustomed as he was to the American way of life, was troubled when the women did not turn up to the meal, though he said nothing. It was hot in the dining-room; over their heads a punkah fan turned slowly. Mrs Regan and Mollie came in from the kitchen and placed a huge dish on the table with two legs of hot roast mutton in it, with boiled potatoes, sweet potatoes, and cabbage, and retired to their own place. The men ate in virtual silence; conversation at meal times was unknown on Laragh Station. The Countess slopped around in bare feet, huge, black, smiling, and shapeless in a cotton frock worn very evidently with nothing underneath it, removing used dishes from the table and carrying them out to wash. Mollie appeared and set down a big steamed pudding with a bowl of hot lemon sauce, and went out to the kitchen again. Perspiration broke out on the American's forehead and his temples began to throb as he manfully tackled the pudding.

They said goodbye to the Regans after lunch and set out for their location to make camp before nightfall, having refused an offer of the shearers' quarters. 'I guess we'd better camp out where the work is,' Stanton said. 'Fourteen miles is a little far to go and come for meals, 'n we'd be needing gas most every day if we did that.'

Mollie and Mrs Regan appeared shortly before they left. 'Be sure now to let us know if we can do anything for you,' the mother said. 'The laundry, now. What will you be doing about the wash?'

'Do it ourselves,' said Stanton. 'We always do that.'

'Ye'll be carting water all the time. Why don't you run it in here every couple o' days, and let the gins do it along with ours?'

The offer was too good to refuse. 'It certainly would help us if we could do that,' said the American. 'It's mighty kind of you.'

'It's no trouble. They wash every day saving Sunday. Just bring it in and dump it in the wash house, and they'll do it.'

Mollie said, 'Can Ma and I come out one afternoon and see what's going on, Stan?'

'Why, certainly,' he said. 'Come any time you can. I don't suppose we'll have much to offer you, except ice cream.'

'Ice cream? Where on earth would you get that from?'

He was a little surprised. 'We make it. We've got a freezer in the truck.' A considerable power plant was necessary to their seismic observation, and the current from this could be used to run a variety of domestic electrical appliances. It would have been hardship indeed to the seismic crew if they had missed out on their ice cream in the outback.

She laughed. 'What flavours have you got?'

'I'd say only strawberry and vanilla,' he said apologetically. He called to the camp cook, 'Hey, Ted! What flavours of ice cream do we have?'

'Strawberry, maple, and vanilla, boss.'

'I'll have a maple,' said the girl. 'I've never tasted maple ice cream.'

He smiled at her 'I'll have it ready for you.' He climbed up into the driver's seat of the truck. ' 'Bye now.'

He drove off from the station buildings with Donald Bruce riding in the seat beside him; the Australian directed him on to a faint wheel track that scarred the red earth. 'This is actually the road to Lucinda Station,' he said, 'where David Cope lives – the young fellow that you met at Mannahill. The best way for us is to go out to the boundary, by the Chinaman's grave, and then turn north along the fence. It's two sides of a triangle but there's a track all the way. It's a bit rough if you try and go direct over the hills.'

Stanton nodded, and the truck rolled on in the shimmering heat, following the jeep tracks that wound in and out of the biggest clumps of spinifex. The other two vehicles followed in his dust. After half an hour a gallows-like erection appeared on the horizon. 'That's right,' said Donald Bruce in slight relief. 'That's the cemetery.'

'The cemetery?'

'Yes. There's a cemetery here.'

The geologist drove on in silence. Presently they came to the erection he had seen in the distance. Two vertical posts supported a cross member which carried a painted board above a gate between the posts, and on this gate was painted,

SHIRE OF YANTARINGA
CEMETERY

A single strand of barbed wire supported on tumbledown posts cut from the bush stretched away into the distance on each side of the gate. Inside the enclosure a single low mound, untended, was marked by a vertical post of sawn timber.

The geologist slipped the gear out and brought the truck to a standstill, surveying the scene. 'I guess there's not much business,' he said. 'Who gets buried here?'

'Nobody,' said Mr Bruce.

'Then why have a cemetery?'

'Aw, look,' said Mr Bruce. 'It's this way. All this land is held on pastoral leases from the state – it's not freehold.

The Regans hold Laragh Station on a long pastoral lease. Well, it's a law of West Australia that no one lessee may rent more than a million acres. Some time back before the war they made a survey checking up on some of these properties, because they reckoned that the station owners had been grabbing a bit here and a bit there till they'd got too much, 'n anyway they weren't paying enough rent. It's not much they pay, anyway – about three and six a thousand acres. Well, they found the Regans had been paying rent on about seven hundred thousand acres, but they were actually occupying a bit over the million, so they had to get rid of some. Tom Regan wasn't going to give land to a neighbour, of course, on principle. So they picked on this Chinaman who happened to be buried by the track here, 'n said the Shire must have a cemetery or shift the body off their land. The Shire reckoned it was cheaper to accept a few hundred acres, especially as Tom Regan said he'd look after it and fence it. So we've got a cemetery.'

The geologist said, 'Well, who was the Chinaman?'

'I don't think anybody knows. He died of thirst along the track – oh, a long time ago. When Tom Regan made the cemetery he didn't like to put a cross up on the grave because he might not have been Christian – probably he wasn't. So he just put up that bit of straight timber.'

'Uh-huh.' The other sat staring out over the grey-green landscape, shimmering in the heat. 'What did you say the rent they pay is? Three and six?'

'That's right.'

'Forty two cents? For a thousand acres, for a year?'

'That's right.'

Stanton slipped in the gear. 'Well let's get rolling. I guess I've seen everything now.'

'Don't kid yourself,' said Mr Bruce. 'You've not seen half of it.'

A mile past the cemetery they came to the boundary fence that ran between Laragh and Lucinda. It consisted of three strands of wire loosely supported on bush timber. A gate crossed the track, and this was adorned with a notice board, with ancient, half-obliterated lettering painted by some angry man in bygone years

SHUT THIS
BLOODY
GATE

'That's the way on to Lucinda,' said Mr Bruce. 'It's about ten miles to the homestead. Just follow the tracks and you can't go wrong. We turn right here, along the fence.'

Stanton swung the truck round and began to follow the line of the fence; faint wheel tracks ran beside it where a jeep from Laragh had run occasionally loaded with posts and wire for repairs. 'He seems a nice sort of a young fellow, the one who lives at Lucinda,' he said. 'I met him last night at Mannahill Station.'

'That's the one,' said Mr Bruce. 'He's bought himself a packet of trouble with that property. There's practically no water at all on it.'

'There's not much on this one.'

'You're wrong there. Laragh's got good water – bores all over the place.' He pointed to the vanes of a windmill faintly seen in the distance, three or four miles away. 'Look, there's one there.'

'Quite a ways from here.'

'Not so far. You're never out of sight of water on this station. It's very different on Lucinda.'

'Does he live alone, or is he married? What's his name, again?'

'David Cope. Yes, he lives quite alone, but for the blacks. He's always over at Laragh nowadays. He's got his eye on Mollie.'

The American said nothing to that. He drove on for a minute in silence, studying the road. Then he said, 'I guess I'll go and see him one day. Or will he come over to our camp?'

'He wouldn't do that,' said Mr Bruce. 'He wouldn't come

on Laragh Station without asking the Regans – they're a bit touchy sometimes. I know he'd be glad to see you over at his place. It must be pretty lonely there at night.'

'It will be a long time before I go wandering about this country in the night,' said Stanton. 'If I go, I'll go in the daytime with a compass and a navigation outfit to take shots of the sun.'

'It won't do you any good,' said Mr Bruce. 'The sun at midday's just about overhead.' He turned to the American. 'That's one thing you want to remember, Stan. It's no good looking at the sun around midday to get the north. If you get bushed, the shot is to camp and wait for sunset, and go by that. It's all right going by the stars at night, of course. Best time to travel, anyway. But middle of the day, the sun's no good to you.'

'I'd say it's not much good to you any time in this country.'

They drove on another five miles by the fence. Then Mr Bruce directed the American to bear in to the right. 'I get it,' said Stan. 'That's the big limestone outcrop in the air photograph.'

'That's right. I've not been this way before. It looks all right for the trucks, though. Take it easy. When we were here before we came down from the north, and then went over the hills to Laragh homestead. We were travelling in jeeps, though.'

Stanton drove the truck carefully across country, threading his way around the occasional boulders and around the thickest clumps of spinifex, too busy to take much note of the geological formations they were driving over. Presently the Australian directed him down from a spur towards a piece of flat country seamed by a dry river bed, beneath the big limestone spur. 'I'd say a camp down there would be as good as anywhere.'

Stanton stopped the truck, and killed the motor, and sat motionless at the wheel looking at the country ahead of him; the two trucks following him stopped also. Presently they all got out and stood looking over the barren landscape.

There were a few sheep in the valley, but no other sign of life.

'I guess this is it,' said Stanton presently. 'This is what we've come for.'

Hank said, 'Run a line of shots across the valley, boss. See where that limestone goes.'

'Maybe,' said Stanton. 'We'll make our camp down there by the dry river bed, for a start.'

FOUR

A WEEK later Mr Bruce left the seismic crew, to return to Melbourne. Stanton drove him to Malvern Downs via Laragh and Mannahill; at Malvern he got a lift in a truck going into Onslow and from there he went to Perth by the regular airline. One of the first jobs if oil should be found on Laragh Station would be to construct an airstrip near the rig.

At Malvern, Stanton Laird met reinforcements. An American from Texas, Spencer Rasmussen, had come up to take over the management of the camp, freeing Stanton for his proper technical work. Stanton had met this man in Arabia and had got on well with him; he had been a driller as a young man and had worked in the oil industry all his life. At the age of forty-five he had drilled many wells in many countries; he was tough with labour and supremely efficient at the job he knew so well. In his leisure moments, which were few, he liked pitching horseshoes and playing the accordion. He brought with him three more men, a jeep, and a big eight-wheeled truck furnished with a miniature drilling rig to drill the shot holes for the seismic observations.

His arrival at the camp took a great load of organization off the geologist. For the first time Stanton was able to get down to work upon the drafting board in the tent that they had set up as an office, poring over the ground observations of the previous party reinforced by his own observations. He was able to work relatively quietly there for hours on end, clad in a pair of shorts and sandals only, analysing the results of the previous day's observations and laying down the programme for the next day. Gradually, on paper and in his mind, he began to build up a picture of the run of the strata deep down in the earth beneath their feet. Frequently he would take the jeep and drive two or three miles to some spur of the hills, and spend an hour or two with plane table and theodolite. Very soon these expeditions took him close to the Lucinda fence.

He took time off one afternoon, and went out in the jeep to pay a call on David Cope. He had arranged the visit beforehand over the radio telephone after the morning schedule of the Flying Doctor service, and David was waiting at the homestead when the jeep drove up.

Lucinda homestead was a little place of five rooms only, build on the earth instead of up on posts; at some time in the past a layer of concrete had been laid on the bare earth floors of the rooms. The structure was of wood supporting a covering of white asbestos sheets; inside, the walls were lined with some synthetic board, dark yellow in colour and unpainted. There was no verandah, a considerable deprivation in that climate, for the house was small and very hot.

David greeted the American warmly. 'Come on in,' he said. 'The house isn't much – not like the Mannahill or Laragh, I'm afraid.'

Stanton said, 'It's a palace to me, Mr Cope. We're living in tents.'

'David's the name, Stan. It's what they do in this country. They're bloody touchy about names.'

'I know it.'

'I expect your tents are a damn sight more comfortable than this house. But do come in. I've got a kettle on the stove for tea, and I got the gin to make some cakes. I don't know what they'll be like.' They went into the house. 'The

85

folk at Laragh haven't broken you in to rum yet?'

The geologist laughed. 'Not yet. Say, do they always drink it that way in this country?'

'They seem to in the outback. Not down in Perth – it's just like England there.'

'I wonder they're not all nuts, the way they drink that stuff.'

'It's the climate or something,' David said. 'Or else it's the way they shoot it down with a chaser of water. It doesn't seem to hurt them, like it would you or me. The Regans are good graziers, you know.'

'I know it.' Stanton laughed. 'That's the part that I can't figure out.'

The sitting-room, so called, that the front door opened into was very sparsely furnished. A deck chair, a steamer chair, and a table, all rather soiled and old, made up the only furniture. 'I'm afraid it's not much to look at,' David said apologetically. 'I got this place walk-in, walk-out, and this is the only furniture that was in it when I came. I did up the bedroom that I use, but I haven't been able to get around to the rest of the house yet.'

The bedroom door was open, and Stanton glanced in. There was a good bed with a bright, clean bedspread over it, good bedroom furniture, new colour wash on the walls, and a couple of strips of carpet on the floor. It was a clean, decent room to look at, unlike the rest of the house.

David saw the glance and led the way into the bedroom. 'This is the only room I've got fixed up yet,' he said, a little proudly. 'I'm going to get the rest of the house like this within twelve months. Do it room by room, in the evenings. The mugger of it is I haven't got a lighting plant yet, so it's all got to be done with kerosene lamps, and that makes it hot working.'

The American said, 'You've got this fixed up mighty nice.' A bookcase caught his eye, half filled with about fifty books in a uniform binding. He started at it in wonder; there were far more books there than in his home at Hazel. 'I see you're quite a reader,' he said.

86

David took up one and leafed it through. 'Reprint Society,' he said. 'They post you one a month. It's the best way to get books in a place like this, where one's a bit out of touch. Don't you find that?'

'Uh-huh,' said Stanton. 'I get the *Saturday Evening Post* and *Life* mailed out from home each week.' He glanced once more around the room. Three framed photographs stood upon the chest of drawers. Two were of elderly people, almost certainly the father and mother. The third one, very simple and rather appealing, was a portrait of Mollie Regan.

David led the way back through the sitting-room into the kitchen. He had laid the kitchen table in anticipation of his guest; the chipped cups, the discoloured pewter spoons, were neatly arranged upon a clean tablecloth laid on the battered, soiled old table. A kettle was boiling on a Primus stove that stood on the blackened, wood-burning range. An ancient, rather rusty kerosene refrigerator added to the heat of the room, and there were many flies.

David made the tea in a chipped enamel teapot, blackened with soot on the bottom, poured it out, and offered his guest one of the unpleasant rock-cakes of the gin's making. 'I'm afraid it's all a bit rough,' he said. 'It's coming good, though. You come along in six months' time and you won't know the place.'

'Sure,' said Stanton. 'There must be a lot to do when you take on a place like this.'

David sipped the hot tea. 'Well, of course – there is. I'm at it all the time, from dawn to dusk. It's a bad property, of course,' he said candidly. 'If it was a good one I wouldn't be here running it, at my age. Three hundred and twenty thousand acres, but very little water. There's over a hundred thousand acres up your end that we can't use at all.'

The geologist blinked at the figure. 'Can't use it?'

David nodded. 'There's not a puddle on it. Everything that falls soaks straight into the ground.' He paused. 'I've never seen most of it.'

'Never seen it? A hundred thousand acres?'

'That's right. I'm always meaning to take the jeep and

drive across, but I've been too bloody busy on the parts that are some good.'

The geologist asked, 'Would that be the part towards our camp?'

'That's right. I can't run any stock between this homestead and your camp. All the good part of the property is west from here.'

Stanton smiled. 'Maybe you won't be so mad at what I'm going to ask, then. The strata on the Laragh side are falling to the west, so far as I can see, and now I'm working close up to your fence. The Department haven't asked for us to prospect on your property, have they?'

David shook his head. 'I haven't seen anything. You're quite welcome, though.'

'You wouldn't mind if we go wandering around with plane tables and levels, with a jeep?'

'Of course not.'

'What about some lines of shot holes for a few seismic readings? That would mean a couple of trucks on the land, and a few little explosions.'

'I can't stop you,' said David, 'and I wouldn't want to. I mean, we've only got a pastoral lease, and if the Department write and say they want you to come here, we can't say no. But, letter or no letter, Stan, you're very welcome. We've got no sheep there because there's not a drop of water for them, and most of it I've never seen myself. If you go on it I'll be glad to know what's there.'

'That's mighty nice of you,' said the geologist. 'I'll certainly tell you everything we find.' He paused in thought. 'It could be that we might know something about the water prospect in this district by the time we're through.'

'I wanted to ask you about that,' David said. 'You *do* prospect for water as well as oil?'

'Uh-huh,' said Stanton. 'It's one and the same thing. There are porous kinds of rock strata and impervious kinds of rock strata, just those two. Water or oil or Coca-cola – they'll soak down into the porous strata and get trapped by the impervious strata. Once I get the undersurface picture of this whole locality set down on paper, then maybe I'll know where water might lie or where oil might lie. Till then I'd just be guessing.'

'I'd be very grateful for anything that you can tell me about the chance of water on Lucinda.'

'It doesn't look so promising right now,' said the geologist. 'But there – that's only guessing. How deep would you drill?'

'Some of the bores on Mannahill go down two thousand feet. I don't think they go as deep as that on Laragh.'

The geologist opened his eyes. 'You'd go as deep as that, though?'

'If we knew that there was water there I think we would. It'ld pay to do so. It's just a matter of finding the capital then.'

Stanton nodded slowly. 'I guess that might not be so easy in these parts.'

'It's not impossible,' said David. They chatted for a quarter of an hour and then the geologist got to his feet. 'Time I was getting back to work,' he said. 'The boys 'll be wondering what happened to me.'

They went out to his jeep. 'Come over to our camp some time, David, 'n take a look around. We got nothing much to offer you except ice cream. Miss Regan said that she'd be over to have some of that, but she hasn't shown up yet.'

'I'd like to do that, Stan,' the boy said. 'I'd like to have a look at how you make these seismic observations, too.'

'Certainly.' The geologist stood by the jeep, looking around. The low hills of red earth, covered in the greenish, dusty-looking spinifex, swelled up towards the south in the golden light of the descending sun; did that show an anticline? He paused in thought, looking around, and then turned to the Englishman.

'You got a mighty lot of country to pick from,' he said. 'There should be water here some place.'

David grinned. 'We could use it.'

'Let's keep our fingers crossed,' said the geologist. He got into the jeep and started the motor. ' 'Bye now.'

He drove back following the track that led to Laragh, passed through the Bloody Gate and shut it carefully after him, and turned north between the cemetery and the boundary fence. A few sheep grazed on the spinifex within the cemetery area, and as he drove a kangaroo got up and bounded away between them. He stopped the jeep and watched it as it ran away over a low rise; it checked in its bounding run and swerved to the right, and then went bounding on till it was lost to sight. He wondered what it was that had made it swerve like that. It looked as if the spinifex there was a different colour, sort of dead-looking.

He was in no hurry. He stopped the motor and got out of the jeep, and walked in the direction taken by the kangaroo. He walked about a quarter of a mile, and a faint odour in the air assailed him, a very familiar smell. On the crest of a small rise he found what he was looking for. There was an area of ground, only about ten yards square, an outcrop of sandstone with a little granitic conglomerate. There was a fissure in the rock, and a smell of natural gas.

He bent to the fissure, sniffed it carefully, and tried to light it with a match, but it would not burn. He stood up thoughtfully, and looked around. It was within the cemetery area; the single strand of wire ran about two hundred yards to the north. There was nothing with which he could mark the place, and he had no instruments with him. He studied the fence line carefully, and walked towards it at right-angles, counting his paces; when he got there he tied his handkerchief in a firm knot on the wire. Then he made his way back to the jeep and drove on to his camp.

There was a strange jeep drawn up by the tents, and as he drove up he saw the bright colours of women's print frocks. He realised that Mrs Regan and Mollie had driven over to visit with them, and he quickened his pace. He drove in and got out of the jeep and went to meet them.

'I'm real sorry I wasn't here when you came in,' he said. 'I picked this afternoon of all afternoons to go visiting at Lucinda.'

'Don't fash yeself, Mr Laird,' said Mrs Regan. 'The boys have been looking after us and giving us ice cream.'

'I invited them to stay for supper, Stan,' said Spencer. 'The trouble is there's only strawberry ice cream in the freezer, and you promised Miss Regan she'd have maple.'

Stanton was distressed. He turned to the girl. 'I'm real sorry, Mollie,' he said. 'We had maple quite a while, waiting for you to come, 'n then the boys got kind of tired of it, so we switched.'

'I got some maple in the freezer now, boss,' said Ted. 'It'll be hard in about an hour.'

The girl laughed. 'It's terrible nice of you to take so much trouble. I've had about half a pound of strawberry already. It's awfully good ice cream.'

Relieved, Stanton turned to her mother. 'Would you be able to stay 'n have supper with us, Mrs Regan? The boys would like it if you could.'

'We'd be pleased to, Mr Laird. It's all cold at home, and the Countess can give that to the men. We'll have to be back by eight o'clock, though, or they'll be sending out a search party.'

Spencer Rasmussen glanced at his watch. 'The six o'clock schedule will be on in half an hour,' he said. 'We can speak to them on the natter session after that.' He meant, on the radio.

'Oh, that would do fine. I'd better speak myself if you can get them.'

'I'll take care of that,' said Hank. He usually operated the set. 'I'll come 'n tell you when they're on.'

Mollie turned to Stanton and said, 'What did you think of Lucinda, Stan?'

'It's kind of small,' he said. 'I guess he'll get it pretty nice, though, by the time he's through. He's certainly a worker.'

She nodded. 'I know. It's such an awful pity that he hasn't got a better property to work on. There's hardly any water there at all.'

Mrs Regan had gone off with Ted to the cook tent, where he was showing her his stainless steel kerosene pressure cooking stove, his cadmium-coated aluminium freezer, and his water softener and cooler, with great pride. Stanton piloted Mollie to follow them, thinking that she would take an interest in these things, and this gave him an opportunity to say a few words aside to Spencer Rasmussen.

'You know what?' he inquired. 'There's a gas seepage, a little one, between here and the Bloody Gate, 'bout a quarter of a mile east, in the cemetery.'

'There is?'

'I'll show you in the morning.'

'It wouldn't be a decomposing body? Seems like that cemetery's getting kind of crowded.'

'I don't reckon that it's that. I know gas when I smell it.'

He joined the ladies at the cook tent. They were amazed at the fine quality of the equipment with which Ted worked. 'There isn't a thing hardly that's not stainless steel or aluminium,' Mrs Regan said in wonder. 'Even the table's got a stainless steel top ...' She stood looking around her. 'It must all have cost a fortune. I've never seen so many stainless steel things in one place.'

The Americans were slightly embarrassed. 'Don't you have stainless steel things in your kitchens, Ma'am?'

'Oh yes, we do. But not so much as this, or such good quality.' She picked up a stainless saucepan. 'It's got a ground bottom and all, but it's so *light.*'

Stanton asked Ted, 'What do we get for supper tonight?'

'Fried chicken, sausages, and hot cakes, boss. I got some biscuits in the oven. Fruit salad 'n ice cream. Coffee.'

'I guess that 'll do.' He turned to Mollie, smiling. 'Sounds like a real American meal,' he said. 'I hope you'll be able to eat it.'

'It sounds delicious.'

He took them round the camp, into his own sleeping tent first. Again they were naïvely astonished at the comforts with which the Americans had equipped their camp, which seemed so natural to them. The pressure water system in the showers conserving water by the use of fine, high-power jets intrigued them. 'It's better than we've got at Laragh,' Mrs Regan said. 'I never saw a camp fitted up like this before.'

'Maybe it's the sort of work we do,' said Stanton a little apologetically. 'We use some mighty delicate instruments, and they need mighty delicate maintenance. I guess you've got to live a bit differently if you're going to do fine work in camp.'

He took them to the observation truck and showed them the galvanometers, the gravimeters, and the magneto-meters. For a time he tried to explain to them how these things worked and what they were each for, but he soon gave that up. The scientific principles were outside their experience; to them it was as if he had been speaking in a foreign language when he spoke of matters that were his normal life and work. He had experienced this before in his own family; his mother had never been able to grasp exactly what he did or how he did it. He was content to leave it so, only demonstrating to them the complexity of the instruments to make his point about the camp.

'It's just like the insides of a clock, only much more deli-cate,' Mollie said. 'If that goes wrong, have you got to put it right?'

'Either that, or send eleven hundred miles to Perth for another one.' He shut the case of the gravimeter carefully and put it back into its dustproof box. 'You want to be clean and cool and in good shape before you start 'n pull that down,' he said. 'I guess that has a bearing on the camp equipment that we take along.'

She nodded. 'I see what you mean.'

He took her to the office tent, where his drawing board was set up, and a table that supported the black cases of the radio transreceiver. Hank was there, tuned in and wait-ing; a low chatter of medical consultation came from the loud speaker. He disregarded that, and showed them the plan upon his drawing board, the sections of the strata so far as he had been able to deduce them at that stage. The drawing meant little to them, but the air photographs meant more, and now he was able to explain to them upon the photographs a little of what happened underground.

Ten minutes later, Hank said, 'Natter session coming on now, Stan. I told them a while back we wanted Laragh.'

'Okay. Let us know when you've got them.'

He took his guests through into the mess tent next door, a marquee with a long table down the middle, a couple of deck chairs, and a side table with a litter of magazines on it. Presently Hank shouted that Laragh was on the air. Stanton took Mrs Regan back to the set, leaving Mollie in the mess tent, thinking that the older woman might need help in operating a radio telephone. He need not have worried; the set was as normal to Mrs Regan as her kitchen stove. She spoke for a few minutes to the Judge, telling him where they were and giving him instructions about supper to retail to the Countess. Then they went back to the marquee.

They found Mollie engrossed in the advertisement pages of the *Saturday Evening Post*. She looked up as they came in, but did not put the magazine down. 'You do have lovely things in America,' she said. 'Tell me, are these pictures real?'

'Real?'

'Do you really have cars like that?' She pointed to the long, flowing lines of a big convertible in a glamorous setting.

He studied the picture. 'I guess so,' he said after a minute. 'Don't you know?'

'I was just trying to remember,' he said. 'I'd say that's about right. Sometimes an artist might exaggerate, make it look longer than it really is. No, I'd say that's about right for an Olds.'

She studied the picture for a moment or so longer, and then leafed the pages through slowly, looking at the television sets, the electric toasters, the electric blankets, the brightly coloured bedspreads. The advertisements, designed to catch the attention of a population accustomed to discount their advertising, were positively dazzling to her. She put the *Post* down reluctantly, afraid that she was being

94

rude to her host. 'You do have the most lovely magazines,' she said.

He was a little surprised at the note of yearning in her voice, because these things were normal to him; he liked the *Post* for the articles and stories, but he paid little attention to the advertisements. 'Would you like to borrow some of them?' he asked.

She withdrew a little. 'Oh no. You've got nothing else to read.'

'I think the boys have read most of these,' he said. 'There's a fresh batch comes in each week with the mail.' He wanted her to have them very much, and her sincerity in not wanting to deprive them of their reading pleased him. They were obliged to the Laragh people for doing their washing; if now they could give pleasure to this girl it would be something in return. The *Post* was his own property, but there were many others on the table. He called through to the office tent, 'Hey, Hank? You finished with the September *Cosmopolitan*, if I lend it to Mollie?'

'Sure,' said Hank. He appeared in the mess tent. 'Look, she can take these others, too.'

She could not avoid their generosity, nor did she really want to; there was little to read at Laragh but the books she bought herself or borrowed from David Cope. The Americans made up a bundle of about a dozen magazines for her and put them in the Laragh jeep, and her thanks were more evident in her gleaming eyes, her raised colour, and her slight excitement than in her words. Stanton, pleased himself at her pleasure, became aware that he was talking to a very lovely girl, a lovelier girl than he had seen in Hazel during his vacation.

Supper in the mess tent with the Americans was a new experience for Mollie, as it was for her mother. The Americans, however, were more accustomed to the change in manners than the Australians. 'I guess we don't eat the way you do,' said Stanton to the girl, laughing. 'See, this is what you do with it. You lift it up, so, 'n put some butter in, 'n then the maple syrup, 'n then a bit of fried chicken, 'n a

95

bit of bacon, 'n a hot biscuit and jam on the side. Then you just eat with a fork.'

She laughed with him. 'Mayn't I use my knife, Stan?'

'I guess you can,' he said generously. 'Back home you wouldn't use it the way people do here.'

'I'll try and do it your way.'

'That's a girl,' said Spencer Rasmussen. 'Make believe you're eating with Chinese and using chopsticks.'

'It's not like that a bit,' she said. 'I think it's rather a nice way of eating. But we don't eat sweet things with meat so much as this.'

'We eat more sweet things than you do, I'd say,' said Stanton. 'That might have something to do with the climate back home. We don't hardly ever get it hot like this, but it gets mighty cold in the winter in some parts of the States.'

'Is it very cold where you live?' she asked.

'Most winters we'd have a foot of snow for around three months,' he said. 'A bad winter, or in a blizzard, it might be two feet.'

'Is that fun, or is it horrid?' she inquired. 'I've never seen snow.'

'I'd say that probably depends on how old you are,' he said. 'If you're at High School or home from college on vacation, 'n go ski-ing or on sleigh rides, then it's fun. I always liked the winter when I lived at home. I guess you'd get to look at it differently as you got older.'

In the hot outback, in a tent pitched on the red earth, it all seemed very distant, very beautiful, and as refreshing as the Americans' ice cream. 'You really do use sleighs to go about in, in the snow?' she asked. 'With horses, with bells on the harness?'

'Only on the farms,' he said. 'The main highways, they get the snow ploughed, 'n you change to your snow tyres for winter. But in the country districts they use sleighs still. Not much, but enough to find one for a ski-ing party when you want it.'

After supper the Regans started off for home, Mollie

driving the jeep. It was a fine night with a rising moon, and the track, though faint, was clearly visible in the silvery light. Mrs Regan and Mollie protested that they were perfectly capable of driving back to Laragh by themselves, as indeed they were, but the Americans would not hear of it. To them the wide expanse of the station properties was still menacing and journeys in them were expeditions to be undertaken with some thought and some provision for disaster. It was unthinkable to them that two women should be allowed to venture out at night to drive home fifteen miles without an escort, and they were unyielding on the point. Accordingly Spencer and Stanton got into their jeep to follow the ladies. They drove behind them till the shearers' camp of Laragh came in sight; then they pulled up alongside, waved and shouted goodnight, and wheeled around to drive back to the camp on the oil site.

Mollie Regan went to bed with an armful of American magazines and with a lot to think about. A whole new world was opening before her. She had never in her life been outside West Australia, had never been further from her station home than Perth. Throughout her education at the convent school and at the University of West Australia she had been brought up to believe that England was the seat of all learning, all wisdom, and all culture in the world. Everything stemming from her own country was immature and puerile compared with that which stemmed from England. As regards America, her opinion was formed entirely on the movies and the movie magazines. For fifteen years, the majority of her short life, the dollar exchange shortage had prevented any Australian from visiting the United States unless on dollar-earning business. In consequence Mollie Regan had never spoken to anybody in her life who had visited America. The picture of America that had been placed before her was that of a country uninterested in simple pleasures and devoid of simple virtues, brash, over-luxurious, dissolute, ignorant, uncultured, and hagridden by gangsters.

She had accepted this picture of American life without

question; now she was having to revise it. She had found these Americans, mostly men in their late twenties or early thirties, to be simple and unaffected people. Half of them did not drink at all, all were generous to a degree that she had seldom met before, and it had not escaped her wondering notice that the only book in Stanton Laird's tent had been a Bible. She did not understand their work, but it was quite clear that they were highly educated people and very competent in the outback, strange though it was to them. Her mother had offered to do their washing and they came in with that every other day, and to collect their mail; apart from that they had not asked for anything, and needed no help at all from Laragh Station. Their equipment was superb, but she could not hold that against them; if they were clever enough to invent a shower that ran for three minutes on a gallon of water they were not to be despised for the achievement. Physically they were very like the people that she was accustomed to see on the movies, and they had the same sort of names, but in behaviour they seemed totally different, and a great deal nicer. Especially their leader, Stanton Laird.

David Cope, coming to Laragh to meet Spinifex Joe next mail day, found the verandah table littered with American magazines, and Mollie deeply engrossed in them. 'The things they have!' she said. 'Look, there's a toaster that makes the toast pop up and turns itself off when it's done! Isn't that a good idea?'

'You can get those in Perth,' he said.

'Not like that – where they pop up and turn themselves off.'

'Yes, you can.' He named the make. 'I'm not sure that they're not made in Australia.'

He convinced her in the end about the toaster. She said, 'Well, look at these sheets. They're made with a sort of pocket that the mattress tucks into.'

He grinned. 'You can get those, too,' he said.

'Oh, David, you can't! I know you can't.'

'You can.' He told her the name of the shop.

'Well, anyway, you can't get a car like *that* in Perth.'

He laughed. 'I don't suppose you can in America, either. I should say the artist's had a go at it.'

'He hasn't,' she informed him. 'I asked Stan, and he said an Oldsmobile really was just like that.'

He had to accept defeat about the car. He picked up one of the magazines and leafed it through, a little enviously. 'I believe we've got most of these things,' he said. 'Not the big cars or the television of course, but most of the rest. But they do advertise them well, don't they?'

She was unconvinced. 'I don't believe you can get half these things here in Australia,' she said. 'I think they're beaut.'

Presently the mail was sorted, and it was time for him to get back to Lucinda. 'What about the movies?' he inquired. 'Mannahill on Saturday?'

'Some of the Americans are going,' she said. 'They're coming here at about four o'clock to pick us up. I don't know who'll be going over from here. I told Stan to come through with his party and have a cup of tea, and we'd go on after that. You'd better join up with us here, David, and we'll all go on together.'

He hesitated for a moment. 'All right.'

Back at the oil site the Americans were now paying a great deal of attention to the land around the gas seepage in the cemetery. They spent some days examining the surface outcrops and correlating them, so far as they were able, with the more detailed knowledge they had gained of the sub-surface structure round their camp, three miles to the north. It was evident to them that the strata underneath the cemetery ran up in a gentle fold to the north end, but they had no means on the surface of estimating the extent of this fold, or the amount of gas or oil that might be trapped in it. In the circumstances there was only one logical course for them to pursue.

'We'll have to run a line of shot holes right across, 'n take some seismic readings,' Stanton said. 'The only thing is, I don't know that we've got the right to go in there.'

99

'Hell,' said Spencer Rasmussen, 'who's to stop us?'

'It doesn't belong to Laragh Station now. It belongs to the Shire.'

'All the better. They don't take no interest in it.'

'I guess we'd better get permission from the Shire Office.'

The Shire Office was in a little town called Yantaringa about a hundred and seventy miles to the north of them; it boasted a hotel with three dormitory bedrooms, a store, an airstrip, and sixty-three citizens. Spencer Rasmussen grumbled a good deal, but drove over one day in the jeep, arriving in the metropolis after eight hours' hard driving. The Shire Clerk, he found, was also the storekeeper, Clerk to the Justices, Shell agent, aerodrome manager, postman, and registrar of births, deaths, and marriages.

Spencer Rasmussen explained his business. 'Aw, look,' said the Shire Clerk. 'Do what you like so long as you don't disturb the Chinaman.'

'We'll be operating at the other end, more than half a mile away from the grave.'

'Good-oh. You won't wake him up.'

Spencer Rasmussen got into his jeep and drove a hundred and seventy miles back in a fury. Next day the Americans moved up towards the cemetery and commenced to drill a line of six shot holes in a position laid down to a yard by Stanton Laird, the last two of which were within the cemetery area. To run their big trucks in they removed a section of the nominal, single-strand, barbed wire fence.

While they were doing this a half-caste on a horse appeared out of the blue, herding half a dozen sheep before him on some obscure mustering errand. This was Joseph Plunkett, one of Pat's sons by the Countess Markievicz. He waved to them and reined in, smiling broadly, and exchanged a few words with Hank, accepting a cigarette. He stayed with them for an hour, watching the drilling in progress, and then remounted, gathered his sheep together from their grazing in the cemetery, and made off over the horizon with his little flock, singing as he rode.

At Laragh Station that evening, in the forum of the

station store, sitting on the floor or on the boxes drinking rum out of enamelled pannikins, the men discussed this new development. 'Aren't they the queer fellows?' asked Pat Regan. 'It's a strange thing that with all the length and breadth of Australia laid out before them, they must choose a cemetery to make their holes.'

'It will bring them no luck,' said Tom soberly. 'No luck at all. No good ever came to men who desecrate a cemetery.' There was a long silence while his words sank in. 'Ye remember the strongpoint in Kilgorran cemetery made by the English – the curse of Cromwell on them?'

'I do so,' said Pat. 'We had them destroyed entirely. James Doherty crept up beneath the wall and threw in two grenades. There was only two of them not killed or wounded, and they lepping the walls like mountain goats till the rifles got them. No good ever came of desecrating a cemetery.'

'Sure,' said Tom, 'only the Black and Tans or the Americans would think to do a thing like that.'

The Judge stirred. 'How very right you are,' he said quietly. 'God's acre has to be protected from unscrupulous and thoughtless men. I take it that the cemetery is clearly marked?'

'Wasn't there a fine board painted with the name, unless it's blown down or somebody has taken it to make a fire,' said Pat. 'I painted it with these same hands, not more than eight years back.'

'I saw it last summer. It was still there then,' said Tom. 'And a fine strand of barbed wire, hardly rusty even, all around.'

The Judge said gravely,

> *Yet even these bones from insult to protect*
> *Some frail memorial still erected nigh,*
> *With uncouth rhymes and shapeless sculpture decked,*
> *Implores the passing tribute of a sigh.'*

'That's a lovely piece of poetry,' said Pat Regan. 'A lovely, lovely piece.' He savoured it. ' "Implores the passing tribute of a sigh." ' He reached out for the rum bottle and poured about two inches into the Judge's pannikin. 'The loveliest piece this side of the black stump.'

The Judge took the rum and shot it down, following it with a pannikin of water. 'It is a very dreadful thing that the cupidity of man should reach out to disturb the dead,' he said. 'The greed for money is a terrible obsession.'

'It will bring no luck,' said Tom. 'It's destroyed that we'll all be, we and they together.'

'What would you think, now,' asked Pat Regan, 'if we were to write a letter and tell Father Ryan the way they're digging up the dead?'

Tom replied, 'He'd say that he'd have nought to do with you while you were living in mortal sin.'

'Sure, and I know he would. He's been saying that the last sixteen years, and Father O'Connor before him. But would he not pay attention to a sacrilege?'

'It's not his sacrilege. He never blessed it, because he wouldn't come on to the station.'

'Sure, someone must have blessed it. Would the Protestants have blessed it, would you say?'

Tom Regan spat. 'I wouldn't know what the heathen would be after doing.'

The Judge said, 'God speaks in divers ways, in divers centuries. In ages past He spoke through the mouths of the prophets. In these times He speaks through the mouths of the common people of the country. God will not suffer His word to be mocked, nor the faithful to be disturbed in their eternal rest.'

It was several days before Spinifex Joe arrived in his semi-trailer to take the mail, and the Geraldton *Advocate* was published only once a week, so that it was nearly three weeks before the startled populace of Geraldton learned from the correspondence column what was going on within five hundred miles of them. Then they read,

Sir,
In these troubled times a voice raised in an endeavour

to protect the simple decencies of Christian life may be, indeed, a voice crying in the wilderness. Yet I have confidence that when the readers of the *Advocate* learn of an act of desecration carried out in their vicinity they will rise up in their wrath and sweep away the wrongdoers.

In the Shire of Yantaringa, in a district seldom visited by newspaper correspondents, there is a cemetery. If judged by the number of burials it is not large; indeed, in numbers it is even smaller than that most famous cemetery of all time, Stoke Poges where Thomas Gray wrote his immortal Elegy. God's Acre, however, is not to be judged by numbers or by size; an act of desecration is unaltered by the numbers of the graves.

It is unfortunate that this small island of the Christian faith lies in the path of Topex Exploration Incorporated, an American company now carrying out explorations for mineral oil resources by arrangement with the Government of West Australia. No doubt the Americans look upon these matters in a different way from those of us who are blessed by membership of the British Commonwealth. Be that as it may, the fact remains that drilling operations to find oil are now going on within the precincts of the cemetery, to the undying shame of every citizen of West Australia. There are imponderable verities, the true foundations of our faith, more valuable than oil.

Can nothing be done to throw back the forces of cupidity and evil in their onward march?

I am, sir,

Pro Bono Publico.

The Editor of the *Advocate* was well aware that his readers liked the correspondence column, and he did his best to keep it interesting for them. A certain Judy Halloran, aged twenty, had recently inserted in his paper an announcement of her engagement to Ted McKie, which had seemed innocuous enough till her mother had written in a fury to say that Judy wasn't engaged to anyone, least of all to Ted McKie. He had printed that letter, and Judy's answer to her mother, and had carried on the dispute for some weeks with a noticeable rise in circulation till the correspondence had terminated with a final shot from Judy on her twenty-first birthday. Since then the column had been in the doldrums, so that the letter from PRO BONO PUBLICO came as a refreshing breeze. He checked the facts with a call to the Shire Clerk of Yantaringa, and put it in the paper.

It caused a minor rumpus, and then raised a laugh. The letter was picked up by the Perth *Observer*, and the editor rang Mr Colin Spriggs, the Topex manager in Perth. Mr Spriggs knew that Stanton Laird and his crew had got permission to take seismic readings in a cemetery, but was under the impression that the cemetery was disused. He promised to get further details without delay, and the editor agreed to hold the story.

Mr Spriggs spoke to Stanton Laird that evening, faintly, by long-distance telephone and Flying Doctor radio. It took him some time to get the full story of Yantaringa cemetery because at first he did not believe the words he heard and assumed that the faint line was distorting the message. When he at last put down the receiver he sat for a few moments in puzzled thought. In his younger days he had seen service in Central Arabia, Venezuela, and in Canada, but he had never struck one quite like this before. He was very conscious that he was a stranger in a strange land, and that it was necessary for him to behave with circumspection.

He picked up the receiver again, and rang up the editor. 'Say, Bob,' he said. 'I've just been talking with our geologist, Stan Laird. I guess it's partly right about the cemetery, but it's a kind of a funny story.'

'What kind of funny story?'

'Say, do you know a part of the country that they call the Lunatic?'

The other laughed. 'In the East Hammersleys?'

'That's right. This story comes from there, and I'd say it's about the only place it *could* come from.'

When they met a quarter of an hour later over a drink in the Adelphi Hotel, the editor was inclined to agree with Mr Spriggs. His reaction was that it was time that he ran another feature story on the search for oil in the outback. It seemed uncertain if the Yantaringa cemetery was consecrated ground or not and so he killed the story, but a gas seepage in a new district was news in an oil-starved Australia whether it was consecrated or not. He asked Mr Spriggs if he had any objection if he were to send up a reporter and a photographer. Mr Spriggs had none.

The two newspaper men came to the Lunatic from Perth in a Land Rover in four days of hard travelling. They reached Laragh Station about midday on their last leg to the Topex camp, and were invited to stay to dinner by Mrs Regan and Mollie. Pat and the half-caste boys were away out on the property, but Tom was there, and the Judge appeared at the lunch table. The newspaper men said nothing about the cemetery but made small talk about the weather, the chance of rain, and the ram sales. They found conversation with Tom Regan while he was pre-occupied with his dinner to be an uphill job, but the Judge was more forthcoming.

'I have sometimes found it in my heart to envy you gentlemen of the Press,' he said. 'So great an influence is yours. And yet, I suppose that your responsibilities must weigh upon you very heavily at times.'

Phil Patterson, the photographer, felt that some confirmatory interjection was required, and so he said, 'Too right.'

'Indeed, I am sure that it must be so. To lay down your pen and read again the words that you have written with such anxious care, changing a colon for a semi-colon here, a comma there – and then to reflect that the words which you have written will take the wings of Ariel and fly around the world, changing the lives, perhaps of unseen people in Natal, of unknown people in Hong Kong or Somerset. It must take great courage, sometimes, to put forth the message from your desk.'

Duncan Mann, the reporter, thought of the drunk-in-charge stories, the bathing-beauty stories, and the New-Australian stabbing stories that were his daily work, and repressed a smile. 'The editor takes most of that responsibility,' he said.

'Indeed. I should have thought of that.' He turned and breathed rum at them with great charm. 'I am afraid that I am very ignorant of the newspaper world.'

Mr Mann laughed. 'Perhaps that's the best way.' He paused, and then said, 'Are you the book-keeper here, sir?' He wondered why he had added the 'sir'.

'Book-keeper and schoolmaster, book-keeper and schoolmaster. I sometimes fear my book-keeping is not all it might be, but Michael is a tower of strength. Yes, a very tower of strength. But schoolmaster – that I am. I know my limitations, and I know my capabilities. I can teach boys and girls, of any age – anything.'

Duncan Mann felt queerly that he was on to something big, but there was no story that he could see. 'Was Michael one of your pupils?' he asked. He wrinkled his brows. 'That wouldn't be Michael Regan, down in Perth?'

'Indeed he is. Michael Regan was one of my first pupils when I came here. A very gifted boy, very, very gifted. He should have been a mathematician, but he became a chartered accountant.'

The reporter recalled the accountant; he must be close on thirty years old, he thought. 'You must have been here a long time,' he said.

'Twenty years,' the Judge said. 'Twenty years next March. It does not seem a long time, but I suppose it is.'

Phil Patterson said, 'I suppose you get away sometimes for a holiday.'

The Judge shook his head. 'I fear that I am growing just a little old for holidays,' he replied. 'I went to Perth in 1944, but I did not find it very satisfactory.' In fact, he had been drunk for three days, had spent a night in the cooler, and had been fined a pound. 'I find it more comfortable to live quietly here.'

'It's ten years since you left the property?' asked Duncan Mann.

'Oh dear no. Mr Rogerson at Mannahill puts on an exhibition of cinema films on Saturdays, and we go frequently to that. Sometimes I go with Mr Regan to the ram sales at Onslow. But for the most part I live quietly here, teaching the children.'

'How many children do you teach?'

'Thirty-two, at the moment.'

'All coloured?'

'All but two. There was a time when I first came here when I had as many as nine white children from this property and two more from Lucinda, and a great number of half-castes. But we are all growing old here now, and there are fewer white children, and correspondingly more half-castes and full-bloods. They differ in their abilities and their desire for education in proportion to their colour. I teach Euclid and Euripides to the white children, carpentry and harness-making to the full-bloods, and a little of each to the half-castes. But all are equally rewarding.'

Tom Regan finished his pudding, got up from the table, muttered something unintelligible, and went out of the door. The others followed him. The Judge bade a courtly good-bye to the reporters and went off to the store; for the moment the two newspaper men were left alone on the verandah.

'Well, anyway,' muttered Duncan Mann to his companion, 'we know who Pro Brono Publico is now.'

Mrs Regan and Mollie came out on the verandah. The newspaper men thanked them for their hospitality, and said that they must get going now to the Americans' camp.

'Och, that's nothing,' said Mrs Regan. 'Come in again on your way back to Perth. Ye wouldn't rather sleep here and go out to them from here? It's only about fifteen miles.'

Duncan Mann said, 'I did think of that. It's very kind of you, but we've got stretchers and blankets in the truck, and Mr Spriggs said they could put us up in camp. It's probably better for them if we talk after dark. We don't want to interrupt their work.'

'As you wish.'

'Tell me, how do we get there?'

'Ye see the shearing shed? Well, out past that ye'll see the wheel tracks on the ground. Ye follow them for fourteen miles, and then ye'll find the cemetery and the gate into Lucinda. Turn north along the fence about three or four miles, and there's the camp. Ye can't mistake it.'

Mollie said, 'I'd better go with them, Ma. It's not very easy for a stranger.'

The newspaper men protested that they could find their way, but Mrs Regan approved the idea. 'Take her along,' she said drily. 'It might save sending out a search party. The boys out there, they'll drive her back tonight.'

'I'll get some ice cream, too,' the girl said. She went off and changed into drill slacks and shirt, and got into the Land Rover, and went off with the men.

When they got to the cemetery the reporter stopped the car, and sat looking at it. 'So that's it,' he said.

She was a little surprised at their interest. 'There's nobody buried there,' she remarked. 'Only the Chinaman.'

'The Chinaman?'

She told them what she knew about the cemetery, which was not very much; she had never taken a great deal of interest in it. Presently they drove on to the Americans' camp.

Stanton Laird came out to meet them as they drove up. She made the introductions, and they went into the office tent out of the sun.

Duncan Mann said, 'I'll tell you what we've come about, Mr Laird. There was a letter published in the Geraldton *Advocate* that said that you'd been drilling in a cemetery. We came to the conclusion there was nothing in that story, and my editor killed it when he'd talked about it with your Mr Spriggs. What did interest us was this news of a gas seepage you'd discovered, which came out while my editor was talking to Mr Spriggs. Now that's real news, here in

108

Australia. My editor thought he'd better send us up to write a feature or two on what you're doing here, take a few photographs, too.'

The geologist nodded. 'That's okay,' he said. 'I did hear there'd been a letter. Do you know what was in it?'

'I've got it here.' The reporter pulled out his wallet, extracted a cutting, and spread it out upon the drawing board for them to read.

Stanton Laird said slowly, 'Well, what do you know!'

The girl said, 'Oh, Stan!'

The geologist asked the reporter, 'Do you know who wrote this?'

Duncan Mann smiled broadly. 'We've just had dinner at Miss Regan's homestead. I might make a guess.'

The girl said, 'He shouldn't have done it. He gets a sort of bee in his bonnet sometimes. I'm so sorry, Stan.'

The geologist smiled. 'That's okay, Mollie. He didn't mean any harm.' He turned to the reporters. 'I guess it was kind of unusual to go running seismic soundings through a cemetery, but we did get permission. We were only on the ground three days. We made eight holes in the area about half a mile away from the grave – the only grave there is – 'n set off a pound of gelignite in each. And then we did a few more outside.'

Mr Mann said, 'We're not reporting this, Mr Laird. My editor was definite on that. It's off the record. But while we're talking about it, do you know if it was consecrated ground?'

'I reckon not. There's nothing religious on the notice, and they didn't tell us anything at Yantaringa.'

The reporter glanced down at the letter. 'He doesn't say specifically that it was consecrated ground, although he talks about desecration. Maybe that's just a way of writing like he thinks. In any case, it doesn't matter; the story's dead.' He turned to the geologist. 'This gas seepage, though – *that* story's not dead. Can you tell us anything about that, Mr Laird?'

'Why, certainly.' The geologist turned back the cover

sheet and exposed his plans and diagrams upon the drawing board. He started to explain the layout of the strata to Mr Mann. Phil Patterson, the photographer, attended for a minute or two, and then moved back, unpacked his camera and equipment from their black leather case, and took a couple of flashlight photographs of the men as they talked at the drawing board. The girl moved away, not wanting to be in the story, and went and drank a Coke with Ted in the cook tent.

All afternoon Stanton and Spencer were busy with the journalists. They drove them out and showed them the terrain, both in the region of the big limestone outcrop and in the region of the cemetery. In the fading light they sniffed at the gas seepage. It was arranged that the visitors should stay in the Americans' camp and take a series of photographs next day, probably leaving for the south again in their Land Rover in a couple of days' time. In the fading light they offered to drive Mollie back to Laragh.

'That's okay,' said Stanton. 'I'll run her back home after supper.' He turned to the girl. 'You'll stay for supper, Mollie?' He smiled. 'We're on maple ice cream, regular, this week.'

'I'd love to,' she said. She wanted to be driven home by Stanton, because the Judge's misdemeanour was very much on her mind. She ate her stewed steak with hot cakes, her peach pie and ice cream, with a pre-occupied mind, and drank her coffee thoughtfully. Somehow she must let him know that at Laragh they really did appreciate the Americans, in spite of what the Judge had said in his letter.

She sat in thought while he drove her home in the jeep, not knowing how to broach the subject that she wanted to discuss; moreover the oil men's jeep had seen hard service. It rattled over the unmade track with a shovel and a couple of chains banging about in the back, and the dust swirled round her, making conversation difficult if not impossible. When they topped the last low rise and the white roof of the shearing shed appeared in the bright moonlight a mile ahead of them, she felt she had to do something.

She said, 'Stan, stop here a minute. I want to talk.'

He pulled up and switched off the motor. 'Kind of difficult to talk in this jeep.'

'I know,' she said. 'Stan, it's about the Judge. He's not really like that, you know.'

He smiled down at her. 'Don't think of it,' he said. 'He didn't do us any harm.'

'That's not the point,' she said. 'I wouldn't like you to think that he was trying to do you any harm. He's English, you know. He's awfully English, although he's been here so long. I should think in a country like England every cemetery must be full of bodies, and consecrated and all that. He'd think of it as making an oil well all in among the tombstones.'

'Wouldn't he have seen it?'

'Oh, I shouldn't think so. He can't ride a horse, and he doesn't often go out on the station. I don't suppose he's ever seen it in his life.'

He glanced at her. 'Mind if I ask something?'

She looked up at him. 'No.'

'Is he a bit nuts?'

She shook her head. 'He's got a very clear mind. He's a wonderful teacher, you know. All of us, when we left here to go to school, we were really interested in getting to know things. We wanted to do lessons. We just shot ahead of all the other kids in school. It's all because of how he started us.' She paused. 'He gets a bit confused sometimes, but that's just the rum.'

He laughed. 'If I drank that much rum I'd be confused all the time.'

She looked up in surprise. 'He doesn't drink a great deal. Daddy drinks twice as much.'

'That's what I can't figure out,' he said. 'Back home, if any person drank like people drink out there, he'd be right on the skids. But this is a good property. Everybody I speak to tells me that Laragh's a station that's well run. I can see that for myself, even though I don't know the first thing about sheep. It just doesn't make sense to me.'

She recalled the advertisements of whisky in the American magazines that he had lent her. 'Americans aren't all teetotal, are they?'

'The States is a big country,' he said. 'I come from a small town in the West. Back home where I come from we don't drink alcohol at all, hardly. My family, they don't, and none of our friends, either. I guess it's different in the Eastern States, and in the cities.'

'I don't drink it, either,' she said. 'I don't like it much. Most station people drink round here. I think perhaps we may drink more than most, at Laragh.'

'You don't think it hurts?'

She shook her head. 'Ma cuts it down when she thinks they've had enough. Daddy and Uncle Tom do what Ma tells them.' She turned to him. 'Ma knows about the grog. She was a barmaid before she married Uncle Tom, you know.'

'I didn't know that,' he said.

'She was. She was a barmaid before she married Mr Foster, and then when he died she was a barmaid again before she married Uncle Tom. Ma knows all about men and drink. That's probably got something to do with it.'

'I guess it might have.' He turned to her. 'You know what?' he said. 'I always thought Mr Pat Regan was your father.'

'He is,' she said. 'I suppose we're rather a difficult family for strangers to understand. You see, after Mike and Charlie and Bridget were born, Ma and Uncle Tom didn't get on very well together, so Ma left Uncle Tom and married Daddy. It makes us rather a complicated family, but that's how it happened.'

He blinked. 'Didn't that make things kind of difficult? I mean, did they just go on here together, just the same?'

She laughed. 'I don't know, Stan. I wasn't born. It seems to have worked out all right. Only, of course, Father Ryan says that Ma and Dad aren't married. We're all Micks here, you know.'

He blinked again. 'Didn't they get married?'

'They can't, because we can't get a divorce. Father Ryan says Ma's still married to Uncle Tom, but of course that's not right. It's all a bit of a muddle.'

He smiled. 'I'd say it might be. They didn't have a civil marriage, or anything like that?'

'I shouldn't think so,' she said. 'You'd have to go to Perth for that, wouldn't you?'

'Maybe. I wouldn't know.'

'I'll ask Ma sometime. I shouldn't think they did, though. It's over a thousand miles.'

He nodded. 'Quite a way.' He sat for a moment looking out over the rolling downs of spinifex. 'I'm mightily glad you told me all of this,' he said. 'It kind of helps to get the picture straight – about the Judge and all that.'

She said, 'We're a kind of a muddled up family, I suppose, if you include the Countess and her sons.' She looked up at him a little wistfully. 'Does it all seem very terrible to you, Stan?'

She was very appealing to him in that moment. 'Not a bit terrible,' he said. 'It's just kind of different from things at home. But then, the whole country's so different.'

'People don't live like we do in America?'

'No,' he repeated. 'Everything's quite different back home.'

'But you've got a lot of empty country, with big stations like we have, haven't you?'

He shook his head. 'We've got nothing like this country. Back home there'd be roads all over, and little towns every so often, with a few stores and a movie theatre and a church, maybe. It's all quite different.'

'Do we seem like a lot of savages to you, Stan?'

He turned to her. 'I guess people are the same all over.' He smiled down at her gently in the dim light. 'If you wore pedal-pushers instead of these long pants you'd be just the same as any girl in my home town. Only a whole lot prettier than most.'

She drew a little closer to him in the jeep, and when his arm slipped round her shoulders she did not protest. 'Tell me about your home town, Stan,' she said. 'What's it called, and where is it?'

He told her, and she said, 'What's it like in Hazel? Is it like Carnavon, or like Geraldton?'

He shook his head. 'It's not like either of those. It's sort of cleaner, and more dignified.' He began to tell her about the home town that he loved so well, the mountains and the pastures and the rivers full of trout. He told her a little about his family, a little about his father's business, a little about his friend Chuck, a little about his home. She listened entranced to the description of a new world, a world that matched the magazines she had been reading, lulled by the warm comfort of his hand upon her shoulder.

'It must be marvellous to live there,' she said. 'I wonder you can bear to leave it and come away to places like Australia.'

He smiled. 'I guess Australia's not so bad as that,' he said. 'But I'd say this is probably my last assignment outside the States.' He went on to tell her of the offer that his father had made him; it was an easing and a relief to talk it over with the girl. 'I think I'll be writing to the old man pretty soon, 'n say that I'll be joining him next year.'

Presently she stirred in his arms. 'It's getting pretty late, Stan,' she said. 'I love hearing you talk about America, but don't let's start anything with Ma or Daddy.'

He laughed and released her. 'I'd just as soon not start anything with your father.'

She wriggled her shirt straight upon her shoulders. 'One thing, Stan,' she said. 'Why do you say that you'll be joining your father next year? Why not now, if he wants you to help him?'

'We got to make a hole first.'

'Here?'

'Uh-huh. It's just a question now of fixing the exact location. I'd say we'd have the drilling rig up here within a month. I couldn't go away until we've drilled the well.'

He started the motor and drove her to the homestead. She got out, and turned to bid him goodnight. 'It was awfully nice of you to drive me home,' she said. 'Thanks so much.'

'You know somethin'?' he inquired. 'I'm kind of glad I haven't got to go away at once.'

'So am I,' she said.

He raised his hand. ''Bye now.' The jeep vanished in a swirl of dust in the night air.

FIVE

In the next few weeks the oil activity on Laragh Station increased enormously. Great trailer trucks began to come through, manned mostly by Australians, bringing huge loads of the components of prefabricated buildings, pre-drilled girders for the great tower of the oil rig, tanks, pumps, diesel engines, cement, pipes, cooking stoves, beds and furniture, cases of foodstuffs, drums of diesel oil, great quantities of earth for drilling mud imported from America, and everything else needed for a camp of nearly a hundred very highly paid men about to drill a hole that might be two miles deep.

All this was normal to the Americans, a routine that they had been through many times before. Even the camp plan was normal to them; the cookhouse and messroom went here, the recreation room there, the showers and toilets here, the septic tank there, the two rows of two-bed cabins here, the office there. The camp was the same camp that they had made from Texas to Palembang; if you knew the camp at Abu Quaiyah you could walk blindfold in the camp on Laragh Station. In consequence it all went up incredibly quickly, because the key men knew exactly where each bit had to go.

To the Regans the growth of the camp was little short of magical. One week there was nothing there but the tents of the survey party; a fortnight later the place seemed full of houses and a party were laying a pipeline to the nearest bore at the rate of about a mile a day; a fortnight after that there were eighty or ninety men accommodated in the camp erecting the steel tower of the rig and installing pumps and tanks and diesel engines.

'Sure,' said Pat Regan in the evening session, 'ye'd think all the devils in hell were chasing after them, biting at their tails. Aren't they the restless fellows?'

The Judge said, 'It is the greed for gold, the curse of the modern age. Avarice kills more men than any physical disease, I am afraid. These men will not make old bones.'

Tom Regan, who was worth ten times as much as any American on the site and who worked, when he worked at all, sitting in the driver's seat of a jeep or in the easy chair of a saddlehorse at the walk, said, 'That's a true word. They'll all be dead in ten years time. What use will all the money be to them then?'

They wagged their heads gloomily together over the perdition awaiting the avaricious Americans, and shot down another rum.

The growth of the camp was as fascinating to Mrs Regan as it was to Mollie. Most days they drove over in the jeep, with the two younger children in the back, to park on the hillside above the camp out of the way, and to watch the buildings going up. The speed with which the men worked was a continual amazement to them. 'It's what they do in America, Ma,' Mollie said, armed with the superior knowledge of her magazine-reading. 'Everybody works like that in the United States.'

'Ye'd think they'd sit a while, and drink a cup of tea or else a drop of rum,' her mother said.

'I don't believe they drink at all,' the girl said.

'They'd be better to relax a little now and then,' her mother observed. It had not escaped the notice of the ex-barmaid that the American camp was dry except on Saturday nights, when beer flowed. No hard liquor was allowed in camp at all. 'It makes for accidents,' Stanton Laird told them. 'The casualty rate is very much higher if hard liquor is allowed in camp.'

'And the dithers is much higher if it isn't,' Mrs Regan retorted. 'I've been watching that wee laddie over there. Watch him twitch – now.'

Stanton watched him, flushing a little. 'Maybe he needs a spell.'

'Maybe he needs a rum,' the barmaid retorted.

'I guess we'll have to disagree on that,' said the geologist. He hesitated for a moment, and then said, 'Mind if I ask you something, Mrs Regan?'

'Go ahead.'

'We run this camp the American way, without hard liquor, and that gives us the results we want,' he said. 'I'd appreciate it if you wouldn't give hard liquor to the boys if they come to see you at the homestead.'

The ex-barmaid thought for a moment. 'All right,' she said. 'I'll see they don't get served.'

Mollie said, 'It's going to be a bit difficult if they come back with Uncle Tom or Daddy, Stan.'

'I'll see they don't get served,' her mother repeated.

In all these new interests and excitements Mollie found that she was seeing a good deal less of David Cope than in the months before the Americans had come to Laragh. Before their arrival he had called for her nearly every week to take her to the movie show at Mannahill, but after they arrived the Americans had taken to going over in a body, welcoming Mollie and David and anybody else to join them in going to the party in one of their big trucks, which from David's point of view wasn't the same thing at all. Now with the growth of the American camp beside the drilling rig they had instituted their own movie show in the recreation room on two evenings a week, with better films than Clem Rogerson could produce and a much shorter distance to drive; moreover, the oil drillers welcomed visitors to meals at any time. Mrs Regan and Mollie fell into the habit of going to the movies there at least once a week; the men seldom came with them, preferring the slow discussion of things that they were well acquainted with to the complexities of thought induced by movies of a foreign land.

Mollie met David Cope at these American shows, and often sat with him to see the film, but the old community born of the long drives to Mannahill in his jeep had been broken. He seldom saw the girl now to speak to alone, and he was very conscious that she was seeing a good deal more of the American geologist than she was of him. The old days when he had shyly asked her for her photograph and she had shyly given it to him now seemed a long way away; with the coming of the Americans they had drifted apart, and his life was the emptier for it.

Early in February she came to the movie show alone, driving in the jeep. There was now no danger of getting lost when driving by night between the oil site and Laragh homestead, for the constant passage of big trailer trucks and the complaints of the truckers had galvanised the State of West Australia to send a couple of graders to the district to smooth out the worst potholes, so that a graded road, unmetalled but a road in very truth, now led back to the homestead. Civilisation, disturbing in its impact and its implications, was advancing on the outback in the wake of the oil search.

Stanton Laird had gone to Perth for a conference, or she would hardly have been free to talk with David Cope after the movie. She bade her hosts goodbye and thanked them for their hospitality, and walked with David to where their jeeps were parked side by side in the bright moonlight. She felt guilty about David and a little self-conscious; she did not much want to be alone with him, but there was no escaping it.

As they went, she asked him, 'How's the rain been on Lucinda?' The district was on the edge of the monsoon country and normally they got an inch or two of summer rain in January, though the bulk of their ten or twelve inches of rain fell in June.

'Not too good,' he said. 'We got about ninety points at the homestead.' He meant nine-tenths of an inch. 'I think it was a bit better at the far end.'

'We did better than that,' she said. 'I think we got about

three inches. Uncle Tom says we won't get any more now.'

'You always get more than I do,' he remarked. 'It's better country.'

'It doesn't do us any good,' she said, seeking to ease the subject for him. 'It goes straight down into the ground. You never see it lying in a pool, however hard it rains. All the water that we've got comes from the bores.'

'I suppose in America,' he said a little bitterly, 'it falls straight into the sheep's mouth.'

She laughed because it seemed the best thing to do, but the implication annoyed her. 'It doesn't really,' she said. 'So far as I can make out, they run their grazing properties, their ranches, very much the same as we do. Only they seem to have a lot more water than we have, and much smaller stations.'

'Better land, in fact,' he said. 'Everything's better in America, isn't it?'

'If it is,' she said hotly, 'it's because they've worked to make it so. I've never seen men work so hard as these people, and you haven't either. They've got a lot of things against them in their country that we haven't got – snow and ice in winter. If they've got better land than we have, it's probably because they work harder.'

He nodded. 'That's right. I just sit on my arse and smoke a pipe all day.'

She softened suddenly. 'I didn't mean that personally, David. You work harder than anybody in the Lunatic. You know I didn't mean that for you.'

'That's all right,' he said. 'But I must say I get a bit tired of these Supermen.'

'Don't you admire them, though?' she asked, a little wistfully. They seemed to be drawing very far apart.

'What for?'

'I don't know – everything,' she replied. 'They *achieve* so much. Here we've been living with oil underneath our feet, all these years. *We* could have found it, but we didn't ever think of it. *We* could have done all that they're doing here, but we just aren't up to it. Then they come along and show us how Australia should be developed, and we hate their guts.'

'You don't, anyway,' he remarked.

'No, I don't,' she retorted. 'I think they're fine people. They don't drink on the job and a lot of them don't drink at all. Lots of them don't even smoke. They work hard, and they read the Bible. The only thing that people have against them is that they show us up.'

'That's not what I've got against them,' he replied. 'I don't mind them showing us up over oil, because that's not what I do. When some American comes here and shows me how to run four thousand sheep on two dud bores and does it better than I can, then I'll sit up and take notice. But that's not what they do.'

'What *have* you got against them, David?' she asked. 'Why don't you like them?'

He paused for a moment in thought. 'I think it's because they're so *ignorant*,' he said. 'Ignorant of everything outside their job. I'm no great shakes myself because I left school when I was sixteen, but I do take an interest in other things besides sheep, besides my job.'

She was silent for a moment. 'I think they do, too,' she said, but a little doubtfully. 'It's just that we don't know them well enough.'

'How many books do you think they've got in their camp?' he asked scornfully. 'Outside the Bible? A few paper-bound crime stories, perhaps, and a lot of glossy magazines. But how many real books, bound books, books that you'd want to read again in ten years time?'

'I don't think they'd bring books to a camp like this in a strange country,' she said slowly. 'They may have them at home.'

'I bet they haven't.'

'Books aren't everything, anyway,' she said.

'That's exactly what they are, so far as I can see,' he retorted. 'If you want to learn anything, you've got to turn to books – unless you like to take it from the radio. And even the Americans can't get much joy out of the reception here.' He paused. 'That one – the manager – Spencer Rasmussen – he was round at my place last week looking at that book of modern French art. You know – the one I got from home last year with all the oil paintings, in colours.' She nodded. 'I said something about Matisse. He thought I said mattress. God knows, I don't know much about oil paintings, but I do take an interest.'

'It's probably not his line, David,' she said.

'What *is* his line?' he asked. 'The live Theatre? Poetry? Sculpture? World Politics? Music?'

'Music,' she said. 'He plays the accordion.'

'I'll give you that one,' he said slowly. 'He does like music. Dance music. He goes all classical and highbrow sometimes and plays *South Pacific* – that's about the top end of his range. But he does like music, and he makes it for himself. I'll give you that one.'

'He's probably got a lot of other interests that you don't know about, David,' she said. 'Be fair.'

'He pitches horseshoes,' he remarked. 'A lot of them do that. They brought the horseshoes with them from America.'

She smiled. 'How do you pitch horseshoes?' she inquired. 'How's it played?'

'I don't know,' he said. 'Hit them with a baseball bat, for all I know.'

'Anyway,' she said, 'Spencer Rasmussen *is* keen on music.'

'That's right. Ask him to play a bit of Beethoven on his accordion and see what happens.'

She was suddenly angry with him. 'I'm going home,' she said. 'You're just looking for any excuse to pick on them, to run them down. I think they're straight, decent people. They've brought a bit of America into the Lunatic and it's done us all good. We've even got a road because of them. If they find this oil there'll be a town here some day – a real town, with shops and hairdressers and cafés and picture theatres and a church or two. That's what they're doing for us in the Lunatic, and we ought to be grateful. But all we do is to sneer at them, and run them down.'

'I don't run them down,' he said. 'I never say a word to anyone about them. I'm very glad they're here and doing what they are. It's very good for all the rest of us. It's only when you start to run them up and talk of them as Supermen that I get a bit riled.'

'I never talk of them as Supermen,' she said hotly.

'Yes, you do.'

'No, I don't. You're just making that up in order to be nasty about them.'

He grinned at her. 'I think perhaps we'd better change the subject.'

'I think we had.'

'Mind if I ask something? About something quite different.'

'What is it?'

He folded his arms and leaned back against the mudguard of the jeep. 'Will you marry me?'

She stared at him, astonished and deflated. 'Of course not. If that's a joke, David, it's a pretty poor one.'

'It's not a joke,' he said. 'I'm serious.'

'But, David – you can't be!' Where was the soft music, the gentle touch that she had read about in books and seen so often on the movies? David must know the drill; he too had read the books and seen the movies. He couldn't really be serious, but if he was, he wasn't going to get away with that.

'I'm quite serious,' he said quietly. 'I'd have asked you six months ago, but for the fact I thought I'd probably be going broke this year. Lucinda's not the best property in Australia, or even in the Lunatic. I've been in love with you for a long time, as well you know.'

She dropped her eyes. He had never tried to kiss her, or spoken the soft words of love that she had thrilled to read about; their conversation, when it touched on sex, had been of ewes with twins or impotence in rams. He hadn't played the game according to the book for reasons of his own that seemed to her of trivial importance, yet he was quite right: she had known that he had been in love with her.

To gain time she asked, 'What made you ask me now, then? Is Lucinda looking up?'

'I don't think it is,' he said. 'In fact, at the moment it's looking down. If we'd had another sixty points last month it would have made a difference.'

'Then what made you ask me now, David?'

He grinned at her. 'Just to remind you I'm still here.'

'Because I've been going about with the Americans?'

'I suppose so.'

'Oh, David!' She felt at a loss, not knowing what to do. She valued David Cope, but wider horizons were opening before her, horizons that led across the Pacific to the countries of the glossy Kodachromes in the big magazines she had been reading. She knew from her half-brother Michael that money was no barrier to a Regan if she wished to travel half across the world, and it was understood that she would go to England, France, and Italy before very long. A daring notion that had occurred to her which she had not mentioned to anybody yet, that on her way home from England she might visit the United States and see with her own eyes the country of the *Saturday Evening Post* and *Cosmopolitan*. She had friends and contacts in America now, the families of Hank and Ted and Tex, and, most of all, of Stanton Laird. She valued David Cope and she respected him for his achievement, but all this had to be balanced against life at Lucinda with sheep dying all around beside the waterholes for lack of feed, and myriads of blowflies, and a rusty kerosene refrigerator that smoked and smelt of hot oil.

'I'm not marrying anybody yet,' she said. 'I suppose some day I'll want to get married and settle down, but that's not now. I don't know why you asked me this now, David, and I'm rather sorry that you did. Because the answer's going to be, no.'

He had expected nothing else, but her words gave him pain. 'I thought you'd say that,' he replied, a little bitterly. 'Well, let's forget it.'

'Why *did* you ask me now, then?' she inquired. 'Whatever made you do it, if you thought I'd say no?'

'Because I thought I'd have even a worse chance if I waited till next month,' he replied.

'I don't know why you should have thought that,' she retorted. 'I just don't want to marry anyone, now or next month or any time. As soon as Elspeth gets through college, in a year from now, I want to go to England.'

He said nothing, and they stood in silence for a minute. 'It's all right for you,' she said. 'You've travelled about the world. You know what England's like, but I don't. You've been to France. I want to go to France, and Italy, too. You've been to other places, and seen how other people live. I've only seen Perth. I want to see what happens in the rest of the world, outside the Lunatic.'

It was in his mind to say that she wanted to see America, but he had the good sense not to. He stood with her in the moonlight very conscious of her, slim and straight beside him. 'I suppose that's reasonable,' he said reluctantly, at last.

'Of course it's reasonable,' she said. 'There's another thing, too.'

'What's that?'

'I wouldn't want to marry you, David. Not that I don't like you. But we'd fight like cat and dog, right from the word go.'

'I don't think we would.'

'I'm quite sure we would. We were fighting like cat and dog only a minute ago.'

'That's different. That was over the Americans.'

'If it wasn't the Americans it would be something else. We don't get on well enough to marry, David. It wouldn't work.' She paused. 'There's only one reason why you asked me to marry you.'

'What's that?'

'Because I'm the only girl here in the Lunatic, just at the moment.'

That stung him. 'If that's all you think of me, we'd better cut this short,' he said.

'I didn't mean to be nasty,' she said gently. 'I didn't really, David. It cuts both ways, you know. If I married you, I suppose it would be for the same reason, because there aren't so many young men in this part of the country. But that's not the right way to set about a thing like marrying. One might make a terrible mistake that way. And I'm a Catholic; when I marry, I marry for good.'

'I suppose it's a point against me that I'm Church of England,' he said a little bitterly. 'I haven't been for the last three years, but I don't suppose that matters.'

She shook her head. 'That wouldn't worry me,' she said. 'I suppose we aren't very strict at Laragh. But I certainly wouldn't marry anyone unless I was absolutely sure that it was going to last.'

'I *am* sure,' he said.

She looked at him doubtfully, a little shaken by the conviction in his voice. 'You can't possibly be,' she said. 'How many girls have you met in the last three years, David? Really met, I mean, to talk to like this?'

He was silent. 'Not very many,' he said reluctantly at last.

She nodded. 'You ought to get away from here,' she said. 'Get away for a holiday, David – go down to Perth, go to dances and parties and get to know some girls.' She smiled at him. 'If you did that and still wanted to marry me, perhaps I'd take it as a compliment. More than I do now.'

'It was meant as one.'

'I know it was, David. It was very sweet of you. But the answer's no, just the same.'

They stood in silence for a long time. At last he said, 'Well, that puts the lid on it. I suppose you'd rather that we didn't go on meeting?'

She thought for a moment, reluctant to break off the friendship. 'I'd be sorry if that happened,' she said, 'but it's up to you. So long as you can realize that I'm not marrying you or anybody else for a long time, I don't see why we shouldn't meet. There aren't so many people of our age here in the Lunatic. But if you think it's not going to work out, we'll have to give it away.'

'Okay,' he said heavily, 'we'll leave it like that.' He turned towards his jeep.

'Goodnight, David,' she said in a small voice. 'I'm terribly sorry.'

They got into their jeeps, the starters groaned, and the jeeps moved off towards the track beside the fence, David following in her dust. They parted where the tracks diverged beside the cemetery, and the girl drove home along the graded road to Laragh. In the moonlight at the homestead she parked the jeep in the yard, and went down the verandah to her room. She went to bed troubled and upset, conscious that she had done the right thing, distressed for the pain that she had caused, uneasy that she might conceivably have made a great mistake. It was some time before she slept.

At Lucinda, David hardly slept at all. Towards dawn he fell into a restless slumber, but he was roused at seven by his aboriginal housekeeper, who said Jackie was waiting to see him. Jackie was his half-caste overseer, who brought him a report of fifteen sheep dead around the No 2 bore with fifteen hundred others looking on and not looking too good. One of the water tanks had sprung a leak and had wasted five hundred gallons in the night; most of the horses had escaped out of the horse paddock; Sammy, one of his black stockmen, wanted to go walkabout and proposed to leave that morning for an indefinite period, and his jeep had a flat tyre. He put on his clothes, went to breakfast, and discovered that the lamp of the old refrigerator had blown out and all the food in it was bad. He set about his daily work, jaded and depressed.

That afternoon he had a visitor, Mr Duncan Mann, the journalist from Perth. The photographer had returned to the head office, but Mr Mann had been instructed to stay on with the oil men to cover the erection of the oil rig, writing feature articles. He had stayed on till he had written himself dry. He had covered every aspect of the oil men's camp and work, and still no order had come through for him to return to his home in Perth. Finally, when the fifth birthday of his eldest child was drawing very near and it seemed imperative to him to get home without further delay, he had turned in a story about the pet kitten at the oil rig, an Australian kitten that was developing a taste for American hot cakes and syrup. That did it, and he received a telegram from his editor ordering him back to Perth. He drove over to Lucinda Station to say goodbye to David Cope before starting off in his Land Rover on the journey home at dawn next day.

A little ashamed of his kitten story, it had occurred to him that David Cope might make a feature article – *British Boy Managers in the Far North*, perhaps. Over a cup of tea he set himself to draw David out, and David was so miserable, and the journalist worked with such skill, that David never realized that he was being interviewed at all. He told Mr Mann all about his upbringing upon the farm, about the requisition of their land, about their emigration and the farm at Armadale. Mr Mann, warming to the story, quietly resolved to go and see the family at Armadale, and set to work to draw David out about his father. The fact that he had served at Gallipoli in 1915 made a close and obvious tie with the Australian forces, greatly strengthening the story from Mr Mann's point of view, and he asked one or two questions designed to find out if David's father had had any previous contact with Australia before his emigration.

'I don't think so,' David said. 'He was in the Black and Tans for a time after the war.'

'What's that?' asked Mr Mann.

'In Ireland,' David said. 'It was sort of being in the police, the Royal Irish Constabulary. Only they were armed like soldiers – tanks and everything. It was a full-scale war against Sinn Fein, the Irish rebels, for a couple of years. Worse than a war, I think. Very bitter.'

'What happened in the end?' asked the journalist.

'Oh, the Irish won. They got their independence. My Dad went home and took a farm near Newbury. He often used to talk about the war in Ireland.'

'Did he consider coming to Australia then?'

'I don't think so.'

Mr Mann stayed for half an hour, bade David goodbye, wished him luck and a good rain, and went back to the oil rig for the night. He left at dawn next day and breakfasted at Laragh Station with the Regans, or rather with Pat and Tom Regan and the Judge, for Mollie and her mother had their breakfast with the children in the kitchen. Light conversation was not normally a feature of the breakfast table at Laragh and Mr Mann, who had been awake for two or three hours, found the atmosphere depressing. Thinking to raise interest and stimulate some small exchange of words, he said, 'I looked in at Lucinda yesterday afternoon and had a chat with Mr Cope. He was telling me about his father's time in Ireland.'

Tom Regan spoke for the first time that morning. 'And when would that one's father have seen in Ireland?'

'After the First War,' said Mr Mann brightly. 'He was in some sort of an armed police force, fighting the rebels.'

If his intention had been to raise interest he had certainly achieved it. There was a pregnant pause, and then Tom Regan asked, 'And what rebels would they have been?'

Mr Mann became aware suddenly that he might be skating on thin ice. 'I suppose he meant the Irish when they were fighting for independence,' he said.

Pat Regan laid down his knife and fork. 'Ye say that this was after the First War?'

'That's right.'

'And that one's father was in Ireland fighting for the English, the curse of Cromwell on them?'

'That's right.'

Tom Regan asked, 'Was it the murdering Black and Tans that that one fought in for the English?'

Mr Mann wished very much that he had not raised this subject, but there was nothing to be done about it now. 'That's right,' he said. 'Something to do with the Royal Irish Constabulary, I think. After that he took a farm in England.'

'In the Name of God!' said Pat Regan. 'Do ye sit there to tell us that one's Dad was raising up the hand of murder against poor boys fighting to drive out the English from their country, and they with nothing but a rifle or maybe a hand grenade itself to throw against machine guns in an armoured car?'

'He didn't tell me what his father was doing in Ireland,' said the journalist uncomfortably. 'I've probably got it all wrong.'

'But ye say that that one's father was in Ireland in the Black and Tans?' demanded Tom Regan.

'I think that's what he said. But it's a long time ago, and he may have got it wrong himself.'

The Judge spoke for the first time. 'It's a very long time ago,' he said. 'There is a Statute of Limitations, gentlemen, a law which states that no legal action may be initiated after a lapse of seven yeaars. I would add to that, perhaps, and say that nothing really matters after twenty years.' The quiet, even voice went on: 'I have proved that from my own experience – nothing really matters after twenty years. And these events that you are speaking of were thirty years ago, or more.'

Pat and Tom Regan sat staring at the Judge. The thought passed suddenly across the mind of the journalist that this drunken and disgraced old reprobate was no negligible man. Pat Regan said, 'There's none the like of that one for black treachery, taking the hand of kindness, and the young girl off with him to the pictures in his jeep in the dark night, and he the son of a black-hearted Black and Tan.'

The Judge said evenly, 'He is an honest and a clean lad, fit for any girl to go with. Would you like to be judged now, Mr Regan, for things your father did in politics ten years before you were born?'

There was a long silence. Then Tom Regan got up from the table and walked out without a word. Pat Regan said heavily, 'Sure, it will have me destroyed entirely,' and got up and went out after him.

Mr Mann sat in silence with the Judge for a minute. Then he said, 'I'm very sorry that I raised that subject, sir.'

'It will pass,' the Judge said. 'They live much in the past, very much in the past. But they will grow accustomed to the new idea, and they are both goodhearted men. You have no occasion to distress yourself. It will all pass.'

Mr Mann got into his Land Rover and went upon his way. It would have made a first-class feature article, but he rejected the idea.

At the end of February the oil men commenced to drill. No ceremony marked the start of the hole; as soon as their somewhat complicated equipment was installed, as they had installed it so often before, the big three-wheel drilling bit was attached to the drill collar and with no more ado the drill began to turn, the drilling mud to circulate, the spoil brought up from the hole to flow on to the screens, and Stanton Laird to inspect and examine all the particles that came up to the surface. They worked a daylight shift for the first week until the rig had settled down and all the bugs had been ironed out; then, warming to the work, they began to work the rig in shifts all through the day and night, sinking at the rate of about five feet an hour.

At the end of March, Stanton Laird got news from home which was a great blow to him. It was contained in a letter from his mother, and it read,

MY DEAR SON,

I'm afraid that what I have to tell you will be very bad news, because Chuck Sheraton was killed flying last week. Aimée came around last night and told us how it happened. It has been a terrible shock to everyone in Hazel and I am sure it will be one to you because you were such great friends with Chuck but God knows best. He was stationed at a Base called Harrisburg in Texas instructing cadets in night flying training and I suppose it was test flying or something because he was flying with another instructor a man called Ed Sparkman at night and it must have been low test flying because they collided with a train. Aimée was all broken up of course she said it was a terrible accident because the wing hit the smokestack of the locomotive and the airplane rolled up in a ball and burned beside the track right by all the people in the coaches looking on. Dan and Aimée have gone down to Texas she never did like flying and I suppose this put her off so they went by the Limited and get in Thursday morning so that they'll arrive too late for the interment but I'd say that's a good thing it was such a terrible accident and they'll be able to make arrangements for a beautiful monument Aimeé said she thought white marble would be nice. They rang Ruthie and talked a while but they said she was all broken up of course everyone in Hazel is all broken up too and so terrible because he did so well in Korea and then to get killed just on a training flight you just can't explain it. I think white marble would be elegant and Dan took his Kodak to take photographs of the monument and when they come back I will ask him for one to send to you.

It seems a dreadful thing that we shall never see Chuck again and I am so terribly sorry for poor Ruthie and all those little children I don't know what they will do and nor does your father. Dr Atheling said some lovely words about poor Chuck in his address this morning I wish I could remember all he said something that he had died for the United States just as surely as if he had died in combat in Korea and that he was fighting the Reds just the same it was so lovely of him to say that and God only can decide who shall be taken and who left.

I am so sorry this news comes to you when you are so far away from us all. But now that you have decided to come home and help your father he is so busy and making all kinds of plans and the house is full of catalogs of dozers and graders and Euclids I wish I knew what they were all for that he hardly has time to look in on the *Ford Theater* and he missed *I Love Lucy* altogether last week. I am so glad you have decided to come home, son, because it is at times like this that all Chuck's friends should be in church together.

All our love, son, and come home soon,

MOTHER.

When Stanton Laird got this letter he read it through twice in the privacy of his cabin, and then went to the wash-basin and wet his face-cloth and wiped his eyes, because it was time for him to go up to the laboratory hut beside the rig to inspect the samples brought up by the last shift. He did his routine tests with the fluoroscope, washed and scrutinized the samples from the screen, and wrote up the day book. Then he went out, and took his jeep, and drove up on to the limestone ridge two miles from the rig. Here he parked, and read his mother's letter once again.

Chuck was dead. Never again would he sit with him in the Piggy-Wiggy café sucking a Coke or licking an ice cream. Of all the men that he had met, in all his life, Chuck had understood him best; perhaps in turn he had understood Chuck best. The circumstances of his death were no mystery to Stanton Laird. Chuck had been killed in practising his own particular joke, probably initiating one of the other instructors into the jest; he had met his death with laughter in his heart and one landing light on. In all his grief Stanton felt instinctively that it was better so. Chuck would never have grown old graciously, and now he would remain for ever young.

There would be no more packhorse trips up into the Hazel mountains with Chuck, to look forward to. Never again would he see Chuck rise slowly to his feet behind a tree in the clear mountain air to shoot his arrow at a buck. Never again would he lie under the stars beside Chuck, re-calling the blazing ardours of their first youth, the touch-last crash, and the disgrace that had brought them so close together, that had made them lifelong friends. He had never had so close a friend as Chuck. As he sat there, lonely in his jeep, looking out over the drab spinifex and the red earth beneath the bright Australian sun, he knew that he would never have so close a friend again.

He could not work that day. He felt a great need to get away out of the camp, to find somebody to talk to about Chuck, someone who would understand. There was only one person in the district who would be willing to listen to him in this trouble; perhaps if he went over to Laragh Station he could find an opportunity to talk to her alone.

He got into his jeep again and drove down to the camp. He picked up three copies of his own magazines from the recreation room to serve as an excuse for going over, said a word to Spencer Rasmussen, and drove out on the graded road that led to Mollie Regan.

As he drove up to the wool shed and the yards of Laragh he saw the men doing something with a mob of sheep held in the yards, and the huge, red-headed figure of Pat Regan with them. He hesitated, and decided that it would be discourteous to drive past to the grazier's homestead, and so parked his jeep and walked across to where the grazier stood exhorting his two sons as they crutched and anointed the fly-struck sheep. The old red-headed man stood hatless in the blazing sun, his grey collarless flannel shirt open down his hairy chest, one hand tucked into the leather belt that held up his soiled trousers, the other gently stroking the kangaroo mouse on his shoulder with one finger.

The geologist said, 'Good afternoon, Mr Regan.'

'God save you,' said the other. 'Have ye come to tell us that ye've found oil down in the deep earth?'

Stanton shook his head. 'Not yet. I wouldn't say we would before we get down to the second anhydrite. We're bring up shale right now.'

'How far down would the oil be, then?'

'If there's any oil at all. I'd say it might be around seven thousand four hundred feet. I'd say we'd probably bring up some gas when we get that far down. Whether there's oil there, I just don't know.'

'How deep would that be down, in miles?'

'About a mile and a half.'

'Well, isn't that a great way to be sinking a bore down into the earth! It's day and night you're working, so herself was telling me.'

'It suits us better to keep going,' Stanton said. 'It takes a long time to start up the plant and get the mud moving.' He paused. 'They're changing the drill head this afternoon,'

133

he explained. 'I brought some magazines over for Mrs. Regan and Mollie.'

'Ye'll find them within.'

'You've still got the mouse, I see.'

'Aye.' The grazier put up his hand to the creature on his shoulder and rubbed its side gently with a gnarled forefinger; it leaned towards the rubbing with little chirrups of pleasure. 'Wait now, while I show you.'

He left the yards and went into the shade of the wool shed, the geologist following him. The grazier lifted the mouse down from off his shoulder and set it gently on the floor by the wool press, and retired a few yards over to the bins. There he squatted down upon one heel, ringer fashion, and called quietly, 'Hop – Hop – Hop! Hop when I tell ye, ye little divil. Hop!'

The mouse paused for a moment and then hopped towards him in two-foot bounds, hopped on to his knee, his elbow, and up on to his shoulder. The red-headed old man took the tin box of matches from the pocket of his belt and opened it, and took out a screw of paper laid on top of the matches. From this screw he extracted a few morsels of rotten beetle and cheese which he proceeded to feed to the mouse on his shoulder, swearing at it gently as he fed it. 'Take that, ye wicked little bastard . . .'

The American said, 'You know somethin'? If I'd read about that in a book or magazine I'd have said it wasn't possible. I mean, to tame a critter like that.'

The grazier got to his feet. 'Ye'll not see the like of it, not if you searched the whole wide world,' he said with simple pride. 'Not all the Cardinals in their red robes within the sacred city would show you the like of that, nor the Holy Father himself. She's the kindest hopper in all West Australia, the kindest hopper this side of the black stump.'

Stanton walked back with the old man to the yards, got into his jeep and drove on to the homestead, leaving Pat Regan with his sheep and his half-caste sons. The Countess, shapeless and very black, was languidly sweeping out the dining-room; she poked the fly door open with the handle of her broom and looked out at him. 'You want Missis or Missy?' she inquired. 'I go tell 'um.'

It was the middle of the afternoon, and they might be taking a siesta on their beds in the heat of the day. 'Don't bother them,' he said. 'I'll just wait here. What time do they have tea?'

'Bye 'm bye,' she said.

'I'll just sit right here till you bring tea.'

'No call Missy?'

'No. Leave her be.'

The Countess hesitated, perplexed at the strange ways of the white strangers, inhibited and repressed. 'That her room,' she said helpfully, pointing to a french window opening on to the side verandah.

'Okay. I'll just sit right here.'

The Countess withdrew doubtfully, not certain if she had made herself clear. Stanton sat down in a cane chair on the verandah and lit one of his very occasional cigarettes, an American cigarette made in New Jersey. Chuck was dead and he would never see him again now; in spite of what his mother had said in her letter he was glad that he was not in Hazel at this time. Here in the Lunatic life went on the quiet tenor of its way, a world that Chuck had never known, that had not known Chuck. It helped him with a sense of proportion. In Hazel grief would have been unrestrained, but here the world went on unknowing, a world where an unregenerate old man took simple pleasure in the taming of a mouse, a world where a black woman naïvely assumed that if a young man wanted to go into a young woman's room he just went.

In a few minutes Mollie appeared in a clean print dress; she had been lying awake and had heard all that went on on the verandah, but the Countess was no novelty to her and she paid little heed to that part of the conversation. She said, 'Why, Stan – it's nice to see you. Come over for tea?'

'I guess so,' he said. 'Didn't have anything to do, because they're changing the drill head. I brought some magazines.'

135

She took them from him gratefully. 'Why – you're smoking!'

'I do sometimes.'

'I've never seen you smoke before.'

'No – I don't do it so often. I guess I'm kind of upset today.'

She glanced at him quickly. 'Why – what's the matter?'

'I got bad news from home,' he said. 'Friend of mine called Chuck Sheraton. He got killed, flying.'

He looked up at her, and she saw that his eyes were filled with tears. She said, 'Oh Stan, I'm terribly sorry! That's not the Chuck that you were telling me about, that you went shooting with, with bows and arrows?'

'That's right,' he muttered. 'It doesn't seem any time ago, hardly.'

'How did it happen, Stan?' she asked gently. 'Don't talk about it if you'd rather not...'

'I guess it kinda helps to talk to some folks,' he muttered. 'He got to beating up trains on one-track lines, 'n then last week he hit one.'

She wrinkled her brows. 'Beating up trains?'

'Yeah. He was always thinking up some damfool joke.' A tear escaped and trickled down his cheek.

She did not understand at all what Chuck had done; she only understood that Stanton Laird was in deep distress. At any moment now the Countess might bring tea to the verandah, or her mother might appear; she wanted to spare Stan the embarrassment of meeting her mother till he had got himself under control. The long open shed that housed the trucks and jeeps, the Humber Super-Snipe that the hens laid their eggs in, and the workshop, was not far away; it was shaded and cool, and there they could talk undisturbed. She said, 'Let's go over to the garage, Stan.'

They walked together out into the blazing sun, and as they went he told her what had happened. In the cool shade of the shed he finished his account. 'I guess he had it coming to him,' he told her. 'It's kind of hard to take, though, all the same.'

136

'You were very great friends?' she said.

He nodded. 'Ever since we were in High School.' He hesitated. 'We got in a kind of scrape together, like kids do,' he said. 'After that we got to be real buddies. Went hunting or fishing or on ski trips together, and fixed things after we left school so's we'd both be back in Hazel on vacation at the same time, if we could arrange it.' He hesitated again. 'Chuck got married pretty young, but that didn't seem to make any difference, as it sometimes does. You see, we'd all been in Hazel High together.'

'His wife's alive, of course?'

He nodded. 'She was with him down at this place Harrisburg.'

'Any children?'

'Yeah. He had four children.'

'Oh, Stan, how terrible! Will she get a pension?'

'I guess so,' he said. 'I wouldn't know exactly, but I'd say that she'd class as the widow of a veteran, same as if he'd been killed on combat service in Korea. He was only a lieutenant, so it wouldn't be so much. Her Dad runs the lumber yard back in Hazel. I guess Ruthie'n the kids'll be kind of hard up.'

She let him talk on, and he talked for a quarter of an hour, gradually calming down, gradually building up a picture in her mind of the small town he loved so well. In the end he said, 'I guess I'll have to write to his mother, and maybe to Ruthie too. Apart from that, I dunno that there's much that anyone can do.'

'There's nothing more you *can* do,' she assured him. 'It's the sort of thing that happens, and one's just got to make the best of it.'

'Yeah,' he said. 'Just got to take it.' He glanced down at her. 'It's been mighty nice of you to let me talk like this. It kind of helps.'

'I know it does,' she said. 'You've got to talk to someone.' She had noticed that tea was on the verandah and that her mother was there with the children. The American had regained control of himself now. 'Let's go over and have a cup of tea.'

'Just one thing.' He took her hand and drew her to him, and kissed her on the cheek. He smiled at her. 'That's for letting me talk.'

She withdrew, flushing a little. 'That's very sweet of you, Stan. But I didn't want payment just for letting you talk to me.'

'I guess not,' he said. 'But I kind of wanted to pay.'

They walked together in the hot sun across the sunbaked earth to the verandah of the homestead. 'Stan's got an afternoon off because they're changing the drill or something,' the girl said to her mother. 'I've been showing him the welder.' Later that evening she told her mother about Chuck Sheraton, and of Stanton Laird's distress.

'Aye,' said the Scotswoman, 'always up and down. Highly emotional, as they'd say. They'd all be the better for more self-control.'

'It must have been a frightful shock, Ma,' the girl protested. 'I think he's got plenty of self-control.'

'They wouldn't have thought that in Edinburgh, when I was a child.'

'His great grandfather was a Scot. He's a Presbyterian.'

Her mother looked up in surprise. 'Do ye tell me that! Is that where the name Laird comes from?'

'That's right, Ma. They emigrated from Scotland to the States sometime about a hundred years ago.'

'And the laddie's a member of the kirk?'

'That's right. All his family are Presbyterians.'

Her mother sat in silence, digesting this information. 'Ah, weel,' she said at last in the intonation of her childhood, half forgotten now, 'maybe there's more to him than I was thinking.' She had never complained about the turn of fate that had made Roman Catholics of all her children, and it was many years since she had been inside a church of any sort herself. A fellow Presbyterian could still evoke her sympathies, however, even though he were American and only a very distant Scot.

Stanton Laird drove home that evening rested by his conversation with the girl, very much more at ease. The letters he would have to write tomorrow to Chuck's mother and Chuck's wife were no longer the ordeal they had seemed before; his talk to Mollie had given him back his sense of proportion and he now felt that he could write those letters without tears. He was immensely grateful to the girl, he hardly knew for what unless it was for her kindness in letting him talk. She was pretty, and young, and very, very kind.

He was tired when he got back to the camp. He did not want to meet his colleagues, and he was not hungry; he cut out supper altogether and went to his cabin. He had a cabin to himself, a privilege reserved for senior officials which he shared with Spencer Rasmussen. He was tired now, and sleepy; his distress assuaged, he knew that he would be able to sleep. Chuck was dead and he would never quite be forgotten, but now everything had come into proportion and Stanton Laird could sleep.

He dropped off his few clothes, lay down on the bed and pulled the sheet over him, and reached for his Bible. It was his habit in times of stress to lie and leaf this through before sleep came, seeking for a message, discarding the many irrelevancies till he found a verse comforting in his mood. Tonight he lay for a quarter of an hour till a familiar passage met his eyes:

For I am persuaded, that neither death, nor life, nor angels, nor principalities, nor powers, nor things present, nor things to come,
Nor height, nor depth, nor any other creature, shall be able to separate us from the love of God, which is in Christ Jesus our Lord.

He did not fully understand the reference to angels but he knew that that was due to his own insufficiency. The passage seemed to fit Chuck's death, he did not quite know why, but it comforted him, and he laid the Bible down and turned the light out. There was always a message in the Book if you looked long enough; it had never failed him. Chuck was dead beside the railway track, but God was still looking after him.

How kind that girl had been, letting him talk about Chuck. How sweet she had been when he kissed her. The kindest girl that he had ever met. The kindest ... where had he heard that? The kindest ... Practically asleep, he smiled. The kindest hopper this side of the black stump. That was it.

The kindest hopper this side of the black stump.

He slept.

All through April the drill bored deeper, making good about a hundred feet a day on the average. The cores and the spoil brought up were more or less as Stanton Laird had forecast from his geological survey; he did not expect anything sensational before the end of May, when they should have reached the second layer of anhydrite and the domed anticline below. Early in the month they struck the first layer of anhydrite, a belt of hard-cap rock about fifteen feet thick. This took them several days to drill through; beneath it there was limestone heavily charged with water. This was in accordance with the geologist's prediction and they were prepared for it, but it slowed down their progress because now all casings had to be sealed with liquid cement pumped down between the outside of the steel tubes and the virgin earth to keep the water out, and this necessitated many pauses to let the cement set.

At the oil rig the labour was about seventy per cent Australian, working under the expert directions of the Americans. By paying a wage unprecedented in Australia the Americans had induced Australians to work as enthusiastically as the Americans, and had persuaded them to work through all the many Australian public holidays. Labour Day and Australia Day had been worked normally at the oil rig, but Anzac Day was approaching, and Topex had been briefed by the bureau of Mineral Resources that Anzac Day, the anniversary of the landing of Australian and New

Zealand troops on the Gallipoli Peninsula in 1915, was in the nature of a Holy Day and there might be real trouble reverberating through the whole of Australia unless work stopped for Anzac Day.

'I guess this Anzac Day must be kind of like the Fourth of July, only a durn sight more so,' said Spencer Rasmussen. 'We never stop the drill for Independence Day.'

'I'd say it's more like Easter Sunday,' said Stanton. 'Sort of a religious day. Clem Rogerson from Mannahill, he's going down to Perth for it, taking all his family. Does that each year, so he was telling me.'

'He does?'

'Uh-huh. He was in the combat group that landed on the beaches at Gallipoli, way back in the First War. Seems like on Anzac Day they get up and parade in the middle of the night, 'n stand to arms at dawn, just like they did then before the assault. It's just the same as a religious ceremony, kind of a Midnight Mass.'

'Well,' said Mr Rasmussen in wonder, 'what do you know!'

He was willing to cooperate, however. He made arrangements to stop drilling and close down all work at midnight, with the reservation that he himself and one or two of the leading American hands would use the idle time to conduct a stocktaking and an inspection of the plant for latent defects. He made arrangements with the Australian foreman to paint a scaffold pole white and to set it up as a flagstaff on a piece of level ground for the Australians to parade to before dawn, only to find that his Australian labour needed a good deal of persuading to get up at five in the morning on a holiday. However, the Americans were so sincere in their endeavours to do the right thing that the parade took place at dawn and was reasonably well attended, with a fair sprinkling of Americans standing in the ranks and making the best they could of the unfamiliar words of command. A ball game followed in the morning, a cricket match in the afternoon, and a good deal of beer in the evening. Next morning at eight o'clock the drill began to turn again.

The stocktaking and inspection had revealed a number of

items to be required from Perth, which should be sent up on the next truck. It had not proved economic to arrange an air service to the oil rig, so that the only mail communication that the Americans had with their head office was by way of the weekly mail truck driven by Spinifex Joe. Most of their communications therefore went by telegram via the Flying Doctor radio service; after the medical calls upon the morning schedule the oil men, in turn with the station owners in the district, would dictate telegrams to the radio operator in Hastings, who would pass them to the post office, who would forward them normally over the land lines.

That morning Mr Rasmussen sat waiting patiently with a three-hundred-word telegram in his hand, while the radio operator at Hastings, a Mr Jerry Lee, took down a number of telegrams from various stations, picked at random out of the ether. He sat in the office where the set was now installed, with Stanton Laird nearby standing at his drawing board and poring over the most recent core analyses, correcting the depths marked in neat pencil on his geological surveys. They listened idly while one station sent a telegram reserving two seats on the airline down to Perth, another sent one ordering a water pump assembly for a Chev truck, and a third sent twenty pounds to a daughter stranded without money in Hobart. A fourth, to a stock transport company, was being dictated by a station four hundred miles to the north of them, when a voice broke in, and said,

'I tell you, 'e's cut his bloody throat.'

Mr Rasmussen blinked, looked up at Mr Laird, and said, 'What in hell was that?' He saw that the geologist was looking at the set, and that he had heard the words. He reached out, and turned the volume higher.

In Hastings, three hundred miles to the west, Mr Jerry Lee was alerted, and began transmitting. 'All stations off the air, please. Some station seems to be passing a medical message. Will that station please come in again and give station identification. Everybody silent, please.'

There was a long silence, broken only by the crackling of static in a dozen receivers that happened to be listening in, in a dozen stations spread throughout the breadth of northern West Australia. Presently the voice said again, ''Ullo. 'Ullo.' And then, *sotto voce*, evidently to someone standing by the set, 'The bloody thing ain't working.' Another voice said, equally indistinct, 'Give it them again, Bert.' And the first voice said, ''Ullo. I tell you, we got a bloke here cut his bloody throat. 'E's bleeding something 'orrible, 'n now Jim Copeland's muggered off into the bush.'

In distant Hastings Jerry Lee could hear the carrier wave still going on. He tried his own transmission set, but it raised a heterodyne squeal at once; he switched it off again. Throughout the country the listeners sat tense and alert. One, who recognized the name Jim Copeland, began transmitting, but the words were indistinguishable among the squeals, and presently he stopped.

The *sotto voce* voice said, 'You got to turn that one to hear. Rec means Receive.' The carrier wave stopped.

Mr Lee came on the air at once. 'This is Six Easy Dog, Hastings Flying Doctor Service. We have received your message about somebody who cut his throat and somebody who went off into the bush. Now I want you to tell us the name of your station and some more about what happened. When you want to speak, turn the little switch low down on the left hand side to Trans, and directly you've done speaking turn the same switch to Rec. Don't touch anything else on the set – it's going fine. Now, turn your switch to Trans and tell us what happened. Over.'

The voice said, ''Ullo. This is Bert Hancock, at Mannahill. We got a bloke here cut his throat. He's bleeding pretty bad. 'Ullo. Did you get that?' The carrier stopped.

Jerry Lee came in at once. 'Flying Doctor here. I got your message. I'm going to switch you through to the doctor in the hospital in a minute, but first of all, you said somebody had gone off into the bush. What was that? Turn your switch to Trans now. Over.'

The voice said, 'Jim Copeland, that was. Went off in the

middle of the night sometime. Left a note on the cookhouse table, said he was going back to London. Cookie found it 'bout an hour ago. I'll turn the knob now.'

'Flying Doctor here. Was this man Copeland walking or riding?'

'Walking, I'd say. The trucks are all here. 'E's just a youngster, a Pommie out from home, jackerooing. 'E got a bit full last night. We all got a bit full.'

Mr Lee, sitting in the radio house by the hospital in the little coastal town, thought quickly. He knew the Rogersons were all away from the station for he had passed the telegram booking their airline seats to Perth. In their absence, it was probable that the station hands had got at the grog, and had gone on a terrific bender all through Anzac Day. One was bleeding to death and he must hurry; there was no time to bother over the Pommie youngster who had walked out into the bush. He lifted his post office telephone, got Dr Gordon in the hospital, and switched the reception on his radio through to the doctor, monitoring the conversation from his set.

By their receivers a dozen listeners sat, separated in some instances by hundreds of miles, waiting and alert to help if it were possible. The oil rig was one of the closest to Mannahill; they had no means of telling if the Regans at Laragh were listening or not.

The doctor said, 'You say this man cut his throat with a razor?'

Bert Hancock said, 'That's right, Doc.'

'Where is he now? Over.'

'Out on the verandah, Doc. We got him sitting up, but it didn't seem right to move him.'

'Tell me how long the cut is. Is it still bleeding?'

'I'd say it's about four inches, Doc. It's bleeding pretty fast still. Real nasty.'

Three hundred miles from the patient, the doctor mustered all his energies to help. He said, 'Now look, Mr Hancock. I'll come as soon as I can get the aeroplane, but first of all you've got to get that bleeding stopped. Have you got any sutures? Over.'

The other said doubtfully, 'I don't know what they'd be, Doc.'

'Well, have you got a needle and cotton?'

'I got a housewife, Doc.'

'That's fine. Now what you've got to do is this. Take your needle and thread it double, and tie the ends of the cotton together. Then you've got to sew up that wound in his throat just as if you were sewing up a tear in your trousers. You've got to pull the edges close together, and then make the cotton fast. Then you must get a pad of linen to bind over it. You'd better tear up a clean sheet. Make a pad that will fit close down on the wound, and then tear bandages from the sheet and wrap them round his throat to keep the pad in place. You'd better keep him sitting up, and keep him warm. Don't give him anything – no alcohol. I'll be out this afternoon in the aeroplane, as soon as I can get to you. Now, can you do that? Over.'

There was a long silence. Then the voice said, 'I dunno, Doc. I can't stand blood. Makes me sick at the stomach. Always did, ever since I was a youngster. Gives me a real bad turn.'

In the office at the oil rig the Americans sat listening. Stanton said quietly, 'Maybe some of us should go over, with the first-aid kit.'

Spencer Rasmussen said, 'Take quite a while. The aeroplane with the doctor would make it 'most as soon. Hold it a few minutes.'

Over the air the doctor said, 'You've got to do that, Mr Hancock. If you don't the man will die. I'll be out with you in about three hours' time. I can't get to you sooner. If you don't attend to him, he'll bleed to death. Now, do as I tell you. Go and get your needle and cotton, sew up that wound, put the pad on, and come back and tell me when you've done it. Go and do that now. Over.'

The voice said reluctantly, 'I'll try it, if you say. But I gets sick at the stomach. I chundered once today already.'

The carrier wave stopped, and there was silence but for the crackling of the static. Then another voice broke in and it was the courtly, refined tones of the Judge.

'This is Laragh Station, 6 CO. We have heard the whole of that. Mr Pat Regan and Miss Regan are leaving at once for Mannahill with medical supplies. They think that the journey will take them about an hour and a half in the jeep. I am afraid those poor boys must have been terribly intoxicated. Over.'

Three hundred miles away Jerry Lee said, 'Thank you, 6 CO. I will tell Mannahill when they come on again. Listening out.'

At the oil rig Stanton said, 'I guess I'll go over, take Tex with me. We're not so far away, 'n it might look bad if we didn't show up to help.'

Mr Rasmussen nodded, turned his switch, and said, 'This is 6 QT, Topeka Exploration. We heard all of that. Mr Laird and one other are leaving for Mannahill right now. I guess they'll be there in about two hours. Over.'

Jerry Lee said, 'Thank you, Topex. I'll tell Mannahill. Listening out.'

At the oil rig Stanton grinned, and said, 'I'll say that they were terribly intoxicated. I guess that's what happens in this country when the manager goes off to Perth 'n takes his family.'

'Except at Laragh,' replied Mr Rasmussen.

'Laragh's different,' said Stanton Laird. 'I'd say they're kind of pickled – it don't do them any harm. Besides, they've got an ex-barmaid in the driver's seat.'

'That's right,' said Mr Rasmussen. 'A Scotch barmaid in the driver's seat. Maybe that's what you want to run a ranch here, in this country.'

Stanton went off to find Tex, to collect the first-aid box, fill up the jeep, and get rolling on the new road to Laragh and Mannahill. Spencer Rasmussen sat on by the radio set, patiently fingering his telegram for Perth. He could not send it till this drama was played out, for Jerry Lee was still listening for Mannahill, the doctor still listening at his extension in the hospital.

Presently Mannahill came on the air again. 'This is Bert Hancock here. I think he's dead, Doc.'

146

The doctor asked sharply, 'Did you do what I told you to do? Did you sew up that wound in his throat?'

'There didn't seem no call to, Doc. He ain't breathing.'

A somewhat macabre discussion followed, dealing with the processes of death. The doctor was at first disinclined to believe Mr Hancock and to go and make him do as he was told, but finally he came round to believe that the man probably was dead. That belief raised problems of a different order.

'There'll have to be an inquest,' he said, 'and that means that I'll come out and do a post mortem before you bury him. I'll come out right away in the aeroplane; I'll be with you this afternoon, soon after dinner. Now, you'll have to make the body decent, Mr Hancock. Where is he now? Over.'

' 'E's out on the verandah, Doc, all in a lot of blood. Real nasty.'

The doctor thought for a moment. It was probably asking too much to suggest that they should wash the body. He was inured to such things; better do that himself when he got there. He said, 'I want you to lift him up and lay him out flat on his back, now. Have you got a long table you can lay him out on? Over.'

Mr Hancock said reluctantly 'Well, Doc – there's the dining-room table what we eats our tucker off.'

The doctor said, 'Well – perhaps that's not very suitable. Can you make a trestle table? Have you got any trestles? Over.'

'We got those, Doc. There's some trestles down by the stockyard.'

'All right. Get a couple of those trestles up to the verandah, and make a trestle table with three planks, and put the body on it lying on its back, and cover it over decently with a sheet. That's all you've got to do. I'll be with you in about three hours' time. I'll bring the constable if I can get hold of him, but I think he's out of town.'

So that was arranged; the radio drama was over, and Mr Rasmussen was able to dictate his Topex telegram to Jerry

Lee. On the ground the drama was by no means over; the sense of it was strong in Stanton Laird as he swung the jeep to a standstill before Laragh Station homestead, in a cloud of red dust.

SIX

THEY did not stop for long at Laragh Station, but the Judge was able to give them a little more information about Mannahill. 'I understand that Mr Rogerson employs four white men,' he told them. 'He had a married foreman in addition, but he left last month. I have not heard of an appointment to succeed him. Perhaps it was unwise of Mr Rogerson to leave the station in the absence of a foreman ... But then, of course, it was for Anzac Day.'

'Sure,' said Stanton. 'Who was this guy that cut his throat?'

'I think perhaps that was a man called Airey. He was a saddler and harness maker, a very depressed little man, and with a terrible weakness for strong drink.'

'Well, who's Jim Copeland, then?'

'He is an English boy, jackerooing. He comes from Blackheath, near London. I think he has only been in Australia for a few months. I doubt if he had settled down yet. Perhaps he was homesick.'

'What's jackerooing?'

'Working as an apprentice, to learn the work.'

Stanton thought for a minute. 'There's Bert Hancock, who was on the radio. How many others are there there?'

'I think only the station cook – of the white men, that is to say.'

'What's his name?'

'They call him Fortunate. I never heard him called anything else. Perhaps that is his name.' He mused for a moment. 'If I were to hazard a guess,' he said mildly, 'I

148

would say that he is an Englishman, or perhaps a Welshman, who had jumped his ship, as they say here. Mr Rogerson once told Mr Regan that Fortunate was most reluctant to go off the station, from which he assumed that he was probably in Australia illegally.'

'A hot citizen,' observed Stanton.

'I beg your pardon?'

'That's okay. I just meant that maybe the police would take an interest in him. They seem to be quite a bunch of boys at Mannahill.'

'No better and no worse than on any other property in the north,' the Judge said. 'I am inclined to think that Mr Rogerson made a great mistake in leaving them without a foreman.'

Stanton Laird drove on to Mannahill with Tex, with a slightly enhanced opinion of the Judge. Beneath the ageing and dissipated exterior there was still a good deal of shrewd common sense. For the first time he began to wonder who it was that really ran the excellent property that was Laragh Station, whether it was Tom Regan with his stomach ulcers or Pat Regan with his tame mouse, or whether in truth it was the Scots ex-barmaid aided by the disgraced stipendiary who had once been a schoolmaster at Eton, assisted by the many children. Perhaps it was a combination of them all, a harmonious partnership tolerant of human frailties that had evolved over the years. It wasn't the way that things were run in Topeka Exploration Inc, or in the town of Hazel for that matter, but set in the Lunatic Range of West Australia it seemed to work.

He got to Mannahill at about noon. He came first to the horse yard, and there he found the Laragh jeep, with a good deal of activity going on. Pat Regan, for once without his mouse, was riding bareback on a horse controlled only with a halter, and with two coloured stockmen he was driving a small mob of horses from the horse paddock into the yard, swearing at them volubly. Mollie Regan was carrying saddles from the harness room to the yard.

She broke off when she saw the oil men. 'Oh, Stan, I'm

glad you've come!' she said. 'They're in the hell of a mess here.'

'I know it,' he replied. 'We heard the radio, and came on over.' He glanced at her. 'What are you doing with the horses?'

'It's this boy Copeland, the jackeroo. We've got to find him – he's out somewhere in the bush. Dad says he'll probably be dead by sunset.'

The tropical sun blazed down on the red, arid land out of a cloudless sky, brazen and pitiless. So long as you had shade to work in and plenty to drink it was not unpleasant, but in the bare country with no shade, no water, no horse, and perhaps no hat it was a very different matter. 'Six or seven miles, and then you're finished, in the heat of the day,' she explained. 'Dad says he'll be walking in a circle, but he might have got a long way out from here during the night, keeping straight so long as the stars lasted.'

Stanton nodded. 'What can we do to help?'

'I don't know – the country's too rough for your jeep. I'll ask Dad in a minute. Can either of you ride a horse?'

'Why, certainly,' Stanton said. 'I can ride.'

'Really ride, Stan? Well enough to ride with us all day?'

'Certainly,' he repeated. 'I was raised on a ranch, back home in Oregon.'

'Of course – I was forgetting. Well, that makes one more man. What about you, Tex?'

The electrician shook his head. 'I guess you'll have to count me out. I never rode no horse.'

'Well, that makes five of us, with the two coloured boys. I'll tell Daddy in a minute. We'll want a lot more people. I think you'll have to sit upon the radio, Tex.'

'Okay.'

Stanton Laird asked, 'What's happened to the man who was here – Bert Hancock? And there's a cook here, isn't there – a man called Fortunate?'

'Bert Hancock's flat out on his bed, dead to the world,' she said succinctly. 'Dad threw a bucket of cold water on him, but he just slept on. He probably went back on the grog after laying out Bill Airey. Fortunate's walking about, but he's no good to us.'

Pat Regan rode up to the rails and slipped from the horse, agile in spite of his seventy years. 'Well, Glory be to God, I'm glad to see you, Mr Laird,' he said. 'Ye'd not see the like of this between Dublin and County Kerry, or in the whole of the United States of America, either.'

'Stan can ride, Dad,' the girl said. 'Ride well. Tex can stay with the radio.'

'Isn't that a great mercy, now?' He swung round on the coloured boys. 'Saddle up one more horse, ye black bastards. Five.' He held up all the fingers off one hand, counting them with the thumb. 'Five horses.' He climbed the rails of the yard and came to the jeep, a red-headed, active old man in soiled working trousers and shirt open down his chest, hardly sweating from his exertions. 'We'll go up to the homestead now the way we'll see if we can talk to anybody on the wireless,' he said. 'It's ten more men that we'll be after needing, with their saddles.'

They got into the jeep and drove on to the buildings. They stopped at the bunk house, a row of single cabins opening on to a common verandah with a messroom and the kitchen at the end. On the verandah was the trestle table that the doctor had ordained, with the body on it covered over with a sheet. Beside it was the man called Fortunate, very busy. At some previous point in his career he had held a job as a chef. This morning, after laying out the body, he had dressed himself for the post mortem, putting on his white chef's apron and his tall white cap, newly starched and very clean and white. On the trestle table beside the body he had all his butcher's knives laid out, and he was busily engaged in sharpening them to a razor edge. A bottle of gin stood beside the body, and from time to time he would pause in his work to take a swig from that.

'Holy smoke!' said Tex. 'What in blazes does that guy think he's doing?'

'Sure, and he's away out of his mind,' Pat Regan said. 'He thinks he's going to do the post mortem when the

151

doctor comes. Just leave him be and he'll not trouble you, unless maybe he goes to eat the insides of a clock.'

He jumped out of the jeep and strode into the end cabin. Bert Hancock was there on the bed, snoring heavily. The red-headed old man lifted him by the collar of his shirt and dealt him four stinging slaps upon his face. The head sagged from side to side, but the man did not rouse.

The grazier threw him back upon the bed, lit a wax match from the tin box held in his belt, and held the little finger of the left hand in the flame. The man muttered in his sleep, but did not rouse.

'Sure, he's a grand sleeper,' he said in disgust. 'It's the gin and the whisky does that to a man,' he explained to Stanton. 'Ye'd never see a man the way he is on rum. The rum's a kindly sort of drink, and easy on the stomach.'

They went back to the jeep and drove on to the homestead. The liquor store at the end of the homestead verandah had been broken into, and there were bottles everywhere, half-full bottles of spirits, empty bottles, broken bottles; the place was in a terrible mess. 'Wasn't it the grand Anzac Day the boys were after having?' old Pat Regan remarked. 'Sure, and you'd think that they'd been drinking a wake to the glory of Bill Airey's soul before his time.'

The office door that opened on to the verandah was swinging open, the lock smashed. They went in there and found the wireless set. Tex slipped into the seat before it and found it was already switched on; Bert Hancock must have left it so. There was still current in the battery, however. 'This is Mannahill,' he said. 'Mannahill Station calling. Will anybody listening come in. Come in anybody. Over.'

Immediately Jerry Lee came in; he had evidently been keeping a listening watch. 'Hastings Flying Doctor here, Six Easy Dog. Receiving you, Mannahill, strength three. Pass your message. Over.'

Pat Regan took the microphone and explained the position. He learned that the doctor was in the air and on the way to them; he should be with them in about an hour.

Stations around would be notified that more riders were required at Mannahill immediately. If possible Jerry Lee would get a radio message to the aeroplane in the air, telling it where to land in order to pick up more riders with their saddles. It was arranged that, before starting off upon the search, Pat Regan with the coloured stockmen would drive a few more horses into the horse yard to help the riders who might come by air or by truck later. Tex would remain at Mannahill on listening watch.

'Ye'd better take the batteries from all the cars and trucks that ye can find, the way ye'll keep it going,' the old man said.

They left Tex at the homestead and drove back to the yard. The horses were ready for them, and the old man set the order for the search. The coloured boys, of course, knew every inch of the property and were in no danger of getting lost. He himself would not get lost, but did not know the property. Mollie would not get lost if she were given a road as a lifeline. Stanton would be useless on his own, and of unknown ability as a rider.

'Sure, and the boy might be any place,' he said. 'Just any place at all, and maybe not upon his feet by now but crept into a bit of shade.' He sent one of the coloured boys to the west to work through to north. He himself took the sector from north to east, because that was in the direction of Laragh and he knew the country better on that side. He sent the other coloured boy into the sector from east to south, and he sent Mollie and Stanton to ride together in the sector from south to west because the track out to the coast ran through that sector like a backbone, and Mollie knew the track. 'Ye might find him out along that way, I'm thinking,' he said. 'Drunk as he was, maybe he took the road. Don't stay by the road, for he'd be after leaving it as soon as he got crazed. Watch the road, though, the way you'd see his footmarks in the dust.'

He saw them mounted, and made sure that each had a full water bottle. Then he swung up into the saddle himself and they separated, each going his own way.

Mollie and Stanton Laird rode together out from Manna-hill south-west along the track. They cantered for a few hundred yards to get the freshness from the horses, but the sun blazed down and very soon the horses had had enough and they slowed to a walk. As they cantered the girl watched the American furtively, to see if he could really ride. She was pleased, and faintly surprised in spite of what he had told her, to see that he rode well and had his horse well under control. The saddle was somewhat different from the western saddles that he was accustomed to, and the snaffle was strange to him, but he rode very long, in the way that she was accustomed to see men ride, not gripping with his knees. The oil geologist had told her nothing but the truth when he had said that he could ride all day. Somehow, she had thought that Americans could only ride a car.

They rode in silence, Stanton busy with his own thoughts. At first he was concerned only with the mastery of the strange horse and the strange saddle and the strange bridle, but being satisfied with those his mind turned back to the last time he had ridden, which was with Chuck back home in Oregon. Chuck's riding was for ever over; when he got back to Oregon he would not be able to tell Chuck of this strange ride that he was undertaking now, as he would have liked to tell him, sucking a Coke out of a plastic straw, perhaps in the Piggy-Wiggy café on Main Street with all the Oldsmobiles and Pontiacs parked by the meters in the sun outside. He would have enjoyed telling Chuck about this country, and Chuck would have enjoyed hearing about it, and with that thought he realized that in this country, harsh and arid as it was, Chuck might have found fulfil-ment. Here, Chuck would have found no need to beat up trains at night with one landing light on to achieve a little excitement in a humdrum life of training flight cadets; his daily living might have given him the adventure that he needed.

He turned to the girl, to share the thought with her. 'You know somethin'?' he said. 'I believe Chuck would have liked this country.'

She raised her eyes from the dust that she had been studying for traces of the jackeroo. 'Whatever put that into your head?' she asked.

'I dunno,' he said vaguely. 'I guess things happen here that he'd have known how to handle.' He chuckled. 'Things like that guy Fortunate with all his knives. I'd just not know what to do with a guy like that. But he'd have known.'

'The best thing to do with a man like that is to leave him alone,' she said. 'Keep well away from him, and hope he cuts his own throat with one of his knives.'

He turned to her. 'Wouldn't you be frightened of a guy like that?'

She laughed. 'I wouldn't get myself in a position to be frightened of him, Stan,' she said. 'When a man's in that condition a girl wants to keep well away.'

'I'd say that's right,' he said. There was a saneness in her approach to fear that he could only admire. Things of this nature were not new to her; she had known them and known of them from her childhood, so that they did not terrify. All her life she had lived with men who drank heavily and mastered the drink; inevitably she had known others who did not master it. She had learned from her mother's knee the wisdom garnered by a Scots barmaid in the bars of country towns; she knew all types of men for what they were, and she was not afraid of them.

They rode on together down the road, scanning the dust, the grey-green clumps of spinifex, the patches of red earth that showed between, the gnarled and stunted trees that gave no shade. They stopped after an hour and took a drink from their water bottles; then they decided to ride out and go parallel with the road, one on each side of it, keeping in sight of each other but perhaps a mile apart. In that way they could sweep the country better.

She rode off on the left-hand side, and he to the right. He watched her as she went, a small girl in overalls and a big hat, on a big horse. How well she new the country, how very, very competent she was! And what a girl!

155

They rode on like that for about an hour, and came together again on the road to compare notes. 'I don't see that we can do any better than go on as we're going, Stan,' Mollie said. 'We must be about seven or eight miles out, I suppose. He could have walked as far as this by night, quite easily, although we've not seen any traces. I'd like to go on for another couple of hours, if that's all right by you.' She glanced at her watch. 'Say till five o'clock. We'd better turn back then, but we'll have the road to go home on.'

'That's okay with me, Mollie,' he said. 'I'd certainly hate to think of anybody wandering around on foot in this country.'

'I know,' she said. 'They come out from home, and they don't understand. It takes a long, long time before they understand.'

They separated again, and went on with the search, riding far distant from each other, but in sight. An hour later a dry, sandy river bed crossed the road, a river that ran only in the wet; they rode across this and came together on the road again to compare notes. 'We'll give it an hour more,' the girl said. 'Come back on the track again at five o'clock. If we've not seen anything by then we'll call it a day.'

The sun was already starting to decline towards the horizon. Stanton Laird sat in his saddle gazing down the track that wavered unsteadily to the south-west. He did not answer, but sat motionless.

The girl glanced at him, and asked, 'What are you looking at?'

'I was wondering what that might be in the road,' he said. 'Lookit. Like a stone.'

'I don't see anything,' she said.

'See the first kind of wiggle? Well, on past that, the tree on the left. Just a little way past that.'

She saw the object that he meant, half a mile away. 'It's a stone,' she said.

'I guess it might be,' he admitted. 'But it's kind of rounded for a stone in these parts, and they're mostly red.' He moved his horse on up the road. 'I'll just take a look.'

She followed him. As they came closer the stone turned into a water bottle with a webbing shoulder-strap.

Stanton dismounted stiffly, for the strange saddle was galling him, picked it up and give it to the girl. She pulled the cork out; the bottle was empty. She put her finger in the aperture. 'It's still wet inside,' she said. 'He must have come this way. Well, now we've got to find him.'

She sat upon her horse looking around, taking careful note of the surroundings. 'We must be about twelve miles out,' she said, 'and just past the second creek. Look, hang it on the branch of that tree, so that we'll know this place again. And put a few stones in the middle of the road, in a little heap.'

He did so, and mounted again, and they rode out again on each side of the road. In a few minutes she shouted, and he rode across to her. She had dismounted when he got there, and he found her examining an elastic-sided riding boot, fairly new and in good condition. She passed it to him without comment.

'His?' he inquired.

'Must be,' she said. 'It's what they do. They start throwing off their clothes – when the skin stops sweating.'

She looked around, hesitated, and placed the boot in as prominent a position as she could upon a clump of spinifex. She mounted again. 'I don't believe he's very far away,' she said. 'Look carefully in every bit of shade, Stan.'

He studied the ground. 'I guess this is the trail,' he said. 'I think he went this way.'

They rode on slowly, peering between the clumps of spinifex for any sign. Then they found a khaki shirt on the red earth.

The next thing they found was a wide-brimmed hat, about a hundred yards away.

A quarter of a mile further on, upon a trail that curved around towards the river bed, they found a pair of drill trousers abandoned on a patch of bare earth, where the owner had thrown them down.

'It's what they do,' the girl said quietly. 'He'll be somewhere in a patch of shade, Stan. Very close here now.'

He dismounted and put the trousers prominently in a stunted tree, mounted again, and with the girl began to ride around slowly, in ever widening circles. Twenty minutes later the girl raised her arm, and called quietly across the hundred yards that separated them, 'He's here, Stan.'

He rode across to her, and they dismounted. The body of the boy lay motionless, stark naked, beneath a clump of spinifex. He had burrowed into it along the ground like an animal, parting the coarse, thorny grass, so that only the legs were left out in the sun, the skin dark red in colour, and shiny. They tried to pull him out, but the muscles tightened convulsively and the hands clutched the grass.

'He's alive,' the girl said. 'Look, let's cut it away from on top of him. Have you got a knife?'

'Surely,' he said. It was his habit to wear the hunting sheath knife that he wore when riding on the trails of his home state; he did not use it very often, but in a strange land it was a reminder on his belt of his home town and of the country that he loved. He pulled it out, and began to cut away the grass above the body.

The sun was getting down to the horizon, mercifully, when they got the boy out of the bush. The body was scratched and torn by the spinifex with wounds that did not bleed; the tongue seemed to fill the desiccated mouth, apparently bitten through. But there was still life there; as Mollie held the boy up in a sitting posture and tried to make him drink from her water bottle, he turned from her and from the sun, feebly trying to burrow back under the bush.

There was no shade, so they lifted him and laid him in the shadow of Stan's horse, and went on trying to force water down his throat. Much of it was wasted, trickling down the chin and neck. Stanton was very conscious that their water bottles were practically empty; he had drunk freely from his own and there was little in it now, and from the look of it there was not much more in the girl's.

Watching it trickle down outside the face for the fourth or fifth time, he said, 'Maybe we should go easy on that water. You're not getting much in, and there's not a lot left in my bottle.'

She said, 'We can get more from the river.'

'It looked pretty dry to me,'

She looked up at him, smiling. 'Of course it looks dry. Didn't you see where the kangaroos had been digging? Little holes in the sand? The water's there all right, under the sand.'

'There's water in that river – right there?'

She nodded. 'You've only got to dig where the kangaroos have been digging.' She glanced down at the body in her arms. 'Poor kid – he didn't know that.'

'I guess I didn't, either.' In this country she must lead and he must follow; what was normal and natural to her was strange and menacing to him. 'What would you say we'd better do now?'

She considered for a minute. 'Do you think we could get him to the river, Stan? It's only about a quarter of a mile.'

'Why, sure,' he said. 'I could carry him that far, or we could put him on a horse.'

She nodded. 'If you *could* carry him, I think it would be better. I think I'd like to make a camp down by the river, where there's water. We can't be more than a mile from the road. If we make a fire, somebody will come out looking for us with a truck sometime during the night, and then we'll be all right. I'd like you to collect his clothes, though, first of all.'

She bent to the boy again, and for the first time saw a convulsive movement of the throat. 'He swallowed a bit then.'

He went off and returned after a quarter of an hour with the shirt, trousers, hat, and one boot; he had not been able to find the other boot, and had not wasted time in looking for it. He found that Mollie had unsaddled her horse to get the saddle blanket; she had wrapped the damp sweaty thing around the scorched body of the boy. 'He took a little more water,' she said. 'My bottle's finished now. Could you carry him as far as the river, do you think?'

159

He bent and picked up the young man. It was a quarter of a mile to the river bed and the lad weighed more than ten stone; Stanton put him down once for a spell, then picked him up and went on. The sun was very near to the horizon when they got to the bank, Mollie following behind with the two horses.

She indicated a patch of coarse brown grass. 'Put him down there, Stan.' He laid the body down gladly, drenched as he was in sweat and breathing heavily. The girl glanced around; about a hundred yards upstream the river sand was pockmarked with little holes. She pulled the blanket round the boy. 'We'll want a bit of wood for a spade,' she said. 'Something to dig with. And the water bottles.'

There was no shortage of wood: fallen, desiccated branches strewed the ground under the sparse trees, and on the sandspits there was desiccated driftwood piled in heaps. They found a root piece with a wide, flat end, and walked up to the kangaroo diggings. Stanton began to dig down in the sand at a spot picked by the girl as being probably the centre of a pool. Before he had got down a foot the sand was moist; at two feet there was water in the bottom of the hole, and by enlarging it he could fill the water bottles. They drank deeply themselves and refilled the bottles, and went back to the boy.

The girl stooped, and managed to force a little more water down the throat. They unsaddled the other horse and took the saddle blanket for a pillow; then they had done all they could for the moment. They stood together for a moment looking down on him, both knowing that he was very near to death. 'It's the skin,' she said quietly. 'He's so terribly burnt ...'

He nodded. 'I guess we'd better make that fire, while there's still light enough to see.' He turned to collect wood, and then stopped, struck by a thought. 'You got a match?'

She stared at him. 'No – I don't carry them. Haven't you got one?'

He shook his head. 'I don't smoke, hardly ever.'

'Perhaps he had some.'

They turned to the boy's clothes, but there were no matches in trousers, shirt, or belt. 'We'll have to try and make it like the black boys do,' she said.

'Rubbing two pieces of wood, or somethin'?'

She nodded. 'I've never done it, but I've seen them doing it often enough. They never carry matches.'

She made him find a straight, hard piece of branch about two feet long, and whittle it straighter with his knife. In the north Australian climate with great quantities of bone-dry wood upon the ground it is not very difficult to create fire when you know how. She picked a piece of wood that had been rotten and was now desiccated to tinder, and put it on the ground, and made him give her the leather boot-lace from one of his boots. Then, kneeling down, she held the straight piece of wood vertically on the tinder, the top end pressed down by a pad of wood between her breasts, wound the bootlace two or three times round it, and began to rotate the drill quickly by pulling on each end of the bootlace in turn. After a few attempts a little smoke began to rise, and then there came a glow of fire in the tinder, and presently Stanton was able to light the corner of an air-letter from his mother in Hazel. After that, the rest was easy.

They made the fire out in the middle of the river sand, mindful of starting a bush fire if they made it on the bank, and they made it big to serve as a beacon. When that was going, they lifted the boy and brought him closer to the fire. They judged him to be conscious now, but the swollen tongue still made it impossible for him to talk. They managed to get a little more water down his throat.

Presently Stanton said, 'You know what? We're going to be mighty hungry before that truck turns up.'

She laughed; now that night had fallen their bodies craved the refreshment that they did not need in the heat of the day. 'I'm hungry, too,' she said. 'We've just got to grin and bear it, Stan, unless you like to eat a bit of one of the saddles.'

'Might be kind of tough. How would it be if I was to ride back to the homestead, 'n bring out a truck?'

'It wouldn't be so easy to pick out the track, Stan, in the darkness, without lights. It wouldn't help at all if you got lost.'

'I don't reckon I'd get lost.'

'I'd rather go myself,' she said.

They discussed it for a time, sitting together by the fire. They were only twelve or fifteen miles out from Mannahill Station and not more than a mile from the road, but the moon would not rise for some hours and in the starlight the danger of wandering off the track was quite a real one. It was urgent, however, to get the boy into the hands of a doctor as soon as possible, and imperative to get him to the station and in shade before the sun rose again. They decided to wait till midnight and see if a car turned up to look for them; by that time the moon would be up and one or other of them could follow the track back without much danger.

They sat together in the firelight under the stars, rising every now and then to feed a little more water into the boy, or to put on more wood. Once Stanton said, laughing, 'I guess I've never been so hungry in my life.'

She laughed with him. 'It's the way it is here,' she said. 'You aren't a bit hungry in the daytime, but then as soon as it gets cool you're famished.' She turned to him. 'Come on and sit down and let's talk about something to take our minds off it.'

'Okay,' he said, settling down beside her. 'What'll we talk about?'

Her mind turned to the magazines she had been reading and to the many things that she had wanted to ask him about America. She said, 'Stan, have you ever done any water-skiing?'

He glanced at her in surprise; it was a far cry from the Lunatic, and a boy dying of thirst beside them, to Wallowa Lake in the cool mountains, the flying spray, the weaving flight over the surface. 'You mean, behind a motor boat?' he said. 'I used to do that summers, when I was in college.'

'I've only seen it on the movies, and there was an article

about it in one of the magazines,' she said. 'Tell me, is it tremendous fun?'

He smiled. 'It's quite a thrill,' he said. 'Don't people do that here?'

'It's not very easy without water,' she informed him. He laughed. 'I did see somebody doing it once, at Perth, in the distance. I'd just love to learn to do that.'

'We do quite a bit of it at home,' he said.

'On the lakes around Hazel?'

'That's right.'

'How do you get the boat? Can you hire them on the lakes?'

'I guess you can rent a boat, most places,' he said. 'I wouldn't really know. You want an outboard boat with a pretty big motor, twenty-five horsepower or so. Most people take their own boat along.'

She wrinkled her brows. 'Take their own boat? Have you got a boat like that?'

'Why, surely,' he said. 'Most people in Hazel seem to have a boat in the backyard. On a trailer. Hitch it on behind the car when you go fishing.'

In the aridity of the Lunatic such a possession was beyond her wildest dreams. In the dream world of the magazines people had motor boats and sat about in them in bathers, and fished from them, and tore over the water with hair flying. She said, 'People – ordinary people – really do have boats like that, do they?'

'Why, yes,' he said. 'Folks with families mostly have a boat on a trailer, back home. It's somethin' for the kids to do, on a vacation. We always had one. Used to get a new boat every three years or so, 'n trade in the old one.'

The real world was merging with the dream world of the magazines. 'Did you learn water-skiing behind your own boat, then?'

'Why, certainly,' he said. 'Dad got a big motor, 'n taught us all one summer, up at the lake. We kept that motor for a while, but I guess he's swapped it for a smaller one by now. I don't remember seeing it around the basement. A small motor's better for fishing, 'n lighter to handle when you put it on the boat.'

'Tell me,' she said. 'How *do* you water-ski? What do you do?'

They sat together in the quiet of the outback night before the glowing embers of the fire while he told her. She kept him talking, and he needed little encouragement to keep on talking about the country that he loved so well. He told her about water-skiing and about trout-fishing, about the long horseback trips up into the mountains, about deer-hunting, about the deer that he had shot with Chuck, about his bow and arrows, about the head and antlers that he had not seen, that had now been delivered to his father's house in Hazel. 'Dad wrote that the Bowmen of Hazel elected me a member,' he told her. 'That was certainly mighty nice of them.'

'It sounds marvellous,' she said. 'Aren't you terribly anxious to get back home to see the antlers?'

He nodded. 'I'd kind of like to see them,' he admitted. 'It's too bad that Chuck won't be there, though.'

'I know,' she said gently. 'When do you think you'll be back in Hazel, Stan?'

He was silent for a minute. Then, 'It depends upon the well,' he said. 'Right now it doesn't look so good.'

'You mean, you're not going to find oil?'

'I wouldn't say that,' he told her. 'We got some gas last week, and we thought maybe there'd be oil there underneath the gas, 'n we got all het up about it though we didn't say anything. But all we got so far is traces in the shale, traces that show up on a water test or else in the laboratory, but not enough to get excited about. Nuthin' to come up liquid to the surface.'

'If there's no oil there,' she said, 'what will you do?'

'I guess I'd resign my job with Topex,' he said. ''n go home and help my father.'

'Help your father in the business, like you told me?'

'Uh-huh. He wants me to help run the auto business, so he can go earth-moving.'

Sitting in the quiet night with her, he told her all about it again. 'That way I might be home around July,' he said. 'I'd kind of like to do that, go home and live in Hazel. I guess I've had my fill of hot countries, in the oil business.'

She said quietly, 'And if you strike oil, Stan?'

'I guess if we strike oil here in the Lunatic it might be so important that they'd put in someone over me to take care of it and expand the field,' he said. 'I'd like to have it that way, of course – to go out with a success behind me here. But I don't somehow feel it's going to be like that. I reckon this is a dry hole.'

'Even if you find oil, then,' she said, 'you'd be resigning just the same.'

He nodded. 'I guess so. I want to be back home.'

She sat in silence with him under the stars. The dream world of the magazines was vanishing away. If the oil well were unsuccessful, as now seemed quite probable, everything would disappear. The Americans would go away, headed by Stanton Laird; big trailer trucks would come and take away the oil rig to set it up again in some more promising location. Only a few concrete blocks and platforms would remain on Laragh Station to show where they had been. There would be no more ice cream or Coca-cola in the Lunatic, no more American magazines, no more firsthand stories of the living conditions on the other side of the Pacific Ocean. There would be no chance of a town arising in the Lunatic, a town that would be based on oil, with hairdressers, and shops, and cafés, theatres, and churches. The country would go back to what it was before, the worse for hopes that had been raised and disappointed.

She said quietly. 'We'll all be terribly sorry to see you go.'

'I guess I'll be sorry to go, too, in some ways,' he replied.

She glanced at him. 'Why do you say that? You can't like living in a place like this, after Oregon.'

'I dunno,' he said slowly. 'I hated it when we first came here. But I guess you get kind of used to a place, and folks here have been mighty nice to us.'

'It's made a tremendous difference to the Lunatic, having

165

you all here,' she said. 'You can't think what it's meant. But from your point of view, I do see it, Stan. In your shoes I should just be itching to get back to Hazel, and when I'd got there I'd never leave it again.'

'That's the way I feel, mostly,' he said. 'And yet in some ways I just can't bear to go.'

'Why?' she said. 'What's so attractive about this place?'

He said simply, 'You.'

She turned towards him, and he took her hand. 'I didn't mean to talk this way,' he said. 'I'm eight years older than you, Mollie, and that don't seem right. But ever since you let me come 'n tell you about Chuck I've thought about nothing else, and now that the oil well don't look too good I just can't bear the thought that I'll be going away soon, and never see you again.' He paused. 'I guess there's one thing above everything a man like me wants in his wife,' he said, 'and that's that she'd be kind. And that's what you've been to me – kind.' He smiled at her whimsically. 'What your Dad would say – the kindest hopper this side of the black stump.'

She looked up at him, half crying and half laughing. 'I didn't know that you were thinking about me as a hopper!'

'I wasn't really,' he said. 'That's sort of allegorical, like the black stump. But if I was to tell you, honey, that you were the kindest person that I'd ever met this side of the black stump – I guess that would be true.'

She said, 'Stan – you can't be serious!' The dream world was flooding back again. Behind Stanton Laird, a better man than she had ever met before, came flooding in a wave the Safeway where you could do your housekeeping in ten minutes even on Sunday afternoon, the Buicks and the Plymouths, the hairdressers, the Cokes and the milk shakes in the Piggy-Wiggy café, the mountains, the trout streams, and the cool mountain lakes with your own speedboat flying over them. 'Oh, Stan!'

He drew her to him. 'I'm terribly in love with you, Mollie. I guess I'm older than I'd have liked it to be, and too serious maybe. But I do love you very truly. Will you marry me?'

166

'I think I'd love to, Stan.' Of course she would; in all the world she knew, she would never find a better man than Stanton Laird. She turned to him, and kissed him very fondly.

Presently he said, 'Are you quite sure, Mollie?'

She drew away from him a little, and said, 'I think so, Stan. I think I could make you happy, and I think you'd make me happy, too.'

He said quietly, 'What's troubling you, then?'

She smiled. 'I don't think anything's troubling me, Stan. I'm too happy to be troubled. Tomorrow, or some time, we'll have to be practical, decide how and where we're going to be married, and all that.' She was thinking that she was a Catholic and he a Presbyterian, and a very sincere one, too. Already she could see that there were problems ahead of them to be surmounted. She drew close to him again. 'Let's not talk about that now.'

Presently he said quietly, 'I never thought when I came to Australia I'd go back with a wife.'

'Will your people at home think it very terrible, Stan? You marrying an Australian girl?'

He shook his head. 'They'll be just tickled to death. Of all the countries in the British Commonwealth, I guess the Australians would be the most like us – barring Canada, of course.'

She sat nestling close to him, his arm around her. 'I *am* looking forward to seeing Hazel and meeting your people, Stan. Tell me some more about them, and how you live.'

He did so, for the next hour. From time to time he would get up and throw more wood upon the fire while she attended to the boy wrapped in the blanket. He seemed to be asleep now in the quiet darkness underneath the brilliant stars, or else in a coma; he was very hot to the touch. There was nothing more that they could do for him, however.

Presently he said, 'What had we better do about your own folks, honey? Had I better go and see your Dad?'

'Not yet,' she said. 'Let Ma tell him, Stan ... I'll tell

Ma about us when we get back to the station, and then let you know.'

'He likely to be mad about it?'

She shook her head. 'Not now. He would have been before you came to Laragh, but you've changed all that. He didn't like Americans before, but he does now.'

'Well, what do you know!'

They sat there together, very happy, till about twenty minutes past eleven. Then, when both were beginning to think that one of them must ride to Mannahill, they heard the humming and the clatter of a truck, and saw headlights on the road coming from the station. They got up and stirred up the fire so that it rose in a great blaze, and Stanton pulled a bough out of it and waved the fiery brand. The truck pulled up, and they heard voices hailing them, and they hailed back. Then men were walking up the river bed to them.

It proved to be Pat Regan and one of the coloured stockmen from Mannahill. Mollie and Stanton walked a little way to meet them. 'We've got him here, Dad,' the girl said. 'He's terribly burnt, and he can't talk. He's taken a good bit of water, though.'

'What time was it that ye found him?'

'Just before sunset, Dad. It was dark by the time we got fixed up, and we didn't want to put him on a horse because of his skin. So we camped here till someone came to find us.'

'Ye got water from beneath?'

'Yes. Stan dug for it.'

'There's the good girl. There's many a man died of the thirst beside a river the like of this, and clear, cool water beneath. Sure, his mother should be burning candles to the miracles of God, the way you found him.'

'Stan found him first, Dad. He saw his water bottle in the road, where he'd dropped it. I'd have missed it. I thought it was a stone.'

'May the holy saints reward ye, Mr Laird.'

They reached the fire, and the boy beside it, wrapped in the horse blanket. Gently the red-headed old man turned the blanket back and examined the body. Then he stood up. 'It's the doctor himself is needed for this one,' he said.

'Where is the doctor?' Stanton asked.

'Sure, he's at Mannahill Station, with the pilot, for the night. He flew to bring Cy Peters and three men from Forest Downs, and they riding the country every way save this, an' the doctor cutting up the body out on the verandah with Fortunate to help, and him as crazy as an old Jew selling muslin. I sent Clem Rogerson a telegram in Perth by the Flying Doctor, the way he'd come back to sort out his station.'

Under the old man's direction they set to work to improvize a stretcher. They made a frame of two long branches with two shorter ones lashed across, and to this framework they lashed one of the tough, coarse horse blankets, using one pair of reins and Stanton's bootlaces to stretch it taut. Then they moved the body on to this and, one at each corner and leading the horses, they made their way down to the road.

At the truck, they managed to load the stretcher with one end supported on an oil drum full of water and the other end supported on the tailboard, so that the spring of the branches would absorb much of the jolting and so save the boy as much as possible. Mr Regan sent the coloured boy off up the road leading one horse and riding the other, and Mollie and Stanton got into the back to ride beside the stretcher and prevent its falling from its somewhat rickety support. Pat Regan got into the driving seat, and they started up the road to Mannahill in the clear moonlight.

In the back, in the clatter and dust of the truck, Mollie and Stanton sat holding hands, absurdly happy; once or twice they kissed. Once Stanton said, 'You know somethin', honey? I guess I'm going to remember this night if I live to be a hundred.'

She said, 'We're both going to remember it, Stan, all our lives.'

The truck drew up at Mannahill at about one in the morning. A couple of men who had been sleeping on the boards of the verandah got up as they drove in and came to meet them, and the doctor came out of one of the rooms clad in his pyjamas and a pair of elastic-sided riding boots. They carried the rough stretcher from the truck into one of the bedrooms, and the doctor began his work.

'They'll fly him away out of it at dawn,' said Pat Regan, 'down to the hospital at Hastings.' He went rummaging about the broken-open liquor store until he found what he was looking for, which was a bottle of rum. He poured himself a third of this into a tumbler, and shot it down followed by a chaser of water. 'Isn't it the great mercy that they left the rum?' he said. He turned to Stanton Laird, full of goodwill. 'Sure, there's a time and there's a place for everything, Mr Laird, and with your exertions you'll be after needing a drink. Will ye not join us, now?'

The American hesitated, mindful of the old man who was to be his father-in-law. Mollie came to his rescue. 'I'm going to make myself a cup of tea,' she said. 'Would you rather have that, Stan?'

He said apologetically to the old man, 'I've got quite a way to drive home, Mr Regan. I guess if I had rum I might drive off into the bush, 'n then you'd have another search party.' To Mollie he said, 'I certainly would like some tea. I'll come and help you make it.'

It was arranged that he should drive the girl to Laragh Station on his way back to the oil rig; Pat Regan would stay on at Mannahill until Clem Rogerson got back from Perth to take control of his property. Mollie and Stanton were very hungry indeed. Pat Regan went roaring to the domestic quarters and came back driving a black woman before him like a flushed hen, still struggling into a cotton frock; she blew up the embers of a wood fire very quickly while he stood abusing her, and threw on four enormous mutton chops snatched from the butcher's shop; within a quarter of an hour they were sitting at the kitchen table eating a large meal of grilled meat, bread and jam, cheese, and tea.

At about three in the morning Stanton and Mollie left

for Laragh in the oil men's jeep. They drove sleepily, very close together; the drive took two hours, but it seemed short to them. They came to Laragh Station in the first light of the dawn, when people were already astir; most of the work upon that property took place between dawn and ten o'clock in the morning.

As they drew to a standstill, Stanton said quietly, 'I'll be over around tea time, Mollie. I guess this has been the most wonderful day I've ever had in my whole life.'

She pressed his hand. 'Thanks, Stan. Thank you for everything.' She got out of the jeep, and went to meet her uncle and the Judge on the verandah. Stanton drove on to the oil rig.

SEVEN

MOLLIE slept late that morning. Her mother, looking in at the french window of her room at about eleven o'clock, saw her struggling towards consciousness in the increasing heat, and brought her a cup of tea. The girl took it from her sleepily. Her mother stood looking down on her. 'They're saying on the wireless that ye found the laddie that was lost,' she said. 'You and Stan Laird between you.'

Recollection of the night's events came back to her. 'That's right,' she said. 'Daddy's staying over at Mannahill till Mr Rogerson gets back.'

'Aye, I heard that.' She paused. 'Stan Laird bring you home?'

The girl nodded, with joy in her heart. 'We got home about five o'clock. Ma, Stan wants me to marry him.'

Her mother's expression did not change. 'Oh, aye,' she said. 'I was wondering when that was coming.'

'Aren't you pleased, Ma?'

'Are ye going to?'

Mollie nodded emphatically.

'Ah weel, he's a decent man, and well brought up, I'd say.

171

Does your father know about this yet?'

The girl shook her head. 'It was all in such a mess at Mannahill. I wasn't sure how Dad would take it, either.'

'Ye mean, the laddie's an American?'

Mollie nodded.

'Your father likes him well enough, child. Would ye rather that I spoke about it to him first of all?'

'I would like that, Ma. I was hoping that you would.'

'Oh, aye, I'll take care of that for you. When will he be coming over next?'

'He said he'd be over about tea time.'

'With the fear of the Lord in his heart, nae doubt. Are ye very happy?'

The girl looked up and nodded. Her mother bent and kissed her. 'Well, get up and have your shower,' she said practically, 'an' then go and help the Countess with the dinner.'

The Scotswoman went out on to the verandah and sat down in her accustomed place, but she could not relax. Presently she got up and went over to the store. In the office room the Judge was teaching half his class the elements of reading the English language, teaching a quarter of them how to sew a buckle on a girth, and teaching the other quarter trigonometry, all at the same time. 'Give them something to read, Judge, and come on over to the house,' she said. 'I want to talk to you.'

When he came, she said, 'Mollie tells me that she wants to marry Stan Laird. He asked last night.'

The Judge nodded slowly. 'You were expecting that, were you not?'

'Oh, aye, I've been expecting it.'

'Have you any objection?'

'I have no objection. He's a decent lad. But I'm thinking that his folks back in America might have.'

'Why should they object to her?'

'She's a bastard and she's a Catholic,' the Scotswoman said. 'There's two good reasons, and if that's not enough I could name you half a dozen others.'

'He's a Presbyterian, isn't he?'

'Aye, and a good member of the kirk. I have nae doubt that they're a family that's well regarded back in his own place.'

'She's well regarded here.'

'Aye, but I'm not. Not by Father Ryan, anyway.'

The Judge said heavily, 'Well, this is going to take a little thought.'

'That it is,' the ex-barmaid said. 'Sit ye down, Judge. It's full early, but wait now while I go fetch the bottle and a little ice.'

The Judge took his rum neat with a chaser of ice-cold water; the Scotswoman sipped hers diluted, with ice tinkling in the glass. They say in silent reflection for a few minutes. Then, 'Is she very much in love with him?'

'Oh, aye,' her mother said casually. 'I'd say she's even more in love with the *Saturday Evening Post*.'

'A very remarkable magazine,' the Judge said thoughtfully. 'A very, very remarkable magazine. It never ought to be allowed outside America.'

Mrs Regan glanced at him. 'Tell me, Judge. You've travelled the world. Would ye say that things in America would be like the pictures in them papers?'

He said slowly, 'I would say that they are exactly like. But the pictures are of things – things, not of the minds of people. If the pictures were of the minds of people those magazines would be dull to look at, because the minds of people are very much the same, in England, or in America, or in Australia.'

She struggled to understand him. 'Ye mean, the people over there would be the same sort as us?'

'I would say so. Little differences, little differences, perhaps, but nothing very great. But to look at the magazines, one would suppose that everything would be completely different in America, a hedonistic paradise where human jealousies, depravities, and infamies would be unknown. A land where every woman is young and smiling on a sunny background, a land where every man is young and bronzed and wears an Arrow collar and Stetson hat.' He paused. 'I think, with your permission, Mrs Regan, I will take a little more rum, to rinse the taste of falsehoods from my mouth.'

She wrinkled her brows as he downed another rum. 'Ye mean, they get old and they get tired and they get wicked, just the same as us?'

'Just the same as us, Mrs Regan – just the same as us. But, to read the magazines, one might think they would be different. That is because the magazines in their advertisements show things alone, and things are merely toys. An adult mind grows tired of toys in a few days, and a child does not take much longer. But I would say that Mollie has an adult mind, for all her youth.'

'Ye mean, that she'd grow tired of all the new things she sees in America, in a short time?'

'I think she would. I think that then she would begin to discover the people, and she might discover them to be exactly as we are.'

They sat in silence for a time. 'Do ye mean this, Judge? If we was to set our minds upon a small town in Australia, the same as this town Hazel in America, a town with the same number of people, raising grass seeds, maybe, just the same? And if we was to set our minds upon a Presbyterian family in that town, well regarded and good members of the kirk? And if we was to think of Mollie settled down in such a place, would that be the same?'

'I think that is precisely right,' the Judge said. 'I think it would be exactly and precisely the same.'

There was another silence. 'It's an awfu' and a sobering thought,' the mother said at last.

'The more so,' the Judge observed quietly, 'because she'd be nine thousand miles away.'

'Is it that far?'

'I have not measured it exactly. But I would think that that would be about the distance.'

The Scotswoman got heavily to her feet. 'Well, I must think on it. It's a long, long way from her own folks for a lassie to be unhappy.'

174

Stanton Laird came to Laragh at about five o'clock that afternoon. As he got out of his jeep he hoped that Mr Pat Regan was still over at Mannahill; although he had become on friendly terms with the grazier he had a notion that initially the mother would be easier to deal with, a notion which was to be proved quite erroneous. Mrs Regan and Mollie were seated on the verandah; the girl got up and came out into the sun to meet the jeep.

'Good afternoon, Stan,' she said, a little shyly.

He got out. 'Afternoon, honey,' he said. He took her hand, and looked into her eyes. 'Sorry about anything yet?'

She shook her head, smiling. 'Not yet,' she said. 'Are you?'

He took her hand. 'Not yet,' he repeated. 'In fact, I'd even say I'm kind of glad.'

She laughed outright.

'Your Dad back yet?'

'Not yet. I told Ma, Stan – about us.'

'Fine. I guess I'd better go and let her give me the once over. How'd she take it?'

'Very well,' the girl said. 'She thinks a lot of you, Stan. The only thing she seems sorry about is that we won't be living a bit nearer. She seems to think America's so far away. I told her it was only two days from Sydney in an aeroplane, but I don't think it really registered.'

'It *is* quite a way, honey. I can see it from her point of view.'

The girl tossed her head. 'It's not as if I was an only child. She's got nine other children living in Australia. She can spare one.'

He smiled. 'Did you tell her that?'

'I did.'

'What did she say?'

The girl hesitated, and glanced at him. 'Ma's a bit outspoken sometimes.'

He laughed. 'I found that out already. What did she say, honey?'

'She said if I was going to talk like that she'd better set about having a few more kids as spares.'

He laughed. 'I guess there's no answer to that one.'

She turned towards the verandah. 'Come on in and talk to her. Stan. She's all right.'

They went together to the verandah. Stanton said to Mrs Regan, 'Good afternoon. Mollie says she told you about us.'

'Aye,' said the mother, 'she did that. I told her you were too good a man for her, an' that I thought the worse of you for asking, but it all flowed off her like water off a duck's back.' She motioned to a chair. 'Sit ye down, Mr Laird, and tell us whatever made ye do such a daft thing.'

He laughed, and sat down. 'I guess everyone goes a little daft when he's in love,' he observed. 'But I'd say that this is the most sensible thing I ever did in all my life.'

Mrs Regan smiled at him kindly. 'Ah well, she's a good girl, an' let's hope that you won't live to regret the day.' She turned to her daughter. 'Mollie, go off and start getting the tea. I want to have a talk with your young man alone.'

'Can't I stay, Ma?'

'No, ye can't. Be off with ye.'

She went reluctantly. When she was gone the Scotswoman turned to the geologist. 'Now, Mr Laird, we'll talk practical politics. I'll have ye know, in the first place, they ye've a good name here, and that I could'na wish a better man for Mollie. Ye need not think that I'm against you, nor her father either. But there's one or two things to be settled before this goes any further.'

He nodded. 'I'd say there might be.'

'In the first place, when were you two thinking of getting married?'

'I haven't talked about that with Mollie yet, Mrs Regan,' he replied. 'It's all pretty new. But I'd say my job here would be finished within three months from now, and I was planning to resign from the oil business then, and go back home to help my father. He owns a garage and engineering business back in Hazel, 'n he wants to turn that over to me, mostly, while he goes road-contracting.'

She nodded. 'Mollie told me that. It sounds like a good opening.'

'It's a good opening all right. With the share of profits I'd be earning around twenty thousand a year – dollars, that is. That's quite a bit more than I'm making now.' He paused. 'I haven't talked this over with Mollie,' he repeated. 'But I'd say that the right time for us to get married would be before I leave here to go home.'

She sat in silence for a minute, studying her sewing. Then she said, 'She tells me you're a Presbyterian.'

He nodded, sensing trouble. 'That's right.'

'She's a Catholic. I would not say that she's a very good Catholic, with three hundred miles to go to attend Mass. But she's a good girl, and she'll want to do the proper thing. Were ye thinking that you'd have a Catholic marriage?'

'I haven't thought about that yet. Perhaps a civil marriage would be better.'

'Aye,' she said quietly, 'if you're both willing to give up your principles, which she's not and I don't suppose you are. However, leave that be, and let's suppose that we get Father Ryan to come here and marry you, for all the ill he thinks of Laragh Station. Would your father or your mother be coming to the wedding?'

'I wouldn't say so,' he replied. 'It's quite a way to come.'

She nodded. 'It is that.'

She sat sewing in silence. Presently she said, 'What that means, then, Mr Laird, is that Mollie would be married to you here and go off with you to a foreign country, to a country that she's never seen but only read about, married to a foreigner, to go to settle down alongside relations that she's never seen at all. It's a big jump in the dark you're asking of her, Mr Laird.'

He nodded slowly. 'I hadn't thought of it that way.'

'Ye'd better start thinking of it, then, and thinking hard. I tell ye, Mr Laird, for all that you're well respected in these parts, I think you're asking too much of a decent lassie if you ask her that.' She paused. 'Many a girl has taken a big chance like that and come well out of it, but there's some that haven't.'

'Do you think she ought to pay a visit to us first, in Hazel?' he asked. 'My folks would like that.'

She nodded. 'Aye. I was thinking the same thing. I was thinking perhaps if she went back with you and stayed three months or so, and then for you to be married in Hazel.' She looked up at him, smiling. 'Maybe I'd come over for the wedding, an' see America myself.'

He sat in thought for a few moments. Although he had been the first to propose this plan, it was vaguely distasteful to him, as though Hazel and himself would be on trial. 'I'd like to talk it over with Mollie, Mrs Regan,' he said. 'I see it from your point of view, and I think it makes sense, but it does mean a pretty long engagement.'

Her mother shook her head. 'It does not,' she said. 'She'd not be engaged to you until she makes her mind up that she wants to get married, and I wouldn't want to see her do that till she's met your folks and seen the way you live.'

'You wouldn't want us to get engaged now?'

'I would not.'

'Why not, if she wants to marry me?'

'She doesna know enough about you, Mr Laird. Maybe when she sees the way you live in your own place she'll want to change her mind.' She glanced at him. 'Be easy, now. She may not want to change it, and I hope she won't. I've told you you're well regarded here. But if she went with you to meet your folks as an engaged girl, then it's going to be difficult for her to change her mind if she should want to. Now, that's what I won't have.'

'I'd like to talk it over with Mollie, Mrs Regan.'

'Aye, ye can do that. An' I'll talk to her, too. She can go with ye to America and stay as long as she likes, but she goes as a free girl, Mr Laird – a girl who's free to get into the train an' come home, or go on to England, any day she likes, and no promise broken, and no harm done to anybody.'

'It's going to put her in a kind of an unusual position, Mrs Regan,' he pointed out. 'I mean, she'd be travelling halfway around the world with me and staying in hotels, in all kinds of places. Some folks might think that kind of strange behaviour.'

'If you're thinking of her reputation, Mr Laird,' her mother said, 'ye can put your mind at rest. She comes from Laragh Station, so she's none to lose.' She bent a stern eye on him. 'But while we're on the subject, Mr Laird, I tell you there's to be no funny business or I'll see to it she never marries you at all. Ye needn't think ye'll put a chain on her that way. We're well acquaint with bastards upon Laragh Station, an' we can always use another.'

He was appalled at the turn the conversation had taken. 'Say,' he protested, 'you got me all wrong, Mrs Regan. I wouldn't ever do a thing like that.'

She sat in silence for a minute. At last she said, 'Well, maybe not.' Her doubts if this was the right man for Mollie were reinforced. 'But if the thought should come into your head one day, ye'll just mind what I say.'

'I can assure you,' he said earnestly, 'she will be safe with me. I do think it might be better if we were engaged before we start travelling around the world together, Mrs Regan – it makes it more regular. But if you think it best the other way, well, I'd agree. But I want to hear what Mollie thinks about it first.'

'Aye,' she said tranquilly. 'Nae doubt ye'll get together after tea in some dark corner. Do na' distress yeself, Mr Laird, and do na' take offence from my rough tongue. We all like you fine, but Mollie's our first care, an' there's a lot to be got over an' smoothed out before you two get married.'

'I certainly do appreciate the way you look at it,' he said. 'She'll be my first care, too.' He sat in silence for a moment, then said, 'Would she be the first of your children to get married, Mrs Laird?'

She shook her head. 'Mike's married, down in Perth,' she said. 'Mike Regan, that is – by my second marriage. He married a young lady from Melbourne; she was up here once, but she didn't like it and she's never come again. Phyllis married a man in Adelaide last year, a wool broker he is; she was my first child by Mr Foster.'

'One of your children is in England, isn't he?'

'Aye, that would be Charlie, Mike's brother. He's a doctor, in a place called Harley Street, but he's not married.'

Pat Regan arrived back from Mannahill in time for tea; Mr Rogerson had returned at midday in a plane chartered from Carnarvon. 'Sure, he was tearing into them like a madman the time I left, as though he was the Lord Bishop and him preaching against drink,' he said. 'He flew in just as we finished the burying, with the doctor himself reading a service over the poor lad, or what was left of him when Fortunate was done. But there'll be no wake at Mannahill this night.'

'What happened to the jackeroo, Daddy?' Mollie asked. 'Is he going to be all right?'

'Aye, he's doing fine. He sent a message to you, to thank for finding him.'

'What's happened to him now?'

'The doctor's after taking him to hospital, in the aeroplane.'

'Will he be coming back to Mannahill?'

'He will not. He wants to go home to England.'

Stanton Laird said, smiling, 'Well, what do you know!'

Mrs Regan said placidly, 'Aye, there's some that's fit for working in the Lunatic, and many more that's not.'

'There's a true saying,' said her husband.

She turned to him. 'Mr Laird here has been asking for Mollie,' she said.

'May the saints preserve us! Would he be after wanting to wed her?'

'I guess that's right, Mr Regan,' said the geologist. 'That's the way it is.'

The grazier stared at him. 'Well now,' he said affably, 'isn't that a great wonder, that the like of you would want to wed a girl like her! Was it in the dark night ye asked her now, and the two of you sitting by the wood fire under the bright stars, waiting while I came to find ye in the truck?'

Mollie laughed. 'That's right, Daddy. That's when it happened.'

'Sure, and I had my suspicions,' her father said, 'and you with all the starlight in your eyes. Go and get the bottle, girl.' He turned to the other. 'This is the one time ye'll take a drink, Mr Laird, even if it lays ye flat as all the boys at Mannahill.'

Stanton Laird compromised. 'It'll have to be a very small one, Mr Regan.'

'Aye.' The grazier winked at his prospective son-in-law. 'Just a quarter of the bottle.'

Stanton escaped with two fingers of rum drowned in a tumbler of water, and found it not unpleasant. He discovered that the new relationship occasioned no particular surprise; at Laragh Station with its many children, marrying and giving in marriage, whether formally or informally, was an everyday matter. It did not occur to Mr Regan to inquire into the American's position or his ability to support a wife, or even to inquire if he had ever been married before; such things in his view were matters that concerned the contracting parties alone.

Stanton Laird commented on that later that evening, as he walked arm in arm with Mollie beneath the stars in the direction of the wool shed. 'You know somethin', honey?' he said. 'It's quite different here from how things are at home. Back home you'd be getting up an engagement party, 'n you'd show your ring to all your friends, 'n I'd have to go meet them all. And then there'd be all the relations to meet, yours and mine – a kind of social whirl. But as things are, I haven't even got a ring to give you right now.'

'If you give me one, Ma says I'm not to wear it. She doesn't want us to be engaged till I've been to America with you.'

'I know, honey. How do you feel about that?'

'I think it's rather silly, Stan,' she said. 'I'm not a baby, and I know exactly what I'm doing.'

'I guess that's true,' he said. 'I'd say your mother was right if it was in the United States, where you could come and visit with my folks before we got engaged. But as things are, it's going to look mighty funny for you, if you travel with me to the States.' He hesitated.

'Funny in what way, Stan?'

'Travelling together, honey – in hotels. We'd be spending quite a few nights in hotels on the way – at Perth, at Sydney, maybe at Honolulu and quite probably at Portland or Seattle.' He thought for a minute. 'It might be possible to fix it so we stayed in different hotels.'

She said, 'It 'ld be all right if we didn't stay in the same room, wouldn't it?'

'You wouldn't mind travelling like that?'

'Of course not, Stan. Two rooms would be perfectly all right.'

'You wouldn't be afraid that folks might talk?'

'Of course not, Stan. You can't make love through a brick wall. Besides, its nothing to do with anybody if we did.'

'I guess that's right,' he said doubtfully.

She glanced at him, aware that he was still troubled. 'I'll travel any way you think best,' she offered. 'Tell me, will it start a lot of gossip in Hazel if we travel like that? It wouldn't do so here.'

He smiled down at her. 'I'd say things might be just a little bit different in the Lunatic from what they are in Hazel,' he observed. 'I wouldn't say that people gossip back at home. It's not a place like that. But at the same time, it's not like the Eastern States, New Jersey, or Connecticut, or places like that. Hazel's a small town, honey, where everybody knows all about everybody else, and not much else to talk about.'

They strolled on in the darkness. 'It's like that here, of course,' she said. 'We've got nothing else to talk about here except what goes on on the other stations – or up at the oil rig. I don't suppose there's much difference between this place and Hazel.'

'Maybe not,' he said, still a trifle doubtful. 'Maybe it's the kind of way you look at things that's different.'

She pressed a little closer to him. 'We're foreigners, of course, Stan, for all that we speak the same language. We'll have to work quite hard to get to understand each other.'

He stopped, and took her in his arms, and kissed her.

182

'I wouldn't say that's going to be difficult,' he said. And presently, when they were walking on again, he said, 'I've been wondering about one thing, honey.'

'What's that, Stan?'

'It's about your mother, when she was married to your Uncle Tom, and then she was married to your father. Didn't that make things kind of difficult when they all went on together, living under the same roof? Back in the States, in Oregon at any rate, it wouldn't hardly be possible.'

'I wasn't born, of course,' she said slowly. 'I can see it might seem funny to you, but it worked out all right. I can't ever remember any trouble; we were all a very happy family, I think.' She paused. 'I don't think Uncle Tom was the man for Ma at all. She probably only married him because she was having a bad time after Mr Foster's death, working in the bar with two children to look after. Daddy was much more Ma's type, but of course she never met him till she came back here with Uncle Tom.'

'And there wasn't any trouble? Back home the two men would have been out gunning for each other.'

She shook her head. 'I'm sure there wasn't anything like that. For one thing,' she said thoughtfully, 'there was the Mauser.'

He wrinkled his brows in perplexity. 'The Mouser? You mean, some kind of a cat?'

She glanced up at him. 'No – the Mauser. General O'Brian's Mauser pistol. It's sort of half a rifle and half a pistol; it's got a sort of wooden holster that fits on the back of it to make a stock. Hasn't Uncle Tom shown it to you?'

He shook his head, puzzled at the change of subject. 'Not yet, honey.'

'Oh well, he will,' she said. 'He's awfully proud of it. And it really is a sort of holy relic. I'll ask Uncle Tom to tell you the story.'

'What story, hon?'

'Uncle Tom or Daddy can tell you better than I can. But it was General Shamus O'Brian's own Mauser that he carried at the start of the Troubles, in Easter Week 1916. He was a terribly fine man, they say, and Uncle Tom and Daddy were with him when he was killed.'

'Killed, honey?'

She nodded. 'On the top of Jacob's biscuit factory. The English worked round behind them somehow and opened up on them with a machine gun from the rear. Daddy and Uncle Tom weren't hit because they were behind a chimney or something, but the General was hit and several of the others. Daddy and Uncle Tom got the General down with them behind the chimney, but he died in a few minutes. Before he died, he gave his Mauser pistol to Daddy and told him to go on fighting the damned English. Daddy carried it all through the Troubles and cut a little notch on the stock for every man he killed, in memory of Shamus O'Brian. Fourteen of them. But you must get him to tell you himself.'

Stanton wrinkled up his brow. 'But what's all that got to do with your mother, though?'

'Uncle Tom always wanted the Mauser,' she explained. 'He should have had it in the first place – Daddy admits that – because Uncle Tom was senior to Daddy in the IRA. But the General was dying and I suppose he gave it to the first man he saw. So when Ma changed over, Daddy gave Uncle Tom the Mauser.'

He stopped dead in his tracks. 'You don't mean that, honey? You don't mean that your uncle swopped your mother for an old pistol?'

She laughed. 'I wouldn't put it quite like that myself, Stan. But I think perhaps it eased hard feelings when Daddy gave him the Mauser. There were just the three great Irish generals in the Troubles – Edmund Pearse, Rory O'Connor, and Shamus O'Brian, and Uncle Tom always says that O'Brian was the greatest of them all. The Mauser means an awful lot to them.'

'I guess it would,' he said. They walked on in silence for a few minutes, the geologist thinking very deeply. Here in Lunatic an eccentricity that verged on lunacy made good sense. When a woman transferred her affections from one brother to another there was nothing much that anyone could do about it. Sensible brothers, used to getting on together in a district hundreds of miles from any civilization, would not go gunning for each other over a thing like that. Stanton Laird was now beginning to appreciate Pat Regan, to appreciate the depth of sincerity and good feeling that lay in the old Irishman. In such a situation a right-thinking man would willingly part with his dearest possession to ease the hurt pride of his brother and a right-thinking brother would recognize the sacrifice, and be mollified. The dearest possession happened to have been an old German pistol. It might equally well have been, on Laragh Station, a Rolls-Royce motor car or the Countess; the personal sacrifice involved would have been the value of the gift. Still, it wasn't the sort of story about his mother-in-law that he'd like to have talked about back home in Oregon. No reason why it ever should be, though.

David Cope, at Lucinda Station, heard the news from Ted next day. Ted was the head cook in the Americans' camp, and he was the only one at the oil rig who thought his time well spent if it was spent in reading a book. He had fallen into the habit of visiting the young Englishman once or twice a week, driving over in one of the jeeps. Usually these visits were for social courtesy and he would usually take with him an enormous peach pie or an angel cake, together with a tin or two of cream to liven up the somewhat pedestrian cooking of the Lucinda gins. Actually he went to return a book and to borrow another one, as well as for a change from the oil rig.

Ted was now David's only contact with the Americans. As Mollie's intimacy with Stanton Laird had ripened he had found the company of the oil men increasingly distasteful and it was now nearly two months since he had visited the rig to see their movies or for any other reason. Moreover, Lucinda was by now in a bad way for lack of rain. The Lunatic lies at the southern edge of the monsoon, the summer rains of North Australia. Usually the country got eight or ten inches of winter rain in June and July, and most years it could look for a few inches of summer rain from the monsoon in January and February. Lucinda with its few bores, however, was a marginal station; unless it got the summer rains it was difficult to carry any stock through from the end of the winter rains in August to the beginning of the next year's winter rains in June. That year, for the first time in David's tenure of Lucinda Station, the summer rains had failed. Altogether they had totalled less than an inch, and that in three separate falls that had evaporated practically as soon as they touched the hot earth. Lucinda Station was in the grip of a drought, a drought that had hardly affected Laragh with its rather better rainfall and its many bores.

David was now trucking water to his sheep. He had plenty of water running still from his two bores, but the feed around these bores had long been eaten out. He had, however, an old three-ton truck and a thousand gallon tank, with a number of portable troughs. He did not dare to put more than five hundred gallons in the tank when driving across rough country, for the truck was his lifeline; if he broke a spring and put it out of action for a week all his sheep would die. He had about four thousand sheep, diminishing in number every day, and his aim was to take two gallons of water to each sheep each day, a total of sixteen journeys every day. He had moved his sheep out from the water progressively into country where there was still feed for them till now they were eight or ten miles from his bores, so that to reach his target he now had to drive three hundred miles a day. To fill his tank at the bore took nearly half an hour, and a quarter of an hour to empty it at the other end, so that it was now only just theoretically possible for him to carry two gallons per sheep if the truck were to run unceasingly for twenty hours a day. Actually, he was falling far behind his target for a variety of practical reasons, and he was now delivering less than a gallon and a half each day to each sheep. They were helping him, however, because the deaths were mounting rapidly.

He had plenty of fuel and tyres for the truck, and Jackie,

his half-caste overseer, was a good driver; they shared the work between them. So far as possible they avoided the hottest part of the day because there are limits to human endurance, and because the evaporation from the troughs was greatest then. They had fallen into a routine whereby Jackie started driving at about three in the afternoon and went on till midnight, when he would take over from David and the stockmen any movement of the sheep on to fresh feed that might be going on. David would commence to move the sheep on to fresh pasture at sunset and then take over the truck from Jackie at midnight, continuing to cart water till about nine o'clock in the morning, when he would eat something and get what sleep he could in the heat of the day in the torrid little house that was Lucinda homestead. He had been living like this for a month, and he was getting very thin and haggard. And his sheep were dying on him all the time.

Ted knew this routine, and aimed his visit for about half past four in the afternoon, when David would have finished sleeping and would be preparing for the night's work. He drove up in the oil rig jeep, and David left his meal and came out to meet him.

'Hi-yah, fellow,' said the cook. 'I just stopped by to see if you were still alive enough to eat a piece of cake.'

The Englishman grinned. 'Just about,' he said. 'I don't suppose I'll be next week, if this goes on.'

The American got out of his jeep. 'Any sign of it letting up?'

David shook his head. 'Not a hope. June the 10th – that's the first date we can expect a rain. Nine weeks to go.'

'How're the goddam stock holding out?'

'Lost about three hundred last week. Jackie says more, but I don't think it was.'

The American wagged his head. 'Jeez! I guess you won't have many left by June the 10th.'

David said, 'It gets easier as they die off, because there aren't so many to water. I think we'll probably get through with about two thousand, or a little under.'

'Out of four thousand you started with?'

'That's right.'

'Quite a loss.'

'I know,' said David. 'We'll be back to where we started. It's a pity, because we'd been doing pretty well and I was planning that we'd sink another bore or two. But now we'll have to wait a bit for that.'

The other wagged his head in sympathy. 'That's kind of tough.'

They turned to the house. 'Come on in. I'm just going to have tea before going out to work.'

'I guess I won't stay.' the American said. 'I got a lot of guys back at the rig'll want their chow.'

'Well, come on in and have a drink. I've got some whisky.'

'You have? Oh brother!'

While David got the whisky and the glasses, Ted said, 'I brought back *The Cruel Sea*. Those guys in the North Atlantic certainly had it tough. Mind if I take another book?'

David said, 'Go ahead and take your pick. In the bedroom.'

Ted went through into the bedroom, glanced at the framed portrait photograph of Mollie that still stood upon the chest of drawers, and stood looking absently at the row of titles. He stood there so long in thought that David came in to look for him, carrying a whisky bottle and a glass in one hand, and a gin bottle full of cold water from the refrigerator in the other. 'Here you are.'

The American took the whisky and poured three fingers into the glass. He hesitated for a moment, and then said, 'She your girl?'

David shook his head. 'She doesn't think so.'

'Uh-huh. You heard the news?'

'What news?'

'I don't know if it's true, brother. But they're saying at the rig she's going to marry Stan Laird.'

David nodded slowly. 'It's probably true enough.' He had been expecting nothing else, but when the news finally came it was painful just the same, because it meant the end of hope. He said mechanically, 'I suppose I'd better take that down.' He reached for the portrait.

Ted said, 'I wouldn't do that yet, fellow. Not until she's married.'

'Do you know when that 'll be?'

'He's going to the States in June. I guess it might be then.'

'He's going whether there's oil here or not?'

The other poured a little water on the whisky and downed half of it. 'There's no goddam oil here. This is a dry hole, a busted flush.'

'Is that right?'

'I guess so. They're going on drilling for a while, but all we got so far is gas, and not so much of that.'

'Isn't the gas any good?'

'Sure it's good, if you can use it. Lay a pipe twelve miles and you could heat this house with it, if you want it any hotter. Light the street lamps of a town with it, if you had a town with any streets. No, it's a busted flush, if you ask me.'

David said heavily, 'Well, Stan Laird's a good sort of chap.' He turned back to the living-room, and poured himself a whisky. He did not usually drink when he was alone, but in the circumstances it was both theatrical and comforting.

The American picked a book at random from the shelf, and followed him. 'Sure, Stan Laird's a good guy, as good as they come. They don't come any better.' He downed the last half of his drink. 'Too good for me, I guess. Drive me nuts to live with him.' He turned to the door, showing the book. 'I'll take this one, if I may. So long, boss, 'n thanks for the shot. Be seeing you.'

He went off in his jeep, and David sat in dejection with his whisky. The gin came and laid the table, and put down a sodden mess of overcooked mutton before him with a couple of tinned potatoes on the side and a slather of tinned carrots. Her duty finished, she withdrew and went away to the stockmen's quarters to nurse her youngest child at her capacious breasts, and David sat picking at the un-appetising meal in the great heat, and drinking the whisky. Once a tear trickled down his nose and he brushed it away irritably, because it was babyish to cry. Stan Laird was an older man, a better man, and a man who could provide a good home for a wife, which David knew that he could not. There were times when a chap had to keep his chin up and show what he was made of, and this was one of them. Self-pity never did anyone any good, and God knew that he had nothing to give away at this time, with all the bloody sheep dying like flies.

He had sent his three stockmen out to the sheep with Jackie an hour before, and now he followed them in the jeep, driving across country over the red earth in and out of the brown clumps of spinifex and the desiccated, scattered trees. It was time, he thought, to take stock of his plans. With Mollie at his side he would have battled on for ever to make something of Lucinda; it would have been their property, their challenge to meet side by side. Clive Ander-son, the bus operator in Perth who had gambled the small capital required for the venture, was fed up with his unpro-fitable investment. If he had married Mollie the Regans might quite probably have bought Clive out; Lucinda then would have been their very own. He would never have asked them for help, whether married to Mollie or not, because in the Lunatic a man stood or fell on his own feet, but inevitably the association would have helped him to success. If this truck broke down now all his sheep would die in a few days, but with Mollie at his side in such a catastrophe a truck would have materialized, un-asked for, from Laragh. It was not for this he would have married her, but without her he could view the prospects of success at Lucinda Sta-tion more objectively, and the prospects were not good.

Two days later he went over to Laragh in his jeep to fetch the mail. He had missed fetching it the week before through pressure of work and because he was expecting nothing but personal letters; he took time off to go this time because he wanted to hear for himself that Mollie was engaged, to kill the nattering of hope that lingered on from Ted's information.

Mollie saw his jeep coming in the distance as they sat on the verandah studying the letters brought by Spinifex Joe, and went out to meet him. She was troubled and uneasy about David, the more so for the reports of his drought troubles that had drifted into Laragh. It is bad manners to go upon a neighbour's property unless you are invited, so that the Regans had no direct knowledge of his difficulties, but there was some movement of the stockmen's coloured wives from station to station, and some information of affairs at Lucinda had reached Laragh from the oil rig. With the comprehensive knowledge of the country that they had, the Regans were very well aware of what David was up against. As Mollie went out to meet the jeep, she was hating herself for what she had to tell him, at this time.

He parked behind the big diesel semi-trailer so that they were screened by it from the verandah and could talk for a few minutes in some privacy. She was shocked by the change in his appearance since she had seen him last. 'Morning, David,' she said awkwardly.

He smiled, a little wryly. 'Morning,' he said. 'I hear I've got to congratulate you.'

She nodded, relieved that she had not had to tell him. 'That's right. I came out to tell you, David.' She hesitated. 'I thought you ought to know.'

'Nice of you,' he said. 'It *is* Stan Laird, isn't it?'

She nodded.

'When's it to be?'

'Not for some time,' she said. 'Ma's being a bit awkward.'

His interest was aroused. 'Why? Doesn't she like him?'

'Of course she does,' she replied, a little annoyed. 'Everyone likes him. It's not that. But she thinks I ought to meet his people in America before we even announce an engagement. So we're not engaged, but we're going to be married. That's how it is.'

'Well,' he said, 'that puts it on a par with everything else in the Lunatic, anyway.'

191

She glanced at him, and laughed uncertainly. 'You *are* a fool,' she said. 'David, you're looking like death. Are things bad over at Lucinda?'

'They're not good,' he said. 'We'll probably get about half of them through to the rains. Just enough to keep from going broke, and to encourage us to go on till it happens again.'

She nodded, because this was what she had expected from the gossip of the station. 'Come on over and have a drink,' she said.

'I think I will,' he replied.

Most of the Laragh party were on the verandah examining the mail. Mr Pat Regan turned to greet him, the kangaroo mouse on his shoulder. 'God bless ye, Mr Cope,' he said. 'Will ye take a drop of rum?'

'I'd rather have whisky, Mr Regan, if you've got any.'

'We have nothing but the Scotch,' the grazier said 'The Irish lies softer on the stomach but ye'd walk your heart out before ye'd find that in Australia. If ye'll heed me, ye'd do better on the rum.'

'I'd rather have the Scotch.'

Her father turned to Mollie. 'Go on and get a bottle of the Scotch, girl, and a bowl of ice.'

When she brought them, David filled a glass half full of whisky with a little water and a lump of ice on top. He raised his glass. 'Here's to the happy pair,' he said. 'Here's to one couple that's escaping from the Lunatic.' He drank.

Mollie laughed, a little self-consciously. Mrs Regan said quietly, 'Sit ye down, Mr Cope, an' take a look through your letters. There's three here came last week for you, that I saved till ye came over.'

He sat drinking his whisky and looking through the letters. There was nothing much for him to stay for now, and he was urgently required for half a dozen jobs on his own property. The truck that was his lifeline now had a flat tyre and a dubious magneto; he had spare tyres and spare points and condensers, but the work had to be done, and done in the heat of the day before carting water began again at three o'clock. With the whisky, however, he could relax and feel the fatigue soaking out of him; the nervous tension that had gripped him for a month was easing up. It would not hurt to sit a few minutes longer.

Presently the Judge said, 'I think if that is a bottle of Scotch whisky I would like to try a little for a change. I find sometimes that I grow tired of rum.'

Pat Regan said, 'Sure, it'll eat holes in your entrails the way they put holes in a colander. But take the whisky, Judge, an' the Lord have mercy on ye.'

The Judge rose and poured himself half a tumbler. He said to David courteously, 'May I refill your glass, Mr Cope?'

It was urgent for him to get back to Lucinda, but for the first time in weeks he felt rested and at ease. He said, 'Thanks.'

The Judge poured him a very generous glass, adding the ice and a little water, and sat down beside him. 'You said something just now about escaping from the Lunatic,' he observed. 'I find it a most peculiar thing, but now I do not want to leave the Lunatic. I remember when I first came here I used to make plans to get away and seek other employment, in an Australian school, perhaps. But now I feel at home here, and I would not wish to go away. Perhaps it is that each and every one of us discovers in the end his own place of fulfilment.' He swallowed half his whisky.

'That's all right for you,' muttered David, swallowing his. 'You aren't going broke.'

'But I *am* broke,' said the Judge placidly. 'I went broke a great many years ago because whenever I found myself in a hotel I spent my money, all the money that I had. So now I don't have any. It makes life very much simpler.'

David said thickly, 'Is it going broke that hurts? When you're down and out it doesn't hurt any more?'

The Judge said, 'The pain comes from losing what once you had. When there is no more to lose, I find that one can live quite happily.'

David sat in silence for a minute. Then he jerked himself awake; he was getting sleepy and there was a truck tyre to be changed at Lucinda. 'Roll on the next three months,' he said genially. 'No more pain after that.' He got unsteadily to his feet, with the best part of half a bottle of whisky inside him. 'I must be going on.' He tripped down the steps of the verandah, miraculously stable, and found his way round the diesel semi-trailer to his jeep. The engine roared into life, tearing its heart out as he revved it up, and drove off erratically on the track that led up to the oil rig and Lucinda. From the verandah they watched him go in silence.

'Yon laddie's got his skinful,' Mrs Regan observed quietly.

Mollie flushed. 'I've never seen him like that before,' she said.

'Ye've never seen him facing ruin before,' her mother retorted. 'From what they tell me there'll not be a sheep alive upon Lucinda come the rains.'

Pat Regan said, 'Sure, and the drink will do him good. He's destroyed altogether with the troubles that he's after having, and he'll be the better now with a drop taken.'

His wife said, 'Ye should help him, Pat.'

'Why would I be after helping him?' the old man demanded, 'the way he'd go on like a man with gold coins in the bank itself until next time the rains come light as morning dew and I'd be after helping him again? No man can run four thousand sheep upon Lucinda Station, not the Holy Father himself.'

Tom Regan made one of his rare utterances. 'That's a true word,' he said, and added lugubriously, 'It's all a part of it.'

'I think ye should help him, all the same,' their wife repeated quietly.

'In the name of the Almighty God,' declared the old man crossly, 'what for would I be after helping him, and he the son of a dastardly murdering Englishman that fought against Ireland in the Black and Tans? That sort would creep into your house in the dark night to slit your throat with the cold steel, and you sleeping like a babe in innocence, dreaming of the blessed saints in Heaven. Didn't they murder Jack Mullavy so, and he sleeping upon sentry in the glen with the rifle and the bottle at his side? What for would I be after helping a heretic the like of him, and with the Holy Mother looking down to see what I was doing, and Satan himself looking up and laughing?'

'Please yeself,' his wife repeated, 'but I think ye ought to help him.' The old man stumped off angrily down the verandah, well aware of the action of water dripping on a stone.

That afternoon Pat Regan was down at his stockyard breaking a new horse, or rather, sitting on a rail and supervising while James Connolly did so. The half-caste had it on a long rope to the halter and tapped it with a long bamboo from time to time to make it trot steadily around the arena, while his father kept up a running commentary. He was so engaged when Mollie came to him.

'Dad,' she said, 'may I speak to you?'

'And why not?' he replied. He made room for her, and she climbed up on to the stockyard rail beside him.

'It's about David Cope,' she said. 'Could we do anything to help him, do you think?'

'Well, Glory be to God!' her father said. 'Why would we be after helping him against a normal sort of summer drought, girl? If it was 1939 itself, the like of which you'd go for fifty years and never seen another the way no drop of rain came down for nineteen months, then I'd say help a neighbour if ye've help to give. But the like of this, sure, if we help him this time he'll be coming to us and expecting help every third year when the rain comes short.'

'I know, Dad,' the girl said. 'I would like to help him this time, though.' She hesitated. 'You see, I had to be rather unkind to him. It's not the time to be unkind to anyone when all his sheep are dying off like flies.'

'Was he wanting to wed you?'

'That's right,' she said. 'I had to tell him I was marrying Stan Laird.'

'The blessed saints preserve us! Is that a reason why we'd take four thousand sheep upon the property, and they so starved they'd eat as much as bullocks?'

'It is, if we can do it,' she said stubbornly. 'I've been unkind to him when he's having a bad time already. If somebody from here was kind to him for a change, it'd even
things up. How many sheep would we be running now?'

The old man sucked his lip. 'Thirty-three – thirty-four
thousand. It's hard to say.'

'*Could* we take his sheep and not get into trouble ourselves?' She paused. 'It's not four thousand, Dad – he's lost
about a thousand. It's more like three thousand now.'

He glanced at her from under his bushy red eyebrows.
'Are ye still thinking of him, girl?'

She flushed a little. 'Of course not. I'm going to marry
Stan. But I feel a bit as if I've kicked him when he's down.
Could we help him, Dad?'

He sat in silence for a time. It was hard to refuse her, for
she was the first white child that he had ever had, to the
best of his knowledge, and so he had taken more interest in
her than any of the others. His wife's insistence that the
children should be well educated and go to good schools
had seemed irrational to him at one time, a Scotswoman's
whim that had to be indulged for peace and quiet in the
house. Yet as this child grew up he had taken pride in her
as quite a little lady. It was a disappointment to him that
she meant to make her life nine thousand miles away, that
he would seldom see her again.

He called to his half-caste son, 'James Connolly! Let the
mare rest, and come on out of it.'

The stockman tied the rope to the rail and walked over
and stood below them as they sat on the high rail in the hot
sun. 'Listen to me, James Connolly,' the old man said. 'How
much feed would we be after having up at the top end,
around old Number Nine bore, and way over by Fourteen
and beyond?'

'Pretty good, boss. Missa Tom was saying maybe move
the mob around Six bore to old Number Nine next week.'

'How would it be round Number Ten?'

'Bit of feed there, Missa Pat. Not much.'

The old man sat in thought for a minute. 'Listen now,'

he said at last. 'We'll drive up there tomorrow, the way I'll see what's going on. Get the horse truck filled up tonight, with a drum of petrol and a drum of water. Start and load my roan horse at four o'clock, with a horse for you. I'll be after bringing tucker from the house.'

The half-caste nodded, and went back to the young mare. The girl turned to her father. 'Thank you, Dad.'

Her father grunted. 'Ye'll be bringing bankrupt ruin on the lot of us.'

Three days later he drove out in the jeep alone. He passed the cemetery that housed the dead Chinaman, passed the graded road that led off to the oil rig, and went through the Bloody Gate on to Lucinda. He saw no people and no sheep as he drove on to the homestead, because there was no water on that portion of the property. It was evening when he got to the homestead and David had already left wearily for the unending job of moving sheep and troughs on to fresh ground, in the stench of rotting corpses. Pat Regan got directions from one of the gins, and drove on.

He came to men working just before sunset. David left the trough that he was loading in the truck and came across to him. He was already exhausted, with the night's work before him.

The old man sat at the steering wheel of his jeep, and David stood before him. 'God save ye,' said Mr Regan. 'I drove across to see if ye'd spare me a few minutes.'

'Spare you any time you like, Mr Regan. I'm afraid I've nothing to offer you here, though.'

'Ah, be easy.' The old man glanced around, at the truck, the troughs, the weary men, the emaciated sheep, the swollen stinking corpses. One glance was sufficient, for he knew it all from his younger days before hard work and careful management had brought Laragh Station to its present state. 'Ye'll be after having strife, I'm thinking.'

The young man flushed. He hated to have a neighbour on his land to see his sheep, his business in this state. 'We'll be all right,' he said defensively.

'We'd all be right and have great times if we'd no sheep,'

Mr Regan said. 'Would it help ye, now, to put them over on to Laragh on agistment for a while? There's feed around our Number Fourteen bore at the top end would hold them till the rains.'

David stared at him, incredulous, his tired brain unable to take in the offer. 'How many could you take, Mr Regan?'

'How many would ye be after having?'

'I think we've got about three thousand altogether.'

'We could take that many.'

David blinked uncertainly. 'I don't know what to say, Mr Regan. It's a very kind offer, and I'd like to take you up on it at once.'

'Ah, be easy. Ye've the womenfolk to thank, and they tormenting me each day till I'm destroyed entirely. Ye'd better pick a mob out of the strongest and start moving them over to my Number Two tonight. Ye can hold them there a day or two, and then on to my Number Seventeen, and then to Fourteen.' He ran his eye over the sheep. 'Ye'll be after needing trucks?'

Dazed, David said, 'It would be a help.'

'I'll be sending Joseph Plunkett over with our big truck in the morning, and James Connolly with the five-tonner. Ye'll have to use your own men to tend them. Ye can make an out-station at Fourteen bore.'

'I don't know what to say,' David repeated. 'I don't know why you should do this for me.'

'Sure, I don't either,' said the grazier affably. 'It's crazy that I must be getting in my later years, and you the son of a black-hearted, murdering Englishman that fought old Ireland in the troubles. I told herself, it's crazy I must be.'

David laughed. 'Crazy or not, it's very kind of you. Tell me, what shall I owe you for the agistment, Mr Regan?'

'It's hard to set a figure on it,' said the grazier, 'and the women will be tormenting me again over the money. Let you give me a case of overproof rum, and leave the rest be.'

EIGHT

By the end of May the oil drillers had reached a depth of about nine thousand feet, the last two thousand of which had been through shale impregnated with oil traces. They had brought no oil to the surface, however, and now it did not look as though they would do so. At the top of the shale they had found quantities of gas trapped underneath the second layer of anhydrite, but in the Lunatic this gas was singularly useless. All that they had discovered in five months of work was that there had once, in the far geologic past, been oil in that shale bed, and they had discovered with equal certainty that it was not there now.

Stanton Laird went down to Perth for a conference at his head office. It was not a particularly depressed conference, for this was normal in the affairs of the Topeka Exploration Company. This highly profitable concern drilled, on the average, four useless wells for every one that turned out to be a good producer, but that one showed profits that would pay for a dozen of the others. Topex, in fact, were more accustomed to failure than to success; their day-to-day business was in drilling and abandoning dry holes, and no particular disappointment or discredit accrued to anyone for the dry hole on Laragh Station.

They decided to abandon the venture and to investigate a new and more promising prospect in the Kimberleys. At this point, Stanton Laird put in his resignation from the Company. He had already warned the Topex representative in Perth, Mr Colin Spriggs, of his intention, and he had now but to confirm it in writing. 'I guess this is it, Mr Spriggs,' he said, in handing him the formal letter. 'I kind of hate to let go of the oil business, but this opening my Dad's got for me in my home town is one a fellow just can't pass up.'

'Sure,' said Mr Spriggs. 'Mr Johnson's going to be real sorry when he sees this letter, but I'd say you're right. Ford and Mercury are doing mighty well back home.' He glanced at the geologist, smiling. 'I reckon you won't be sorry to see the last of the Lunatic Ranges.'

For some queer reason that he could not understand himself the remark irritated Stanton a little; there were things he now knew about Australia that Mr Spriggs would never understand. 'It's quite a place,' he said quietly. 'But I could use a river, and the sight of snow on a mountain.'

He went on to have lunch with Mike Regan, the accountant, on Mollie's suggestion. He found her half-brother to be both affable and competent, and they got on well together. They discussed the matter of Mollie's passport. 'She'll have to have a passport and a visa from the American consul,' the accountant said. 'I'd better get going on that right away.' He sat in thought for a moment. 'It's just a little bit complicated, and it may take some time,' he said. 'I suppose you know she's illegitimate?'

'She told me,' said Stanton shortly.

'I'll have to see how that affects her passport. She must be able to get one ... She'll have to have a birth certificate, but I don't suppose she's got one of those. I'm not sure that any of those children had their births registered. In the eyes of the Law she's probably not there at all.'

'She's there so far as I'm concerned,' said Stanton warmly.

The accountant laughed. 'Too right. Well, the first thing that I'll have to do is to register the birth. Then we'll see how we get on after that.'

Stanton got back to the oil rig three or four days later. Already drilling had stopped and dismantling of the rig had commenced; the Americans did not believe in wasting time. Stanton talked for a while with Spencer Rasmussen, and then got into the jeep and went over to Laragh.

He found Mrs Regan and Mollie together on the verandah shelling peas; the mother made some excuse and went off to the kitchen, leaving them together. He kissed her, and then said, 'Well, honey, it's all over at the rig.'

'All over, Stan?'

He nodded. 'Stopped drilling last night, dismantling to-day. We decided there's no sense going on at this site.'

She had known that this was coming, but that hardly softened the blow. 'There isn't going to be an oil well here at all, ever?'

He shook his head. 'Not here, honey. There's no oil.'

'Oh, Stan!' There would never be a town here in the Lunatic. The shops, the churches and the movie theatres, the hairdressers and the cafés and the bitumen-paved roads were all to remain mere dreams, mere disappointed hopes that might have been. The Americans were all to go away with their ice cream, their magazines, and their movies; everything would go back to what had been before. All the hopes that had been built up over the last eight months were brought to nothing. Laragh and Lucinda would go on just as they had before.

He knew her well enough by that time to feel her dis-appointment. He drew her to him. 'It's too bad, hon,' he said quietly. 'I know just how you feel. But you're the only one who's going to miss it, really. And you won't be here. You'll be back in the States, with me. And believe me, that's a country doesn't need no oil to make it good.'

She smiled up at him. 'I know. But it's awful to think there's never going to be a town here, after all.'

'I guess your Dad and everyone at Laragh will be pretty glad about it,' he observed. 'It's going to save them skads and skads of headaches.'

She nodded thoughtfully. 'I suppose that's right. They're probably too old to change their ways. But it's an awful pity, all the same.'

He released her and they sat down together. 'I saw your brother Mike,' he said. 'He's a real nice guy; I liked him quite a lot. He's getting to work now on your passport and your visa for the States.' He pulled a mass of coloured litera-ture from his hip pocket. 'I got these plane schedules from the airline offices.' He showed them to her, and she bent over the maps, enthralled at the strange-sounding names, Nandi, Canton Island, and Honolulu.

'I can't seem to take it all in, Stan,' she said at last. 'I've never been outside Australia, you know. I thought only rich people ever went to places like Honolulu – not people like us.'

The financing of her journey to America was, in fact, a matter of some perplexity to the Regans. It was almost thirty-five years since Tom or Pat had seen the world outside Australia or thought much about it, and over thirty-five since Mrs Regan had left Scotland. The Judge's knowledge was wider, for in his youth he had travelled a good deal on the Continent, and he had left England as recently as 1930, a mere twenty-five years ago. His experience, however, had been narrow, being limited in the main to literary, mountaineering, and scholastic matters. None of his experience was very pertinent to the requirements of Mollie Regan on her journey across the Pacific Ocean to the United States.

The men discussed the matter at their storeroom forum after tea one Saturday night, as they sat around on boxes or upon the floor, leaning against racks of store goods in the light of an incandescent petrol lantern on a box. 'This letter Mike was after writing to the Judge,' Pat Regan said. 'It's wanting money he is, the way he'll take a ticket for her on the aeroplane with Stanton Laird. How much was it he'll be wanting?'

'Three hundred and thirty-six pounds, Mr Regan.'

'Sure, that's a power of a lot of money,' said Tom Regan. 'A power of a lot of money.'

Pat Regan poured himself his standard measure of rum, a quarter of a bottle. 'What would that be the price of, now, Judge?'

The accountant was accustomed to his employer's methods of assessment in matters of finance. 'That would be about thirty-five drums of petrol,' he said.

Pat Regan paused with the drink in his hand, the other hand upon the gin bottle of cold water from the refrigerator. 'Thiry-five drums? Sure, that's no great matter at all. I mind the times we've used twenty drums in two weeks, trucking to the coast.'

'It's a power of a lot of money,' repeated Tom.

'Sure, it's nothing at all to spend upon the girl, and her going to be wed. How much would a Land Rover cost now, Judge?'

'I am not very sure,' said the accountant. 'I think it would be about three times that amount, though.'

Pat Regan turned to his brother. 'What was I after telling you? A third of a Land Rover, 'tis nothing at all.' He shot down his rum and followed it with a chaser of cold water. 'Thirty-three per cent,' he said academically. 'Thirty-three per cent of a Land Rover. Sure, and it wouldn't be so much as that of a Rolls-Royce. 'Tis nothing at all, I tell ye.'

'It's a power of a lot of money,' Tom repeated gloomily. 'But there, it's all a part of it.'

Pat turned to the accountant. 'Tell me now, would that be for her to go there, or to go and come back if she wants to?'

At that time of night the Judge required notice of that question. He stumbled slowly to his feet. 'I will see if I can find the letter, Mr Regan.'

He lifted the petrol lantern from the box and crossed to the high, Uriah Heep desk where the correspondence of the station was kept till time had marched on and it could be burned, a ceremony which took place once a year. He fumbled to put on his spectacles, fumbled till he found the letter, and read it slowly through. 'That is the single fare, Mr Regan,' he said at last. 'That is the price of the tickets to go from here to this place Hazel in America. Not to return.'

'And how much would it cost to come back if she took a thought to? Would that be the same, now?'

'I think it would,' said the accountant. 'There might be a small reduction if she took a return ticket before she went.'

'To go and come would be two-thirds of a Land Rover? 'Tis nothing at all.'

'There's a true word,' said Tom, a little surprisingly. 'What would you be after doing with two-thirds of a Land Rover if ye had it? Sure, it would be no value without the other third.' He gave the matter some deep thought. 'Six hundred and seventy-two pounds,' he said at last. ''Tis the power of a lot of money to be giving to a child. Ye'll have us in black ruin, begging in the streets of Perth for bread to fill our empty stomachs, if ye scatter money like that.'

Pat Regan was a little alarmed. 'God save us, Tom,' he said. He turned to the Judge. 'Tell me now, how much money would we be having in the bank?'

The Judge, who had just sat down, got painfully to his feet again, took the lantern, and went back to the desk. He found the black folder of bank statements, put on his spectacles again, and turned the pages slowly till he found the last one. He read the figure at the bottom of the page. 'One hundred and ninety-eight thousand, seven hundred and twenty-two pounds, nineteen shillings and fivepence,' he said slowly. 'That was at the first of last month.'

'And how much of that would we be owing, for petrol and the like of that?'

The Judge flapped his hands a little helplessly. 'I find it difficult to guess, Mr Regan. Perhaps the outstanding invoices might total about five hundred pounds.'

Tom said, 'We'll have the income tax to pay, the seven curses on it.'

'We paid this year's income tax last month,' the Judge said. He peered at the page. 'It's down here as having been paid. Thirty-eight thousand and twenty-two pounds, four shillings and ninepence.'

The men sat trying to unravel these figures. Pat Regan reached out for the bottle. 'Tell us in plain language, now. How much money would we be after having to spend?'

'About one hundred and ninety-eight thousand pounds, Mr Regan.'

'What would that be the price of, now?"

The Judge cast about in his bemused mind for a comparison, rejecting with regret the Restoration Fund of Dunchester Cathedral, the only sum of a like magnitude that had ever come his way. 'You paid just under seven thousand pounds for the big diesel truck,' he said. He searched for a pencil and began a difficult sum in long division.

'Sure, that's a lovely truck,' said Tom Regan thoughtfully. 'A lovely, lovely truck.'

The Judge finished his arithmetic. 'I think that makes twenty-eight,' he said a little uncertainly.

'We could buy twenty-eight trucks the like of that?' asked Tom. 'Sure, ye could do the power of a lot of trucking with twenty-eight big lovely trucks the like of that.'

'Come on out of it, and sit ye down after your labours,' said Pat to the Judge. 'Give yeself a drink out of the bottle. Wait now – fetch another bottle while you're on your feet.' And when that was adjusted he said, 'Tell me now, Judge. If Mollie went with Stan Laird to America and then got setting down to think she'd have no part of it, 'twould only be a little piece of the money would be needed for her to come home? A little piece, the way a man would never notice it was gone?'

'That is quite correct, Mr Regan. You can pay her fares each way without worrying about it at all.'

Pat turned to his brother. 'What was I after telling you?' 'Tis no matter at all.'

'I'm thinking that it's not the end of it,' Tom said. 'Sure, you'd not send the girl out into the great world to live with strangers, and her with not a penny piece to rub between her fingers in the pocket of her dress? It's new clothes she'll be needing, and new shoes, and a pound or two for spending money. It's all part of it,' he added gloomily.

This was a new angle on this difficult matter. Pat turned, as always, to the Judge for help. 'Tell me now, what would things the like of that be after costing?'

'I have no idea, Mr Regan. I think Mrs Regan might be able to tell you more what she would want.'

Pat Regan poured another rum in his perplexity. 'There's many would be looking at her in America itself, and her coming as a stranger from Australia. I'm thinking she should not go in a torn dress, or else maybe with a hole showing at the heel of her stocking.' He paused in thought. 'She should have money for her spending, too, the way she'll not be asking anyone for anything till she gets wed. Would ye think now, Judge, we could spare the value of a truck for spending money? Sure, and we'd have twenty-seven of them left to work with.'

'That would mean giving her seven thousand pounds for spending money, Mr Regan. That would be about the value of seven Land Rovers. I really think perhaps that might be a little excessive for a young girl.'

Tom Regan said. 'Ye might as well trust a murdering Black and Tan as trust a woman with money. She'll have you destroyed entirely, and you not knowing what hit you.' He paused, gloomily. 'It's all a part of it.'

The Judge said, 'If I might make a suggestion, Mr Regan, I should give her a return ticket so that if she decided that she wanted to come home she could get on to the aeroplane without having to ask for help from anybody in America. And then for spending money and for clothes, I would think about five hundred pounds. That would be about fifty drums of petrol.'

Pat Regan nodded slowly. 'I mind a dress I bought for Mrs Regan two years back cost thirty-five shillings in Carnavon, good enough for a Cardinal to buy in the Holy City itself. Sure, a girl could buy the power of a lot of clothes for fifty barrels of petrol.'

The Judge said, 'There will be other things besides clothes, Mr Regan. She will have to pay hotel bills on her journey, and other little expenses such as that. But I think that if you gave her five hundred pounds she should be able to put up a good appearance in America and not be short of money.'

Pat Regan struggled slowly to his feet. 'I'm thinking that you're in the right, Judge,' he said. 'And now I'm off to my bed. Will ye write to Michael in the morning, and say that's what she's to have for clothes and money in her pocket.'

A week later Mollie and Mrs Regan travelled down to

Perth together. They went in the little-used Humber, the hens and droppings having been removed from it by the Countess and the car dusted out. James Connolly drove them out to Onslow to fly down to Perth. Mike Regan met them at the Guildford airport with his wife Sylvia, and they drove to the very pleasant house off Bellevue Terrace where the Regans lived, looking out over the Swan River. It was a better house than so young a couple would normally be able to afford, for a small fraction of the profits of Laragh Station was devoted to helping the many children at the outset of their lives. In the case of Mike, however, his early success had removed him from the list the year before.

Mollie and her mother stayed in Perth for a week, getting a birth certificate, getting a passport, getting an American visa, and buying clothes and luggage. They left Perth in a rainstorm to return to Laragh about the middle of June. It had been raining at Onslow and throughout the country in their absence; when James Connolly came to meet them at the aerodrome he came in their old Army truck with four-wheel drive and he brought with him a suitcase full of khaki slacks and shirts for them to change into, thoughtfully packed for them by the Countess. For two days they wallowed and splashed their way into the Lunatic from the coast, staying for a night at Malvern Station on the way.

It rained steadily from Malvern to Laragh. As they approached Mannahill they passed the place where Mollie and Stanton Laird had found the jackeroo, but already after a few days' rain the country was very different. The dry creek where they had dug for water only six weeks before was running now from bank to bank, over a foot deep as they splashed through it in the truck. Mollie pointed it out to her mother and to James Connolly, but it was difficult even for her to realize it was the same place. Already in the hot and humid conditions spears of bright green grass were showing, covering the damp red earth with a thin film of green. She knew it all, but each year it came as a fresh surprise.

'The feed's coming again,' she said. 'I wonder if David's got it like this on Lucinda yet?'

'It's a dry country, that,' her mother said. 'There should be feed there before long. He'll be taking his sheep back on to his own place then.'

'I'm glad Daddy did that for him,' the girl said. 'I'd have felt awful, going away, if we hadn't.'

'It's a poor, starved place, Lucinda,' said her mother. 'A good laddie on a poor station. I doubt he'll stay long, after this experience.'

Stanton Laird came over to Laragh the first afternoon after they got back. Spencer Rasmussen and many of the men had already departed to other ventures, and Stanton was in charge at the oil rig, or what remained of it. 'I guess there's not much left there to see now,' he said. 'The derrick's down 'n dismantled for transport and most of the other gear. I'd say it would be quite a while before it can be got away, though, on account of the roads. They tell me that we won't be able to bring heavy trucks in before September.'

Mollie asked, 'Will you have to wait so long as that, Stan?'

He shook his head. 'I can go now most any time I like. How're you fixed, honey?'

'I can go any time, Stan. I'd rather go soon, now that I've got everything.'

'What say I write to Mike, and see if he can get us reservations leaving Perth July 4th? That's a Monday. Be in Sydney Tuesday, leave on Wednesday and get to Honolulu Wednesday. That's a day later, but you cross the date line 'n it all goes haywire. Stay two days in Honolulu, 'n go on to Portland by Northwest on Saturday. Maybe my folks might drive over to meet us there, but anyway we'd be in Hazel Sunday.'

'That sounds beaut,' she said. 'Why do we stay in Honolulu for two days, though?'

'Kind of a nice place,' he said, 'and quite a ways from home, so you don't get to see it very often. Time we get there you'll have been travelling the best part of a week after leaving here. I thought maybe you'd like to stop off there, so's you'd be fresh and rested before meeting my folks.'

She smiled at him. 'You think of everything.'

'That's what I'm here for, honey.'

After that the days passed very quickly for Mollie. Sorting clothes, mending, packing, weighing luggage, unpacking, packing again, telegraphing to Michael Regan, consulting Stan Laird: these things filled every minute of her day. Laragh Station was thrown into a turmoil and the men made themselves scarce. In the middle of all this David Cope took his sheep back on to his own property, where new feed was now beginning to appear. It took him a week of hard work in the intermittent rain, but they got back on to Lucinda in considerably better shape than when they had left. He came over next day to thank Pat Regan for the help, which he did rather awkwardly, in the wool shed.

'Be easy,' said the grazier, 'and don't think on it. I mind the days when we first come here or soon after that, in 1929 maybe, we started off with eleven thousand sheep before the dry, and finished with three thousand and they not worth a shilling each. It's all a part of it, as Tom says, but sure, it comes good if ye keep on at it.'

The boy said, 'Did that really happen, Mr Regan – here on Laragh Station?'

'God save us! It's many the time we'd have no stomach for our dinner for the stench of the dead sheep, and many the month when we'd eat sheep meat only with a little bread, the way we'd have no money to buy stores. Sure, and we all go through it, but the blessed saints walk with us and it comes good in the end.'

David Cope went thoughtfully to the homestead. Mollie was busy ironing dresses, for she was to leave in three days' time, but she came out to him in the verandah. 'I just looked in to thank your father for the agistment, and to say goodbye,' he said a little awkwardly.

'That's very sweet of you, David,' she said. 'Got all your mob back on Lucinda now?'

He nodded. 'That's right. I'd have been sunk but for your father's help. As it is, we've only lost about a thousand.'

'I'm so glad,' she said. 'You'll make that up and more next year.'

'Unless we get another drought,' he said a little wryly. And then he said, 'Your father told me he only did it because you and your mother kept on plaguing him.'

She flushed a little. 'Nonsense,' she said. 'He'd have done it anyway. He just used that as an excuse.'

He smiled. 'Anyway, I'm very grateful to whoever thought of it,' he said.

There was a little pause.

'You're going away this week?' he asked.

She nodded. 'On Friday. It's quite a long way. It's going to take us a week to get to Stan's home, even flying all the way.'

There was nothing more to say, really. 'Well, the very best of luck,' he said. 'I don't suppose we'll ever see each other again.'

'Oh yes, we shall,' she said. 'You know, I'm beginning to hate the thought of leaving the Lunatic for ever. It's going to be marvellous in America, but I shall want to come back here for a visit every five years. When I come back you'll be on your feet, I expect. No more agistments.'

He smiled. 'Maybe.' And then he said, 'I brought you over a book as a wedding present. I've got it in the jeep.'

'Oh, David, how kind of you! What is it?'

'I'll go and get it.' He went out to the jeep and fetched the parcel, and returned and put it in her hands. 'That's for you both,' he said, 'with the best of luck.'

She tore the paper off. '*A Shropshire Lad*,' she read. She opened it. 'It's all poems, is it?'

He nodded. 'I like it quite a lot.' She turned to the flyleaf, and saw that he had written, 'For Mollie and Stanton, with every good wish from David Cope.'

She fingered it appreciatively. 'Stan will love this. You know, this is our first wedding present, our very first.'

He smiled. 'Fine. Well, I'll have to be getting along,

Mollie. There's quite a bit to do over at Lucinda now we've got the mob back.'

'Won't you stay and see Stan, David, and show him this? He'll be over this afternoon.'

He shook his head. 'I wish I could, but I think I'll get on.' He hesitated, and held out his hand. 'Goodbye, Mollie.'

She took it, a little sadly. 'Goodbye, David. Will you write now and then and let me know how things are going in the Lunatic? Nobody here except Ma ever writes a letter if they can help it.'

'I might,' he said. He dropped her hand. 'Well, I must be going on.'

He turned to the jeep, got in, and drove off down the muddy, graded road that soon would be graded no more. She turned back to her ironing, depressed. With all America before her, it was absurd to feel so badly about leaving the Lunatic.

She showed her book with pride all day to everybody, including Stanton Laird. Later, in bed, she read a little of it. Leafing the pages through, she found a poem with a faint pencil mark against it.

Oh, when I was in love with you,
Then I was clean and brave,
And miles around the wonder grew
How well did I behave.

And now the fancy passes by,
And nothing will remain,
And miles around they'll say that I
Am quite myself again.

She put the book down with moist eyes. It was absurd to feel so miserable about leaving the Lunatic.

Next day she weighed the book, and threw out a pair of shoes to make room for it in her air luggage.

When it was time for her to leave, it was a relief to her. In the last three days she was plagued with regrets, irrational regrets at leaving the arid, unsatisfactory, and uncivilized place that was her home. With her intellect she knew that she would have a happy life with Stanton Laird, a happy life in America, but she was unhappy at leaving the country she had been brought up in. Her mother sensed her trouble but did nothing about it, for everybody has to learn to live their life in their own way and from their own experience. Only on the last evening did she let fall a word or two in her dry manner.

'Now mind what I say, Mollie,' she said to her daughter. 'Ye're not to go marrying in America without ye let us know in good time to come over for the wedding. I'm thinking that the Laird family are decent, upright people who would think ill of us, and of you, if no member of the bride's family were there to see her wed. I'm minded to come myself, for all that it's a long weary way. I doubt we'd get your father to come, and maybe it's a better thing he shouldn't. But you mind what I say. If ye get wed, ye get wed in a decent fashion with your mother in church, for all you've been brought up on Laragh Station.'

She left next morning. Stanton Laird came to fetch her in the oil rig jeep which he had spent half a day in washing and trying to make a little presentable for the occasion, for a jeep was now the only vehicle that could be depended on to negotiate the morass of the roads down to the coast. He had arranged to leave the jeep at Onslow, to be picked up by another member of the Topex staff coming to the oil rig as his replacement in the final stages of dismantling. She went dressed for the road in khaki shirt, slacks, and gumboots, with her clean new luggage wrapped around in tarpaulins to keep it from the mud. 'One thing, honey,' said Stanton as they piled these bundles into the back of the jeep. 'You'll never have to travel this way again, back in the States.'

'I suppose not, Stan,' she said. 'It's going to be marvellous.'

Her leavetaking was a short affair, for they had a hundred and fifty miles to go to the station where they had arranged to stay the night, and to travel that distance over the flooded roads would be all that they could manage in daylight. She kissed everybody all round including the Countess, got into the jeep, and sat in a depressed silence as Stanton drove her from her home. He realized her mood and did not bother her with talk. Within a quarter of an hour, however, she was jerked roughly from her depression, for a watery slough a quarter of a mile long stretched ahead of them on what was called a road, and Stanton judged it better to go bush and drive across country with the jeep in four-wheel drive, rocking and swaying over the clumps of spinifex and coming back to the road half a mile ahead. From that time onwards she had plenty to do and no time for regrets.

They flew down together from Onslow to Perth two days later. The accommodation in the Onslow hotel had left a good deal to be desired, and she elected to travel in the Dakota still in her shirt and slacks, with the worst of the mud brushed off, rather than risk her fine new clothes. On that outback air service this attire was normal and aroused no comment, but at Guildford airport she felt shabby and out of place. From the airline office in the town they took a taxi to Mike's house, and here Stanton left her while he went to his hotel.

When he came to her again that evening she had had a bath and washed her hair and done her face, and had put on one of her new costumes in his honour. In turn, Stanton appeared in a clean new two-piece suit of a distinctively American cut with very square shoulders.

He stood back and looked at her, amazed. 'Gee, honey,' he said. 'You look like a million dollars!'

She stood back and looked at him, equally amazed. 'Stan darling!' she exclaimed. 'Honestly, I'd never have recognized you. It's the clothes, I suppose.'

He laughed. 'I guess this is the first time you've seen me in a suit.'

'It is,' she said. 'You're always been in that battledress thing before.'

He smiled. 'I'd say we've still got quite a bit to learn about each other, hon.'

He took her to the theatre that evening to see Ralph Richardson appearing in the flesh in *Separate Tables*. At the interval Stanton said, 'I guess there's something about a play the movies haven't got. I kind of wish we had some more of them at home.'

'Don't you have a live theatre in Hazel?' she asked.

'Oh – no, honey. Hazel's quite a small town, you know. Matter of fact, it's got to be a pretty big city in the States to have a play on all the time. There's lots of theatres in New York, of course, and two in San Francisco. I wouldn't think you'd ever find a regular theatre in a city the size of this, though. They haven't got one in Portland, and I don't think in Seattle, either.'

On the next day, which was Sunday, Mollie went early to Mass, a thing she hadn't done for lack of opportunity for quite a time. Later, she drove out with Stan to visit her old school and to take her sister Jean out to tea at the Regans'. They returned her at about six o'clock and went on to a farewell party given for Stanton by the officials of the Topex organization in Perth. Most of the Americans and Australians drank Scotch, Stanton and one or two other Americans drank Coca-cola, and Mollie elected for beer. She said to him, 'Will I have to stop drinking beer in Hazel, Stan?'

He hesitated for a minute. 'Women don't drink it the way they do here,' he said. 'But, shucks – anyone can drink beer back home. There's skads of people do.'

They left for Sydney on Monday evening, after a day of last-minute shopping and re-arranging of baggage. Sylvia and Mike drove them to the Guildford airport to see them off on the night flight across Australia in the Viscount. It was the first long flight that Mollie had ever made and she was thrilled by the experience, and deeply impressed by the comfort of the aeroplane. Already the Lunatic seemed far behind her, and America very close at hand. She turned to Stanton at her side as the engine note reduced after the take off.

'We're really off, now, Stan,' she said.

'That's right,' he replied. 'We're on our way. Happy about it, hon?'

She nodded emphatically. 'It's going to be wonderful,' she said. She looked around her. 'It's so *comfortable*.' She fingered the ashtray at her side, the airline folders on her lap.

He smiled. 'Think you'll be able to sleep later on?'

'I should think so.' She put the reclining seat back experimentally. 'I should think I'd sleep like a top. But it's too exciting to sleep.'

He smiled again. 'I don't sleep so well in an aeroplane, myself,' he said. 'But this is a pretty quiet plane I'd say. Quieter than most.'

She nodded. 'It's much quieter than the ones that go up to Onslow.'

The hostess came with a light meal on plastic trays for Mollie to marvel at and to eat every scrap of, and then she came with rugs and pillows and advice. Mollie kissed Stanton goodnight, and composed herself for sleep, but it was some time before sleep came. She lay in comfort watching the slow march of the stars above the firm line of the wing, completely happy. Life with Stanton Laird in America was going to be wonderful.

Before leaving Laragh she had had a letter from Stanton's mother welcoming her for the visit, a pleasant, cordial letter that had told her little, partly because Mrs Laird had been uncertain how far they were committed since they were not engaged, and partly because she wasn't a very fluent writer at the best of times. She had written in a similar strain to Mrs Regan and Mollie knew that her mother had replied to it; everything was secure and happy and arranged for her new life. She lay there looking at the blue immensity beyond the window, wondering if the stars would be the same in Oregon. Presently she slept, and did not wake until the hostess roused her to do up her safety belt before the plane touched down to refuel at Adelaide.

It was still dark when they got out to stretch their legs and drink a cup of coffee in the lounge. She had slept better than Stanton, who looked tired as he fetched her coffee and biscuits, a fact which did not escape her notice. She fussed about him a little, and when he confessed to a headache she made him take a Veganin from a tube she carried in her bag. Then they were summoned to the aeroplane, and they were on their way again.

She did not sleep again, but sat and watched the dawn creep up ahead of them as they flew on to Sydney. The hostess brought them breakfast for her to marvel at again, and after that there was hardly time for a cigarette before they were down to circuit height on the outskirts of Sydney and coming in to land at Kingsford Smith.

It was the middle of the morning before they found themselves in adjacent rooms in their hotel. Both felt a little washed out after the night flight. They strolled out for half an hour before lunch, but the streets looked very much the same as the streets of any other city. They lunched back at the hotel, and in the afternoon they took Mike Regan's advice and went on the ferry from Circular Quay to Manly, a journey down the harbour that took the best part of an hour and showed them a good deal of the waterfront. They found Manly to be a prosperous seaside resort with a magnificent bathing beach; they walked about it for a little, had tea in a café, and took the ferry back again, glad to sit and to enjoy the genial winter sunshine and the moving panorama of the harbour.

They dined in the hotel before going early to bed, for another twenty hours of flying lay before them. Over dinner Mollie turned to Stanton, and said, 'Tell me something, Stan. Are you sorry to be giving up the oil business?'

He hesitated, and replied, 'I guess the answer to that one would be both yes and no, honey. The oil business is a fine thing to be in 'n mighty big; it makes you feel you really are somebody. But it sure means you have to spend your life in rugged places. Hazel's a small town and folks who move around might say the job's not so important as the one I'm quitting. But it's a happy little town to live in, full of nice people, 'n a go-ahead place, too. I guess we're going to make

216

out better home in Oregon than if I went on in the oil business, 'n always going off for years to Arabia or Patagonia or some other goddam place.'

She laughed, and touched his hand. 'Or to the Lunatic. I'm glad you came there, anyway.'

He pressed her hand upon the table. 'I couldn't agree more, honey.'

They started after breakfast on the tedious formalities that must precede an international flight. Finally they got into the Pan American Stratocruiser at about midday and took off on the long flight to Fiji. A subtle change in the voices of the hostesses and in the food upon the trays told them that they were travelling in a little part of the United States.

'She said, "Are you-all comfortable?"' Mollie remarked. 'I haven't heard that before.'

'We don't say that in Oregon so much,' he told her. 'I'd say she's from Kentucky or some place in the deep South.'

They flew on for eight hours, seemingly motionless above a sea seen intermittently through layers of cloud far below. They read a little, talked a little, dozed a little, and ate a little, suspended in the tubular room in space. Night came as they nosed downwards to the clouds; they broke through at about three thousand feet to see a rocky coast in the moonlight and then they swept in low over the sea and touched down on the airstrip of Nandi, the airport of Fiji.

As they went down the steps out of the aeroplane the heat hit them like a blow, a warm wind scented with salt and with the smell of tropical flowers. They walked across the road and through the garden of the airport hotel for dinner, a hotel with bamboo decoration in the lounge, with straw hula skirts and brassières for sale in one corner among the picture postcards, the Siamese silverware, and the souvenirs of Fiji. They dined in the draught of many fans, served by native boys with the great shock of upstanding hair that she had seen in travel books, and then sat over their coffee in the lounge. It was totally different from anything that Mollie had ever seen before.

Stanton said, 'We got another ten or eleven hours to go this time before Honolulu. What say I get you a little drink of something, honey? Make you sleep better?'

She turned to him, smiling. 'I will if you will, Stan.'

'I guess I'd just as soon stay on Coke, or somethin'. But you have it, hon.'

She said, 'I won't unless you do, Stan – on principle. When we get to Hazel I'm going to be as dry as a bone until I see what other people do. But I do think it might be a good thing now. If I have one will you have just a little tiddly bit, in your Coke?'

He laughed. 'Okay.' And then he asked, a little helplessly, 'What'll I get? Some wine?'

The barmaid's daughter said, 'When we were very tired sometimes, Ma used to give us ginger ale and brandy. That's the only drink I know anything about, except the rum the men drink. I only tried that once, and it made me sick. Get a Coke and a ginger ale, Stan, and a little brandy in another glass.'

When he came back from the bar she poured about a quarter of the brandy into his glass, and the rest into her own. Sipping his Coke and feeling a bit of a devil, Stanton said, 'I tell you what, honey. I think it makes a better drink this way.'

'It does when you're tired, anyway,' she said. 'And we're both a bit tired now.'

'Only one more hop to Honolulu,' he said. 'You'll be able to rest there a while, 'n freshen up.'

Presently they got back into the aeroplane and sat perspiring freely in the confined heat of the cabin till they were off the ground and climbing up to cruising height. Gradually they grew more comfortable, and as they grew more comfortable, more drowsy. Presently the hostess came with rugs and pillows, and they lay back and slept.

Dawn came, and breakfast as they hung poised in space, more reading, and a very early lunch. Then as they lost height towards the sea land appeared on the port side and they regained the sense of speed; they slipped along the coast and Stanton pointed out Pearl Harbor to her. Then they were down upon the runway, and taxi-ing into the airport of Honolulu.

It was by far the busiest airport that the girl had ever seen. Great silver aircraft stood around or taxied about; between the tarmac and the sea a wide car park housed all the motor cars she had seen in the magazines, and over all there was an indefinable sense of being in another country. On every side she heard the accent that she was familiar with as Stanton's; here he was at home, and she was a stranger and a little ill at ease. This feeling was accentuated by the immigration formalities, for as a US citizen he was called for first and passed through quickly and ahead of her, while she had to wait in line and answer a good many questions before she could go through to join him. When finally she did so she was hot and sticky with worry and with the humid heat, and very glad indeed to be with him again. With him she could relax and look around to savour her first sight of America, the country where the cars were bigger, the people busier, the sea more sparkling and the sun brighter than any place that she had ever seen before.

Presently the formalities were over, and they got into the airport limousine, an outsize vehicle that looked like a car but seated about ten people, and were driven through the town to the hotel near the beach at Waikiki. As they went, Stanton said, 'Well, this is it, honey. Is it like you thought it would be?'

'It's just exactly like the pictures,' she said, eyes gleaming. 'Stan, look at that pineapple up there on stilts! Whatever is it?'

He laughed. 'That's a water tank, belongs to that factory.'

'Why is it like a pineapple?'

'They fix it up that way for advertising,' he said. 'I guess they make canned pineapple, or somethin'.'

She stared at it in wonder. 'It's awfully good ...' And then she said, 'Everything's so different here.'

The foyer of the hotel was small for the amount of traffic

in it, very modern and well decorated. She was glad to stand back against the wall while Stan stood in line to claim their rooms, watching the Japanese and Philippino boys handling the baggage, a little dazed by the many American voices. Then they were going up in the elevator to the quiet of the upper floors. They had two rooms on opposite sides of a corridor; when the boy was gone they went into each other's rooms to inspect, and then parted to change and take a shower and relax.

Her two days in Honolulu were a delight to Mollie. The humid heat was relieved by a perpetual trade wind, and her room was designed to take full advantage of it, with louvred windows and a louvred door, permitting the cool, scented wind to blow through by day and night, ruffling her hair gently as she slept. To her amazement and delight the room was furnished with a little refrigerator, very small and white and cold, for the provision of ice and cold water, and for the storage of fruit. Her room looked out over the sea and over the hotel swimming pool, set in a shaded garden with many deck-chairs and tables, the water very blue in the bright sunlight. They bought nylon Hawaiian shirts and straw sandals to be in the fashion, and bathed in the pool, and sat around with Cokes in bathing costumes in the warm sun and wind. Stanton hired a car for the two days, a very easy thing to do in Honolulu, and they drove to the yacht harbour and to Coral Gardens; the dined at The Reef and after dinner walked and kissed in the moonlight upon Waikiki Beach with a hundred other couples doing the same thing.

Everything was new to her, and yet she knew it all beforehand. When they went to buy a pack of cigarettes she spurned the hotel shop and walked out to a real drug store, the first that she had entered, and had a milk shake in it with Stan to mark the event. She wondered at the many Japanese shops, so well patronized so soon after the war; nothing in Australia had prepared her for such fraternization. The affluence and the slow, restful tempo of the place were a delight to her, tired as she was after their long flights. The great, brightly coloured motor cars parked thick beside the sidewalks on every block amazed her with their size and pleased her eye, and she discovered very soon that these were Stan's weakness, too. 'Whatever folks can say against the United States,' he observed once, 'and maybe they can say plenty – we certainly do know how to build automobiles ...'

Briefed by her mother back in the distant Lunatic, she insisted upon paying all her own expenses, even down to splitting the bill at The Reef and the hire of the Hertz car, much to Stanton's distress. She discovered on their last evening that she had spent nearly a hundred dollars in the two days, and her enjoyment of Honolulu was tempered a little by the reflection that twenty pounds a day was quite a lot of money, though, to be sure, she had a Hawaiian shirt and a pair of straw sandals to show for it. As she drifted into sleep that night the Scot in her began to assert herself; lovely as Honolulu was, and it was certainly by far the loveliest place that she had seen, it was in no sense a permanency. It was a place to come to and enjoy and go away from: a place as different from real life as a theatre set. America, she felt, in some way would be different to this.

Next morning they flew on to Portland, Oregon. They took off soon after dawn after a very early breakfast in their rooms, breakfasted again in the air, and dozed and read magazines and ate all day, in the manner that they were now accustomed to. In the evening towards sunset they crossed the coast losing height fast, swept round over a great river, and landed on the airport of Portland.

As they walked over to the enclosure, Stanton said, 'Say, honey – there's Mom and Dad, come to meet us!' She looked where he was pointing, and saw a stout man in a grey suit lift a hand to them in salutation, and a grey-haired woman, who must be his mother, waving.

As they passed through the gate, Stanton said, 'Hi-yah, Mom!' and kissed his mother. She said, 'Oh, Junior, it's good to have you back!'

He turned to the girl. 'Mom, I want you to meet Mollie Regan.'

His mother caught one of her hands affectionately, 'Well now,' she said, 'isn't this just lovely?'

NINE

MOLLIE found the kindness of the Lairds quite inexhaustible. They drove from the airport to the Congress Hotel in the family Mercury, and as they got into it Mrs Laird presented Mollie with a Pendleton jacket of tartan wool, very cosy and comforting. 'It's such a hot place that you've come from, dear,' she said, 'and Honolulu's hot, too, so they tell me. It can get mighty cold here in the evenings, and you want to be careful, driving. Slip it on now, so you don't catch cold. I'm afraid maybe I got it just one size too big, but we'll be passing through Pendleton tomorrow and they'll change it.'

The girl slipped it on over her light summer frock. 'It's terribly kind of you, Mrs Laird', she said. 'It really is a lovely thing.' She wrapped it round her appreciatively. 'It *is* quite a bit colder here than it was this morning.'

'I guess the colour's about right, Mom,' said Stan's father. He turned to the girl. 'We had quite an argument, Mom and I. Junior said in a letter that you had bronze hair, 'n I said a two-tone jacket in a kinda brown would be the best. But Mom said green. I guess she was right, too. You certainly look mighty nice it it, Miss Regan.'

She laughed, and flushed a little. 'It's beaut,' she said. 'I've not got much to wear except hot weather things, and I know I'm going to wear this a lot.'

Mrs Laird said, 'I think it suits you. You've got such pretty lights in your hair. But I'd say just one size smaller might be better. We'll stop off on the way home tomorrow and see if you like one a size smaller. Now you get right in here in the back with me, dear, and let Stan drive in front with his father, and you tell me all about your trip. My, haven't you come a long way!'

In the hotel Stanton's mother took the girl up to her room. The well furnished, standarized hotel room was embellished with a great bowl of roses, and a little assortment of new bottles of lotions and Eau de Cologne stood on the dressing table. 'I didn't know what you use, dear,' the older woman said a little diffidently. 'But I kinda thought perhaps you might be tired. Oh, they're nothing. I reckon a hotel room's just plain miserable without flowers.' By the easy chair, on the floor, stood a pair of new suède, sheep-skin-lined boots, calf length and zip-fastened. 'Just try them for size, dear. We got quite a way to drive tomorrow, and my feet always get real cold driving, even with the heat on.'

Impulsively the girl kissed the older woman on the cheek. 'You're so kind,' she said. 'I don't know what to say.'

Mrs Laird patted her shoulder. 'I think it's brave of you to come such a long way,' she said. 'We went once to New York, but Dad was telling me you've come three or four times as far.' She hesitated for a moment, and then said, 'Jun wrote and told us about you not being engaged,' she said. 'I think that's sensible.'

The girl said, 'I think it's a bit of nonsense, Mrs Laird. Stan and I wanted to get married. But Ma said we weren't to be engaged until I'd stayed with you a bit, so that's the way it is. The only difference is that I haven't got a ring.'

Mrs Laird said, 'Your Ma's right, dear. If Junior wanted to marry a girl from Florida or Mississippi, I'd kind of like her to see how we live up here in Oregon with coloured people riding in the same coaches and going to the same schools, 'n everything, before they got engaged. Folks live differently in different parts. Now, I'm going to call you Mollie. I guess you'd better not call me Mom, though everybody else around the place does. You can call me Helen.'

The girl laughed. 'I shall call you Mom.'

'Don't do that, dear. Your Ma mightn't like it. You just call me Helen.'

They dined in the hotel, in a room that delighted the girl with its decoration. She did not talk much, content to stay quiet and listen to Stanton's conversation with his parents, to study the new style of eating with a fork alone, the novel order of foods, the novel foods themselves. Although she had had an introduction to these matters in Honolulu there was still a good deal to be learned, and a good many old habits to be forgotten, if she was to enter into the social life of Hazel without rousing comment.

Once Mrs Laird said, 'It was so dreadful about Chuck, Jun. I just hated to have to write and tell you about it.'

Stanton nodded. 'Just one of those things, I guess,' he said heavily. 'Too bad it had to happen. Where's Ruth now? She back at home?'

'Not yet,' said Mrs Laird. 'Seems like they rented an apartment at this Harrisburg place for a year or something. There's not really room for them back with the Eberharts without they do some building, with all those children. Aimée's staying down there for a while with Ruthie while Dan makes some alterations to the house; they're turning the outside garage into a kind of cottage for her.'

'Quite a lot of work,' said Mr Laird, 'making it over. Putting in a furnace, bathroom, 'n two more rooms. It's going to cost Dan plenty.'

'When's it going to be finished, Dad?'

'I'd say in about a month. Dan told me Ruthie would be back in Hazel in the fall.'

'She got any money?'

'Not a lot. I guess they're kinda worried about that as well. But Dan don't say much.'

There was little to do after their meal but sit around and talk, and after half an hour of that Mrs Laird suggested that their visitor might want to go to bed early. Mollie resisted the suggestion for another half hour though she was growing very weary; then she accepted it at about nine o'clock and Stanton escorted her to her room. As they paused in the corridor to say goodnight, she asked, 'How am I doing, Stan?'

He drew her to him. 'You're doing fine, honey. You just knocked them cold. Dad said you were like someone from the Eastern States, Connecticut or some place. I guess that's quite a compliment.'

'They're terribly nice, Stan,' she said. 'I think your mother is a dear. She's been so kind – she thinks of everything.'

He kissed her. 'You don't have to worry about a thing,' he said gently. 'Not a thing. Just sit back and enjoy life from now on.'

'It's going to be marvellous,' she whispered.

Presently they parted, and she went into her room to go to bed. The room was warmer than she liked and she turned off the register, and opened a window. The mutter of the city came up to her from below, a continuous murmur of great cars that moved in the street, effortless, continuous. On the building opposite a neon sign flashed in unceasing sequence, and there were many others round about; the rotating beam of an airways beacon swept the horizon monotonously, and now and then an aeroplane crossed the sky, sliding down towards the runway at the airport. For a moment she thought with longing of the great quiet, the great stillness, around Laragh Station, of the huge, silent panorama of the starry skies, and banished the thought. This was America, and it was marvellous.

The bed was softer than any she had slept in before, the linen finer, the bedside light more convenient, but she did not sleep very well. There was so much that was strange to her, so much to get accustomed to, so much to enjoy. It was after two in the morning when finally she fell asleep.

Next day they drove two hundred and fifty miles inland to Hazel. For much of the day the road ran beside the Columbia River, a river bigger than she had imagined that a river could be, flowing through a gigantic valley. For most of the day she rode in the front seat while Stanton drove, his father and mother behind. The scale of the country amazed her; she had known with her intellect that rivers and mountains in America were big, but the reality was nevertheless a surprise. They stopped for half an hour at

Celilo Falls to watch the Indians scooping salmon from the rapids with nets and spears, and then drove on all day through an undulating country largely given over to wheat farming, a big-scale country with ranges of mountains and snow-covered peaks usually to be seen in the distance.

In the middle of the afternoon they came to Pendleton and stopped to change her new jacket for a smaller one. As Mrs Laird fussed around her in the store Mollie made a diffident, halfhearted effort to pay for the jacket, but the proposal was turned down so emphatically that she withdrew it, afraid of creating an offence in face of such kindness.

They came to Hazel in the dusk after a long drive from Pendleton through forests of firs, over a low range of mountains. The little town lay in a bowl of the hills, in a wide valley of farm land with high mountains rising up towards the east in the direction of Idaho. They slipped in past the grassy airport, over the railway tracks, up Main Street, turned up between the Safeway chain food store and a Texaco gas station, and found themselves in a district of quiet, prosperous homes, incredibly like scenes that she had seen upon the movies. They drew up finally before the Laird home on 2nd Street.

Stanton killed the motor, and turned to the girl beside him. 'Gee, honey,' he said very quietly, 'it's nice to be back.'

It was a house of two storeys and a basement, a white modern frame house, fairly large. It was a well built house in a small area of well kept garden with a number of shade trees, open to the sidewalk and innocent of fences. A path of crazy paving led up to the front door and a wrought iron gate decorated this path at the sidewalk end; there were wrought iron lamps each side of the white front door. At the side of the house a ramp led down into the basement, housing the two cars beside the furnace as is necessary when the snow lies deep. A sprinkler played on the front lawn, and from the back of the house a black and white cocker spaniel came bounding out to meet them, alerted by the sound of the car.

They got out of the car and a middle-aged woman came down the path to greet them, and was introduced to Mollie as Auntie Claudia, Mrs Laird's sister. 'My,' she said, 'you must be real tired after travelling all that way with Junior! How ever long did it take?'

The girl said, 'About a week. But we stopped off for two days in Honolulu.' Already she was picking up the idioms.

They went into the house. Inside the door the hot air hit her like a blow, for the Lairds were proud of their thermostatically controlled furnace and regulated it to keep the rooms at the same even temperature, winter and summer. She found that it was the normal habit for the men to take off their jackets when entering the house and sit in their shirt sleeves, and normal for the women to wear light clothes. Her first action in her room on that warm day was to open the window and turn off the heat.

They had given her the guest bedroom on the ground floor, a pleasant room looking out over the garden, with its own bathroom. She was to discover later that the house had three bathrooms. Here she unpacked her luggage, made herself at home, and settled down to grow accustomed to America in the Laird family.

They found her surprisingly ignorant of many things that were normal to their daily life. She had never seen a dishwasher or a washing machine, and had to be taught how to use them. This was strange to them, because Hazel High School ran a domestic science course and every boy and girl learned all about these things at school in their early teens. The electric kitchen stove was a great white thing controlled by no less than twenty-six coloured plastic keys like organ stops which lit up and glowed when they were on, arranged in a long row beneath a time clock. It was weeks before she learned to play this instrument, accustomed as she was to cooking on a wood-burning stove stoked by one of the gins. The refrigerator was normal to her, but the deep freeze was a novelty and she had little idea how to deal with food that had been kept in it. They found, however, that she was anxious to learn, and she spent most of her mornings doing housework with Helen Laird.

Her attitude towards the men's laundry amused them. It was normal in Hazel for unmarried men to do their own laundry, washing it in the washing machine and ironing their own shirts, collars, and handkerchiefs. It seemed to her a terrible thing that a man should waste his time on chores like that; at Laragh it would have been unheard of. She took charge of Stanton's laundry from the outset, glad of the opportunity to show Helen Laird that she could do one thing well at any rate, and one Saturday when she found Mr Laird ironing a shirt she took it away from him.

'Shucks, Mollie,' he said. 'I like doing it. I do this all the time.'

'I think it's terrible,' she said. 'What am I supposed to do? Sit and twiddle my thumbs and watch you?'

'What 'ld I do if I wasn't doing this?' he asked. 'Sit and listen to the radio?'

She took the iron from him. 'Go out and earn some money,' she said. 'Go out and have a drink – anything. But give me that shirt.'

He surrendered. 'I got enough money,' he said. 'I wouldn't have if I sat in the saloon drinking.' He paused. 'You know what?' he inquired. 'Mom and I were wondering if you'd like it if we got in a few cans of beer. Junior told us that you drink beer back at home.'

She smiled at him. 'That's awfully sweet of you, Mr Laird,' she said. 'I do drink it at home, but I'm perfectly all right without it. I'd rather do what other people do.'

'I guess I'll get in a few cans anyway,' he said.

She spread the shirt out on the ironing board. 'Don't do that just for me,' she said. 'I wouldn't want to drink alone. Besides, it 'ld look funny if Helen went into the Safeway and asked for half a dozen cans of beer to carry home down the street.'

'I wouldn't ask her to do that,' he said seriously. 'I guess I'll get Jake Feldman to bring them along to the office in a parcel and shove them in the trunk of the Mercury. Then

I'd take them out in the basement and put them right up in the pantry, at the back.'

He grinned at her boyishly. 'I'd kinda like to have an empty can to stand on Claudia's windowsill among the flower pots, so people 'ld see it from the sidewalk, and think she'd been drinking beer.'

She laughed at him. 'You are a baby! I won't be any party to it.'

For the first few days after they arrived in Hazel, Stanton devoted himself to her, took her driving round the countryside, introduced her to friends and acquaintances. Gradually, however, the work claimed him and he began to spend more time down at the business, and in a sense she was glad of it. Her job was to get to know Hazel as a resident and as a wife-to-be, not as a visitor to be escorted round, and this she could hardly do with Stanton at her side. It was better for her to spend her time in shopping and in housework with Helen Laird all day and to go with Stanton to the movies in the evenings, or drive out to some mountain stream or lake with him to fish at the weekends.

She was touched by the fact that the Lairds, staunch Presbyterians, made it easy for her to go to Mass. She went early in the morning on the first Sunday and returned in time for breakfast, and fell into the habit of going at that time each week. The Lairds, she found, were regular churchgoers in the winter when there wasn't any fishing, attending the morning service at the Presbyterian Church. In the summer Helen Laird was the only member of the family who showed up regularly at church. The men went fishing, and Mollie went with them.

The outboard motor boat was there upon its trailer, just as Stan had told her. They took it up one weekend to Wallowa Lake and she braved the cold water, incredibly cold to her after Australia, to try water-skiing on a board first of all. She tried water-skis once or twice but never mastered them, mostly because she found the water and the wind so cold that she could only bear it for a little time. 'I think you've got to be about fourteen years old for this,' she said.

Stan laughed. 'I guess that's right. It's better down in Florida, 'n places like that.'

He taught her to fish for trout with a spinning rod in the swift waters of the Hazel River, or to troll for them in the lake behind the boat, and she caught a few small fish with great glee. These were the amusements of the weekend; in the week they used to go together to the outdoor drive-in movies in the Ford sedan which he had acquired through the firm, sitting together very close in the love scenes. Sometimes they would spend an evening at home looking at the television, but though this held the attention of the Laird family and provided a topic of conversation with the neighbours next day, the girl from Australia found little interest in it and came to regard it as a somewhat trivial way of spending an evening. However, she did it with the rest.

She found that The Frontier was a very real thing to Oregonians. Chatting to Sam Rapke in his hardware store one day after buying a new can-opener for Helen, he said, 'I guess you find things kinda rugged here after Australia. Of course, this country ain't been settled for so long, and we've quite a ways to go before we catch up with the Eastern States. My Granddad, he came over with the first settlers, way back in 1859. Hazel was a frontier town then, and I guess it's one still.' She looked out through the door at Main Street while he rambled on and saw the paved road with the traffic lights, the air-conditioned movie theatre, the big cars parked, the gas station, the drugstore on the corner, its window full of electric razors, cameras, and hot-water bags. She said politely, 'I guess that's right.'

Making orange bread with Claudia one day, the older woman said, 'Of course, way over in the Eastern States I reckon folks don't cook at home the way we do. The Frontier was just forest country eighty years ago. My mother used to say when she was a girl the flour used to come in sacks by ox cart right from Omaha on the Missouri River through Nebraska and Wyoming, and it took three months to get here. Women had to learn to cook in those days and not waste things, 'n that's why we do it still. Over in the Eastern States I guess you just go out and buy orange bread any time you want.'

'It's pretty much like that with us still,' the girl said. 'Our flour comes from Geraldton by truck – that's about eight hundred miles.'

Auntie Claudia stared at her. 'But you get bread delivered?'

Mollie shook her head. 'We live in the country, quite a way from any town.'

The explanation satisfied the older woman. 'Folks here living upon ranches, they have to come into town to buy stuff, too.'

Little by little, as the weeks went by, the Frontier began to get her down. She made a trip or two with the Laird family on horseback up into the mountain reserve, and quickly realized the virtues of the western saddle on the steep mountain trails. She learned the use of chaps to keep the legs dry when riding in an uncertain climate, and once or twice she saw a rider with a six-shooter belted at the waist, and was properly impressed. But when she commented upon it, she was told that it was carried from habit and for an occasional shot at a cougar, a mountain lion which preyed upon young calves. It was patently obvious to her that there were no bad men or hostile Indians around Hazel for loyal ranchers to defend themselves against by force of arms. If there were any bad men the local motorcycle cops looked after them, and as for Indians, she found that they lived in reservations at the expense of the tax-payer, and were paid a few dollars now and then to dress up in their ancient glory to walk in parades that glorified The Frontier, while the tourists photographed.

Little by little she developed a distaste for Western movies and TV.

She walked round once or twice with Mr Laird to visit with Dan Eberhart, and to inspect the building that he was converting from a garage into a home for Ruth and her four children. She liked Mr Eberhart, as indeed she liked most people that she met in Hazel, a grey-haired, somewhat worried little man who ran a small sawmill and was reputed to drink whisky in the privacy of his home. She watched the building to completion and with Helen Laird went round to help him with the curtains, his wife being away with Ruth. The family were due to arrive back in the first week of September, and Helen Laird and Mollie spent a busy week before their arrival machining curtain material and going round to put them up and to see how they looked.

'I guess you folks made it look real pretty,' said Mr Eberhart one evening, surveying their labours. 'It looked kind of mean before, but now it certainly looks homey. Ruth and Aimée will be mighty pleased.'

As Ruth's arrival drew near, Stanton Laird became vaguely concerned. He had never told Mollie of his teenage escapade, preferring to forget it, but now he felt uneasily that some explanation might one day be necessary. It was all over now, and half forgotten in the dim past, of no concern to anybody, yet there was no denying that Chuck's first-born son was getting to look very like himself. He did not think it likely that Mollie would notice it or that anyone would call her attention to the likeness, yet it was indisputably there, and it was something that she should know about before they married. He did not want to marry under any false pretences, and one day it would be necessary for him to tell her all about it. Yet he shrank from doing so because there never seemed to be a very good opportunity, and as the time of Ruth's return drew near he grew thoughtful and depressed.

Early in September Mollie got a letter from David Cope. She had heard once or twice from her mother, rather stilted, laborious letters that did not conceal the effort of the writing or the affection that lay behind them, but which gave her very little news. She found the letter from the English boy more informative. It ran:

DEAR MOLLIE,

So far as I can make out nobody seems to be writing to you very much from home so here goes. The last of the Americans have gone away now and there's nothing left but a few slabs of concrete on the ground and the septic tank, and three three-thousand gallon water tanks which I bought off them with some piping and brought over here. Got them for only a couple of quid each, a snip, but they didn't want the trouble of carting them away. Most of them have gone to a place called Camp Hill on the coast near Broome; they're sinking another trial well there. I got a letter from Ted last week; he says the mosquitoes are hell and they've tried spraying the whole area with DDT from an aeroplane.

We had a really good rain this winter after you went and all the creeks are running, kind of makes up for the rain we didn't have last summer. The sheep are doing well, what's left of them. You've got some marvellous feed on your place out past your Fourteen bore, saved my bloody bacon and I'll never forget it.

Clem Rogerson sacked Fortunate about the time you went but he wouldn't go away until they threatened to get the constable out from Onslow. The cops got him anyway because he got drunk in town and started playing with his knives in the bar, so Sergeant Hamilton knocked him out and put him in the cooler, and we heard that he was headed for the looney-bin. But that wasn't right because I heard last week he was working in the hotel at Five Mile Crossing as barman, so there'll be some fun and games there before long.

Your Dad and the Judge went down to Onslow for the ram sales and the races and on the first day the Judge put fifty pounds on Laramie Girl to win and lost it. He was a bit full and said later that he thought he was putting five pounds on but he put fifty which was all he had, so after that he hadn't got any money for grog except what your father gave him and that wasn't very much so he came back in pretty good shape. Mike was up here for a week doing the year's accounts with the Judge just after you went. I asked him how much Laragh was losing each year, but he sort of grinned, so I don't think they're losing very much. Wish I could say the same.

I've been going over to Laragh quite a bit since you went away. They love getting your letters and hearing all about America, so go on writing even if they don't write much themselves. Pat has been teaching me to drink rum his way with a chaser; I haven't got up to his quarter bottle tot yet, but I'm still alive, anyway. It's been dull here since you went away, but your father says he'll find me a yellow girl or a good-looking gin, if you can imagine such a thing, so I'll be right.

All the best,
DAVID.

The girl from Australia treasured this letter, though she did not answer it for some time. It seemed disloyal to be carrying on a correspondence with David Cope when she was virtually engaged to Stanton Laird. Yet the letter brought a breath of the wide spaces that she had grown up in, and that she was beginning to miss. She did not show this letter to anybody because there were some things that could not be explained. She could never hope to make Helen Laird or Claudia understand about the Judge, or her father's way with rum, or Fortunate, or David's deplorable remark about the yellow girl. There were some things that she would never be able to talk freely about to her new relations in Hazel, kind and affectionate though they were. There were some things in her background that they would never understand.

She kept the letter to herself, and read it once or twice a day in private. It was lovely to get news from home.

Ruth arrived back in Hazel a few days later, with her mother and the four children. The car had been sold and they came wearily and economically by train from Texas, a three-day journey through El Paso to Los Angeles and so up through San Francisco to Portland and to Hazel. They arrived early one afternoon and Helen Laird went down with Claudia to meet them at the depot and assist them home to the new cottage in the back yard of the Eberhart home. They returned later with a depressing tale of two worn, haggard women and four weary, fretful children, all in urgent need of rest and kindness in the haven that was Hazel.

'They're just plumb tired out, all of them,' Aunt Claudia said. 'It's quite a ways to come by railroad in this weather, and it must be mighty hot still down south. I'm going to set right down now and make four fruit pies. I just can't imagine they'll be wanting to do any cooking for a day or two.'

'I guess I'll make a kettle of soup that she can give the baby,' Helen Laird said thoughtfully. 'Potato soup, with some of the chicken stock. I'll take it over in the morning and see if I can do the shopping for them while they get themselves settled.'

Mollie said, 'Is there anything that I can do, Helen?'

The older woman turned to the girl. 'She brought back a whole sack of dirty diapers. I know she'd appreciate it if somebody would put those through the washing machine, 'n hang them out.'

The girl nodded. 'I'll go round and get them right away.'

She walked out in the warm September sunshine and round the corner of the shaded street, and up two blocks to the Eberhart home. She walked round to the back and in at the back door, as they were used to doing. In the kitchen she ran into a strange woman, a tired woman of twenty-nine or thirty with white scars on her forehead and one cheek, cooking up some baby food over the stove.

Mollie said, 'I'm sorry – my name's Mollie Regan. I'm stopping with the Lairds. Helen said there were some diapers here wanted washing.'

The woman smiled wearily. 'I'll say there's some diapers. About seventy or eighty. I'm Ruth Sheraton. Have you come to do them?'

'That's right,' said the girl. 'I'll take them and do them in our machine, and bring them back as soon as they're dry in the morning.'

'They're all yours, sister.' She went and fetched a bulging sack of waterproof cloth. 'This is mighty nice of you,' she said. 'You don't want to carry them, though. Wait till Pa comes back with the car, 'n he'll drop them off at the Laird house for you.'

'I can carry them,' the girl said. 'They're no weight.'

'You don't mind walking down the street with a sack of diapers?'

'No. I don't mind.'

The woman looked at her with interest. 'Say,' she said, 'you're English or somethin', aren't you? You wouldn't be the girl came back with Stanton from Australia?'

'That's right,' she said.

'Well, what do you know! Say, I'm real glad to know you. Chuck and Stan were mighty good friends.'

'I know,' said Mollie. 'It was a terrible blow to Stanton when he heard.'

The woman nodded. 'It would have been ...' And then she said, 'Chuck always had lots of fun, whatever he was doing. But when you go having lots of fun in aeroplanes, I guess things are liable to happen, and that's all there is to it.'

The girl nodded. 'I suppose so.' She picked up the bag. 'I'll let you have these back as soon as they're ready, to-morrow morning at the latest.'

'I'll be real grateful,' said the woman. ''Bye now.'

Stanton, coming to the house from work, found Mollie hanging out row after row of newly washed diapers on the clothes lines at the back of the house. 'Say,' he remarked. 'Getting a bit ahead of the game, aren't you?'

Aunt Claudia, overhearing, said, 'Stanton Laird! How dare you say a thing like that! You start right in now and apologize to Mollie!'

'That's all right,' the girl said equably. 'I'm used to that kind of a remark.'

'I never heard such behaviour! Make him apologize, Mollie.'

To keep the peace, Stanton said, 'Guess I'll apologize.'

'Apology accepted.'

'Say,' he asked, 'are these all Ruthie's?'

'No,' she said. 'They're the baby's.'

Aunt Claudia, disgusted, went indoors.

He grinned. 'That's mighty nice of you, Mollie. I just looked in to see how she was making out, and she told me you'd been over.'

The girl said, 'I'm so glad to be able to do something to help. She looks as if she's had a rotten time.'

'I guess she has ...' He picked up a few moist diapers and began hanging them on the line with her. 'It'll be better for her now she's back in her home town.'

She nodded. 'It was probably a mistake staying on in Texas, wasn't it? I mean, the associations?'

'Uh-huh. It's been kind of difficult for them all round. They had to live somewhere till Dan got the cottage ready for them.' He paused. 'He was in the office today, wanting to sell his Ford.'

'Sell his car? They've only got the one, haven't they?'

'That's right. Fifty-one model. He won't get so much for it.'

'Is that to pay for the cottage, Stan?'

He nodded. 'I guess it'll be pretty rugged going for them for a while.'

'But she gets a pension, doesn't she?'

'That's right. But a lieutenant's pension ain't so much, honey. She's reckoning on finding some kind of a job later on, when things get settled down a bit. Half time.'

He wanted to talk to Mollie about Ruth and her first-born, but no opportunity arose that night. In the Laird home the plight of the Eberhart family was the main topic of conversation at supper, as it was in many of the homes in Hazel. The girl from Australia found this open discussion of another person's troubles to be distasteful, an invasion of privacy that ought to be respected. Yet there was no denying the sincere good feeling and desire to help that lay behind it. The women talked of nothing else all evening, but through all the talk ran a current of plans to assist. Even Mr Laird said once to his son, 'You know somethin'? I guess I'll offer him ten fifty, 'n be prepared to go up to eleven hundred.'

'It's not worth that much, Dad. The motor's just about shot.'

'We might not lose on it. Anyway, it's a coupla hundred more'n he'd get any other place.'

When Stanton went to bed that evening he was troubled and unable to sleep. He was deeply concerned with the plight of Ruth, but even more concerned that he had not told Mollie yet about their early escapades. He felt that he had drifted into a position of duplicity without in the least intending to do so. He knew now that he should have told Mollie about Ruth much earlier, back in Australia before ever she had come with him to the United States, and yet it had not seemed important then, an old trouble that was practically forgotten. It was going to be far more difficult to tell her now, but she must be told. Somehow or other he must find an opportunity to tell her the whole thing next day, or on the day after at the latest. In far-away Australia he had never dreamed that a position like this could arise.

He lay in deep distress, wondering how he could get Mollie alone next day and broach this difficult matter. About midnight he reached out for the Bible by his bedside and began to leaf it through in search of guidance. He found nothing relevant to his particular situation and was growing drowsy through the comfort of the familiar verses, when one that was strange to him jerked him suddenly awake:

Nevertheless, I have somewhat against thee, because thou hast left thy first love.

He stared at the words aghast; surely they did not refer to him? He read the context; they very well might. He had looked for a message in the Book, and he had got it with a vengeance.

He did not get a lot of sleep that night. He lay tossing restlessly in bed till it occurred to him that he was hot, and he got up and turned the heat off at the register, and half an hour later he felt cold and got up and turned it on again. He went on exercising the thermostat all night, and still he couldn't sleep. When dawn came it found him thick in the head and tired to death, but completely resolved that he must tell Mollie all about it, and tell her at once.

He did it after breakfast. He said, 'Say, Mollie, come out in the garden. I got somethin' I want to tell you.' She followed him, wondering, and he led her round behind the barbecue where there was a little privacy. And then he said, 'Say, did you ever get in trouble when you were at school?'

'Lots of times,' she said.

'I mean, in real trouble. Like when somebody gets killed, or has a baby, or gets liable to go to the reform school or the penitentiary. Did you ever get in real trouble, Mollie?'

She shook her head. 'I never did, myself. I know people who did, of course. What's this all about, Stan?' She looked at him keenly. 'Are you all right this morning?'

'I guess I didn't sleep so good,' he said miserably. 'I got to thinking about things, and then I thought maybe I ought to tell you. I got in real trouble one time, 'n you'd better know about it. I guess I should have told you long ago.'

'Lots of people get into trouble,' she said quietly. 'Tell me if you want to, Stan, but sometimes it's better to let things be. How long ago did this happen?'

'Thirteen years,' he said. 'It was in 1942.'

'Thirteen years!' she exclaimed. 'But you ...' She thought quicky. 'You were just a kid then. You were sixteen?'

'That's right,' he said. 'We were all sixteen. I guess you're old enough to get in plenty of trouble by the time you're sixteen.'

She smiled. 'Tell me about it if you want to, Stan,' she said. 'But I shan't lose much sleep over anything you did before you left High School.'

'You'd better wait till you hear it,' he observed. 'Maybe you'll be so mad you'll never want to see me again.'

There was only one thing that could upset him so, she thought; born and brought up on Laragh Station this was no novelty to her. 'What did you do?' she asked. 'Get a baby?'

At least he hadn't got to beat about the bush with her. 'I dunno,' he said unhappily. 'Sometimes I think I did and sometimes I think I didn't. But that's not all of it. Somebody got killed.'

To her, that was much more serious. She reached out and took his hand. 'Tell me about it, if you want to. I shan't get mad at you.'

He hesitated, uncertain how to begin. 'I guess you must think I'm a straight-laced kind of a guy,' he said at last. 'Only drinking Cokes and like that. I wasn't always that way. Chuck 'n me, we went kind of wild when we were kids together, in high school. Both of us had old torn-out jalopies. We used to get bottles of rye 'n drive out some place in the country, 'n get tight. Used to take the girls along, 'n they got tight, too. And then we'd get to playing tag on the way home ...'

She wrinkled her brows. 'In the cars?'

'Uh-huh. First I'd bump him just a little, 'n then drive away lickety-split while he tried to bump me.'

She smiled. 'Sounds a good game.'

'Maybe. I guess we didn't know the chances we were taking. But that wasn't all we played, taking the girls along, 'n getting tight all together.'

She nodded. 'I don't suppose it was.' A light began to dawn on her. 'Do I know any of the girls?'

'Ruth Eberhart was one,' he said unhappily. 'The other was a girl called Diana Fawsitt, but she got killed.'

'Got killed, Stan?'

'Uh-huh. We got in a tangle, corner of Roosevelt Avenue and Fourth Street, both going about seventy. Those scars on Ruthie's face are where she went through the windshield. Chuck 'n me got away with it, only broken ribs and

240

like that. I guess that's because we had the wheel to hang on to. But Diana, she got thrown out on the sidewalk. And she died.'

She pressed his hand. 'Oh, Stan!' She knew the corner so well. She passed it every day on the way down to Main Street, an innocent suburban corner with grass borders and mountain ash trees, covered in red berries now. It seemed incredible that tragedy could happen there. 'Was she any relation to Mr Fawsitt at the jewellery store?'

He nodded. 'His daughter.'

She said quietly, 'I'm so sorry, Stan.'

'I guess kids get to doing things that are plumb crazy,' he went on. 'Like smoking marijuana cigarettes – we used to do that, too. We were all pretty tight, of course – Diana too, poor kid. I dunno how we dodged the penitentiary. Chuck 'n me got the Reform School but the Judge suspended sentence, and we went on at High. But after that I gave up liquor. It doesn't do you any good, that stuff.'

'Not when you're sixteen, anyway,' she said. There was a pause, and then she said, 'But, Stan, that's all over and done with now.'

'That's not the whole story,' he said. 'When they started digging into things, they found Ruth was going to have a baby.'

'I see,' she said. 'A lot of people have done that before.'

'Mostly they get married first,' he said.

She smiled at him kindly. 'Not in the Lunatic. I'd say it's about fifty fifty there.'

'I guess it's different in Hazel,' he remarked. 'Or anyways, folks like to cover up a bit more here.'

'Was Chuck responsible?' she asked.

'Honest, Mollie, I dunno,' he said. 'Chuck, he allowed he was responsible, but I was just about plumb certain it was me. We spent all one afternoon trying to get it figured out when we got out of hospital, in the Piggy-Wiggy café.'

She burst into laughter. 'In the Piggy-Wiggy café?'

'That's right. It was the best place to meet, in the middle of the afternoon when most folks are off the street. You see, our jalopies were sold for scrap.'

'Over a couple of milk shakes, I suppose?'

'Chuck didn't go much for milk shakes. He liked ice cream.'

'I see. Well, what was the result?'

'We agreed we'd leave it up to Ruthie to say. Her folks were at her, anyway. We wrote a note in the café and gave it to the janitor at the hospital to give it to her. She took quite a while making up her mind, 'n then she said that it was Chuck.'

'I see; he was the bad boy. Is that when they got married?'

'Uh-huh. They got married about a month after she got out of hospital. I never did know how she settled it was Chuck and not me. Sometimes I kinda get to thinking that she settled it wrong.'

She eyed him keenly. 'How do you mean, Stan – settled it wrong?'

He said, 'Her first boy, Tony – he's grown up to look a lot like me.'

He was glad, very glad, that it was over. Now there was nothing more to tell, no more to be revealed. But he was not prepared for her to burst out laughing again, and he was hurt. He said, 'I don't see nothing much to laugh about.'

She said, 'Stan, it's just the sort of thing that might have happened in the Lunatic!'

He was silent, very deeply concerned. The Lunatic was in a foreign country, where people lived to standards that were wholly alien to the United States, drank to excess in an outlandish manner, swapped wives for pistols, and cohabited with native women. It was the way of foreign countries to behave like that, and he could readily believe from his reading that worse things happened in France, but it was not the way of the United States. It was deeply insulting to suggest that things that happened in his home town could be in any way comparable with things that happened in the northern part of West Australia. Hazel was a part of the United States.

He must be patient, because she was a foreigner and would naturally take some time to learn their ways, and be-

242

cause he loved her. He said quietly, 'I guess it's kind of different here, honey.'

To her there was very little difference between his situation and that of a white stockman disputing with a friend the paternity of a yellow baby, but she didn't say so because she knew that she had hurt him by her laughter, and because she loved him. Moreover, his case was worse, far worse, than anything in her experience that had happened in the Lunatic, for through his action and his games with Chuck a young girl had been killed. Girls might have casual babies in the Lunatic as they did elsewhere, but they didn't casually get killed in the course of a drunken game as they seemed to do in Hazel. In the Lunatic, at any rate, a girl's life was safe.

She said, 'I'm sorry I laughed, Stan. It's really nothing to laugh about, is it.'

'I'll say it's not,' he said.

'Is that what you wanted to tell me?' she inquired. 'Just about Ruth's boy – what's his name? Tony?'

He nodded. 'I guess you must think me a heel.'

She smiled. 'I don't think that, Stan. I'd like to meet him. Is he a nice kid?'

'He's okay. Honest, Mollie, I dunno if he's mine or not. But if he is, would that make any difference between us?'

'Of course it wouldn't, Stan. It happened such a long time ago, and you were only sixteen.'

He breathed a deep sigh of relief. 'Gee, it's swell of you to take it that way, Mollie. I been lying awake nights over it, thinking that I should've told you way back, right at the beginning. But honest, I never thought about it. It all happened so long ago, 'n then she married Chuck.'

She pressed his hand. 'Don't think about it any more.'

They stood together in silence for a minute under the speckled shade of the elm tree, its leaves already turning to gold. 'Tell me one thing,' she said presently. 'The other girl, Mr Fawsitt's daughter. She got killed?'

He nodded.

'What did you say her name was?'

243

'Diana. Diana Fawsitt.'

'Was she killed at once?'

He hesitated; what morbid curiosity was actuating her? 'I guess she was killed almost at once,' he said. 'I think she died on the sidewalk before they could get the ambulance.'

She pursed her lips; so she hadn't died at once. There was no sense in prying further into details, but her imagination could reconstruct the scene; the smashed cars, the children pulled from the wrecks by the horrified neighbours, the smashed body of the child Diana dying in a pool of blood on the grass verge between the paved sidewalk and the road, in the slanting light of the evening sun, under the flowering mountain ash trees, in the prim decency of Roosevelt Avenue. 'What a terrible thing, Stan,' she said.

'Uh-huh,' he said. 'Too bad it had to happen.'

She recoiled a little, but he was a foreigner and looked at things differently. She had to know a little more about Diana, though. 'Did the Fawsitts have other children?' she asked.

He wrinkled his brows. 'Well now – I'll just have to think. There was Sam in the Senior class the year I went to Hazel High ... 'n then ... 'n then there was another one. What was his name? I just forget what he was called, Mollie.'

'Another boy?'

'That's right.'

'Was she the only daughter that they had?'

He thought for a moment. 'I'd say she probably was. I think there were the two boys and Diana.'

'It must have been a frightful thing for her parents.'

He nodded. 'I know it. Getting smashed up in a couple of old jalopies.'

She recoiled from him again, but the beauty of the cars that had surrounded her in America had influenced her, too. In the six weeks she had come to understand the enormous part the automobile played in his thinking, in the thinking of all Hazel. She could understand him, though she could not go along with him. She became very conscious that she was a stranger in this country, that she must be very careful what she said, or she would offend again.

'Is she buried here?' she asked.

He wrinkled his brows; why did she keep harping on this old tragedy? 'I guess she must be.'

'You don't know?' she asked a little sharply.

'I never gave it much thought, Mollie,' he said. 'You think I'm kind of callous, or somethin'?'

'I think you might have put some flowers on her grave sometimes,' she said with sudden bitterness. 'After all, you killed her.'

He stared at her in amazement and concern. 'Say ...' he exclaimed, 'that's not right. It was an accident! Folks get killed in auto accidents every day!'

She bit her lip, and was silent though the red-headed indignation was rising in her. If she was to marry him and make her life in Hazel she must learn his way of thought and not go flying off the handle because Americans in this small town didn't think exactly as she did. She was silent for so long that he said, puzzled, 'You mad at me, or somethin'?'

She raised her head. 'I'm not mad at you.'

'What's eating you, then? You better tell me, Mollie.'

She was still silent.

'Come on, honey,' he said gently.

'I don't know how to put it, Stan,' she said slowly. 'We've both got a lot to get accustomed to, about each other. We've been brought up pretty differently. You thought that I'd be worried about Ruth's son. Well, I'm not a bit worried about that. After all, I'm not too legitimate myself; I'd be an awful hypocrite if I was bothered about Ruth. But I can't get over this other girl, Diana Fawsitt.'

He wrinkled his brows, trying to understand. 'You didn't mean it, when you said I killed her? We were all having a game. Nobody meant to do it.'

She looked at him in the eyes. 'You'd better understand the way I see it, Stan,' she said. 'So far as I can understand it, you were all sixteen. That's very important, because a kid of sixteen can't be held entirely responsible for what he

245

does. I suppose that's why you didn't go to prison. In my country I believe you would have done. Apparently you got a lot of liquor, you and Chuck, and took these two girls out and got them full. I don't mind about you seducing them; that's probably the girls' fault as much as yours, and anyway it's not important. What is important to me is that you got into a drunken game and killed one of the girls. You and Chuck were driving, and you were responsible for her, and you killed her between you. And you don't seem to care a thing about it.'

She paused, and he looked in silent consternation at her strange attitude. 'I'm going to remember that you were sixteen,' she said. 'I'm going to try and forget all the rest.'

He looked down, kicking the turf. 'I think you're being kinda rough on us, Mollie,' he said. 'All accidents, they happen because somebody does somethin' silly.'

'I know they do,' she said. 'Don't let's talk of it again.'

'Okay.' He glanced at her. 'And you don't mind about Ruth's boy? I never was just sure if he was mine or Chuck's.'

She smiled. 'I'll tell you when I've had a look at him.'

They went back to the house, and he went to the works, and she went on with the household chores with Helen Laird. In the middle of the morning a boy of twelve strolled in.

'Hi-yah, Mrs Laird,' he said. 'Mom sent me over to get the diapers.'

Mollie took one look at him, and endeavoured unsuccessfully to control the laughter that was twitching her face at the ridiculous thought of Stan's uncertainty. 'Hi-yah,' she repeated. 'You must be Tony.'

'That's right,' he said. 'You the Australian girl come back with Stan?'

'That's right,' she said. 'I've got the diapers right here.'

'Gee,' he said with interest, 'you look just like an American. What are you laughing about?

To cover up, she laughed out loud, and said, 'Did you think that I'd be like a coloured girl?'

She had embarrassed him with her laughter. He said resentfully, 'I seen pictures of Australians and they were coloured. With spears. They throw things called boomerangs that come back.'

'That's right,' she said. 'But there are a lot more whites than coloured in Australia. Just like there are here.'

'I guess I didn't know that. Mom said she'd be around this afternoon to visit with you, and say thanks for the diapers.'

'Tell her that'll be lovely,' the girl said.

He turned to go, the sack of diapers flung sturdily over his shoulder. ' 'Bye now.'

She watched him go a little fondly; Stanton at that age must have been exactly like this boy. There was still laughter in her eyes at the absurdity of an uncertainty about his parentage when she turned back to the kitchen, and found Helen Laird looking at her apprehensively.

She had to say something. 'Nice kid,' she said casually.

'Sure ...' the older woman said a little faintly.

She looked so unhappy that Mollie took pity on her. 'It's all right, Mom,' she said. 'Stan told me all about him.'

A wave of relief passed over Helen Laird. 'He did?'

The girl laughed out loud. 'I'm so sorry, Mom, but I can't help laughing. Stan said he wasn't sure if he was his or Chuck's – and he meant it, too! As if you couldn't tell by looking at him!'

The older woman said faintly, 'He's Chuck's son, Mollie.'

The girl laughed again. 'He can't possibly be, Helen. Stan must have been exactly like him when he was that age!'

Helen Laird said dully, 'You never saw Chuck, Mollie. I guess they were pretty much alike.' And then, to the girl's consternation, she turned to the corner of the room and began to sob bitterly, her face hidden in her hands.

The laughter faded from the girl; though this was amusing to her it was a bitter tragedy for his mother. She crossed the room and put her arm round Helen's shoulders. 'It's all right, Mom,' she said gently. 'It's not going to make any trouble, whoever his father was. Stan told me all about it, and I don't mind a bit. Honestly, I don't.' She pulled out a handkerchief tucked in the waist of her skirt and gave it to the older woman. 'It's quite all right. Come on and sit down, and I'll get a cup of coffee.'

Helen Laird wiped her eyes. 'He *is* Chuck's son,' she said tearfully. 'Ruthie always said so, and she must know.'

'It doesn't matter who's son he is, Mom,' the girl said. 'He's a nice kid and that's all that matters. I'd like to get to know him better.'

Helen Laird stared at her in tearful perplexity. 'You wouldn't want him around about the place if he was Stan's. But he's not Stan's, Mollie. Stan was never wild, like poor Chuck.'

The girl led the older woman to the table and switched on the electric coffee pot. 'Sit down,' she said gently. 'If he were Stan's, it wouldn't matter a bit to me, Mom. Stan was only sixteen, and he told me all about it.' She busied herself to get the cups and saucers, the carton of milk from the refrigerator, the sugar.

'I dunno how you young folks look at things,' the old woman muttered. 'You surely couldn't bear to have him round the place if he was Stan's. Or if you could, what would your folks say? But he's not Stan's, Mollie. I'm quite sure he's not. Cross my heart.'

The coffee pot began to sing and the girl switched it off, and brought it to the table. She poured out the cups of coffee. 'Don't worry any more, Mom,' she said gently. 'I suppose it might matter with some people, but not with me. We're quite used to this at home. We live a long way out in the bush, you know, on Laragh Station, and things happen there that wouldn't happen here. I've got a whole family of half-caste half-brothers and half-sisters living with us on the property, that we don't talk about too much. Honestly, this doesn't mean a thing to me.' She paused. 'And it wouldn't mean a thing to Dad and Ma, either. They'd just laugh.'

Helen Laird stared at her incredulously. 'What did you say, about half-caste brothers?'

'I've got three of them,' the girl said, 'and two sisters – yellow girls. There weren't any white women in the district when Dad and Uncle Tom first went to Laragh after the First War, and they lived with the gins – the black women, you know. Of course, they gave that up when mother came along.' She sipped her coffee. 'I suppose we're really a lot worse than you are here,' she said. 'But honestly, you needn't worry about this any more, Mom. Just forget about it.'

The other woman stared at her in perplexity. 'But Stan wrote us about your brothers and sisters. He said one was an accountant down in Perth, and one getting to be a famous surgeon in England, and another, a girl, doing Oriental languages, or somethin'.'

Mollie laughed. 'That's quite true, Mom,' she said. 'But I've got a lot of others we don't talk about so much. I suppose there's not much else to do up in the Lunatic, except breed children.'

Helen Laird said, 'But, Mollie – let me get this straight. You don't really mean you've got coloured people in your family?'

Aware for the first time of a pitfall opening before her, Mollie said, 'Dad and Ma are white, of course, and I'm pure white. But I've got half-brothers and sisters living on the property, and they're coloured.'

'You mean, real coloured, like the coloured people here?'

'That's right.'

There was a long pause. Then Helen Laird said quietly, 'Stan never told us that.'

'I think he might have done,' the girl said. 'But does it make any difference?'

Helen Laird passed her hand across her eyebrows wearily. 'I dunno, dear. It's all been so sudden, first the one and then the other. Guess a boy's folks kind of like to know before he marries into a coloured family.'

The girl kept her temper with an effort. 'We don't call ourselves a coloured family,' she said. 'Not that I'd mind very much if we did. Perhaps you ought to have a talk with Stan, Helen. He'd be able to explain things better than I can, because he'd see them more the way you do.'

'Maybe that's right, dear,' said his mother heavily. 'I guess I'll have to have a talk with Stan.'

The girl went up to her bedroom, depressed. Everything today was going wrong, in every kind of way. First Stanton, with his unconcern over Diana Fawsitt's death which had so shocked her, and now his mother's shocked reaction to the news of the Countess and her family. Having grown up with them from childhood, Mollie had accepted her half-brothers and sisters as a part of Laragh; infinitely kind and loving guardians in her childhood, people to whom she was deeply attached, and yet who were quite different to herself. Could she ever make the people of this town, the generous, affectionate people who were her hosts – could she ever make them understand about the Countess? And what about the Judge? If she lived here, would he hang permanently above her head like the Sword of Damocles? Or must she disown him, too?

She got out the letter from David Cope for comfort, and read the well known words again. When she came to the end, the part where David had said that her father was going to find him a nice yellow girl or a good-looking gin, she wondered how that joke would appeal to Helen Laird.

The atmosphere of the delightful little town of Hazel wrapped her round, pretty and civilized and stifling. For the first time since leaving home she was acutely homesick for her own country.

Down at the works, Stanton Laird sat in his office, doodling and distrait, doing no work, unconscious of the trouble brewing in his home. He had been puzzled by Mollie's ready acceptance of the fact that Tony might well be his son, and deeply wounded by her charge that he and Chuck had killed Diana Fawsitt in a drunken game. That had never been said to him before and it had never entered his mind; an accident was an accident, and that was all there was to it. Now that it had been said, it wounded him more deeply for the realization that there might be truth in it; it was one way of looking at things, anyway, and a very unpleasant one. A guy's girl ought not to make herself quite so unpleasant as that, even is she was a foreigner. There'd be quite a few allowances to be made in the future.

He sat in idle unhappiness, and in the background of his mind were seared the words of the Book, revealed to him in the night:

Nevertheless, I have somewhat against thee, because thou hast left thy first love.

It was real difficult to know what was the best thing to do sometimes. You went on doing what you thought was right, and then you found that it was all wrong in the eyes of God.

That afternoon Mollie sat down in the privacy of her bedroom to answer the letter from David Cope. She wanted to pour out her mind to somebody she knew, to free herself on paper from the restraints that were beginning to gall her. She started by telling him all that had happened since she had left the Lunatic. She wrote on page after page, telling him about Sydney, telling him about Honolulu and the long flights she had made. She told him about the Laird family and their great kindness to her, she told him about the lovely country that was Oregon, and the delightful little town of Hazel. And then she said,

It's all so lovely here, and everybody's been so kind, I really feel ashamed of feeling homesick. I mean, it's just marvellous here. The country is so pretty, the people so nice, the shops so full of everything one wants, the roads so good, and the motor cars so lovely, just exactly like they are in the advertisements. It's all the opposite to Laragh and the Lunatic, so that it's crazy to be always thinking of home. I wish you'd write again sometime and tell me more of what they're doing. I know I'm going to be terribly happy in this lovely place, but it's going to take a little time to settle down. My love to the yellow girl, or is it girls?

Yours,
MOLLIE.

Downstairs, as she was writing this, Ruth Sheraton was visiting with Helen Laird and Claudia. She had found them upset, and in the atmosphere of free discussion that prevailed in Hazel it was not long before she had discovered why.

'Say, Mom,' she said in amazement, 'that can't be right! Stan wouldn't ever do a thing like that! I think she's a real nice kid. I liked her quite a lot.'

Aunt Claudia said, 'Sure, she's a sweet girl, Ruthie. It's been just lovely having her to stay. But that doesn't alter the fact she's got coloured people for brothers and sisters.'

'Half-brothers and half-sisters,' Helen Laird said. 'That's what she said.'

'What does that mean, half-brothers?' Ruth asked. 'How can you have half a brother, anyway?'

'Same father or same mother, isn't it?' Helen Laird inquired. 'I'm so confused I don't know what to do.'

'Half or whole, it's all the same to me,' said Aunt Claudia. 'I knew a girl one time could pass as white, anyplace, even right down South. She got married to a real nice young man in Duluth, Minnesota, and first thing you know, they had a black baby. Real black it was, as black as any nigger.'

Ruth Sheraton said, 'Aw, be your age, Aunt Claudia. I'm sorry to speak like that, but things don't happen that way. I don't say she didn't have a black baby, but if she did she had it by a black man, 'n not her husband. I reckon it's not right to talk that way about Mollie. Stan's a good guy and I'd say this girl's a good one, too. I guess we better show a little confidence in them, and quit talking about it.'

Aunt Claudia sniffed. 'I'd feel a whole lot better about doing that if she wasn't a Catholic.'

'What if she is a Catholic?' Ruth demanded. 'I got some mighty good friends, Catholics, down in Texas.' She paused, thoughtful, for a moment. 'I learned quite a lot, when Chuck got killed,' she said. 'When you're a long ways from home and things like that happen, you're liable to change your views a bit. About friends, Catholics, and all that.'

When Mollie came downstairs she found them chatting amicably about the Shakespeare Festival that the Teachers College in Eugene were organizing, and drinking coffee. Presently Ruth rose to go. 'I got four hungry mouths to stuff some chow into,' she said. 'I'd better go along.'

'I got the fruit pies ready in the basket,' said Aunt Claudia. 'Two peach and two blackberry and apple. I'll just go get them.'

'That's lovely of you.'

Mollie said, 'I've got a letter to post. I'll walk with you to the mailbox.'

As they stepped out on to the sidewalk, Ruth Sheraton looked at her quizzically, and said, 'Mind if I tell you somethin', honey?'

'Of course not.'

The older woman said, 'This is a small town. It's a real nice place to live, except it's small. I guess I never knew how small it was till I started travelling round airbases and like that with Chuck. I dunno that I want to live anyplace else. But when you live in a small town, you got to live and talk the way they do. You've been shooting off your mouth too much, about coloured people in your family. You don't mind me telling you?'

'Of course not.' The girl bit her lip, and walked on for a moment in silence. 'I realized afterwards that I'd done the wrong thing in mentioning them,' she said. 'It was silly of me. But Helen was so upset.'

'What was she upset about?' asked Ruth.

The girl walked on in silence, wondering miserably how she could get out of that one. Whatever she did today, she seemed to put her foot in it. 'Nothing that mattered,' she said at last.

'That's a funny thing to get upset about,' Ruth said. She paused in thought, and then she said kindly, 'You better come clean, honey. Was it anything to do with me?'

'Not really. It wasn't anything.'

'I'd appreciate it if you'd tell me. It kind of makes things easier if you know what gossip's going around.'

They walked in silence for a moment. 'If you must know,' the girl said at last, 'it was about Tony.'

The other nodded. 'I've been expecting that, of course. I guess that must have been quite a shock to you. What say we walk around the block a little way, 'n talk this out?'

TEN

THEY strolled together down the pleasant, shaded avenue beside the white-painted homes, each standing in mown lawns. Ruth said, 'You met Tony this morning?'

Mollie nodded. 'He's a nice kid, Mrs Sheraton. I liked him. I really did.'

'You might start calling me Ruth, honey. You notice anything about him?'

The girl smiled. 'Well, of course I did. Stan told me of the trouble you all got into. I don't mind about him. Honestly I don't.'

'What did Stan tell you about Tony? I never knew what Stan thought about it it, 'n not so much of what Chuck thought, either.'

'Stan told me he was never sure if Tony was his son or Chuck's,' she said. 'They tossed up for it, or something, in the Piggy-Wiggy café.' She broke into a smile. 'As if one couldn't tell by looking at him!' She glanced at the older woman.

Ruth nodded. 'It's got to be a lot more noticeable these last few years ...' They strolled on for a few minutes in silence. 'I guess we were real wicked in those days,' she went on presently. 'Wicked and crazy. We thought that we were smart. Some kids are like that in High School. The war was on, too, and our folks too busy to look after us, maybe. And then we got to smoking those reefers ... Those cigarettes! The things they make you do!'

The girl said, 'I don't want you to think that I'm upset

about it.' She stopped and looked at Ruth squarely in the eyes. 'I really do mean that. I come from a different sort of place to this, you know. More irregular, I suppose. This is the sort of thing that happens all the time at home. Or it used to. I don't know that it would now, or not so much. I tried to make Helen understand, but I only made more trouble.'

'Was that about coloured folks?'

The girl nodded. 'I don't know if you can understand any better than she could.' She paused. 'We live in the outback,' she said. 'We live three hundred miles from the nearest town, and that's only got two stores, two hotels, and an airstrip. We're nine hundred miles from a paved road, and three hundred miles from a gas station. Our property is just under a million acres – that's about fifteen hundred square miles. The priest comes to see us once a year. Things are different in that kind of place to what they would be here.'

Ruth nodded slowly. 'I'd say they might be. A property of ten thousand acres is a big place here.'

'Ours is a hundred times as big as that.' The girl paused. 'Everybody here talks about the Frontier, and says this is a Frontier town. You're pretty proud of that. But you've forgotten what the Frontier's like, honestly you have.' She glanced at Ruth. 'When your first tough guys broke through the Rockies from the East and found this lovely place, they married Indian girls. You know it, and you're rather proud of it. It's part of the Frontier legend. Well, the Frontier's moved on. Our country is the Frontier now. But when I told Helen this morning that I'd got a lot of half-caste brothers and sisters she nearly threw a fit.'

'I'll say she did. Have you explained it to her, honey – like you have to me? About the Indian girls, and that?'

The girl shook her head, depressed. 'I don't think that they'd ever understand.'

'Claudia wouldn't. I think Helen might.'

The girl said, 'Anyway, that doesn't matter. What I was trying to explain is that I don't mind about Tony – not a bit. Where I come from things are different. In the old days, not so long ago, very few white women could live in the outback. It was all too hard. The ones that could were really tough, strong women, like my mother. People like that get married when they can, but they're not fussy. We get a good few illegitimacies, both white and black. I'm one myself, for that matter.'

'You are?'

The girl nodded defiantly. 'Yes, I am. So what?'

Ruth looked at her, laughing. 'Does Helen Laird know that?'

'Not unless Stan's told her. He knows, of course.'

'I bet she doesn't. Say, have you got any cupboard hasn't got a skeleton in it? Just one teeny-weeny one?'

'I shouldn't think so,' Mollie said. 'I come from the Frontier.' They walked on a few steps in silence. 'I do want you to understand,' she said. 'If Tony is Stan's son, it doesn't mean a thing to me. It might be a terrible shock to an American girl, but it's not to me.' She glanced at the other. 'He *is* Stan's son, isn't he?'

'I guess he is.'

'Did you know all the time?'

Ruth said, 'I dunno. I suppose I did, but I kinda hoped he might be Chuck's.' She walked on in silence, and then she said, 'Stan's a real nice guy, Mollie. He always was, or I'd never have gone with him, however tight I was, even when I was a silly kid like that. But Chuck – well, Chuck was different. Everything Chuck did was real good fun. He wanted to pilot aeroplanes and go places, 'n he did, and I went with him. We were always broke, we drank a lot of rye, had a lot of kids, and had a lot of fun together.' She paused. 'Maybe it was getting us down just towards the end,' she said. 'Always being broke, 'n nothing in the future. Maybe in another ten years it wouldn't have been so good. I dunno. Maybe I did wrong when I told everyone the baby would be Chuck's. But I guess I'll never be sorry that I did it.'

'Of course you won't,' the girl said. 'Nobody's any the worse for what you did.'

They walked on slowly till they came round again to the mailbox; the girl dropped her letter into it. She turned and faced Ruth. 'You've given me a lot to think about,' she said. 'I'll think about it tonight. Would you like me to do the diapers again tomorrow?'

'You thinking about Tony, honey?'

She shook her head. 'No. About the Frontier, and all the skeletons in my cupboards.'

'I was only joking when I said that. Forget about it.'

The girl stood in silence for a minute. 'Your tough men and women who broke through the mountain chains and found this country. Do you think they all went back to the small towns they came from in the Eastern States and settled down to live there happily?'

Ruth wrinkled her brows in perplexity. 'Why, no – why should they? They had opportunity here, 'n everything. Guess they'd have died of boredom back in those small Eastern towns, after the Oregon Trail.'

The girl nodded. 'That's what I was thinking. Shall I come along in the morning for the diapers?'

'Don't make a thing of it. But if you're doing nothing else, I'd certainly appreciate it, honey.'

The girl turned back to the Laird home. 'I'll be round. Goodbye.'

' 'Bye now.' Ruth walked on towards her new cottage, somewhat puzzled. Stan certainly had got himself a strange kind of a girl out in Australia. Real nice she was, but mighty strange. You never knew what she was going to say next.

Mollie walked back through the quiet, shaded streets, deep in thought. She had been shaken that morning by Helen's reaction to the news that she had coloured half-brothers and sisters. She had never asked Stan what he had told his parents about her background in Australia; she now knew that he had told them very little. No doubt that was from consideration for her, but it wouldn't work. Some day his parents must learn all about her whether they approved or not; she did not feel she could go on in Hazel under false pretences. Stan would have to understand that; if she married him she would do so candidly and honestly, with nothing concealed. After all, she had done nothing to be ashamed of, nor was she ashamed of anyone on Laragh Station.

She walked back rather sadly to the Laird home.

That evening they sat watching a Western on the TV after supper. The hero, a Federal agent sent in disguise to root out a gang of cattle rustlers, appeared in the small cattle town as a bank robber with a price of five thousand dollars on his head, dead or alive. Posters advertising the reward with a picture of this miscreant were displayed all over the town, and he spent a busy forty minutes evading the bullets of the loyal citizens while he wormed his way into the confidence of the bad men prior to arresting the lot single-handed and handing them over to the sheriff, whose daughter, rescued from a fate worse than death, fell into his arms. Cutting the set before the commercial and switching on the lights, Mr Laird said comfortably, 'I thought that was a real nice show.'

Aunt Claudia said, 'What that poor girl went through! How ever can they think of such things?'

Stan laughed, and said, 'There's something about a Western. It's the horses, or somethin'. However much you can't believe in it, it gets you just the same.'

Mr Laird laughed, and said, 'I guess it must be pretty unnerving to see your own picture stuck up all over town, five thousand reward, dead or alive.'

Mollie said casually, 'My father had a price on his head once. Just like that.'

Stan coloured, and said nothing.

Mr Laird said, 'You say your father did?' He laughed.

She nodded. 'Daddy and Uncle Tom both had a price on their heads. They were gunmen, you know – members of the Irish Republican Army, in the Troubles. Daddy's always been a bit sore because Uncle Tom's price was bigger than his – a thousand pounds for Uncle Tom and only five hundred for Daddy. There were pictures of them outside every police station in Southern Ireland, just like that. Dead or alive.'

Mr Laird stared at her, the smile fading a little from his face. 'Did the cops get them?'

She shook her head. 'They got away to Australia. It was quite a long time ago, of course – about 1921. But they talk about it still, and how it felt to see the posters.'

Helen Laird said, 'But what did they do, Mollie? They didn't shoot people?'

The girl said, 'Oh yes, they shot a lot of people. Black and Tans and British soldiers. It was in the Rebellion, you know. Just like a war, only nobody called it a war.'

Mr Laird moistened his lips and forced a smile. 'Was the price ever taken off? The price on their heads?'

The girl wrinkled her brows. 'I really don't know,' she said. 'I don't know if they'd still be in trouble if they went back to Ireland. They won't ever go, of course.'

Aunt Claudia leaned forward earnestly. 'You mean to sit right there and tell us your own father could be tried for murder if he went back to Ireland?'

'I'm really not quite sure,' the girl said equably. 'He won't go, so it doesn't matter much. At one time, in the Troubles, if he'd been caught he'd have been put up against a wall and shot right away. I believe it's different now, though. All forgiven and forgotten.'

Aunt Claudia said, 'I don't suppose the mothers of the poor boys he killed will have forgotten.'

The girl coloured and was about to say something impetuous, but Stan interposed quickly. 'I guess it takes a long time for the feelings a war raises to cool down.'

Helen Laird said, 'That's right. Well, I'm going to bed. That was a real nice picture, Dad. I liked it a lot.' And the tension passed.

Next morning Mollie walked round to the Eberhart home, chatted for a time with Ruth, and brought back the sack of dirty diapers and put them through the washing machine. While she was so engaged Aunt Claudia went down to the town, shopping. Mollie hung out the diapers, busied herself about the house with Helen Laird, and wrote a short letter to her mother. The men came back to dinner as was their habit, and after the meal Stan said to Mollie, 'I got to go over to Enterprise this afternoon. You like to come along for the ride, honey? It's real pretty country out that way, 'n I won't be more'n a few minutes there.'

She said, 'I'd love to, Stan.'

They set out in the Ford. When they were ten miles from the town and driving up on to the foothills of the Wallowa Range, he slowed the car, and said, 'Mind if I say somethin', Mollie?'

She said, 'Of course.'

'There's quite a lot of talk going around the town,' he said.

'About me, Stan?'

'Uh-huh.'

'What are they saying? Stop the car a minute.'

He parked on the crest of a rise, with a view out over the wide, undulating, park-like countryside. 'It's nuthin' very much,' he said. 'Maybe you want to be a bit more careful what you say in front of folks.'

'What about?'

'About your coloured half-brothers and like that. And now it's that your father was a gunman once.'

'Is that all over town?'

He nodded.

'Aunt Claudia?'

'I guess so,' he said unhappily. 'It's the way of folks to talk in a small place like this, honey. You can't stop it. It's just that I don't want it to make you unhappy.'

She nodded sadly. 'I did it on purpose, Stan.'

He stared at her. 'On purpose?'

'Not the first time,' she said. 'Not about the Countess and her family. That sort of slipped out, when I was talking to your mother about Tony. But afterwards, Ruth told me that I'd made a great mistake in telling them I'd got the coloured in my family, and then we got to talking about things. She's awfully nice, Stan.'

He smiled at her. 'What did you talk about?'

260